Praise for

Where the Fire Falls

"Written with an artist's sure strokes, *Where the Fire Falls* captures every hue of adventure, romance, and danger."
—REGINA JENNINGS, author of *Holding the Fort*

"Karen Barnett has fashioned a story filled with color, complexity, and rich imagery. Readers of *Where the Fire Falls* will not only find friends in Olivia and Clark but also become enamored with the enchanting Yosemite National Park. Barnett has given her readers the gift of a heartfelt story that is delightful and hard to put down. I can't wait to read what she shares next!"
—SUSIE FINKBEINER, author of *A Cup of Dust, A Trail of Crumbs,* and *A Song of Home*

"Yosemite National Park is as stunning and unforgettable as this book's leading lady, artist Olivia Rutherford, in this lush, atmospheric blend of visual and natural art. Karen Barnett's deft prose sweeps each page with the same delicate touch as Olivia's brush so that the 1920s-era park comes to life. Armchair travelers will sense every sight, smell, and touch thanks to Barnett's inimitable spirit of place."
—RACHEL McMILLAN, author of the Van Buren and DeLuca series

"Capturing the grandeur of Yosemite National Park with words is a bit like harnessing the wind. Yet this talented author does just that. Karen Barnett's story drew me in on the first page, her descriptions of Yosemite took my breath away, and her well-developed characters kept me turning pages until the end. I loved *Where the Fire Falls*!"
—GINNY L. YTTRUP, award-winning author of *Words* and *Flames*

Where the
FIRE FALLS

Where the FIRE FALLS

A VINTAGE
NATIONAL PARKS NOVEL

KAREN
BARNETT

WATERBROOK

WHERE THE FIRE FALLS

All Scripture quotations are taken from the King James Version.

This is a work of fiction. Apart from well-known people, events, and locales that figure into the narrative, all names, characters, places, and incidents are the products of the author's imagination or are used fictitiously.

Trade Paperback ISBN 978-0-7352-8956-7
eBook ISBN 978-0-7352-8957-4

Published in the United States by WaterBrook, an imprint of the Crown Publishing Group, a division of Penguin Random House LLC, New York.

WATERBROOK® and its deer colophon are registered trademarks of Penguin Random House LLC.

Library of Congress Cataloging-in-Publication Data
Names: Barnett, Karen, 1969– author.
Title: Where the fire falls : a vintage national parks novel / Karen Barnett.
Description: First edition. | Colorado Springs, CO : WaterBrook, 2018.
Identifiers: LCCN 2017050265| ISBN 9780735289567 (softcover) | ISBN 9780735289574 (electronic)
Subjects: LCSH: Women artistsFiction. | BISAC: FICTION / Christian / Historical. | FICTION / Christian / Romance. | FICTION / Christian / Suspense. | GSAFD: Christian fiction. | Love stories.
Classification: LCC PS3602.A77584 W48 2018 | DDC 813/.6–dc23
LC record available at https://lccn.loc.gov/2017050265

Printed in the United States of America
2018—First Edition

10 9 8 7 6 5 4 3 2 1

To my brothers: Mark, Chris, and Scott.
Thank you for giving a little girl the first
glimpse of what a hero should be.
I will always look up to you.

It was like lying in a great solemn cathedral, far vaster and more beautiful than any built by the hand of man.

Theodore Roosevelt, 1904

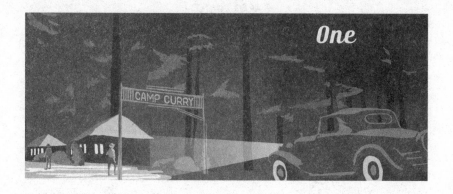

One

July 2, 1929
Sacramento, California

O livia Rutherford applied lip rouge the same way she painted—with bold, broad strokes. Anything to distract from the truth. She leaned toward the mirror in the gallery's tiny powder room, admiring the cosmetic's resemblance to the cadmium red she'd chosen for her latest painting. *Girl with Scarlet Poppies* was sure to be a success at tonight's showing. She, on the other hand? Olivia placed a hand against her chest, her heartbeat obvious to the touch. The shingled bob, the expensive beaded dress, the black hair dye—she'd become her own canvas, and it demanded every penny she had. If tonight's shindig flopped, she'd be hoofing it home on an empty stomach. Again.

Her art dealer, Frank Robinson, always insisted she attend. "Buyers like to meet the talent behind the artwork. Just act the part. We want them to think you're modern and sophisticated, not some starving bohemian."

She adjusted the feathered headband, the final piece of her carefree charade—such a contrast from her backwoods roots. When she'd changed her name, she'd left everything behind. Olivia Rudd died the moment she signed the paperwork at the county courthouse. If she played her cards right, Olivia *Rutherford* would provide her sisters with the life she'd missed out on. It would also ensure she never needed to step outside a city again.

Frank knocked and ducked his head inside, a grin lighting his lined face. "You ready, Liv? I've got a line of hot prospects for you tonight." He brushed a lock of gray hair from his forehead.

Liv. Only Frank called her that anymore. Olivia glanced in the mirror to check the finished product. From behind those kohl-lined eyes, the truth peered back. "Ready as ever."

"You look like a million bucks. They're going to fall all over you, as always." Frank squeezed her shoulder. "If I were thirty years younger, I'd marry you."

"I need this to go well."

"You've mastered the routine, sweetheart. Keep it up and these *nouveau riches* will be tripping over themselves to acquire your work. Everyone in this room is as fake as a schoolchild's clay creation masquerading as a Rodin sculpture."

Olivia tugged at the fringed hem of the short dress. If only the facade could soak in, permanently blending with her own colors like paint on a page. Her popularity might be growing, but the paybacks remained meager. Hardly enough to mail one check a month to her aunt. She needed to find a way to scrape up extra money because Aunt Phyllis had already given more than her fair share to her twin sisters. She'd agreed to take them in for a year, and how many had it been now? Six.

Olivia was no closer to being able to care for Frances and Louise than she'd ever been. The thought tightened around her throat like her imitation pearl choker. She ran a quick finger between the necklace and her skin. To make matters worse, her aunt had sent several complaint-filled letters in recent months. But really, how much trouble could two fourteen-year-old girls be?

Well, tonight she would pretend to be bold and affluent, if only for their sake.

Following Frank into the gallery, she glanced around at her paintings—as though her heart was on display for everyone to see. No matter how she dressed or acted, at the end of the day, only her talent mattered. For years, watercolor artistry had been ruled by masters whose highly detailed pieces mimicked reality. She painted what was in her mind's eye, her emotions leading the brush. The results had surprised the local art community, and her reputation was spreading. Or Olivia Rutherford's was, at least.

The idea of an exclusive showing this early in her career sent a giddy thrill through her. At one time Frank had a wide array of clients, and he'd served as a distinguished matchmaker between artists and collectors. But in recent years, he'd grown far more demanding and melancholy—an exacting taskmaster for those artists who remained in his circle. Many had drifted away.

The changes only made Olivia more determined to please him. Art lovers were often known for being moody and unpredictable. Why should dealers be any different? He paid her well—in compliments and promises. The lure of wealth still dangled just out of reach, but that would come in time.

She made the rounds, offering practiced smiles and sparkling conversation. A portly older woman sporting an exquisite diamond necklace waved Olivia over. "Miss Rutherford, join us, please."

"Mrs. Dixon. You look divine." Olivia dropped an air kiss just short of the lady's powdered cheek.

"You're too kind, my dear. I'm anxious to introduce you to some of my friends from the club." Mrs. Harold Dixon clamped onto Olivia's arm and addressed the women with her. "Ladies, this is the creator of all these lovely paintings you've been admiring—Miss Olivia Rutherford. Isn't she a rare beauty?" She introduced each woman in turn.

"I'm enchanted to meet you." Olivia nodded to each, the names slipping through her mind like paint rinsed from a brush. "I hope you're enjoying the showing."

The youngest of the group tipped her head, her glistening Marcel waves putting Olivia in mind of Goldilocks from the story of the three bears. "Your artwork is quite avant-garde. Where did you train? Paris?"

A tightness spread through Olivia's chest. Why must that always be the first question? "Oh, here and there."

An older woman wrinkled her penciled brows. "No wonder I don't see the mark of a master on your style. I'm surprised Mr. Robinson didn't insist on additional schooling, particularly for one of your tender years. How old are you, anyway? Twenty? Twenty-one?"

"I prefer to plow my own path, you could say." Olivia chose to ignore the question of her age. What did it matter?

"I see." The socialite tucked a clutch studded with iridescent beads under her elbow. "But raw talent should be guided by a firm hand, don't you think?"

Guided? More like crushed. Art school had taken the last of her mother's money, and Olivia hadn't even lasted a term. The teachers treated her like a lump of clay to be reshaped into the form of artists who had gone before.

The blonde sighed. "Must you always find fault, Gladys? Miss Rutherford's paintings are the cat's meow. These are so much better than the stodgy old canvases my husband collects." She ran a gloved finger along her jawline as she studied Olivia. "Do you do portraits, by chance?"

The idea twisted in Olivia's gut. The woman possessed nice lines, but creating commissioned pieces was worse than art school. Last time she'd attempted one, she'd invested a fortune in supplies and spent weeks perfecting the final product. In the end, the insipid woman refused to pay. "No. I'm sorry."

"Of course she doesn't." Mrs. Dixon clicked her tongue. "Miss Rutherford is far too successful an artist to lower herself to working commercially. Not like one of those pitiful, starving artists we see on street corners."

"I wouldn't have paintings done by such trash in my home." The other woman sniffed. "Imagine the filth."

"One can't be too careful." Olivia watched the silver tray of delicate appetizers slip by her, balanced on the hand of a passing waiter. Chasing the server down for a morsel of food would probably place her in that dreaded class. Hopefully there would be some tidbits left over when the gallery closed.

A tall gentleman in a pinstriped suit took a canapé from the selection before glancing her way and tipping a fine Panama hat.

Olivia froze. Was that Marcus Vanderbilt? The man had bought more art in the past five years than anyone else in the Bay area and often turned around and donated some of the most valuable pieces to hospitals, libraries, and museums. She forced her hands to her side so as not to flap them like an overexcited child. If her work caught his eye, she'd be on easy street. Maybe she could even afford that ritzy private school the girls wanted to attend.

He started in her direction but walked by without a second glance, stopping only to press a kiss to Goldilocks's cheek. "Sophie, I was worried you'd be bored, but it looks like you've made some friends."

She turned back to Olivia, her blue eyes shining. "Marcus, for once I met the artist before you. Miss Rutherford, may I present my husband, Mr. Marcus Vanderbilt?"

Olivia's mouth went dry. Her husband? Had she been introduced as a Vanderbilt? Olivia stuck her hand out like a hayseed salesman. "Pleased— I'm—m-meet..." She slammed her lips shut. *Compose yourself.* "I'm most honored to make your acquaintance, Mr. Vanderbilt."

A smile lit his aristocratic features as he took her hand. "Miss Rutherford. I must say, I'm impressed with what I've seen. You've a keen eye and an innovative technique. I especially love your use of the female form."

She swallowed and tugged her skirt lower to cover her trembling knees. "Thank you. I do prefer to use people in my work. I feel it provides life to a scene." Her thoughts raced. Had she actually refused to paint Mrs. Vanderbilt?

"I quite agree." He nodded. "Your model in *Girl with Scarlet Poppies* is particularly lovely."

She bit her lip rather than admit it was a self-portrait—her former self. Paying a model was out of the question. "I was just thinking how Mrs. Vanderbilt might be ideal for my next watercolor—if she'd be willing to sit for me."

The young woman grasped her husband's arm. "Oh, Marcus. Wouldn't that be a dream? I could be in a painting."

He ran his fingers along her cheek. "You're already a piece of art, my dear. I'm not sure I could share you."

Exactly. Then he'd buy the picture, regardless. Olivia pressed on, despite her quavering voice. "With those exquisite features, an artist couldn't go wrong. It would be such an honor to have Mrs. Vanderbilt in one of my scenes."

Mrs. Vanderbilt beamed. "Perhaps by the sea?"

"I recently visited a penthouse balcony adorned with flowering bougainvillea," Olivia countered. "They'd look lovely with your fair skin." She'd had her fill of fresh air as a child.

Frank wandered up to join them. "Marcus, so good of you to come. I couldn't help overhearing. I think it's a splendid idea. And I've got the perfect setting for this masterpiece."

The art collector raised an eyebrow. "What did you have in mind?"

Olivia stepped back. Her dealer had never told her where to paint.

Frank glanced at her before smiling at the Vanderbilts. "I'll need to beg you to excuse us for a moment, and I'll speak to Miss Rutherford. Once all is arranged, I'd be delighted to fill you in on the details."

Olivia followed him to a quiet corner of the room. "What could be so important you'd pull me away from someone like Marcus Vanderbilt?"

He clasped his hands in front of him. "I just finished speaking with an editor from *Scenic Magazine*. He wants you to do some illustrations for an upcoming travel piece."

"I thought you didn't want me taking on commercial jobs."

"This is different. *Scenic* goes out to thousands of subscribers all over the West. They pride themselves on their artwork. If you do well, you might even land the cover."

Her spirits rose. Most great artists did work for hire at some point in their career; why should she be any different?

"And—you'll like this—all expenses are included." He grinned. "You won't pay for a single thing. He's going to set up everything. They're allowing an entire month for the trip."

"A month?" Olivia's heart jumped. With that sort of help, she'd be able to send all of today's proceeds to Aunt Phyllis. But could she manage the pretense for such a long period? "What sort of trip? France? Italy?" Images of posh hotels, restaurants, and museums flooded her imagination.

Frank scrubbed a palm over his mouth and chin. "Not quite so glamorous, I'm afraid. More of a grand adventure." He met her eyes, an unspoken plea almost hidden in his gaze.

Something about the way he said "adventure" sent a quiver through her belly. "Where am I to go?"

"I've already agreed to the deal, Liv, so don't get upset. This is the opportunity of a lifetime."

A wave of heat prickled across her skin. He'd committed her without asking?

"We need this gig, sweetheart. You need it. Your name is hot right now, but it'll only stay that way if we fight to keep you in the public eye. Most folks would call this place a paradise."

"Where did you tell *Scenic* I'd go?"

He averted his eyes. "Yosemite National Park."

She backed up two steps, her knees weakening. She'd long ago stricken that name from her memory. "I can't, Frank." Her voice shook. "You know that. Anywhere but there."

"Keep it down, Liv; people will notice." Wrinkles formed on his brow.

The memory of trees closing in clouded Olivia's vision. She wouldn't return to the mountains. Not for *Scenic,* not for Frank, not for anyone.

"You need the exposure."

Exposure is exactly what she feared. Olivia reached up and tugged off her necklace, unable to draw a decent breath. People were turning to stare. No amount of lipstick and hair dye would save her reputation if she melted into a puddle here in the middle of the gallery.

Hurrying from the hall, she retreated to Frank's office and slid the lock into place. Gulping air, she laid her head against the wooden door and tried to banish the image of giant tree limbs blocking the sky. Her father had fled into those forests a wanted man and never emerged. The mountains had claimed their revenge—a life for a life. What made Frank think she'd ever set foot there? Even the name sent a stream of fire coursing through her soul.

Olivia yanked off the headpiece and let her hair fall loose.

A basket of red poppies sat balanced on the edge of his desk. Another of Frank's rash purchases? Poppies never made good cut flowers, typically wilting less than a day after they were collected. They couldn't maintain their appearance any more than she could. What had made her think she could live this masquerade forever? Her father's choices would always drag at her footsteps, no matter how she chose to present herself to the world.

A rap on the door cut through her unpleasant memories. She willed her breathing to slow. Frank had been her rock for years, transforming her from the girl who survived by selling caricatures outside the gate of the state fair to the sophisticated woman at the center of tonight's posh showing for the area elite. If he thought this was a good idea, she owed it to him to at least hear his arguments. She unlocked the door and swung it open.

Marcus Vanderbilt stood on the other side of the threshold, his pale blue eyes commanding her attention. "Miss Rutherford, we saw you leave, and Mrs. Vanderbilt grew concerned. I do hope nothing is amiss."

Olivia pressed a hand to her throat, struggling to push her practiced persona back into place. "I'm sorry to have worried you. I needed a moment alone. I had some rather shocking news."

He placed a hand on the doorframe, filling the narrow space. "The Yosemite trip? I couldn't help overhearing."

Her throat tightened. How many others had heard?

"I take it you've never been there. It's well worth the visit." He straightened. "I fancy myself quite the outdoorsman, actually."

"I-I'm pretty much a city girl, I'm afraid." *A half truth.* Olivia Rudd might have ties to the mountains, but Olivia *Rutherford* had never left the streets of Sacramento.

Mr. Vanderbilt took a step inside, the fragrance of Brylcreem obvious in his wake. "Perhaps you'd allow Sophie and me to accompany you? I would love to show my bride the beautiful park, and it would give you an opportunity to paint the portrait you were tempting me with."

"Was I so obvious?"

He smiled, tipping his head forward. "It was well played. I respect that. And Sophie is quite charmed by you." He shrugged. "And to be perfectly honest, I'd do anything to make her happy. So if you're willing to paint her portrait at Yosemite, we'd be honored to come along. Should I speak with your dealer regarding your fee?" His kindness chased a bit of the chill from the room.

A commissioned portrait. A month of all expenses paid. The enticement of a potential magazine cover. She'd be a fool to turn down such mind-boggling offers. Olivia Rutherford may be nothing more than a paper-thin illusion created by her dealer, but she also had bills to pay.

She nodded. "I'm sure he can come up with a fair price."

Mr. Vanderbilt ran a hand down his pinstriped lapel. "As long as my Sophie is happy, I'm not concerned about the expense."

Her life had been nothing but one expense after another for as long as Olivia could remember. Perhaps the Vanderbilts could help her achieve the status she already pretended to enjoy.

And Yosemite? She closed her eyes for a moment. The place held no allure for her. No draw. All it contained was the secret of what her father had done; the day her life crumbled.

Could she go, if only to wring from its landscape the money she needed to protect her sisters' future? She opened her eyes and took a deep breath. "I'd be delighted to have you and Mrs. Vanderbilt join me."

Perhaps Yosemite could return everything her father had stolen.

⟶

July 8, 1929
Yosemite National Park

Clark Johnson secured the General's reins to the wooden post outside the Ahwahnee Hotel, and then he pushed back his hat against the slanting rays of the early morning sun. The breeze carried a chill laced with the lingering fragrance of campfires. Lifting his eyes, he studied the massive granite cliffs framing the boundaries of the Yosemite Valley. The Royal Arches rose sharply in the sky, dwarfing the luxury hotel and perhaps reminding visitors of their minuscule role in this grand place. On a day like this, Clark longed to disappear into the trees, follow the streams to their sources, and not speak to another human soul for days on end.

Unfortunately, another group of tourists probably waited for him. Boorish, overly talkative city folk who spoke of "getting back to nature" and calming their nerves. Didn't they realize the secret to tranquility resided in quiet?

Talk never solved anything—a plain fact he'd learned the hard way. Words held no power to fix lives. For three years he'd explored Yosemite and the High Sierra, hoping for a word from God about his failed calling. Nothing so far. The thought lay heavy on his chest. How long should a man wait? Maybe silence was His answer on the subject. The church had cast him out—who's to say the Lord hadn't as well?

Clark winced. God didn't work that way. That much he knew. But as for the rest?

He turned his back on the view and followed the walkway to the Ahwahnee.

Chief Ranger John Edwards stood out front, one foot propped up on the short rock wall near the entrance. "Glad to see you made it back. How did your group handle the wild weather last night?"

"Mad as wet hares this morning. You'd think I controlled the climate."

"Well, you do have a direct line with the big guy."

"The superintendent?" Clark said wryly.

"That's not who I'm referring to, and you know it." The ranger shrugged.

It never failed. Once people discovered he'd been a minister, they had trouble seeing him in any other light. "So, what've you got for me today? Tell me it's not more pencil pushers in search of adventure."

"I wanted to talk to you about that. You know the transportation department is hiring a professional guide service—"

"Next year."

"I'm afraid it's been moved up to next month."

A lump settled in Clark's throat. "I've been running trips for almost three years now. The pack mules and I are out on our ears?"

"The mules belong to Yosemite; they'll be fine. It's you I'm worried about." John rubbed a hand across his chin. "You sailed through the civil service exam, Clark. I've been holding that ranger position for you, but I can't stall much longer. You need to make a decision."

"And put on the flat hat?" He glanced up at John's Stetson, the stiff-brimmed and high-crowned hat marking him as National Park Service even more than the gold badge on his chest.

"I've got men clamoring for the honor. I don't understand why you're hesitating. We don't want to lose you. You know this park better than almost anyone."

A jolt of pain went through Clark's chest. The staff had become like family, but was he ready to join their ranks? He pushed aside the question. "You haven't answered me. What've you got for me today?" He'd deal with tomorrow, *tomorrow*.

John folded both arms across his chest. "You've been booked special for the next month. That'll take you through the end of your contract. *Scenic Magazine* is sending out some artist—a painter. You're going to be the escort. After that, the new team takes over."

Clark ran a hand across his sore shoulder muscles. "A whole month? How many pictures does this person plan on painting?"

John shrugged. "I'm just the messenger. She arrives this afternoon."

"She?" A familiar squeeze gripped Clark's heart. "I can't take a woman into the backcountry alone."

"I know, you're not so good with the ladies."

Or too good. He'd succeeded in barely speaking to a woman outside his tours for months, and now he'd be saddled with one for four weeks? He'd rather guide a grizzly sow. "Can you spare someone to come along? How about that lady ranger, Miss Michael? This artist might like some female companionship."

"You're afraid of women, so you ask for more?" His friend shook his head. "Enid is busy putting together a wildflower display for the museum. And I'm told the artist is bringing a couple of chaperones—wealthy art connoisseurs. So there's no need to panic."

"I'm not afraid of women." Clark thrust his hands into his trouser pockets. "They're just a highly unpredictable species. One minute they're sweet as honeysuckle; the next you find yourself up to your kneecaps in hellfire."

John laughed. "I suppose there's a grain of truth to what you say. At least about some women. But truly, you don't know what you're missing, my friend."

Easy for John to talk. He'd snared a wife as steady as a mule but pretty as a ray of sunshine. No ranger could ask for a better helpmate than Melba Edwards. No wonder John smiled so often. "I'm safer keeping my distance— at least until I meet someone I can trust."

"So, what'd she do to you?"

"What are you talking about?"

"Back when we first met, when you were hiding out over by Mount Starr King, I guessed you were on the lam. I thought putting you to work as a guide might make an honest man of you." He chuckled. "Took some time to figure out you'd been a preacher, not some criminal." John leaned forward, a glint in his eye. "Melba thinks a woman put you over the edge. I told her you wouldn't get close enough to a gal for that to happen."

Clark buttoned his jacket, as if it could protect him from both unwanted questions and memories. "*Natural* history, John. That's what you hired me for. Not personal history."

John grinned—an expression so common it had carved deep lines at the corners of his mouth. "If you won't throw us any bread crumbs, Melba and I will have to keep guessing."

With a quick tip of the hat to his friend, Clark hurried back to his horse. If he'd learned anything in his three years at Yosemite, it was never feed the rangers. It only made them more curious.

Is that what God wanted for him? *Ranger Clark Johnson.* It sounded absurd.

He patted the General's rump before digging into the mare's saddlebag. "All right, girl. If we're picking up a lady artist, I guess I'd better at least put on a clean shirt."

Olivia stepped out of the long Packard Phaeton, untied the silk scarf from around her hair, and smoothed her bob back into place. She blinked hard and took several quick breaths to gather her composure. She couldn't allow the Vanderbilts to see her undone by a few cliffs, trees, and clouds—even if the panorama had left her heart a quivering mess. Could she somehow capture that emotion on paper?

Sophie hopped out of the car behind her. "It's chilly. I should have brought a warmer coat." She gestured to the valet, still holding the door. "You'll make sure our bags are brought up straightaway, won't you?"

The pale man nodded, his cap slipping forward on his head with the motion. "Yes ma'am. Right away."

Olivia shook off the strange feeling that had captured her the moment they entered the valley. "I'll take my paint box. I don't want anyone else to handle it."

Mr. Vanderbilt trotted around from the other side of the vehicle. "I'd be happy to tote it for you, Miss Rutherford, if you don't trust the help."

A flicker traveled across the valet's face, but he turned toward the luggage compartment without a word.

Sophie tittered. "You're wasting your time, Marcus. Olivia already informed me she doesn't let anyone near her case. It must contain holy relics or something."

Olivia strode to the rear of the automobile and grasped the handle of the heavy container. "Thank you, Mr. Vanderbilt, but I barely trust myself with it. My whole life is wrapped up in this box." More than anyone knew. An elegant lady would probably allow a gentleman to carry her belongings, but she couldn't chance anyone finding the old newspaper clippings and letters hidden under the paint tray.

"I imagine this place is filled with eligible bachelors. I fully intend to pick a companion for you." Sophie flung a cashmere wrap about her shoulders with an exaggerated shiver, her ploy drawing Marcus like a wave to the sand. The woman had perfected the wide-eyed act, but Olivia surmised she was more perceptive than she let on. "Though I imagine a fellow would have to be pretty colorful to snare your heart. I don't believe you'd marry just any handsome face."

Olivia propped the box on her hip and surveyed the grand hotel entrance. "Every human form is a piece of art, if you look through the right eyes."

Marcus slid an arm around his wife's slim waist. "And you two are prettier than any picture."

Olivia followed the pair down the long promenade and into the hotel. Sophie's lively chatter had already eased a little of the tension from Olivia's shoulders. She'd brought the wealthy couple along primarily to validate her reputation, but was it possible they could actually become friends?

A rough-looking man leaned against the hotel's reception desk, one booted foot kicked out before him. He held a coiled rope over one broad shoulder, arms folded across his chest.

What a perfect specimen of Western manhood. Olivia tightened her grip on the box, the image of this fellow posed against the Yosemite cliffs flashing across her mind. But painting could wait. First she needed to find her room and splash some cold water on her windburned cheeks. Olivia forced the gentleman's rugged visage from her thoughts and approached the long counter.

The clerk jerked his head upward. "Checking in, miss?"

Frank said the magazine had arranged everything. She'd expected a bit more of a reception. "My name is Miss Olivia Rutherford."

The man she'd been appraising a moment before turned and stared right at her. "The artist?"

A quiver raced through her stomach. "Yes." She wouldn't expect someone of his physique to be an art connoisseur. "Are you familiar with my work?"

A smile lifted his lips, easing the harsh expression from his face. "Clark Johnson. I'm the guide for your pack trip."

"The—the what?"

He hiked an eyebrow. "Your guide. You're the magazine artist, aren't you? They hired me to escort you and your party through the valley." Mr. Johnson glanced back at the Vanderbilts and pushed back his hat. "Sir, ma'am, we can head out whenever you're ready." His eyes traced them from head to foot. "You might want to change first."

Olivia's heart picked up speed. It would take a pretty big change to entice her out onto the trail. She'd agreed to travel to Yosemite, not trek through its woods. "I'm afraid you were misinformed, Mr. Johnson. My art dealer said I could paint from the hotel balcony. We have no intention of setting foot on any dusty trails." She focused on the desk clerk. "Now, about our accommodations."

The clerk studied the registration book. "I'm afraid I don't have your name here, Miss Rutherford. You say you're with a magazine?"

A wave of heat crept up Olivia's neck. She knew this situation would be trouble. Hadn't she told Frank as much? She leaned across the counter. "Yes, *Scenic Magazine.* We will need two of your best suites. With balconies and private washrooms."

The man's Adam's apple bobbed as his eyes darted between her face and the book. "If you'll excuse me for a moment, Miss Rutherford, I'll check with my manager."

Sophie let her wrap drape down her back. "Oh, dear." She turned to her husband, running a hand over his lapel. "You'll fix this, darling, won't you?"

Mr. Vanderbilt straightened his shoulders. "Of course. They cannot treat us as such."

The guide propped one elbow on the counter. "You're not in need of my services, then? The magazine scheduled us for four weeks on the trail. I've got my pack mules ready and waiting."

The room wavered before Olivia's eyes. Four weeks—in the wilderness? *Stay calm.* "Mr. Johnson, I am here to paint, to dine, and to dance—in that order. Smelly mules are not on my agenda." Not to mention the bears. And bugs.

He shrugged one shoulder. "The magazine paid for my services, regardless. I suppose my stock could use the rest." The guide turned to leave.

She studied the curve of his bicep as he hiked the lariat over his shoulder. "Wait a moment. They already paid you?" An idea spread through her mind like colors blending on the page. "So you're at my disposal?"

Sophie giggled behind her.

He glanced back, a light simmering in his brown eyes. "I'm not at anyone's *disposal,* miss. But if you want a tour—"

Olivia flicked away his words with a brush of her hand. "No tour. I need a model. And you're perfect. Rugged, manly."

"I—what? No." His jaw dropped.

Sophie placed her hands on her hips. "I thought I was your model."

Olivia turned to her friend. "I'll need more than one, certainly."

The guide had pulled the hat from his head revealing a shock of brown hair. "Ma'am, I'm honored, but I couldn't possibly."

Was that a blush? *How endearing.* Olivia circled around, eyeing him from various angles. "As you said, you've already been paid. It's much less work than hiking all day, I'm sure."

The clerk reappeared, a sheen of perspiration showing on his forehead. "Miss Rutherford, I'm terribly sorry. We have only one room available, and it's not quite what you requested."

Olivia ran her fingers through her bob. What would a proud, affluent woman do in this situation? Probably not dissolve into tears. She tucked the art case under her arm and glanced toward Mr. Vanderbilt. "I'm simply parched. Sophie and I are going to find the dining room and order some lemonade. I trust you'll take care of this. You and"—she turned to the handsome outdoorsman—"Mr. Johnson here can speak to the manager and work out the details. Sophie and I will wait on the patio. I hear the view is splendid."

Two

C lark grunted as he jostled the bags under his arm and clambered up the stairs. *At her disposal?* First chance he got, he'd be setting this little minx straight. He was no bellhop, no personal secretary, and certainly no model. He wouldn't even be a park employee after this month.

Placing himself under a woman's thumb would be a mistake—an all-too-familiar one.

He dropped the bags at the door of the honeymoon suite. He'd never even handled luggage for his tour clients. *You bring it; you load it.* But the manager appeared as if he might suffer a breakdown when he discovered the porter had stepped out for a smoke. It seemed easier to haul the bags himself rather than watch the man fall apart. Of course, a professional bellhop wouldn't have let pride prevent him from taking the lift. For the next load, he wouldn't make the same mistake.

He fumbled with the large key, then thrust it into the lock. The door swung wide, revealing an elegant sitting room with bedrooms attached. Why would a honeymoon suite need more than one bedroom? He dragged the cases inside and left them in the middle of the floor. Was he to unpack for them too?

If the artist and her companions planned to spend the entire visit at the

Ahwahnee, it would be a quiet month for him. She'd bore of his company in a day or two. Perhaps he could sneak away for a few weeks in the backcountry. Maybe that would help him decide what to tell John about the ranger post.

After three years of walking these mountains, Clark still didn't know if he was answering the call of the wilderness or fleeing God's bidding. Considering his disastrous experience in the ministry, a significant part of him wanted to fade into the trees and never emerge.

John might credit himself with returning Clark to the land of the living, but it had really been an encounter with the park hermit, Filbert Logan. Gray-haired and wild-eyed, the old transient was little more than a wisp of smoke from a dying ember. It had taken Clark a month to gain the fellow's trust enough to share a campfire. Another week to get him to speak a single word.

Cold fingers crept up Clark's back. *It is not good that the man should be alone.* The verse from Genesis had never made so much sense.

He strode to the window, the stale hotel air smothering him. After spending several weeks on the trail, it was always difficult to stay inside more than twenty minutes at a time. Clark opened the drapes, the expansive view never failing to make his breath catch in his chest. He wedged up the sash, letting the mountain air cleanse the stuffy room. The group certainly couldn't complain about the scenery. A shame that artist would waste all her time painting from a window when she could be out walking the hills with him.

Not that he wanted her to. With her crow-black hair and painted face, she was less suited for Yosemite than anyone he'd ever seen. And the couple trailing in her wake looked little better. The trio looked as if they belonged in a New York City hotel, not sitting in front of a Yosemite campfire.

The door creaked behind him. Clark spun around.

The artist stood on the threshold, glancing about the room with wide eyes. As her attention settled on him, her contemptuous expression returned like a mask dropping into place. "This is all they had?" She lowered a wooden box to the floor and rubbed her fingers as if the metal handle had taken a toll. "I suppose it'll do."

"Better than you'd get out on the trail with me."

She narrowed her sharp blue eyes. "And fewer bears, I imagine. No, thank you. I'll stay here where it's safe."

"Bears aren't nearly as dangerous as people. I'd rather take my chances out there."

She glanced down toward the rustic wooden box, short hair framing her overly pale face. "You might be right, Mr. Johnson. But I'm more comfortable in a crowd than alone with my thoughts." Miss Rutherford moved toward the window, her painted lips parting as if in surprise. She swung around to face him and waved a delicate hand in the air. "What's the name of the waterfall out there?"

"Yosemite Falls."

Her voice dropped to a near whisper. "It's even taller than I...than I—" she paused and darted a glance toward him— "It's taller than I pictured it. Have you been to the top?"

He cocked his head, studying her peculiar expression. "Sure. Many times. Quite a view. I can take you there, if you like."

"No. No, I couldn't." A long breath of air escaped her lips. "Has anyone ever fallen?"

That was a new one. "I've heard some stories. Gruesome tales I'd rather not share with a lady, if you don't mind." John had told him about recovering a body from the base of the falls. The person hadn't fallen...exactly. Chester Givens, a Sentinel Hotel porter, had been murdered.

"Of course."

He couldn't resist studying the woman, her gleaming white pants drawing attention to the curve of her hips. He didn't much care for the current trend of women wearing trousers like men, but then he'd never seen trousers that draped and clung like these.

Clark took a quick step back and averted his eyes. He still had scars from the last woman who'd turned his head. *I have no business being alone with her.* "If you don't need me, I should return to the...the lobby."

A weak smile brightened her face. "Actually, I could use your services."

"You've changed your mind, then?"

"I still want to paint you. And I thought if you could wait a moment while I freshen up, you could *guide* me downstairs to the dining room. It's such a large hotel, I'm not sure I can find my way."

His stomach hardened. Was she mocking him? "It's down the stairs and to the right. You can't miss it."

She looked at him from under long lashes, the light from the window dancing across her face. "I have a pathetic sense of direction. You wouldn't want me to get lost, now would you?"

A sour taste rose in his mouth. Olivia Rutherford was a bobcat on the prowl. Clark dug in his pocket until his fingers closed around a small metal case. He tossed it onto the table. "Here's a compass. You'll find your way fine."

After the door slammed behind Mr. Johnson, Olivia picked up the silver case and opened it. She ran her fingers across the face, the crystal cold to the touch. He must think her a complete Jezebel. It was wrong to tease the man, but it proved a good distraction from the waterfall. She nestled the object in her palm and walked back to the window, staring out at Yosemite Falls in the distance. *So that's where it happened.*

This job would be even harder than she expected. But perhaps, by capturing her fears on paper, she would banish them from her memory.

Laying the compass on the table, she hurried over to her valise. She'd unpack later, but now she was eager to exchange this ridiculous outfit for something more suitable in which to work. Olivia swapped her crepe de Chine yacht pants for a simple cotton dress. She could worry about her image later. Right now, she needed to paint.

Rust, cadmium, azure, blue… Crouching down, she unlatched the box lid and sorted her colors. She should have laid in a better stock before embarking on this adventure. Her hand shook as she sifted through the tubes. Mr. Johnson's words about exploring the higher reaches of the park trailed through her mind. Could she actually do that? Pack up her paper and paints and set off into the wilderness?

Olivia shivered as a breeze from the open window fluttered the edge of her dress. The sight of Yosemite Falls had touched a vulnerable thread somewhere deep inside her soul. She finished gathering her painting supplies and then slid the guide's compass into her tiny beaded handbag, next to her lipstick. The weight of the gadget was oddly soothing. If only she could have convinced Mr. Johnson to stay a few more minutes. Because when she was alone…she knew who she really was.

Clark rushed out the rear door, drawing in as much air as his ribs would allow. Did he have a target painted on his chest? As a boy, he could never get a girl to glance at him, much less show interest. His life's path had been a straight arrow before his goals collided with the wife of one of his church elders and her sordid lies. Ever since, he'd been little more than a billiard ball, bouncing off one wall after another. If a second woman had determined to knock him off course, he had no intention of cooperating.

Heading for the hitching rail, he thought through his supplies. He'd laid in enough provisions for two weeks, but without clients, it could easily last him a month. Clark gathered the General's reins. "Let's go, girl."

"Taking off so soon? What about your group?" John rode up on his horse from the direction of headquarters.

"They don't need my services."

He snorted. "That's not what I heard."

The words settled on Clark's shoulders like a yoke. News spread fast. "I'm not staying around to be some woman's lackey." Or whatever else she had in mind.

The ranger shifted in his saddle. "The magazine paid good money, Clark, and the superintendent is excited about the publicity this piece could bring to the park. You can't walk out—not if you expect to keep working here."

"You said I was done, regardless."

"Melba and I want you to stay. The Park Service needs men like you. Finish this job before you make any decisions."

Clark tilted his hat down over his eyes. The idea of leaving his friends always unsettled him, but the idea of signing on as a ranger held little appeal.

"Give her some time. She may change her mind about hitting the trail." John smiled. "Besides, she's much better looking than most of the tourists you haul up into the hills. Sounds like a pretty relaxing job to me—sitting there while someone paints your picture. Though why she chose you, I'll never understand."

"I don't understand, myself."

"Stay a few days at least. Give Yosemite a chance to work its magic on her."

"Did you see the woman? She doesn't look like the type to fall under Yosemite's spell. I bet she's never set foot in the woods in her life."

"Then you're just the man to show her how it's done." John eased his black mare back a few steps. "Besides, you hardly ever use your quarters in the village. And Melba would love to have you at our table for mealtimes."

Clark let his hand drop away from the pack. A couple of nights sleeping in a real bed might do him good. And home cooking? "Fine. I'll wait two days—no more. If she doesn't budge from this place, I want you to cut me loose from this contract. The Park Service hired me to guide in the backcountry, not to play model for some woman Michelangelo."

"That's good, my friend, because you're certainly no *David*."

After sitting at the easel for three hours, Olivia's arm ached as though she had hefted a brick rather than a brush. The sunbeams playing along the face of the granite cliffs had held her in rapt focus as she dashed paint across the paper. She sat back and rolled her shoulders. The day was fading, but still the scene beckoned. Perhaps she should have waited and painted sunset over the rock face. Or she could rise early and play with the dawn hues. This one spot could give rise to dozens of paintings as the rays of light washed the stone with colors and shadows, defining some edges and softening others.

She'd been right. There was no need to leave this patio. Certainly she could capture the spirit of the place while tuxedoed waiters delivered pink lemonade and finger sandwiches. Olivia glanced at the small table. A fly buzzed about her untouched food. What good was the magazine's generous expense account if she forgot to eat?

Sophie's champagne-bubble laugh drew her attention. Olivia had chosen to work on scenery alone for the first attempt, so her new friend sat just inside the open lodge doors, entertaining a small circle of businessmen with nonsensical stories. The socialite's hands hovered about her face as she spoke. Was it a canny attempt to direct the male attention or simply an unconscious habit?

Olivia turned back to her easel. She admired Sophie's ability to hold a crowd. Painting had a way of transporting Olivia into an artistic trance. More than once, she'd surfaced to find herself alone. And alone wasn't always a good thing. Anything could happen when she was lost inside her creative mind. She needed the security of knowing someone would be there when she emerged. Preferably lots of someones.

She squinted at the paper. The flat image failed to catch the depth of the valley's grandeur. Even though the color, light, and shadow waltzed together in a seamless dance, the picture lacked a heartbeat. It remained cold and lifeless.

Her mother's stories brushed the edges of her imagination. Mother used to speak of God walking in the garden, breathing life into His creation. Olivia put little stock in the ridiculous legends, but over the years she'd discovered that paintings need breath as well. And she could almost picture God moving through this place, adding touches of living decor here and there.

Dipping the brush into a dark sienna, she dabbed some birdlike shapes in the sky above the massive rocks, hoping for a sense of motion. She sighed. A few clouds? It seemed a shame to mar the agate blue sky. Olivia glanced around, the muse evaporating. Perhaps she should come back to it later. When she got in this sort of mood, she'd pick at a painting until it was nothing but dry bones.

Marcus Vanderbilt leaned against one of the building's granite columns, staring through the open doors at Sophie and her cluster of admirers. Irritated or amused? It was difficult to tell. He balanced a cigarette holder between his fingers, the smoke curling upward.

On the opposite end of the patio, the guide—Johnson, was it?—sat with a novel open on his knee. His head lay tilted against the chair back, eyes closed.

Must not be very engaging material.

She set aside her painting and dug out her sketchbook. Pulling the pad into her lap, she flipped it open and began roughing out the man's shape on the paper.

One leg lay outstretched, the tall laced boot propped against a nearby planter. The other leg bent at the knee, braced as if ready to spring into action at the slightest interruption. His arms were also in disagreement, the left hand clutching the book, the right casually draped over the armrest. She'd never seen a man so divided—even in sleep—as if some inward battle raged for control of his spirit and soul. Only his head appeared in complete repose, eyes closed and lips parted, a faint whistling breath escaping at measured intervals.

Breath. How could she imbue the cold, dead cliff face with this sort of life? She scraped the pencil across the paper, etching the curve of the man's shoulders and the bend of his leg, almost as if her fingers slid along his form in the process. In many ways, sketching seemed more intimate than painting. Drawing a man while he slept felt a little voyeuristic, but the peace on his face was intoxicating.

Slapping the book closed, Olivia rose. She grabbed the lemonade glass, dripping with condensation, and paced over to join Sophie and her circle. She couldn't let her new friend have all the fun, and the two fellows on the porch weren't much company.

Sophie paused her storytelling. "Olivia, I thought you'd never come up for air." She pushed her lips into a crimson pout as she turned to her companions. "This lady works me entirely too hard, fellas. I hope you're willing to show a couple of girls a fun time tonight."

The laughter around the table was tonic to Olivia's crumpled nerves. An evening of amusement and mindless conversation was exactly what she needed to divert her mind from bad memories and stone cliffs. "Sophie, you've not worked a single minute since we arrived. And your husband might protest you dancing the night away with a crew of bachelors."

"Marcus knows I like to have fun. Why do you suppose he married me?" Sophie flicked her hand over her head, waving to her husband. "Now, which of these handsome gentlemen is going to serve as your dinner escort, Olivia? I could make a few recommendations."

Several members of the group sat forward in their seats, as if ready to accept the woman's challenge. A young man with slicked-back brown hair jumped to his feet, running a hand down his silk vest. "Please, allow me, Miss Rutherford. I'm an avid admirer of your work. I saw your showing in Sacramento last November. The still life with oranges was exquisite."

An avid admirer? The words wrapped around Olivia's shoulders like a mink stole. "Well, thank you, Mr...."

"Langley. Joseph Langley." He tipped his straw boater her direction. "It's an honor to meet a talent such as yourself. I'm an aspiring artist as well. Perhaps you could share some tips—tell me how you got started."

The sight of Mr. Langley's eager eyes scattered the pleasant feelings garnered by his words. Talk about her history? Unlikely.

Olivia sat back. "Thank you, Mr. Langley. But I..." She glanced toward the sleeping guide. Turning back to the young man, she smiled. "I promised Mr. Johnson we'd discuss travel plans over dinner. He's quite set on escorting me around the park, I'm afraid. I don't want to disappoint him."

Mr. Langley offered a quick nod. "If you need a tour guide, I'd be happy to oblige. Perhaps I'll see you later this evening at the Firefall."

She couldn't resist studying the good-looking gentleman—purely from an artistic standpoint, of course. "What's a firefall?"

Sophie laughed, laying a hand on Olivia's arm. "Haven't you heard? Everyone talks about it."

Mr. Langley drew a cigarette case from his breast pocket and tapped it on his open palm. "At nine o'clock, the staff push burning embers off the cliff top, near the Glacier Point Hotel. It provides quite a show for the folks down here in the valley. It looks like a fiery waterfall."

A fiery waterfall? Now that would make for a stunning magazine cover. Her mind ticked through the colors she might need to capture such a scene. "They do this every night?"

"Through the summer, yes. Beforehand there will be entertainment here in the Great Hall." A slight smile warmed his face. "I hope you'll save me a dance."

The fellow's soft green eyes melted her resistance. She glanced down at the table to maintain her composure. Blushing at a man's attention didn't match the self-assured image she wished to portray. "I look forward to it."

⌒

Dinner at the Ahwahnee? Clark scrambled to answer the artist's invitation. Most nights he just ate beans warmed over the campfire. Did dining with the touring party count as one of his duties? If so, he couldn't exactly shirk it. At least Mr. Vanderbilt would be there to distract the ladies. "Yes ma'am. I suppose it'd be an honor to join you."

"I thought you could tell me more about your life here at Yosemite. I'd like to paint more than the scenery—I need to capture the *spirit* of the place." Miss Rutherford toyed with her ear bob, the movement drawing his eyes.

He'd spent the afternoon watching her paint, not exactly sure what the magazine folks were paying him to do. One thing was certain: Miss Rutherford's hoity-toity demeanor dropped away as she worked. Her eyes had narrowed into a tenacious stare, her lower lip tucked between her teeth. The intensity with which she labored exhausted him more than a ten-mile hike. Perhaps that's why he'd finally dozed off.

But the moment she put down the brush, the calculating socialite had returned. He steeled himself against her onslaught of artificial charm. "There's definitely a heart to Yosemite. I always say God saved up the best bits of creation and spent them here."

She shrugged her narrow shoulders. "I've worked all day, but I feel the painting is missing something critical. I'd like you to look at it."

"I don't think I'd be of much help. Perhaps one of your friends—"

"My friends tell me only what I want to hear. That's why they're friends. I need an unbiased eye." Her red lips drew into a smile. "You didn't seem to have trouble offering your opinion of me earlier."

He shuffled his feet. "Yeah, I'm sorry about that."

"It's settled then. We'll have dinner, enjoy the evening's entertainment, and then you can look over my first attempt at capturing the waterfall." She still carried a fistful of brushes.

"You can't capture a waterfall. It has the tendency to slip through one's fingers."

"Ah, yes. Like most things in life."

Wait—did she say entertainment? What exactly had he agreed to? Clark tugged at his tie. "I'll meet you in the lobby at six o'clock."

"Also, I have this for you…" Miss Rutherford dug in her handbag. She held out his compass, nestled in her palm. "I'm sure it's a keepsake. I couldn't help but admire the inscription."

Clark's throat tightened. He'd nearly forgotten the words left there by his father. *"Ye have compassed this mountain long enough: turn you north-ward. Deuteronomy 2:3."* Dad had found it humorous to take obscure scrip-ture verses out of context and reapply them in odd ways. Somehow Clark didn't think an instruction given to the Hebrews wandering in the desert could be applied to his own life, but he still missed having his dad around to offer sage—if a little bizarre—advice. What would he think about the path Clark had chosen?

He closed his hand over the compass, still warm from her skin. "Thank you."

"It was kind of you to loan it to me. Even if it was done in jest." She turned and started up the stairway. "I'll see you at six."

"If you can find your way." The jab slipped before he had a chance to think.

The smile she cast over her shoulder sent a jolt of warmth through him. As she departed, he shook off the odd sensation. Casual glances had been the first step toward the cliff edge of disaster in his former life. Under normal circumstances, this feeling of panic would send him running for the hills. Thankfully, his National Park Service contract kept his feet firmly planted. *Lord, keep my eyes on You.*

He glanced down at his rumpled clothing. A quick sprucing wouldn't hurt. He might not want to draw the artist's attention, but he didn't care to embarrass her, either.

~

Olivia entered the elegant dining room, the log framework overhead putting in her mind the image of a Gothic castle. Even with all this beauty, she couldn't help but be distracted by Mr. Johnson trailing two steps behind her. She'd managed not to laugh when she came downstairs and spotted him standing to one side of the lobby, his arms hanging stiffly beside him as if his suit had been soaked in starch. He looked like a fish out of water. But so was she, in a way. Evidently the Ahwahnee served as a middle ground where city dwellers and mountain men could somehow coexist and breathe the same air.

Since he didn't know her history, he probably thought her terribly shallow and helpless. Olivia pushed the thought away. It would be best to keep him uninformed. She couldn't trust him to maintain her charade, now more important than ever. She pressed the portfolio to her side. She'd brought today's painting—rough though it was—but had also included some examples of her better pieces. It made no sense to try to impress the man, but something inside her yearned to do so.

As the maître d' seated them at a table beside the tall windows, Olivia took a moment to study the rugged guide. He seemed a man of few words, though his deeply set eyes spoke volumes. He'd already darted a couple of glances her direction, as if uncomfortable with her scrutiny.

Hopefully he couldn't hear her stomach growling. She had never dined in a place this elegant, but she couldn't let on to that fact. "I've heard the chef here is unsurpassed."

He glanced up from the confusing array of silverware. "I've heard the same."

She paused. "You've never eaten here? How long have you worked in the park?"

"I've been leading a pack string in the area for almost three years."

Olivia opened her menu, her mouth watering as she studied the contents. So many nights going to bed unaware of how she'd afford her next meal, and here she was offered quail, duck, and trout almandine. Would this be her life from now on? "What did you do before you were a guide?"

"This and that."

His words were less than illuminating. Was she to trust her life to someone who refused to share anything about himself? What was the magazine editor thinking?

"What about you. Always been a painter?"

The way he phrased it, it sounded like she painted houses. "For a number of years, yes."

"And before that?" The corner of his lip twitched as he lobbed her question back.

"Before that I…wasn't." This might be a quiet meal.

Mr. Johnson shifted in his seat. "Your friends aren't joining us?"

The tension in Olivia's shoulders eased with the change in topic. "No, Mrs. Vanderbilt had a headache, so they took dinner in their room. I imagine she'll recover in time for the evening entertainment." She draped the napkin across her lap. "I haven't known Sophie long, but she seems to thrive on social affairs."

"I figured you were old friends."

"New friends." The word sank deep into her heart. Were they? Would Sophie give her a moment's notice if she knew the truth? "I plan to include Sophie in a few of the pictures, to add some class."

His brows drew together as he leaned forward to match her stare. "Yosemite doesn't need class." He gestured to the grand windows, framing the view of the massive granite cliffs and Yosemite Falls. "The valley speaks for itself. You just have to have ears to hear it."

The passion in his words pulled at her, and Olivia couldn't help but lean in, like warming her hands in front of a fire. "And what does it say?"

Something flickered in his expression, the light vanishing from his face in a heartbeat. He scooted away, as if the table wasn't enough of a barrier between them. "I suppose you'll have to listen for yourself."

Olivia closed the menu. "I'm an artist. I deal in what I can see. In fact, I was hoping you'd examine what I painted today." She reached for her portfolio. "I have another drying in my room, but this was my first attempt this morning." She glanced over the paper before handing it across to him. It wasn't her best effort, but it was probably a far sight better than most of the artwork Clark Johnson had ever laid eyes on.

He took the paper gingerly, as if it were the *Mona Lisa* rather than a quickly dashed-off piece. "It's Yosemite Falls." He lifted it as if to compare the painting to their window view.

"Yes." She stood and crossed to his side, studying it over his shoulder. "But see this part?" She drew a finger across the upper edge of the picture. "How the light travels across the rocks?"

"Granite." His voice hard, like the stone to which he referred.

She dropped her hand, his voice as encouraging as a splash of river water. "You don't like it?"

"I didn't say that." He set the paper on the table. "It looks like the falls."

Olivia snatched up her work. "Well, I'd hope so. That's what I was hired to paint." She returned to her seat.

"I thought you were hired to capture the spirit of Yosemite. At least that's what you told me earlier."

Her stomach tightened. What did he know? "And so I have." She stared at the image, the painting's merits suddenly fading. "At least, I've begun to. I'm sure there are more vistas to depict. Better ones, perhaps."

"It's not the location." Mr. Johnson sat back in his chair. "Look, I don't know much about art. As I said, I'm the wrong person to ask."

She jammed the picture into her portfolio, not daring to show him the rest. Taking criticism never came easy, but for some reason this one burned. "Then tell me what you mean—about the spirit."

He rubbed a hand across his chin. "Yosemite is a total stranger to you. If you spotted a man on the street, you couldn't tell anyone what made him unique. You could only describe his likeness and perhaps his demeanor on that particular day—but you would know nothing of the God-given spirit that lies within." Mr. Johnson's eyes narrowed. "If you want to paint Yosemite, you need to make its acquaintance. That's what I think. Learn the mountain's heartbeat. Breathe its air into your lungs."

A quiver raced through Olivia's stomach. The truth of his words was undeniable, but the very idea sent ice flowing into her veins. Brave the woods? Walk the trails? Face her memories? She fought for composure, struggling to pull her mask back into place. "That's preposterous. I'm here to paint, not commune with nature. I'm not John Muir."

"That much is certain."

"I think we should cut this meal short." She clutched her portfolio, pushing its sharp edge against her thigh. She certainly couldn't sit through dinner knowing the fellow's disregard for her.

"Fine by me."

She leaned forward, drilling him with a stare. "But I'll have you know, I've painted plenty of perfect strangers. And those paintings hang in homes and galleries across California."

"That may be." He folded his arms. "But what shows in those strangers' eyes? Their souls? No, because they're fictions. You're here to paint the truth of Yosemite—or so you claim."

Am I? Is that why this job frightened her so badly? "What is the truth? No one can know that."

A smile crossed his face, softening the hard glint in his eye. "I do." He stood, folding the napkin and placing it on the tabletop. "And if you're interested, you know where to find me."

⌒

Clark stalked out of the Ahwahnee, the stuffy indoor air giving way to the glory of birdsong and summer breezes. Perhaps he'd been too frank with the artist, but he'd never been good at small talk. Truth? Did he really have the only claim on that?

The arrogance of the statement sank into his gut. He glanced toward the cliff face, the long evening shadows deepening every crevice in the rock. *You are my rock, Lord. My rock and my refuge.* The only truth lay in Christ. But would a woman like Olivia Rutherford ever be interested in such things?

When she'd swept down the stairs in that short black dress, jeweled and sparkling like the night sky, he'd almost forgotten why he'd agreed to accompany her to dinner. He never wasted his time with upper-crust snobs, staring down their noses at the rest of the world. Then when he saw his falls frozen there on the paper, decked out in watery colors, the painting had stolen both Clark's breath and his common sense. Had he actually told her it was no good?

Something about this woman scrambled his brain.

What would he do if she took him up on his offer? He may no longer be a pastor, but that didn't free him from the responsibility of explaining his faith to any who asked.

Then again, she hadn't asked about faith. She asked about Yosemite. And that he didn't mind sharing.

Clark started out across the meadow toward the Edwards's home. He studied the Ranger's Club as he passed, trying to imagine himself living in the dormitory with the other bachelor rangers. He currently had a room— more of a broom closet, really—over in the transportation-staff housing. He spent most nights camped on the trail.

At least for tonight, Melba's cooking sounded much more appealing than any fancy grub the Ahwahnee chef might concoct. She and John were always quick to offer a seat at their table anytime Clark found himself in Yosemite Village.

Melba Edwards pulled open the door to their tiny house, a wide smile brightening her face. "Clark, I thought you were occupied this evening."

John, still in uniform, sat at the table. "Come on in. I should have known you wouldn't survive an entire meal with a lady."

Melba frowned at her husband. "I'll try not to take that personally."

The warmth of their interaction swept over Clark like the glow of a campfire. If only he could find such contentment in his own life. "It's more like she couldn't bear spending the evening with me."

"Oh, baloney." Melba reached out and straightened his tie. "You look handsome, all cleaned up. Shame to let that go to waste."

He shrugged. "It's not wasted. That is if you and John don't mind me mooching at your table."

John pushed out the extra chair with his foot. "You know we keep a seat ready for you. I hope you don't mind that we've already started. With as fast as you eat, you'll be caught up in two bites."

Clark hung his hat on the hook near the door before joining him. "You've got to eat fast on the trail, or the bears might beat you to it."

Melba placed a plate in front of him and dished up a generous serving of chicken and potatoes. "So, what's she like, this artist? The girls at the hotel were all abuzz. John says she's quite a looker." She turned to her husband. "Or did you say she's a 'dish'?"

Clark glanced at his friend. "You think so?" If John's head was turned by someone as fake as Olivia Rutherford, he was a foolish man.

The ranger grinned. "Nowhere as beautiful as my girl, of course. And what I actually said was, I thought she had caught Clark's eye."

Taking a biscuit from the platter, Clark snorted. "You're just trying to pair me off so I'm not here eating your supper. No, that woman is as fraudulent as a backwater medicine show."

Melba paused with the spoon dripping above the gravy boat. "You mean she isn't a real artist?"

"No, I saw the painting she did today. She's good. But…" He gestured at their surroundings. "This is what's real. You and John—you're true, honest." How could he explain what he meant? He set his fork down. "This lady—you look into her eyes, and it's like a different woman is staring back."

Like a hurt child.

The realization settled into his gut like a stone. Was that what had sent him running? He thought back to his interactions with Miss Rutherford.

She'd not said anything about herself—only her art. So why did he sense something amiss?

Melba smiled, a knowing look in her eyes. "You say that, but your face suggests otherwise. My husband was right. She's caught your interest all right. But it's not her looks. It's her heart."

"You've got to be joking." Clark picked up his fork and jammed it into the potatoes. "Did you know she's planning to paint Yosemite without ever leaving the hotel? How can someone come to this beautiful place and not bother to step outside?"

John refilled his water glass. "Not everyone wants to schlepp their way through the woods with you. Some people like their nice beds, fine food, and string quartets."

Melba's laugh rang out like birdsong. "And when have you heard a string quartet?"

"Maybe not." He leaned forward and tweaked her cheek. "But I caught every one of your shows, darling."

She captured his hand in hers for a moment. "I don't think vaudeville counts as high culture, dear. If this lady is as cultured as you suggest, she wouldn't deign to step foot in the Hippodrome. Or Camp Curry, for that matter."

Clark's spirits rose. Melba's act had brought a touch of fun and humor to the camp shows this season. He sometimes accompanied her on guitar, when he was able. "Are you singing tonight?"

"Not this week. They have a new jazz trio in from the city. I thought we'd go tomorrow and listen. Maybe they'll have dancing. I miss doing the Charleston and the Black Bottom."

John frowned. "I may have to work late." As much as the chief ranger loved watching his wife perform, dancing was not among his skills.

Melba narrowed her eyes. "Likely story. Then we'll go to the Ahwahnee tonight. William is playing piano in the Great Hall. And I know you can handle the waltz." She turned to Clark. "You come, too, Clark. You're dressed for it, anyway. It's not often a girl gets a good-looking fellow on each arm. Besides, I want to see this artist for myself. You can introduce me."

"I don't think Miss Rutherford wants anything more to do with me." He shifted in his seat. "I may have insulted her talents."

John laughed. "Put a pretty girl in front of you and what do you do? Stick your foot in your mouth."

Melba cleared the table. "Well, apologize first thing. Then you can sweep her off her feet on the dance floor. Many a good woman fell in love that way." She perched on her husband's knee and tucked an arm behind his shoulders. "I've always said it's a lucky thing this fellow snared me before I realized he had no rhythm."

Clark pushed away from the table. "Well, there's rhythm and then there's grace. Not everyone is blessed with both." And from what he'd seen, Olivia Rutherford was sadly lacking in the latter.

Four

C lark edged around the outside wall of the Great Hall, avoiding the clusters of socialites and high hats. How had he allowed Melba to talk him into this? He should be checking on his pack string, not rubbing elbows with wealthy elitists.

It wasn't hard to spot Miss Rutherford; she was surrounded by preening men vying for her attention. Mrs. Vanderbilt and her husband were already on the dance floor, waltzing to the strains of Strauss emanating from the grand piano. Her laugh carried above the music, drawing all eyes to her. If Miss Rutherford wasn't careful, her model might upstage her.

Melba hurried over from the far side of the room. "John had to go take care of a problem at the campground, so it looks like you're my dance partner for the evening." Her attention roamed the room. "Is that her? In the black?"

Clark focused on the dark-haired young woman, her short dress glittering as if studded with stars from the Yosemite sky. "I'm afraid so."

"She looks like she'd be more at home in a Hollywood speakeasy." Melba touched a hand to her simple blue dress. "I thought I was dolled up, but now I feel underdressed. My goodness, look at all her admirers."

He turned toward his friend. "They're fools. All of them. Don't forget that the critters with the finest fur often have the worst dispositions. Fox. Mink. Ermine."

She shot him a look. "Let's not lead off your apology with that little observation, shall we? And I prefer to reserve judgment on someone's personality until I've gotten to know them."

Hadn't he said something similar to Miss Rutherford about Yosemite? Was he on the same course, but with people?

The artist pulled away from her male company, some sparkly doodad in her hair catching flashes of light from the chandelier. Miss Rutherford moved toward the open doors. She lifted her head, studying the rise of the cliffs in the dusky evening shadows.

Melba caught his arm. "Now's our chance. Introduce me." She dragged him forward, nearly upsetting the glass in his hand.

His stomach dropped. After their disastrous conversation earlier, Miss Rutherford might not be too keen to speak with him so soon. Melba was right—he owed her an apology. And he wasn't too proud to offer it. As to whether she'd accept it, that was another question.

She turned as they approached, blinking hard. The emotion on her face took him by surprise.

"Miss Rutherford, I'm sorry to interrupt you."

She glanced back toward the scenery, brushing a finger along her cheek as if erasing an expression she hadn't meant to share. "You're not interrupting. I thought I'd take another peek at the falls, in a different light. Making its acquaintance—as you suggested earlier."

"I spoke out of turn before. I shouldn't have judged you so harshly." He hesitated, searching for words that might undo the damage he'd inflicted. "I actually quite liked your painting. It was lovely."

Melba patted his arm, whether in approval or camaraderie, he wasn't sure.

Miss Rutherford snorted—a most unladylike sound from one so re-fined. "I hope you don't think I'm sulking because you criticized my work." She rolled her eyes heavenward. "I'm quite accustomed to criticism. It's the nature of my business. I'd already forgotten what you said."

"Still, I am sorry. I hope you can forgive me." He cleared his throat and turned to Melba. "And Miss Rutherford, I'd also like to introduce you to a friend of mine. May I present Melba Edwards? She's quite a local singing talent, and the wife of our chief ranger."

Miss Rutherford turned, a smile illuminating her face. "Mrs. Edwards, it's a pleasure to meet you."

Melba bobbed her head. "I'm honored. Clark here spoke so highly of you."

"Really?" The artist focused on Clark. "Well, that's the second surprise of the evening."

⟳

Olivia excused herself to the powder room, suddenly needing a moment away from the crowd's prying eyes. Running into Mr. Johnson and his friend had rattled her. Something about that man—it was as if he peered straight into her soul. As if he could follow every trail of deceit she'd based her life on.

She'd never considered how physically and emotionally draining this act could become. Wouldn't it be a relief to cast off the facade for one day? Or at least to have one person who knew her as she was? But if anyone discovered she was nothing more than a poor girl hiding from her father's legacy, they'd cast her out in a heartbeat. Maintaining her image meant protecting her sisters and providing them with a proud future. She closed her eyes for a mo-ment, imagining Frances and Louise sporting smart school uniforms and rising to the top of their classes. That's why she was here. Not to find her true self in the wilderness.

Turning the faucet handle, Olivia watched the water roll off her fingers into the small basin, like Yosemite Falls cascading down the cliff face. Her hand trembled even as her thoughts fled back to today's painting. Was it the act of falling that gave the water life? It surrendered all control and submitted to the pull of gravity and motion. She shuddered. She could never do that. She held her life—her talent, her thoughts, her behavior—firmly grasped in her hand, like the brush poised above the page.

The door swung open behind her, and Olivia caught the reflection of the ranger's wife entering the small room. Olivia shut off the faucet and shook the water droplets into the sink. How long had she stood pondering the water? "Miss Edwards, wasn't it?"

The pretty brunette smiled. "Mrs. Edwards, actually. And I'd love it if you'd call me Melba. Everyone around here does."

Olivia turned. The woman's honest demeanor and smile were refreshing.

Rather than slip back into her act, Olivia faltered. "Call me..." *Liv.* She stopped short before the childhood nickname could slip off her tongue. "I'm Olivia."

Melba offered a quick nod. "Olivia, the Firefall is going to start in a minute. Are you planning to watch?"

"Oh, yes. I'd very much like to see it." She followed Melba out of the small room and across the Great Hall. Most of the dancers had already departed.

The young woman took her arm, like an old chum. "Many like to watch from the Solarium, but I prefer to see it from the lawn. Do you mind? If everyone is quiet, you can hear the stentor shout from Camp Curry."

"What's a stentor?"

"A loudmouth, essentially." Melba laughed. "A fellow from the campground hollers up to the fire tenders at Glacier Point, and they shout back to coordinate the drop. They make a whole show of it."

Olivia followed her to the edge of the crowd gathered on the lawn be-hind the hotel. "But it's so far up there. How do they ever hear each other?"

"You'll see." Melba squeezed her arm. "Are you warm enough? It's a little chilly now that the sun is down."

Olivia rubbed her gloved hands up and down her bare arms. The beaded dress had seemed perfect for tonight's festivities. She hadn't realized they'd end up outside. *I should have guessed.* Everyone seemed determined to get her out in the fresh air.

"You'll enjoy this. It's tailor-made for someone with an artist's sensibili-ties. Now John—my husband? He hates it."

"Why's that?"

Melba rubbed her hands together. "He says it's a silly spectacle. And I guess it is."

"You bet it is." Mr. Johnson, the guide, appeared out of the crowd and stood on Melba's far side. "Dumping fire over a cliff? It's a little ridiculous, if you ask me."

Melba lifted her chin. "It's beautiful. And after a long day enjoying God's stunning creation, there's nothing wrong with enjoying a little man-made fun. Is there?"

Olivia felt compelled to support her new companion. "Of course not. And not everything about nature is worthy of adoration. People can add their own touches. Aren't they carving presidents' faces into a mountain in South Dakota?"

The guide's brow furrowed as if she were some sort of puzzle to be solved. "I suppose that's true."

Someone called out from the front. "They're starting!"

A hush fell over the meadow. In the distance, a booming voice carried through the night sky. "Helloooooo, Glaaaaaaaaa-cier!"

A ripple of excitement seemed to travel through the watchers as a distant voice answered from above. Olivia couldn't make out all the words, but it seemed to end with "Curr-eee."

A few more phrases passed back and forth. Melba leaned close to Olivia's ear. "You can hear it better from Camp Curry. And here, too, when the wind's not blowing."

The cool breeze ruffled the hem of Olivia's skirt around her knees, as if in agreement.

Finally a few sparkles of light appeared at the top of the cliff face. They wafted downward as a murmur of appreciation swept through the waiting crowd. Someone bumped Olivia's arm, momentarily distracting her from the scene above. As she turned her eyes back to the cliff, a spray of glowing embers trickled down the rock, followed by more and more. Rather than looking like a glowing stream, the fall resembled the dance of millions of fireflies drifting to earth—some being blown off course to float slightly away from the mingling mass of cinders.

"Is there no fear of the fire spreading?" Olivia whispered.

Mr. Johnson was barely visible in the growing darkness. "Not really. It's all granite up there. Even if a few shrubs get scorched, the fire has nowhere to go. They've been doing this for years."

Olivia fell silent, watching the dancing sparks cascading downward, cutting a growing path of light through the darkness. "It's breathtaking." She took a step closer, as if closing the distance could help her understand the confusion brewing in her heart—an odd kinship with the mirage playing out in front of the crowd. The rippling, flowing stream of flame was as much an illusion as her own life. Somehow the lines between reality and fantasy blurred until no one could distinguish the difference—or cared to. Is that why Mr. Johnson and Melba's ranger husband disliked the spectacle?

Something about the vision made her want to strip off the veil of lies she'd used to decorate herself. Burn away Olivia Rutherford until only plain old Liv Rudd stood like an empty canvas before everyone.

She shook herself, turning her eyes away from the scene. She needed to think like an artist and plan how she'd capture this image in paint. Did it embody the spirit of Yosemite?

She observed the people, their heads raised in unison, eyes glittering with the reflected light. From the oldest to the youngest, everyone seemed consumed by the display. Even Melba and Mr. Johnson stood in rapt attention.

Perhaps human activity had become such an integral part of this grand landscape, no one could separate the place from the community. The people had become a page in Yosemite's story.

On the far side of the crowd, one face stood out from the others. His baggy work clothes and shabby boots put the fellow out of step with the posh gathering. Apparently even hotel employees couldn't help being drawn to the curious sight, no matter how often if was repeated. The curve of his shoulders and the jut of his chin as he stared up at the Firefall sent an odd chill through Olivia's memories. Was that...? She pulled her arms to her chest to halt the breath leaking from her lungs as she recognized the man. He couldn't still work here. It was impossible.

She hadn't seen Gus Kendall since she was twelve, but she'd never forgotten.

Likely as not, her father's best friend hadn't forgotten her, either. Olivia backed three steps, then ducked toward the shadows. She'd grown up, changed her name, and dyed her hair—was it enough?

Any chance that he could spot her was more risk than she desired. Gus Kendall knew her father's crime. He knew everything. And from what she remembered of him, he wouldn't hesitate to use that information against her.

A weight settled in Olivia's stomach. She must have been off her nut to agree to this job. Coming to Yosemite had been a mistake, and she'd recognized as much the moment the park's name dropped from Frank's mouth. If she'd had any inkling her father's friend would be skulking about, she'd never have agreed.

Olivia tightened her fists, inhaling deeply of the mountain air. Now that she was here, she couldn't turn her back on the assignment. It meant too much—to her, to Frank, and especially to Frances and Louise. She couldn't allow someone like Gus Kendall to derail all of her carefully laid plans.

There had to be a way to avoid him.

As applause rang out across the meadow, Clark turned to the ladies. "Another Firefall done." He glanced about. "Where did Miss Rutherford get off to?"

Melba frowned. "She was right here. I didn't see her leave."

He caught sight of her in the distance, huddled in the hotel's shadow. Her shoulders were curved, her head bowed. He hurried across the lawn. "Miss Rutherford, is everything all right?"

She glanced up, her eyes large in her pale face. "I—yes, I'm fine. I apologize. I didn't mean to desert you and Mrs. Edwards."

"Were you disappointed with the Firefall?" Most tourists ate this stuff up faster than ice cream.

"Not at all." She blinked several times, her attention darting back toward the Ahwahnee. "I was a bit overcome. I know it's nothing but a flashy display, but…" She pressed a trembling palm to her cheek. "Maybe it's my artist sensibilities."

Her words sounded a chord in his heart. He'd experienced the same sensation when he'd first beheld the massive cliffs of the Yosemite Valley. "Maybe."

The music had started up again, and the crowd was streaming back inside. Had they been down at Camp Curry, the Firefall would have been accompanied by the song "Indian Love Call," and then the families would wander back to their tents. Here at the hotel, people would probably continue to dance and make merry for a few hours yet. Melba had already gone back inside.

A wave of exhaustion dropped over him. He wasn't cut out for such madness.

Everything about Miss Rutherford suggested a life spent in the limelight, but right now she appeared every bit as tired and haggard as he felt. Almost like a piece of her fine veneer had dropped away with the Firefall.

She opened her tiny pocketbook and pulled out a lipstick, then jammed it back inside without using it. The harsh movement caught his attention. Her focus flicked over to where a handyman was lighting one of the outdoor lamps that had been darkened for the festivities. She turned her back on the fellow and edged closer to Clark.

As much as he wished to slip away, he didn't want to leave her stranded, especially when she appeared visibly affected by the events of the evening. Could she really have been so moved by the Firefall? He'd spent little time with women other than Melba in recent years. What was expected of him in this situation? "You look like you could use a moment of quiet. Would you like a walk?"

She lifted her eyes. "Is it safe—at night?"

He swallowed a laugh. "We won't go far." To him, she was the most dangerous critter in the area.

She latched on to his elbow, her fingers pressing into his arm. "I'd like that, yes."

The sudden touch sent a prickling sensation from his wrist to his shoulder, and it took all his self-possession to not yank away from her grasp. *Easy, there.* He led her across the Ahwahnee's lawn and down toward the river. It wasn't hiking in the wilderness, but a quiet walk by the Merced wasn't a bad way to end an evening—even with an unpredictable female at his side.

The tension in her stance seemed to relax the farther they walked from the hotel. After several minutes, she broke the silence. "I hope you'll reconsider modeling for me."

"I don't understand why you'd want me for that. This place is so full of beauty, I'd only mar the picture. You did a fine job with Yosemite Falls today." He cleared his throat. "Regardless of what I said earlier."

"No, you were right." She shook her head. "I was a stranger painting what anyone could see. I'm determined to go deeper. To find out what makes Yosemite special."

They stopped at the old stone bridge, the sound of the river trickling away below them. She hadn't released his elbow, the pressure of her hand oddly foreign. When was the last time he'd had a woman on his arm? "What does that have to do with me?"

"I was thinking"—she leaned on the railing, gazing out over the dark stream—"there's so much life here. The plants, the animals, the people, even the water, seem full of breath and spirit. That's what I need to capture in my painting."

"I'm not sure anyone can capture that. There's a photographer here. Ansel Adams. He's been working on that for years."

Her expression softened for the first time since the Firefall. "I'd like to meet him. My art dealer made sure I saw his *Monolith, The Face of Half Dome,* before I came." She sighed. "But photography is a rather stark art form for capturing emotion and passion. There's so much more you can do with watercolors. I'm determined to try."

Clark paused. "And you think I can help with that?"

"You are the embodiment of this place." She released her grip and pointed toward Half Dome. "Like the living representation of that cliff face up there."

He glanced up, the moonlight casting enough glow to outline its curved shape against the night sky. Her statement echoed in his chest, a confusing mess of words and images. "I don't have a clue what you're talking about, but I'm happy to help however I can, Miss Rutherford."

"My name is Olivia. If we're going to work together, I think we should be on a first name basis."

He managed a quick nod. "Olivia, it is. And I'm Clark."

"Clark." A brief frown crossed her face. "Like Lewis and—"

"Yes."

A smile teased her painted lips. "No wonder you became a wilderness guide. I suppose you were born to it."

"You would think so, wouldn't you?" A breeze swept up from the river, and he noticed her shivering. He shrugged off his jacket. "I didn't realize how cold it was."

Her face grew somber as he settled the coat around her shoulders. "Clark, I've decided to take you up on your offer."

His throat tightened. "My offer?"

"To see the park."

Of course. "What made you change your mind?"

She pulled the garment closed, gripping the lapels with one hand. "I think in order to discover the spirit of this place, I might have to ramble about like John Muir first did." She paused. "And also, because I think staying here at the hotel"—she glanced back toward the Ahwahnee—"won't help me at all."

Five

O livia sorted through her things, spreading clothes and jewelry on the wide bed. Why had she told Clark she'd go into the wilderness with him? The very idea sent a quiver through her stomach.

Walking with the guide last night, she'd felt safe. She couldn't remain at the Ahwahnee—not with Kendall lurking about—but choosing instead to go on the trail with a perfect stranger? The impulsive decision now hung on her like a dress two sizes too large.

She couldn't let anything distract her from this job. She had a month to come up with six stellar illustrations of the real Yosemite—whatever that meant. The girls were counting on her for tuition money. And Aunt Phyllis? The thought sent a chill through her. She couldn't fail here. Olivia Rutherford had to be a success.

She stared at the ridiculous assortment of clothes she'd brought along. Everything had been chosen with an eye to being seen, not for trudging down a forest path and sleeping on the ground.

Olivia sank onto the edge of the mattress, the walls closing in. Gus Kendall still worked at Yosemite, after all that had happened? The notion boggled her mind. It was almost ten years ago when temporary jobs lured Kendall and her father to the park. Men were needed to help lay railroad line for the dam-building project in the Hetch Hetchy Valley. She and her sisters had stayed home with their mother in Coulterville, a little mining town in the Sierra Nevada foothills. Olivia had never dreamed Kendall continued working at the park.

No matter. She couldn't sit and wait for the past to reveal itself in front of a crowd of well-wishers in the Great Hall. Not when she was on the cusp of success. The girls deserved better. So did she.

A knock at the bedroom door jarred her to her feet. "Olivia?" Sophie's voice sounded as she rattled the knob.

Olivia hurried over and opened the latch.

"You locked me out? Are you expecting hooligans at the door?" Her friend stood in the sitting room, one hand latched onto her hip. "The hall boy said you were leaving. What's going on? Are you deserting us?"

A sick feeling settled in Olivia's stomach. She hadn't thought this through. "I'm going out on the trail with the guide, Mr. Johnson. I decided if I'm going to illustrate the park, I need to see more than I can from the hotel."

Sophie brushed past her, striding into the room and staring at the pile of clothes. She wrinkled her nose. "What's this foolishness? You can't traipse off into the wilderness alone with that mountain man. You've a reputation to maintain. And you still haven't done my portrait." She folded her arms. "If you're going, we're going too."

Olivia's heart jumped. "I can't ask you to do that." Sophie and Marcus Vanderbilt hiking through the dirt and drinking stream water from a canteen? The image was ludicrous.

The woman ran a hand over her golden Marcel waves. "We'll pretend we're going on safari. It'll be a hoot." She picked up Olivia's white yacht pants. "But I think you're going to have to find some new togs. Maybe your fella can help."

"He's not my fella." Olivia bit her lip. "And I hate to ask him for favors."

"I don't see why not. He's delicious. If I weren't with Marcus, I'd be thinking of running off into the woods with him." She sighed. "And if he saves you from a wolf or a bear—all the better."

Marcus appeared in the doorway, his tall frame nearly filling the space. "Who am I saving now?"

His velvety voice made Olivia smile. The man never failed to put her in mind of a film star. All he needed was a turban, and he could be Rudolph Valentino.

"Not you, silly." Sophie rushed to his side, taking his arm. "Oh, Marcus, it's simply too exciting for words. You and I are going on safari with Olivia and that park guide. We'll be trekking up hill and down dale in search of Olivia's next great painting."

Marcus fixed his attention on Olivia. "Are we now? A grand adventure, eh?"

This trip grew more complicated by the moment. Perhaps taking the pair along was not the best idea, but she couldn't face the woods alone either. At least Sophie's lighthearted demeanor would distract Olivia from the haunting memories. "Only if you're sure you don't mind."

He lifted his chin. "I think it's a splendid idea. Why come out to the wilderness and not set foot in it? I come from a long line of explorers. My father made his fortune in the Yukon. This will be a mild excursion at best."

The Vanderbilts' confidence bolstered her own. Maybe they were right. Perhaps the experience would be good for her. Get her over her fear of the outdoors. As a child, the woods had been her playground. Could she reclaim that sense of security? "Very well. I'll inform Mr. Johnson we will all be joining him. Shall we meet downstairs at ten?"

An hour later, Olivia stood in Melba's tiny living room, holding a pair of woolen riding breeches in front of her. "Are you certain you can part with them?"

Melba laughed. "Of course. You and Mrs. Vanderbilt can't ride horseback in those silly cocktail dresses. I've laid out several flannel shirts, as well. Oh, and here—" She pulled a bulky, blue sweater out of her drawer. "I never camp without a wool sweater. It might be July, but the nights get cold. You might not look like a fashion plate, but at least you won't freeze." She glanced up at Olivia's face. "And for goodness' sake, leave the lipstick and face powder behind. Unless you're hoping to impress the mule deer."

The teasing lilt in Melba's voice made Olivia smile. "I don't know how to thank you. You barely know me, but you're going to all this trouble."

The ranger's wife handed her a folded pair of socks. "I want to see those paintings before you send them off to the magazine. Especially if you put Clark in any of them." She grabbed a second pair and added it to the duffel bag she'd set out for Olivia. "Yosemite is a place of healing. It draws broken people—folks trying to understand why they're on this good, green earth. I think you'll find Clark's not so different. He came here in despair, and this land has been slowly putting him back together, piece by piece."

In despair? The guide hadn't seemed troubled. Melba's words settled into Olivia's heart, making themselves at home, even if she didn't completely understand their meaning. "How can a place do that?"

"I'm not certain." She tapped fingers against her chin. "Maybe it's the water or the air—or the enormity of the landscape. It reminds you we serve a big God and our problems are miniscule in comparison. Flies—ready to be brushed away."

Olivia turned away to blink back tears. Problems...miniscule? The woman had no idea.

Melba folded one more item. "Anyway, Clark means a lot to us. I know he'll take good care of you out on the trail. But someone needs to look out for him, too."

"I'll do my best. But I don't think I'll be of much use to him."

Her eyes brightened. "You might be surprised. I think you could do him a world of good. God brought him here for healing, but he's still figuring out who God wishes him to be—seeking his identity and purpose. I'll be praying you find yours, too."

~

Clark walked Old Bess around in a few lazy circles before rechecking her cinch strap and tightening it a third time. The headstrong mule had a habit of tensing while being tacked up. They'd get maybe ten yards down the trail before her saddle slipped sideways. He rarely put visitors on her back due to her ornery nature, but one of his friendlier mules had turned up lame.

Marcus Vanderbilt strode up and tossed his leather grip at Clark's feet, not even bothering to look him in the eye.

Clark nudged it with the toe of his boot. "I'm not a porter, Mr. Vanderbilt. You'll need to put your belongings into one of the bags over there by the supplies." Hopefully, the party had packed light. He still needed to weigh everything and make sure the large pannier boxes were properly balanced for the mules.

The man lifted his chin. "I'll have you know, I'm an avid outdoorsman. Fishing, game hunting—I've done it all."

"Then I'll be glad of your help." Every time Clark heard this speech, his hackles rose. Like so many of the others he'd guided in the past, Marcus

Vanderbilt was a pith helmet short of an African safari. Next thing you knew, he'd be demanding tea from a china cup.

And yet, maybe the fellow would surprise him.

Vanderbilt cleared his throat, glancing back toward the hotel. The women had yet to emerge. He took a step closer to Clark, keeping his voice low and even. "And just so you're aware, the ladies are under my protection." He folded arms across his chest. "I won't have any...misunderstandings. Are we clear?"

Clark set his jaw, swallowing the heat crawling up his throat. Posturing already? "You've no need to worry."

The gentleman stepped back as the ladies appeared on the path. He turned to the string of mules. "I like an animal with a little spirit, not a plodding old nag. Have you got one with some life left in it?"

Clark studied the long-legged aristocrat. *I shouldn't...really shouldn't.* He laid a hand on Bess's neck. "Well, this is one of my best animals, but not everyone can handle her."

Vanderbilt stared down at the mule—a long way down. "It's a little short."

"Good things come in small packages, or so they say." Clark turned to greet the women as they approached.

Seeing the flamboyant artist and her flapper friend dressed like packers brought a grin to his face. Wearing boots and riding trousers, and with hair tucked into felt hats, they looked like they'd done this sort of thing a hundred times before. Olivia's eyes betrayed the truth, however. She glanced about as if she expected a bear to charge out of the brush at any moment.

He reached for the wooden box she carried, but Olivia swung it away before he could make contact with the handle.

She pulled it close. "I'll take it. It's my art supplies."

"You'd best give it to the man." Mrs. Vanderbilt adjusted her cloche hat. "You can't hold it while you ride."

"How about I load your box onto the front mule with the other fragile supplies?"

Olivia bit her lower lip. "Are you sure it'll be safe?"

"I haven't even broken an egg on the last two trips." He gestured to the large mule near the end of the hitching post. "Chieftain's my most sure-footed animal, next to the General—my horse. But she's spoken for."

Olivia wrinkled her nose. "You call your mare the General?"

Clark shrugged. "She's in charge." He gestured to the mule on the opposite end. "And you can ride Goldie."

She held the item to her chest for a moment before carefully passing it to him.

Was the lady always so jumpy? Clark hung the case on the scale before tucking it into one of Chieftain's pannier boxes. Had there ever been anything he feared losing quite so much? He'd already lost his job, his self-respect, and his mission in life. What was left?

The woman watched for a moment and then headed back to Goldie. She reached a tentative hand up to the animal's neck and patted it. Goldie responded with a gentle snuffling sound, bumping the lady's shoulder with a soft nose. Olivia smiled, running her fingers along the mule's cheek and chin. "What a lovely animal. Kind eyes."

Clark resisted the urge to laugh. Not many of his clients seemed charmed by the yellow mule, though he'd always thought she was a lovely thing himself.

Mr. Vanderbilt helped his wife get settled on Smoke, the dainty gray, placing the reins in her gloved hands. "You'll be fine, dear. This looks like a sturdy fellow."

Mrs. Vanderbilt laughed. "I'm not worried, darling. I trust Mr. Johnson —he's the real McCoy. I'm sure he knows everything there is to know about surviving in the wilderness."

Clark balanced and loaded the panniers himself rather than waiting for Vanderbilt's help. After all, the man was probably more familiar with the Windsor knot than a diamond hitch. "I appreciate the confidence, Mrs. Vanderbilt, but I think we'll hit a few of the more famous landmarks in Yosemite rather than trekking off into the wild country just yet. We'll see a couple of the waterfalls and maybe go up to Glacier Point. There's a nice hotel there if you folks would prefer it to staying in tents."

Her lips pursed. "Oh, no. We want the full experience, don't we Marcus? Sleeping under the stars, campfires, scary stories."

Her husband frowned. "Bugs, bears, hard ground? Waking up soaked in dew? Sophie, you have no idea."

She straightened her neck. "I'm stronger than you realize, Marcus Vanderbilt. You mustn't treat me like a porcelain vase sitting on a shelf. I'm a modern woman."

Olivia pulled herself into Goldie's saddle unassisted, a smile playing about her lips. Was it the Vanderbilts' banter or the beauty of the morning?

Something about seeing the artist settled on his favorite mule warmed Clark's heart. She looked nothing like the glamour girl he'd faced down in the lobby.

Vanderbilt placed his foot in Bess's stirrup and hoisted himself onto her back with a flourish that would have put a Musketeer to shame. "And what's this beast's name?"

Clark fought to maintain a steady expression. "Queen Elizabeth."

"Named for royalty, eh?"

Clark led out on the General with Chieftain and the other pack mules falling in behind him. The two women followed on their mounts, but Bess seemed glued in place. Vanderbilt kicked at the mule, quite a feat as his heels nearly dragged the ground. "Move, your highness." He grunted, bouncing in an attempt to get the mule in motion.

Mrs. Vanderbilt turned in her saddle. "Come along, dear. You're going to be left behind."

The man huffed, jabbing his heels into Bess's sides and slapping the reins. Evidently a Yosemite pack mule was a long way from the fancy equines he'd ridden in the past. If he *had* ever ridden.

Clark placed a finger and thumb between his teeth and whistled.

Bess's long ears swiveled forward. She heaved a heavy sigh and plodded after the others.

The animals sauntered down the trail, leaving the Ahwahnee and its fuss behind. Whenever Clark ventured away from the valley's hotels and campgrounds, he felt tension peel away in layers. Something about the mountains breathed life into him, and prayers of gratitude welled up from his soul.

Maybe he should consider John's offer. The idea of leaving this place for good left him hollow inside. But he had always pictured returning to the ministry in some form. Being a uniformed park ranger seemed about as far from his dream as one could get.

He glanced over his shoulder, careful to make sure everyone stayed close. Goldie and the gray marched along at a good clip, but Bess trailed farther and farther behind.

Vanderbilt's face reddened. "What's wrong with this animal?" He hoisted himself higher in the saddle and whacked the reins against the mule's flank.

Bess snorted her displeasure, flattening her ears.

If he did much more of that, he'd find himself on his backside in the dirt. It wouldn't be a long trip, but the landing might not be too pleasurable.

Clark dismounted and walked back until he reached Vanderbilt. "Having difficulties?"

The man's eyes narrowed. "I told you not to give me an old nag."

"Bess is no nag. She's strong-willed and feisty, and she has a get-up-and-go that could curl your hair. You said you could handle a spirited animal."

"This creature has no spirit. It's as if it has lead weights strapped to her hooves."

If only he knew. If Clark allowed Vanderbilt to continue yanking on the mule's mouth, he would find out the hard way. With reluctance, Clark tied Bess's lead rope to the ring on the back of Smoke's saddle. "Let's try this a while. She's accustomed to following the others."

The man sputtered. "I'm not some child on a pony ride."

Then quit acting like one. Clark gritted his teeth. This was shaping up to be a long week on the trail, and they'd only been out for ten minutes.

Leaving the man huffing, Clark strode back to Olivia. "What do you think? Would you like to see Yosemite Falls first?"

Her mouth opened and closed, and she ducked her head. "The falls I already painted?"

"Yes, but I could take you right alongside so you could feel the spray in your face. Let the thundering water speak to your soul. And then tomorrow, we'll visit Bridalveil Fall."

Her lips pressed into a firm line. "It's time to make their acquaintance."

"All right. First stop, Yosemite Falls." He patted Goldie's flank, stopping himself before he did the same to the woman's leg. The base of the falls would make for a short first ride. Enough time to get these folks used to the idea, but not so long as to see them get antsy. If they made it that far without calling for a concierge, they might even survive their first night on the trail.

⟶

Olivia slid from the saddle, the towering waterfall above threatening to scatter every thread of self-control she managed to keep during the short ride to its base. She never imagined she'd be standing in this place. She took a deep breath, staring up at the water coursing down the face of the cliff in a gushing torrent. *It's only a waterfall. It holds no power over me.*

Sophie came to stand next to her. "Isn't it stunning?"

"It is." Olivia closed her eyes, letting the sound of the water soak through her and the misty air chill her flushed skin. She needed to let go of the memories and paint the waterfall as it stood—not as she'd imagined it. Sophie's giggle drew her attention.

Queen Elizabeth seemed to have set her brakes early, and in royal fashion wasn't taking orders from her underlings. Marcus gave up trying to encourage her the last ten feet and jumped to the ground. "Fine, stop there."

Olivia shook out her knotted muscles, trying to dislodge any lingering dread. She was here to paint, not dwell on the past. Besides, every step down the trail had been one step away from the Ahwahnee. Who could possibly know anything about her history clear out here? Her father's mistakes shouldn't keep her heart captive forever.

Taking a deep breath of the mountain air, Olivia strode to the stream, where Clark stood gazing up at the thundering falls.

He turned to her. "What do you think?"

"So wild, so free."

From the Ahwahnee porch, the falls had been a silver line scratching the face of the massive cliffs. Here the water bellowed as it bounced down the rocks, as if laughing from deep in its belly and shouting at the top of its lungs at the same time. The creek had carved a notch into the rock, slicing a path before jumping free to cascade down to the pool below. The top section dropped well over a thousand feet, disappearing into a cloud of mist before reappearing, then splashing over some rocks and casting itself down several hundred more feet as if for an encore performance.

Olivia exhaled, suddenly aware she'd been holding her breath. The energy of the water seemed to flow through her arms, and she had to fold her hands to keep from tracing the water's path in the air with her fingers. "I've already painted this once, but I want to try again." She strode along the edge of the creek, leaving the group a few steps behind. The water beckoned to her with its force. Perhaps the only way to free herself from its memory would be to commit the sight to paper. Then she could look at it with new eyes. At least for a time.

"I'll get my paints out and try to capture a little of this while it's fresh in my mind." *And my heart.*

"You're the boss here, Miss Ru—Olivia. We can stay for as long as you like. Should I retrieve your box?"

The thought jarred Olivia from her reverie. The box. She hurried after him, catching up as he unfastened the straps. "Thank you. I'll take it."

He lowered the wooden box. "Are you certain you don't want me to tote it to your spot? I'm more than happy to do so."

Olivia frowned. What would it hurt? It's not as if he would open the lid and dig through the contents. "All right. I mean, yes—thank you." The warmth in his eyes melted the last bit of resistance from her spine.

"Where would you like it?"

She gestured to the creekside. "We're so close, I think I'll just paint the lower section." She lifted a hand and measured to the top, judging the best angle. "Yes. That would be idyllic."

He set it down in a dry spot, away from the bank.

Olivia pulled her folding easel from the crate and put it in position.

Sophie came to her side. "I don't mean to be any trouble, but what do we do while you're off painting?"

"Aren't you going to sit for me?"

Her friend's eyes lit up. "Really? Do you mean it?"

"That's why you came, isn't it?"

Sophie bounced on the balls of her feet. "Where do you want me?"

Olivia scanned the scene. The waterfall must be primary to the painting, but *Scenic* wanted the images to portray a playground of sorts. Sophie didn't look like the type to try fishing, but it never hurt to have a pretty face in the painting.

"How about right down there on that outcropping?" She gestured to where the creek lapped at the bank, the water taking a quiet turn after its mad plunge. Perhaps she could mirror that with Sophie's presence. "Take a seat on that rock, and dip your toes in the water."

Sophie hurried down to the water's edge, pausing to pull off her boots and roll up her pants.

The guide cleared his throat and turned away, striding back to where the mules rested.

Olivia couldn't help smiling. If the sight of Sophie's bare legs made the poor man uncomfortable, she could probably trust him not to make any untoward moves during their trip.

She clipped paper to the board and filled her water cup from the stream, then used a flat brush to dampen the surface in preparation.

Sophie found a spot on the large, flat stone. She sat on the edge, letting her legs trail down into the water. "Oh, it's cold."

"You don't need to put them in all the time. Let me rough out the other areas first." Olivia swirled her brush in the paint, dabbing the color onto the paper and forming the basic structure of the cliff and the falls, taking her time to let the pigments play. Her heart soared as the sounds filled her spirit, rushing like the blood through her veins. Is that what water was to a landscape? The lifeblood? And the wind was the breath?

Thoughts played alongside her brushstrokes. If Yosemite were a living thing, how would it present itself? A gentle friend? A wild creature? If the falls were any hint, the place definitely had a daring and playful side.

And yet, the water slowed here, too. She drew her brush through the lower right quadrant of the paper, tracing the stream's path to where Sophie waited. Olivia lifted her eyes, studying the young woman as she sat, gazing upstream. Her shoulders were relaxed and languid, one leg stretched in front, the other tucked up with her arms wrapped about the knee. Perfect.

Changing to a smaller brush, she used the finer tip to outline Sophie's shape against the background, smoothing the edges to show her at ease with the scenery.

Every good picture told a story. In this one, the chaos and intensity of the waterfall filled the background, but the quiet pool and Sophie's demeanor served as the antithesis. Olivia couldn't help but smile as she added detail and color to the imagery, letting the light play off Sophie's golden-blond hair and the tan of her trousers mirrored by some warmer tones in the water.

A touch on her back made Olivia jerk, her brush dragging across the painting. She wheeled around, Marcus's face looming directly behind her.

His lips drew down, as if hurt by her reaction. "I'm sorry, I didn't mean to frighten you."

"You—you didn't." She shook off the energy racing through her system. "I was engrossed in my work. I didn't hear you coming."

He stepped even closer, brushing his fingers along her elbow. "I'm sorry I disturbed you then. I hoped for a closer look."

Olivia drew her arm away. "Your wife is doing a fine job."

Marcus studied the painting. He lifted a finger close to the paper and he gestured to her form. "Why don't you add a few curves, while you're at it?" He kept his voice low. "It's the only area in which she's lacking." One side of his mouth quirked upward.

"It's not her figure I'm concerned with." Her stomach tightened. "It's how she portrays Yosemite as a place to retreat from the pressures of life."

"The magazine's editor—he's a man, I assume?"

Olivia dipped her brush in the paint, grasping at the vanishing strains of her muse. "I assume so. My art dealer made the arrangements."

"Then he'll be concerned with her figure. Take it from me."

A sour taste rose in her mouth as Marcus walked away. He'd never seemed anything but devoted to his wife. Olivia brushed away the crawly sensation he'd left behind. As an art connoisseur, Marcus Vanderbilt knew what might appeal to her audience. Perhaps he was right. Did Sophie need a little extra...interpretation? She focused on the painting. The young woman looked lovely framed against the fall's spray—innocent.

Many times she'd taken artistic license with her paintings. Even now, she'd softened the edges of the scene and used large strokes to create extra movement in the water. She lifted her brush, considering how she might enhance the girl's appearance. Olivia glanced back at her friend, sitting with head tipped back, her golden hair catching the glow of the late afternoon sun.

Olivia had changed her own name, dyed her hair, become a new person —all at Frank's bidding. Was this really so different? She tapped the brush's handle against her lips. She had the main aspects of the work finished; she could add details later. Olivia rinsed the paint from the bristles, flicking the excess moisture onto the ground. If only she could wash away the sickening feeling left in her stomach.

Six

C lark undid Goldie's cinch and slid the saddle and blanket off the molly mule. "Short day, girl." Since Olivia had dawdled away several hours painting the falls, he'd only taken them a few more miles before stopping to set up camp. He thought they'd make more distance today, but truth be told, this was one of his favorite places in the park. It sat far enough from the hotels and public campgrounds to offer some peace but remained in the heart of the valley where one could appreciate the sensation of being dwarfed by the rampart-like cliffs rising on all sides.

Perhaps tomorrow they'd take the steep trail up to Glacier Point and give the artist an aerial view of the park. One could never truly understand Yosemite Valley without seeing it from above. It was an Eden, an oasis hidden in the midst of a massive mountain range. How many years had it existed, stashed away, until man had stumbled unawares into its beauty?

The Ahwahneechee tribe would probably argue that its reaches had never been hidden from them. God had provided the land as a refuge from their enemies. Too bad it hadn't protected them from the white man.

Clark laid the saddle over a nearby log with the others. The valley had protected him for a few years now, too, but his time was running out. Soon he'd have to face the world. Then what?

He staked the mule in a lush spot of grass and patted her shoulder. Not that Goldie needed the attention. She and Olivia seemed a good match. He wished he could say the same of Vanderbilt and Bess. Or rather, *Queen Elizabeth*. He might keep the name. It fit her personality rather well. Queenie, perhaps?

Sophie and Olivia's laughter carried through the trees as they headed off to take care of some discreet business. One would think they'd desire privacy, but perhaps that was one of the many things about women he'd never understand. Then again, Olivia seemed particularly concerned with not being left alone. He'd always thought of creative types as being moody loners, but little about that woman fit with his previous assumptions.

He'd set Marcus Vanderbilt to gathering wood for their campfire. The evening was warm enough that they wouldn't need one, but most groups desired hot food at the end of a ride. For that matter, he'd welcome the smell of coffee and some finer fare than jerky and cold beans. Thankfully he'd managed to learn a few tricks when it came to outdoor cooking.

After stacking the iron skillet and other kitchen gear to one side, Clark pulled Olivia's paint supplies from its spot in one of the pannier boxes. Remembering her fussing over the item, he took care as he lifted it free. Craftsmen were generally obsessed with their tools, so it made sense that an artist would be the same.

A shriek in the distance launched Clark's heart into his throat. He swung around, the sudden motion causing the wood to shift in his grip. After a quick juggle, the crate broke free and landed in the dirt, the hinges splintering open on impact. His blood froze at the cracking sound. Olivia would have his hide for a canvas when she saw her precious cargo laid out on the dirt. He stooped, but a second scream knocked the accident from his mind. Jumping up, he dashed in the direction of the women. Had they encountered a bear? A mountain lion?

He never carried a firearm, despite the Park Service offering him a permit to do so. "Olivia?" He ducked through the underbrush, branches pulling at his arms. "Where are you?"

"Over here!" Her voice carried through the thicket.

He changed direction, slowing to give himself time to assess the situation before coming face to face with some creature. Spotting the two women at the edge of a clearing, he stopped. "What happened?"

Olivia pointed. "It's…it's an Indian. Or something. Over there. Sophie spotted him first."

An Indian? *Unlikely.* Clark hurried to Olivia's side, searching the edge of the trees for whoever—or whatever—had frightened them. The only person he ever saw in this area was… Clark paused. "Filbert, is that you?"

The gray-haired man stepped from the shadows, his lanky frame doing little to distinguish him from the tree trunks. He grinned, exposing several gaping holes amongst his yellowed teeth. "Jus' me." He tipped a battered black derby to them.

Olivia gasped. "Clark, you know this man?"

Clark turned back to the ladies. "Yes, I do. And he's harmless; trust me."

Vanderbilt burst into the clearing, brandishing a small pistol. "What is it? Rattlesnake?"

Filbert vanished in an instant, a lifetime of honed instincts taking over.

Clark charged forward, placing himself between Vanderbilt and the others. "Put that away! Everything's fine."

The man gestured with the gun. "I'd like to hear that from the ladies, if you don't mind."

"Marcus." Mrs. Vanderbilt hurried over to her husband. "We're fine."

He returned the gun to an inner pocket of his jacket. "I'm glad you're safe." He took Sophie in his arms, glancing toward Olivia over her head. "And Miss Rutherford?"

"Yes, yes. It was a misunderstanding." She picked her way to where Clark stood. "Who was that man? Is he gone?"

Clark scanned the trees. "A friend. Sort of. Filbert Logan. He's a bit of a hermit, but he wouldn't hurt a horsefly."

Mrs. Vanderbilt clutched her husband's arm. "He looked like a wild man. I've never been so frightened."

Vanderbilt pulled her close, pressing her to his chest. "Don't worry, sweetheart. I'll protect you." His brow furrowed as he frowned at Clark. "You didn't warn us there were crazy men in the woods."

And which one had been brandishing a weapon? "Filbert isn't crazy. Not exactly. He's just a bit eccentric."

Olivia rubbed her arms. "I think we frightened him even more than he did us."

Clark nodded. "That's where you're right. Now we should get camp set up before we lose our daylight." He cast one last glance over the trees. If Filbert was still nearby, he'd need hours to gather the courage to approach again. It had taken Clark months to earn the man's trust. How much damage had Vanderbilt done in ten seconds?

Olivia moved in the direction of camp. "I should hang up my picture and make sure it dries properly."

The box. Clark's breath caught in his chest. "About that…"

She turned, the question obvious in her eyes.

"Let me finish unpacking the supplies first. Why don't you and Mrs. Vanderbilt help gather some firewood?"

Before she had the chance to protest, Clark dashed back to camp. He picked up the box and ran a thumb across the broken hinge. Pulling it open, he groaned at the sight of the jumbled paint pans and brushes. With a shaking hand, he jammed them back into their slots. He'd never be able to return them to a proper order. Would she notice? One of the tubes was leaking. He tightened the cap, the red smears on his fingers putting him in mind of blood.

He clustered the like colors together, fastening the brushes in the slots from smallest to largest. The box's base shifted as he pressed the largest brush into place. Was it a false bottom? He lifted the slat of wood, and then jammed it back into position. Better not to disturb the contents more than he already had.

Smeared red fingerprints remained where he'd touched the light-colored wood. "Blast." He grabbed a handkerchief from his pocket and wiped his hands, then the box.

He was working on the latch when the Vanderbilts' voices rang out through the trees. He jumped to his feet, tempted to push the box in with the other things. *No, that wouldn't be right.*

Olivia appeared a few steps ahead of the other two, her arms laden with broken branches. "Will these do? I'm afraid I haven't done this in years."

The sight of the young woman's smile and the dirt smudge on her cheek made him feel even worse. "Olivia, there's something I need to confess to you."

She halted, her face whitening.

He swallowed hard. "Your box. It fell."

"Did you look inside?" She dropped the wood and hurried over to where the case sat with the other supplies.

"Well, I tried to put your things back the best I could—"

"You opened it?" She flung back the lid and rifled through the contents.

"I'm sorry." Clark stepped back, giving the woman space to go through her belongings without him watching over her shoulder. He had no defense; best not to make excuses. Instead he got on with setting up the tents. Even though Mrs. Vanderbilt had spoken of sleeping under the stars, he'd found most visitors—particularly women—slept better with a canvas roof between them and the elements.

He laid out two tents and carefully pounded the stakes into the soft earth. He wasn't sure if Vanderbilt would share a tent with his wife or if the women would choose to stay together.

Something about the man unsettled Clark. He'd been irritated with the fellow's pretentious attitude since the moment they met, not to mention the way he manhandled the mule. But when Vanderbilt rushed in and frightened Filbert, his actions had snapped Clark's last nerve.

Speaking of… Clark drove the last stake and stood, scanning the clearing for the old vagrant. Either Filbert had hightailed it back to the hills, or he might be three trees away listening to everything they said. No way to know. Clark blew out a long breath. He strode to where Vanderbilt crouched, arranging the fire pit. "I'm going to need your gun." Not only didn't he like the man, he couldn't trust him not to go off half-cocked.

Vanderbilt glanced up. "And why is that?"

"Firearms are not allowed in the national park."

The man stood, his shoulders thrown back. "You're joking. We're in the middle of the wilderness. What happens if we meet a grizzly or a wolf? Or another of your…friends? One not so easily spooked." His eyes narrowed. "Someone must protect the ladies. It doesn't look as if you're prepared to do so."

Clark bit back an angry retort. "I won't have you carrying a gun while we're out in the woods. It's against regulations."

"Regulations? You're no park ranger."

"Then I'll return you to Yosemite Village in the morning, and you can take it up with one of them." Clark turned back to finish the tents. He could attempt to take the pistol by force, but it didn't seem worth the risk. Let John settle the matter. That's why he wore the badge.

Maybe Filbert would stay away tonight, and Vanderbilt wouldn't see the need to use the thing.

Clark glanced back to where Olivia fiddled with her brushes and paints. Good thing she wasn't carrying a weapon, too. After what he'd done to her precious supplies, she might clock him with his own skillet.

⌐

Olivia took several deep breaths as she dug through the box with trembling hands. Nothing seemed out of place, except for a cracked tube of vermillion red. In fact... She studied the layout of the case. It was better organized than usual. The paints were arrayed in the order of the rainbow, red through violet. She usually jammed them in however and organized them afresh with each project. The fellow must have been quite concerned to go to such effort.

Her throat tightened. That also meant he'd spent several minutes at least going through the container. She moved the paint tray to check the wooden slats at the bottom. Red smears of paint decorated the wood. Clark's finger marks? Her pulse raced. Had he seen any of her papers?

She glanced up, checking that everyone was busy with their tasks. Sophie was down at the riverbank rinsing her hands, dirtied by gathering the wood. Clark was working on the tents. Marcus was... She glanced toward the fire pit. Marcus was gone.

At least he wasn't hovering at her shoulder as he'd done earlier.

The scent of wood varnish tickled her nose as Olivia peered into the depths of the box and lifted out the bottom panel. The most recent letters from the girls appeared to be untouched. No red prints. He couldn't have had enough time to go through them. She pulled out the faded scrap of newspaper softened by years of handling and folding. That was about the last thing she wanted anyone to see.

She unfolded the newsprint, the words so familiar she didn't even need to look. *"Murdered Man's Body Found at Yosemite Falls."*

She jammed everything back inside and fastened the thin sheet of plywood over the top. She'd kept this corner of her life under lock and key for so long, it was difficult to see it bleeding into today.

Olivia picked up the box and carried it to the tents where Clark was tying a support line to a nearby sapling. "Clark, I wanted to apologize to you for my harsh manner earlier. I was concerned about my…my things."

"I understand." His eyes softened. "And I am sorry for being so clumsy. I hope nothing's broken."

"Nothing important. In fact, it looks better organized than ever."

"I'm relieved."

"You didn't…" How did she dare bring this up? "You didn't look in the lower section. Did you?"

"No." He looked away, dropping his head like a guilty schoolboy. "I mean, I saw it was there, but I didn't disturb anything."

He probably thought she was hiding money or jewels or some such. She bit her lip. "Thank you. It's just some personal effects. They're private."

The guide drew a step closer, lowering his voice. "Please tell me you're not stashing a pistol as well."

"A pistol?" Her breath caught. "Me? No. Why would you think that?"

"Did you know Vanderbilt carried one?"

"Not until he came charging through the trees with it." Olivia glanced back toward the fire pit. Where had Marcus gone? "It probably wasn't even loaded."

The man's eyes darkened. "Yeah, well, I can't say as I trust him."

"Not trust him?" She swiveled her head, searching the clearing. "Marcus

Vanderbilt is highly respected. He's not just an art connoisseur; he's a philanthropist."

"The man wears his status like a suit. Those are the people who worry me most. The tiniest slight can cause offense."

Olivia's throat tightened. Did he lump her in the same category?

Clark hefted a sack of supplies over his shoulder. "I don't like him having a gun. He's just as likely to shoot one of us by mistake. I'll escort the group back to the Ahwahnee in the morning. He can deal with the chief ranger, if he's determined to keep it."

She grabbed his wrist. "Oh, don't do that. Let me speak to him." Going back and possibly facing Kendall sounded far more frightening than dealing with a simple aristocrat with a gun.

"Very well." He focused on her, the intensity in his brown eyes unsettling. "I hope you know, I'm capable of protecting you—all of you—without his help."

She shivered. Why was she so trusting of this man? Something about him spoke truth, as if he didn't bother with the veil everyone else used to shield their feelings.

Olivia grabbed her heart and tugged it back into submission. She barely knew Clark Johnson. For all she knew this in-your-face honesty could be his disguise. She needed to focus on why she was here—to complete the illustrations, get paid, and go home. She had two girls counting on her. This was no time to get distracted by a handsome face.

⌒

As darkness crept over the forest, the group lounged around the campfire, the occasional spark popping free from the burning wood. Clark had stashed the last bits of dinner and washed the dishes with Olivia's help. He'd obviously misjudged the woman, because much of her standoffish appearance seemed to drop away as they got farther from civilization. Of course, they hadn't actually traveled very far yet. If they were going to see the park, they'd need to get an early start in the morning.

Clark studied the couple beside Olivia. Sophie Vanderbilt leaned casually against her husband's chest. He appeared uncharacteristically relaxed, one arm draped protectively around his wife's shoulder, the glow sharpening his hawkish features.

The man's voice lifted, recounting the incident with Filbert as if the other three hadn't been present. Somehow in his retelling, he seemed a tad more heroic—frightening off the old hermit as Clark stood and watched.

Sophie giggled. "Olivia, you should have seen your face. You looked as white as a bedsheet."

The artist's brief frown vanished before anyone else noticed, replaced with a disinterested air. "You don't expect someone to sneak up on you like that." She glanced toward Sophie's husband.

Clark sat forward, his attention snagged by the little exchange. Was there more reason to suspect Vanderbilt's intentions? He'd sensed the man's casual interest in Olivia but had chalked it up to protectiveness. He definitely needed to keep a closer eye on the two. Clark pressed fingers against his temples, warding off a growing headache. One of the many reasons he didn't like taking women out on the trail.

Vanderbilt huffed. "Who knows what the old coot had planned? At the bare minimum, he was spying on two ladies as they…" He waved his fingers, brushing away the words. "But who knows? He might be scheming to murder us all in our beds."

Sophie's eyes widened, she swiveled around and found Clark across the fire. "Do you think so, Mr. Johnson? Could he be dangerous?"

Clark poured himself another cup of coffee. "Filbert's no more dangerous than any other critter around here. He wants nothing other than to be left alone to live out his days unhindered."

"Then why did he sneak up on us like that?"

"He heard your voices and got curious, I imagine. I don't often bring women tourists out here. You could have been some campers who'd gotten lost. He was probably concerned."

Vanderbilt scowled. "The old fellow was leering like a weasel after a mouse."

Sophie giggled. "A gap-toothed weasel?"

Her husband shifted, repositioning himself on the hard ground. "Yes, well, a man doesn't need teeth to—"

"Oh, that's nonsense." Clark snapped. "Filbert is a decent man with a good heart. Just because he's a little dirty and uncombed—"

"A little?" Vanderbilt scoffed. "He looked as if he hasn't bathed in months. And those rags?" He turned to Olivia. "Can you imagine him walking down San Francisco's Market Street dressed like that, Miss Rutherford?"

She fiddled with her sleeve. "I felt sorry for him."

The man rubbed a hand across his chin. "You're a sensitive soul. I admire that. Perhaps he'd make a good subject for one of your paintings. You could call it *The Derelict of Yosemite.*" He lowered his voice, speaking under his breath. "All you'd be missing is the smell of the old tramp."

Clark stood, brushing the dirt from his trousers. "If you lived alone in the woods for three years, I wonder how you'd fare."

Olivia's brows drew together, her lips forming a heart-shaped bow. "Doesn't he have a home? A family?"

Clark stopped at the edge of the firelight, regretting his words. The last thing he wanted to do was lay out someone else's failings. Especially when these folks seemed determined to use him for mere entertainment. "There are times in a man's life when things can get too difficult to face. Some bear up under the pressure and become heroes. Others..." He paused, the shame of his own existence washing over him. "Others snap. Or just run away."

Olivia's eyes fixed on him, as if reading his thoughts.

A flush of heat swept up his neck. How could she bare all his secrets with one knowing glance?

Vanderbilt laughed. "Runaway is right. He's likely an escapee from the insane asylum. You ladies should watch yourselves."

Clark stalked over to the pile of supplies and pulled out his camp guitar. "How about some music?" Typically he saved his singing for when he was alone with the ground squirrels, but right now he'd do next to anything to shut Vanderbilt's trap.

He couldn't deny that Filbert was a little odd. But the man deserved better than life had dealt him. And he certainly deserved better than to be ridiculed by folks who'd never known a lick of trouble in their lives.

Seven

O livia turned her attention back to the fire, the flame's warmth doing little to distill the icy chill creeping over her. *"Others snap. Or just run away."* He'd never know the effect those words had on her soul.

"You play?" Sophie sat up sharply at the sight of Clark's guitar, a wide smile brightening her pert features. "This trip gets better and better."

Clark settled down on a log, balancing the small guitar on his knee.

Olivia shifted uncomfortably on the hard ground, tucking her legs beneath her. A few rounds of campfire songs might chase away the shadows. What had prompted Clark to say such a thing? Could he know more about her than he'd let on?

The man's face softened as he stroked the strings, his thumb catching every note in turn. He paused to adjust a few strings before glancing about the group. "What should we sing?"

Marcus gestured to his wife. "My darling's favorite is 'Red River Valley.'"

"You remembered." She patted his leg.

Clark launched into the song with a gusto that didn't match his strained expression.

Olivia remained silent as the others lifted their voices. *"From the valley they say you are going. I will miss your bright eyes and sweet smile…."* Would everything remind her of losing someone today? Even as she banished thoughts of her father, the image of Frances's and Louise's faces rushed in to fill the void. Could they ever be together—live as a family?

The songs that followed didn't help. "Down in the Valley," "The Water Is Wide," "The Yellow Rose of Texas." Every song dug deeper into the wound in her heart like a miner wielding a pickax. Maybe that's why she preferred art. Art laid every emotion out end to end, somehow making it easier to see and understand. Music swept you up in the moment and didn't allow you time to puzzle it out.

A stirring in the woods, just beyond their circle of light, drew her attention. She leaned forward, scanning the forest's edge. A whisper of gray appeared, like a shadow slipping between the trees. Clark's friend again? Thankfully, she'd talked Marcus into unloading the pistol and stowing it away.

Clark met her eyes. Without stopping the music, he tipped his head in the direction she'd been staring and then gave her a quick nod. Was he confirming her suspicions?

Hopefully the fellow was as harmless as Clark let on, because having a stranger lingering around their camp was disconcerting.

She glanced back toward the trees, her heart going out to the old man. He didn't worry about the world's opinion of him. What would it be like to live a life without pretense? Perhaps that's the real reason Clark seemed to understand him.

Then again, if such a life meant a lack of bathing, she could probably do without.

After the final notes drifted through the night, Clark cleared his throat. "Okay, one last song. Ladies' choice."

Marcus shifted on the ground. "And what were all the previous ones?"

Olivia settled back against a fallen log, crossing her legs in front of her and letting the blaze warm her toes. Was there anything more handsome than a man with a guitar? Of course, it didn't hurt if the man looked like Clark to begin with. She tipped her head back and gazed up at the stars rather than the guide's rugged face. Perhaps she should paint this scene for her portfolio—a group of friends around a campfire.

Sophie ran fingers over her hair. "Do you know 'Always' by Irving Berlin?"

"Do I?" Clark chuckled. "It's one of my favorites."

Olivia had heard the tune in many clubs, and the melody never failed to dance through her mind like a pleasant dream forever out of reach. Clark's rendition followed suit, especially when he launched into the plaintive chorus. *"I'll be loving you, always."*

His eyes met hers across the fire, the soft light bringing a warmth and gentleness to his face. Tiny laugh lines formed around his eyes. Was he teasing her?

As Clark's voice faded into the surrounding trees, it took a moment for Olivia's breathing to settle back into a near-normal rhythm. She jerked her attention away, a wave of heat burning across her cheeks. *You're not some schoolgirl.*

The Vanderbilts drew her attention as Marcus placed a kiss on Sophie's cheek. Those two were as lovely as actors in a silent movie. The wealthy aristocrat with the beautiful young wife—the perfect match. Could love really be so simple?

Smoke curled upward from the campfire, the musky warm scent wrapping around her like a hug. Clark sat on the opposite side of the crackling fire, still strumming the guitar strings absently as he stared into the glowing embers. The light cast a glow across his face, deepening the shadows behind him as he hummed under his breath.

Olivia listened for several minutes, the melody just out of reach, stuck away between other memories like the chinking in a log cabin's walls. She closed her eyes, stretching through her mind for the forgotten tune. When she opened them again, she noticed him staring at her.

"Getting sleepy?"

Olivia glanced to the side. When had Sophie and Marcus crept away? Had she drifted off? She stretched her arms over her head, her back muscles aching from sitting so long. "Mmm. Yes."

He continued picking at the strings, the gentle tones wooing her back to drowsy land as she wrapped her arms around her knees. The fire's warmth stung her cheeks even as the night air chilled her backside. "I could curl up and sleep right here by the fire."

A faint smile touched his lips. "That's what I'm planning to do, but I figured you'd want one of those." He nodded to the canvas pup tent staked out nearby. "Your friends took the other one. You might want to steer clear."

"Yes, I suppose that will be my abode then." Every muscle protested as she pushed up to her feet. She glanced around, the forest looming dark about them on every side.

He cleared his throat. "Don't worry. Filbert won't bother you. I promise."

The mountain man was the least of her concerns, but somehow knowing Clark would be nearby instilled a sense of calm. "Thank you, Clark."

He set the guitar down, reaching over to toss another log onto the fire. Sparks spiraled upward, lighting the air above.

She paused at the tent flap, glancing back. Olivia couldn't help tracing the line of his muscled arms as he spread his bedroll by the fire. "Clark?"

He glanced up.

"What were you humming earlier?"

He sat back on his heels, his forehead crinkling as if trying to remember. "I think it was 'In the Garden.'"

The words rose like bubbles through her memory. *"I come to the garden alone..."* She could hear her mother's voice carrying through bits of her childhood memories. Even with as hard as she'd had to work, raising three girls by herself, she'd held on to her faith to the end.

Olivia blinked as tears rose in her eyes. She must be more tired than she thought. She slipped through the tent flap, the smell of damp canvas hanging heavy in the darkness.

With all his folks settled for the night, Clark wandered over to check on the stock. The General snorted at him, tossing her dark head as if recounting the humor in the day's activities.

"I know, girl; I know. But you should be glad I didn't put that sap on your back. Bess will punish me for weeks for this. Right, Bess?"

The mule eyed him distrustfully, shifting her weight.

"Don't look at me like that. I didn't do it to be funny." He laid a hand on her back. "Well, maybe a little. But I knew you could handle him. Goldie over there was treated like royalty. If only all riders were so kind." His thoughts went back to the dark-haired artist. She'd proven herself today, not just in her treatment of the mule, but with the way she reacted to Filbert. Obviously the man's appearance had unsettled the ladies, but Olivia had managed to take it in stride.

He patted Bess's back one last time, the idea of parting with the animals weighing on his spirit. Except for the General, the stock all belonged to the Yosemite Transportation Company. When his contract ended, so did his guardianship over them.

Clark gave the camp a quick once-over before gathering some supplies and setting off into the darkness. He'd sensed Filbert lingering around the forest's edge since their earlier encounter. The man did pretty well at caring for himself in the woods, but he did get hungry sometimes. Clark typically made an extra serving with him in mind. Evidently Vanderbilt hadn't proven frightening enough to keep Filbert from a free meal.

Clark balanced the tin plate in one hand as he picked his way down the trail. Less than five minutes out, he spotted Filbert leaning against a large incense cedar.

The old man ran a grimy hand across his mouth before spreading his arms in welcome. "Still here."

"I'm glad to see it, old friend." Clark led the way to a favorite spot, a collection of rocks that served as good seats in a pinch.

Filbert sat down and claimed the tin plate, bowing his head for a few whispered words.

Warmth radiated through Clark's body. He'd spoken to the man many times about God, but in the past two months, Filbert seemed to have latched on to God's love. And in those past two months, he seemed more settled and less haunted than he'd been before. Maybe with a little kindness—and a lot of prayer—the man might find his way back to the world.

"Odd group you got." The old man managed to speak between shoveling bites into his mouth.

"You noticed." Clark hoped he hadn't overheard their words about him. "Yes, one of the ladies is a painter. I'm taking her around to see the park."

Filbert chewed, the process taking a little longer because of his poor teeth. "The crow head?"

"How did you guess?"

"She sees everything. Even saw me out in the woods whilst you was singing. Other gal only looked at you and the fella."

Clark sat back and considered his words. Pretty insightful for a loner. "Best you steer clear for now. The man's a hothead. I don't want trouble."

"No one wants trouble. Has a way of finding us though."

"That may be, but I'd still appreciate it if you gave him a wide berth."

The vagrant shrugged, the motion sending his wispy hair floating above his shoulders. "Ain't no never mind." He shoveled in the last two bites and chewed, eying Clark over the plate. "He one of them industrialists?"

Clark lifted his head. That had to be the biggest word he'd ever heard Filbert utter. "I'm not sure how he made his money; I just know he's got plenty of it."

"Don't trust the industrialist."

Clark laughed. "Sounds like a great name for a song."

"Work us like mules, break our backs, fill us with poison and smoke." Filbert tottered to his feet, the tin plate falling to the dirt. "Cogs in their wheels, that's what we are."

"No, friend." Clark jumped up and placed a hand on the man's shoulder. "Don't worry. There's no one like that here."

The old hermit's attention darted around the trees as if he expected a factory bigwig to come lurching out from the darkness. "Won't go back. No, won't."

"You're safe here. You don't have to go anywhere." Clark kept his voice low and soothing. Whatever demons troubled this fellow, they were of the human sort.

"Don't trust industrialists." Filbert shrugged off Clark's hand and stumbled off into the dark, still muttering. "Man deserves what he gets."

Clark gathered up the plate and the unused fork, doubt settling around his heart. He'd assured the group that Filbert was harmless. *Keep watch over him, Lord.*

Back at the camp, Clark checked each of the tents. All was quiet, so he headed for his bedroll near the fire. This was one of his favorite times of day, after all his clients had turned in and it was just him and the stars. The Yosemite sky was like none other; the silhouettes of the trees and cliffs blocked sections of the starry firmament as if to make him appreciate the bits that God did let him see.

He flopped down on the blankets, drawing off each boot slowly as he studied the tiny pinpricks of light above. *I'm running out of time here, Lord. I wish I knew what You wanted from me.* If he could wrestle that out of God, then maybe he could go on with his life.

Clark leaned back on both elbows, the familiar odors of camp mingling with the scent of the pines. That and…something else. He sniffed, drawing in a lungful of the night air. Cologne? The women wouldn't bother with such ablutions out here, would they? It might draw wasps. A rustle from one of the tents drew his attention. He lay back, pulling the blanket up close to his chest. If one of the ladies was off to relieve herself, he certainly didn't want to get caught spying.

The tall form that slipped from the tent flap certainly wasn't female, however. Vanderbilt paced a few steps away from the tent and lit a cigarette, the flare from the match cutting through the darkness and momentarily illuminating his vest hanging open over his unbuttoned shirt. The man wandered around the clearing, finally coming to a stop at the campfire. He tapped his ashes off into the blaze. Maybe he had more sense than Clark had credited him with.

Clark blew out a long breath and closed his eyes. Why did campfires smell good, but cigarettes stink? Hopefully Vanderbilt wouldn't start the place on fire. The last thing they needed was a flare-up in the valley. He rolled to his side, turning his back. It had been a long day, and tomorrow promised to be every bit as tiring. Something about sitting too long in one place.

A twig cracked behind him. Had Vanderbilt finished his smoke already?

Clark lifted his head enough to see the man circle the fire and head back toward the tents.

The wrong tent.

A sour taste rose in his mouth. Either Vanderbilt was making the mistake of his life or he had dishonorable intentions. Clark's mind raced. Seeing Olivia kick the fellow to pieces like a mule would certainly be entertaining, but he couldn't take the chance. He settled for clearing his throat. Loudly.

Vanderbilt stopped in his tracks, casting a quick glance Clark's direction. His pale face caught enough light to expose his widened eyes. Had he not realized Clark was there? He backed two steps, then turned and headed for his own bed.

The incident settled in Clark's gut like a lead sinker. Maybe it wasn't a mistake or an unwanted visit. Perhaps he and Olivia… Clark couldn't even finish the thought. What did he know of these wealthy flapper types? He'd read that ridiculous *Gatsby* novel when it came out. Was something like that playing out right here in Yosemite Valley? The idea seemed far-fetched, even though these three clearly looked the part. But he was no Nick Carraway, that much was certain.

He rolled to his back, glancing over to make sure Vanderbilt's tent flap remained still. It wasn't any of his business, not really. He wasn't the woman's guardian—not in that sense, anyway. But he couldn't ignore it, either. Especially not with Mrs. Vanderbilt right nearby.

He slammed his eyes shut. Maybe Filbert was right. The man deserved what he got.

Olivia awoke with a start, the darkness pressing in around her. The smell of canvas and campfire smoke rushed her back to reality. Camping in Yosemite. She rolled over. Whatever had possessed her to think this was a good idea? She should be home in her comfortable bed, not here with her shoulder aching from pressing against the hard ground all night. A shiver raced through her. The hard, *cold* ground. It seemed to have sapped every bit of warmth from her body.

But that wasn't what had startled her awake. A crunching sound echoed nearby, like someone walking outside the tent.

She scooted toward the tent flap without unwrapping herself from the blanket. Pushing the canvas aside, she peeped out into the dark night. The campfire coals still glowed red and a half moon brightened the sky. Clark lay curled up in blankets. He must be freezing, lying out in the cold air like that. Why didn't he bring a shelter for himself? She shivered as the chill swept in through the opening. He seemed at rest, his sleeping face lit by the moon's glow. Perhaps she was imagining things. If he was such an expert guide, he'd rouse at the first sign of a disturbance. At least that's how it would happen in the movies.

A second sound came from beyond the Vanderbilts' tent. Was it a wild animal?

"Clark." Olivia whispered, trying to get her shaking voice to carry as far as the sleeping guide. She crouched on her knees, digging through the grass with one hand. Her fingers closed around a pebble. With a gentle heave, she tossed it toward him. The stone skidded across the dirt, bouncing to a stop a few feet away from him.

No response.

She patted the ground as if calling a dog. "Clark, wake up. There's something out there."

The noises deepened, a snuffling grunt emanating from whatever menacing creature approached. Great, they were going to be attacked by bears while their guide snored.

Olivia grasped a second stone and lobbed it.

Whack!

Clark jerked upright, a hand pressed to his cheekbone. He glanced her way with one eye, a scowl darkening his face. "What was that for?"

The shrubs on the far side of the Vanderbilts' tent shook. Olivia placed a finger over her lips and then gestured to the disturbance.

He threw the blanket off and lurched to his feet.

Olivia pulled back into the tent a few inches, thankful the man had worn his clothes to bed.

Clark hurried in the direction she'd pointed, but returned a few moments later. He strode over to Olivia's tent. "Raccoons. Nothing to worry about. And certainly not worth braining me in my sleep." He rubbed his cheekbone, wincing.

Olivia pushed out through the flap and stood next to him. "I'm sorry. I thought it might be a bear." She studied the angry mark on Clark's face. "Oh, my goodness. I'm so sorry. Another inch and I'd have hit your eye." She reached out a trembling hand and touched the skin near the welt. "I honestly didn't mean to hit you."

He didn't brush her fingers away, though his countenance stiffened. "What was your plan, then? Bean the bear with a rock like David and Goliath?" He shook his head. "That's twice I've been woken by the lot of you."

Olivia ignored the jab. "Twice? What did I miss?"

"Your friend Vanderbilt went wandering. Nearly returned to the wrong tent."

"Marcus tried to come to my tent?" *That would have been a rude awakening, indeed.*

"An honest mistake, I suppose?"

She wrapped the blanket tightly around her arms. "What are you implying?"

"Nothing. Never mind. Go back to bed." He turned away.

As if she could sleep after that. Olivia picked her way across the clearing in pursuit. "I don't take orders from you. And I don't appreciate your intimation." She kept her voice hushed, but the captive intensity burned in her throat. "Sophie is my friend. And—and so is Marcus. If he made a wrong turn in the campsite, you shouldn't assume the worst."

"He's your friend?" Clark turned back toward her, his eyebrow hitching up. A second wince followed, and the man pressed his knuckles to the bruise. "You need to choose better companions."

The criticism jabbed. "You barely know Marcus."

He sat down on one of the logs he'd rolled up next to the fire.

She plopped down next to him. "I'll have you know, there aren't a lot of good choices in my circles. And Sophie's been a gem."

"Maybe what you really need is better circles." He leaned over and stirred the ashes back to life, adding another piece of wood.

"And you're the expert on such things, out here in the wilderness? Who are you to advise me? I'm doing very well for myself, I'll have you know." She regretted the bitter words as soon as they escaped her lips. When had she turned into such a shrew? Maybe around the time she became solely responsible for her family's future. But he had no right to be so high-hat about her friends.

He pinned her with an unflinching gaze. "I'm a man who's made the same mistake."

Any further argument died on her tongue. "Meaning what?"

"Put your trust in the wrong person and you find yourself"—he glanced around the dark woods—"wandering around trying to figure out how the rug got pulled out from under your life."

What had happened to this man? One moment he seemed strong and fearless, the next he looked like a wounded little boy. She shifted on the hard surface. "Whom did you trust?"

His face softened as he stared at the fire, poking at the embers with a long stick. "A parishioner."

"A—a what?"

"A parishioner. A member of my church. She was unhappy in her marriage, but when I tried to help, she"—his eyes lowered as his Adam's apple bounced—"she turned on me. Like a cornered animal. Used me against her husband—all lies." He shook his head. "So many lies."

Olivia buried her hands in the fold of the woolen blanket, drawing it up under her chin. "So you're a churchgoer."

"I'm a little more than that, I'm afraid. Or rather, I was." He glanced her way as if sizing up her reaction. "I was a minister."

A minister? She scooted a few inches away from him without thinking. "How in the world—how did you end up here?"

Clark shrugged one shoulder as the fire popped, sending sparks up into the night sky. "I lost my way. My job. My church." He spread his arms. "Lost my whole life—in a sense."

Olivia fell silent, processing this new side to the rugged man, as if someone had touched him with a deep blue brush, swirling his colors in unforeseen directions.

He cleared his throat. "I didn't know where else to go." He gestured to the woods. "Sort of like Filbert out there. Only God wouldn't let me go. Not completely."

Olivia couldn't tear her attention away; she watched the firelight color the man's stubbled chin and lengthen the shadows on his face. *"Others just run away."* Wasn't that what he'd said?

Like her father, only he'd run from the law, not from rumors. God must have turned His back on Albert Rudd. And He'd done a fair job of leaving Olivia on her own as well. "You vanished into the woods? Left everyone behind?"

He frowned. "My church left *me*. Put me out on the doorstep like so much trash."

She swallowed. "You didn't have a wife—or children?"

Clark sat back, his eyes meeting hers for the first time in several minutes. "No. I...I imagine things might have been different if I had."

Without meaning to, she reached for his face a second time, brushing her fingers across the red spot on his cheekbone.

Clark jumped up and moved away, pacing around to the far side of the fire pit. "I don't know why I told you that. I haven't told anyone else."

"Nobody else has thrown rocks at you."

A smile lifted the corner of his lip, his face lit by the campfire's glow. "Is that what it takes?"

She pulled her hand into her lap. Why this sudden urge to touch the man? He was almost a stranger to her. Only now...he wasn't.

"So now you know my secret. Do I get to hear one of yours?"

The desire evaporated. She glanced down at her knees. "What makes you think I have any?"

He tossed a new log on the fire, sending a spray of sparks into the air. "I thought all women had secrets. Course I'm no great expert on the subject."

The man was more perceptive than most. Maybe that came with being a preacher. "You want to hear my confession, then? Is that the kind of minister you are?"

"I'm not a priest." He brushed the dirt off his hands. "Just a listening ear."

Olivia drew the blanket closer around her shoulders as if it could protect her from the darkness. "Marcus and Sophie—they think I'm like them."

"And you're not?"

She swallowed a halfhearted laugh. "No. I'm nothing like any of them."

He tipped his head. "I don't understand."

Her stomach tightened. If she opened this crack and let him in, the whole facade might crumble into a million pieces. "Never mind." She stood. "It's late. I should get some sleep."

"Actually it's early. Sun will be rising any minute."

"Then I'll get my things together. We've got a busy day ahead."

Eight

Olivia coaxed color across the page as the face of El Capitan emerged from the watery hues. After three days and nights on the trail, her hair smelled of smoke and she had dirt—and who knew what else—under her nails, but something inside was singing, particularly when she had a brush in her hand. Sophie and Marcus reclined beside the Merced River in the mountain's shadow, with their backs to her, exactly as she'd arranged them. She painted the couple mainly in silhouette, the lovebirds gazing at the peak in rapture.

That's how it was going on the paper, anyway. In reality, they bickered, their sharp voices carrying over the sound of the water. But at least she had them both where she could see them. In the past couple of days, every time she turned around, Marcus was there. His presence was like a rash one couldn't get over. Likely at home he had other interests to keep himself busy.

Olivia bit her lip as she focused on the top edge of the mountain, managing to capture the light's reflection off the far side of the polished granite.

Clark returned from caring for the stock and glanced at the pair cuddled by the water's edge, their voices raised in irritated jabs. "Trouble in paradise?"

"Mm-hmm." Olivia used a wet brush to dab a little more paint along the dome's face, using a downward brushstroke to drag dark lines along the granite cliff. After several minutes, his lingering presence prickled the hairs on the back of her neck. Was he watching? Rather than pull her eyes from the scene, she cleared her throat. "Everything all right?"

"I was hoping for a peek. You're painting one of my favorite scenes."

A knot formed somewhere between her shoulder blades. "You may look, but I'm not satisfied yet."

He closed the distance. "El Cap looks great."

"But the rest...not so much." She stepped back and stretched her fingers.

Sophie's voice lifted in the distance, the shrill tone unmistakable. After her husband responded, she jumped to her feet and stalked away.

"Oh, dear." Olivia set down the brush. "Now what?"

"Well, I could sit in for her, but I think it might change the painting a bit."

Olivia swallowed a laugh. "No, I don't think that would work."

Marcus glanced back toward them, a bitter scowl crossing his distinguished features. He stood and strode off in the other direction.

"Well now you're really up a creek, I'm afraid." Clark folded his arms across his chest.

Olivia dropped her brush into the rinse cup. "I think their energy was sapping my muse anyway." She frowned at the image on the page. The couple in the foreground looked stiff and unrelenting, exhibiting no more life than stick figures. "This painting is a total loss, I'm afraid."

Clark clutched his chest. "Don't say such a thing. Did you hear me a moment ago? This is my favorite view in the whole park."

"And it's beautiful." Olivia raised her hands and gestured at the granite cliffs rising above the open meadow. "But I can't seem to capture it."

His brows lowered, a tiny red mark still dotting his cheek. "I've been watching you work for days. You become the scene while you're painting.

Did you know that? You don't speak; you don't eat. I'm not even certain you breathe."

"That doesn't suggest talent. It means I focus well."

"Come on." He grabbed her hand and moved toward the stream.

His touch sent a jolt of electricity racing through her arm. She stumbled after him, suddenly unaware of anything other than the feeling of his skin against hers. "What—where are we going?"

Clark didn't stop until they stood where Sophie and Marcus sat moments before. He dropped her hand and gestured to the spot where they'd been arguing. "Sit."

Olivia pulled her fingers close to her chest and lowered herself to the flat rock, its surface warm from the summer sun.

He gestured toward El Capitan. "Now look up there."

She studied the monolith, the late afternoon light radiating off the granite. A few long-winged birds circled lazily in the air high above. "I suppose I could add a little more—"

"No." He lifted his hands, palms outward. "No more thinking. Quiet."

She fell silent, the man's chastisement weighing on her spirit. *Bossy.* When was the last time she studied something without imagining a painting? Appreciating a scene merely for the sake of its own beauty? Leaning back, she let the breeze lift the edges of her hair. She pulled off her hat, feeling the warm sun beat down on her head.

Clark crouched by the edge of the stream, lowering his hand to touch the top of the water.

She closed her eyes, listening to the air breathing through the limbs of the pine trees. There was a heartbeat to this place. That's what she needed to paint. If only she could figure out how to do so.

How long had these mountains stood, their rocky frame curving around this valley like a wall of protection from the outside world? She opened her eyes and looked down at Clark, balancing on his heels beside the water. The sunlight caught the ripples he stirred with his fingers.

The cliffs here had a permanence that love could not replicate. Maybe that's why she struggled with the painting. The Vanderbilts' love seemed a fleeting thing, like the seeds from the cottonwood trees lining the Merced's banks.

Clark had sung of a love that lasted always. Was that only a dream? As she studied him, he lifted his head and gazed up at the monolith, the gentle curve of his shoulder showing a steady confidence in what he saw—and perhaps in what he didn't.

Always.

<hr />

Clark swirled his fingers in the water, the coldness a sharp contrast to the hot sun beating down on his neck. He had a dozen things to do to get camp ready for the night, but Olivia needed this moment of peace. If he walked away, she'd likely jump right back to the easel before he made it ten steps.

She'd been driving herself too hard over the past few days, and he'd felt helpless, unable to do more than watch. He hoped a moment of reflection would quiet her spirit. He didn't know her well enough to figure out what might work.

He glanced back at her. Olivia's eyes were closed, but she held her right hand extended as if she were painting the air. He stifled a laugh. "You can't do it, can you?"

"Not without a brush in my hand." Her voice held an element of mirth as she opened her eyes. "May I ask you a question now, or are you going to order me to be silent?"

"Go ahead." He turned around and settled down into the dirt, cross-legged.

"Yosemite, the cliffs, the water—even the air—seem to have life. You mentioned a spirit. Do you consider Yosemite to be alive in some way?"

He pulled his hands into his lap. "Not in the sense you mean. Yosemite isn't a spirit. It is filled with spirit."

"Like the Indians said? Each tree and bird and squirrel?"

"Well, that's not what I believe. Not exactly." *You were a minister, Clark. This should be easy.* Only, it wasn't. Her focus hadn't wavered since she'd asked the question. "Have you ever seen the Sistine Chapel?"

"In photographs."

"Folks say it's the most beautiful cathedral built to honor God. Near perfection, but built with human hands." He gestured to the landscape. "Yosemite is a cathedral built by holy hands."

She lifted her gaze up to El Capitan.

Clark pushed on. "He hoisted up the cliffs, sculpted them with glaciers, carved the valleys. He set the Merced in its course, here—*Merced* means 'mercy,' did you know that? His river of mercy and grace, flowing right through Yosemite Valley." The idea grew in his chest as he spoke. "God dropped a ridiculous amount of beauty in this one spot. But why?"

Olivia focused on him. "Yes, why?"

"I'm not certain, but I'd like to say it's for us. The two of us here, right now. And maybe it is." He shrugged. "Or maybe He did it for the sheer joy of creating something stunning, whether or not any human ever laid eyes on it."

A smile pulled at her lips. "I've painted like that."

His heart slowed for a moment as her smile melted into him. "And it's probably your best work, isn't it?"

She tipped her head back, the sun's radiance lighting her face. "When I'm creating for me, I don't feel the pressure of pleasing a client or making a sale. I just...paint. And it comes from a deeper place."

"From your spirit."

She pulled a long blade of grass and wrapped it around her fingers. "So you're saying this place comes from *His* Spirit." She closed her eyes. "Then what's our purpose here?"

"Do you ever show those paintings to others?"

"Sometimes."

"Why?"

"Because…because I hope they see it. My heart." She opened her eyes, locking her focus on his face. "You're saying we see God's heart in this place?"

"Here and other places like it." He nodded. "And through that, come to know Him better. Scripture says faith can move mountains, but I've found time spent in the mountains sometimes moves us toward faith."

The artist fell silent once more. She slid over, patting the surface beside her. "Join me. There's no need for you to sit down there in the dirt. If a bickering married couple can share this rock, I imagine two friends can do the same."

Friends. He stood, brushing the bits of grass and leaves off his trousers.

Olivia's arm brushed against his as he took the spot next to her. How far they'd come in a week. From bitter opposites to discussing theology in the shadow of El Capitan. That was one of Yosemite's blessings—bringing people together. It didn't hurt that she sat here in a worn shirt and trousers rather than a glittering evening gown. She was a tiny bit less fearsome dressed like the natives.

A chittering yellow warbler flitted through the nearby cottonwoods, drawing Olivia's attention and giving Clark a moment to discreetly study her. Her fingers twitched as she watched the bird hop from limb to limb, pecking at the stems in search of insects. Was she imagining painting it? Did her mind ever stray far from her passion?

She swiveled around to meet his eyes, as if aware of his thoughts. "Thank you for this."

"F-for what?" He swallowed. *Get it together.* Evidently he'd been out in the woods so long he couldn't sit next to a woman without getting antsy.

She smiled. "For telling me what you believe. For helping me understand this place."

"That's why I'm here." He paused. "Why we're here." *Together.* "To help you understand Yosemite, right? I can't paint it, but I know my way around pretty well."

"You do." She leaned closer. "And I appreciate your help. More than you'll know. I'm sure you're aware I didn't want to come here."

"Yes, you made that painfully obvious."

She laughed, ducking her head. "I'm sure I did."

Perhaps that's why she threw herself into her work with such fervor—to hide from her fears. "I hope I've shown you there's nothing to be anxious about. Once you've spent some time in the wilderness, it will seem like home."

"Home." She dropped her focus to her knees, rubbing her hands up and down her thighs as though the word agitated her.

"If only you could paint yourself."

She slid closer, the disturbance easing. "I can sometimes, from memory. I just have to sear it into my thoughts." She looked at him pointedly. "Give me your arm."

"What?" He choked.

"For the painting. Please?" Her plea scattered his thoughts. Would anyone be able to resist her charms? No sane man would turn her away. A knot formed in his chest. *She doesn't know what she's asking.* Or maybe she did. Which was worse?

She took hold of his arm. Drawing it around her waist, she leaned in, resting her head against his shoulder. "Relax. It's not what you think."

Of course not. Because a woman like her would never be interested in someone like him. A mountain guide. A disgraced minister. Not a black-tie patron of the arts who listened to Beethoven and waltzed in ballrooms. The idea was laughable.

If only she didn't fit so perfectly in his arms.

⟞⟶

As soon as the sun rose the next morning, Olivia was back at the easel, the morning birdsong providing accompaniment to her work. She dipped the squirrel-tail bristles in burnt sienna, adding detail to yesterday's painting.

Clark and Marcus busied themselves down at the river, fishing lines whizzing over the surface of the stream. Occasionally she could hear the voice of one of the men while she worked. Sophie had yet to make an appearance. An early bird, she was not.

The change in the sun's angle didn't matter too much, since she'd captured the upper reaches of El Capitan the day before and was now touching up the couple cuddling by the river.

Her sister Louise would say they were a step from *spooning*. Olivia had been disturbed to discover her fourteen-year-old sisters knew the term. Neither she nor Frances was old enough to consider kissing boys. Not if Olivia had any say in it, anyway.

But as she slid the brush along the contours of the scene, the word seemed apt. She could almost feel Clark's hand resting on her hip, her head nestling into the curve of his neck. She'd gotten cozy with a fella before, but never once had she felt so perfectly...home. As if she could fall deeper into his embrace with each passing moment. What if he had kissed her?

The thought made her breath catch. Clark Johnson wanted nothing to do with her. He'd made that clear. When she'd inserted herself into the protected space between his arm and his chest, she'd sensed his heartbeat pick up pace to match her own. But even as she relaxed into it, his muscles had tensed—the strength of his arm evident against her back.

Her spirit sagged, her hand pulling away from the painting. He must think her an outright vamp, launching herself at him in such a fashion. She'd made excuses about the painting, but he must have known the truth. In light of their intimate conversation, she'd wanted nothing more than to feel his skin, touch the warmth radiating from his shirt. His pull was irresistible.

Apparently hers was not. A lump formed in her throat.

She glanced back to where the two men stood downstream, Clark helping Marcus disentangle his line. *The river of mercy.* What did that even mean?

A sound in the woods behind her drew her attention. She turned, catching a glimpse of something moving in the trees. The hermit, perhaps? The man had lingered in her thoughts since they'd met. He looked like a refugee from battle, his clothes hanging limp on his emaciated frame.

How long had her father wandered—lost, hungry, and alone—before he met his end somewhere in the mountains? He deserved his fate. Did this Filbert person, as well?

Olivia laid down her brush and walked to the crate where Clark stored the food. The biscuits from breakfast were still warm to the touch. She gathered a few in a linen towel, then added a portion of ham and a boiled egg. Clark always made plenty, and Sophie rarely ate anything at breakfast. It would never be missed.

Glancing over her shoulder, she checked that the menfolk were still busy before she slipped away. She made it a dozen steps down the trail before her palms grew clammy. She stopped, the bundle clasped in her trembling hands. She couldn't walk into the woods. Not by herself.

The sounds of the forest closed in around her, the hammering of a woodpecker giving voice to her throbbing pulse. Olivia drew the food close. She couldn't turn back, and yet her feet refused to move.

She took several deep breaths, the smell of the red fir filling her senses. What was she afraid of? Getting lost? Not coming back? She'd grown up in woods like these. Steeling herself, she pushed forward until she was out of sight of the camp.

"Mr. Filbert?" She went a few more yards before stopping. "I thought you might be hungry. I don't mean to bother you." The hum of insect life and the trill of a song sparrow were all she could identify. "I'll leave this here for you. And if I'm just talking to myself"—she knotted the towel around the food and laid it beside the path—"then it'll make a nice snack for some creature. I'm sure it won't go to waste."

Olivia backed away, her heart steadying as she returned to the familiar camp.

Clark walked toward her, the pole balanced over one shoulder. "I wondered where you'd gotten off to."

"I—I needed a moment, alone."

"Mr. Vanderbilt will be fishing for a while yet. There's no hurry to pack up, I suppose."

Four days on the trail, and they still hadn't left the Yosemite Valley—moving barely a mile or two each day. She could sense Clark's frustration simmering under his calm exterior. It was a waste of his time, she knew. They could have stayed at the Ahwahnee and still done these little jaunts, sleeping each night in style.

But he couldn't know what it had taken to get her out this far. Last night around the campfire, he'd spoken of other peaks and valleys, granite scraped bare by ancient glaciers, erratic boulders left in strange formations, and giant sequoias—far bigger than anything she'd experienced. His words sparked a fuse of excitement deep in her artist's soul, but the frightened little girl felt like she'd been plunged into an icy pool. She'd grown to appreciate this protected valley where the granite monoliths surrounded her like a palisade blocking out the world and all its fears.

Here she could breathe. And paint. Who knew what lay beyond these walls?

She lifted her brush and glanced toward Clark, the muscles in his shoulders cording as he stacked a load of supplies near the mules. He knew exactly what lay beyond—every lake, rock, and tree. She turned back to the paper, studying the couple seated by the river, his arm protectively around her waist as she leaned against him in complete trust. Even though their backs were to the artist, she knew their eyes were turned upward, gazing in rapt awe at the beauty of the mysterious Creator of whom Clark had spoken.

She added a little extra color around the edges of the riverbank, near the couple's feet, as if the evening sun cast a hint of its warm rays on their affection. One more fiction, not unlike the life she lived.

If Yosemite was God's masterpiece, made for the sheer joy of creating, shouldn't she take the opportunity to explore every nuance of the place? Perhaps it would help her understand Clark's reverence for the land. And it might chase away the dark memories.

After her mother died, the only person Olivia had counted on was Frank, and his consideration always came with expectations. So why did she now feel compelled to throw her safety in the hands of this mountain guide?

She washed her brushes and then shook the water from their bristles before returning each to its notch in her case. Olivia ran her fingers across the wooden base, resisting the urge to draw out the items hidden within.

As crunching footsteps drew near, Olivia closed the box's lid, struggling with the broken hinge.

"Here, this should help." Clark kneeled beside her and pulled a leather strap around the box, then fastened the buckle.

"Thank you."

"It's the least I can do, considering I'm to blame for its condition." He smiled. "I like what you've done with the painting of El Cap. Quite an improvement."

"Did I capture the spirit?"

"I'd say you got in touch with it." A dimple showed in his cheek when he smiled. How had she not noticed that before? Perhaps she hadn't given him many reasons for the expression.

She pushed down her misgivings. "I'm ready to see the rest of the park. Where should we go first?"

He lifted the box and balanced it under one arm. "I'd like to take you up the hill to Glacier Point. That way you can see all this from above."

"Isn't that where they do the Firefall?"

"That's where they push off the coals, yes. There's a nice hotel there, in case you'd like to wash off some of the trail dust and have a soft bed for a change."

She glanced down at her clothes. "I'd like that fine. Glacier Point it is, then."

Clark offered a quick nod and walked off, her box clutched against his chest.

She watched, the memory of being in those arms flooding her thoughts. Whoever captured that man's heart would be a lucky woman indeed. A wave of sadness cut through her as she brushed a stray lock of hair from her face. Some pretty girl with a ready smile and a sweet spirit. One living without a mask, a secret, and a burning desire to succeed.

⌒

At the turn of one of the many switchbacks, Clark called for the pack string to halt. The steep climb up Glacier Point was tough on Bess. He'd dropped back and allowed Vanderbilt to lead for a time, and from Clark's position in the rear, he could see the mule favoring her right hip. As much as he hated to admit it, the old girl's trail days might be nearing their end. If only he could arrange for a nice pasture where she could retire in style. Most packers simply disposed of their animals when they outlived their usefulness. He didn't have the stomach for that, but she deserved better than to continue working in pain. Hopefully his boss in the transportation office would agree.

Vanderbilt glanced back. "Why are we stopping?"

"Rest break."

The man rolled his eyes skyward. "We won't get anywhere at this pace."

He should make the fellow walk a few miles up these stony trails and see how *he* liked it.

Sophie and Olivia slid down from their mounts, stretching their arms above their heads. Olivia lifted a hand to shield her eyes as she scanned the view. "This is lovely. I'm glad we stopped."

Her friend joined her beside the trail. "You're not going to start painting again, are you? Mr. Johnson promised me a real bathtub at the end of this trek."

Clark took Bess's reins as Vanderbilt dismounted. "How would you like to take my horse for a while?" The idea of feeding the gentleman's ego by placing him on the best mount grated on Clark, but he couldn't let him continue to abuse the small mule. The General could take care of herself.

Vanderbilt straightened. "Might be a nice change from this old nag." He strode off to join the women.

Clark checked Bess's feet and wasn't surprised to find a small stone lodged in her rear hoof. He retrieved a folding hoof pick from his saddlebag and worked the rock loose from where it had wedged itself. "That must have been hurting, wasn't it, girl?" He patted her rump. "Well, don't worry. I'll give you a break for a while. The others can manage. I doubt you'll miss that clod yanking on your mouth, will you?"

The mule blew a loud huff, turning her head toward the cliff face as if giving him the cold shoulder.

A sharp voice from the group drew his attention. The three had turned from the valley view and were now staring past him, up the hill.

Clark gritted his teeth as Vanderbilt drew the pistol for the second time this trip. A fiery surge burned through his chest. Hadn't he already warned the man?

He spun and searched the rugged rock face for what could be causing such alarm. Not even a stray piece of gravel had shifted to alert him. It took a minute for him to pick out Filbert's shape, crouched on the rocky hillside. The disheveled man pointed down at them. "Industrialist!"

Clark kept a firm grip on Bess's lead. "No, Filbert—go back."

A bullet whizzed past Clark's head and nicked a chunk of stone near the vagrant's foot.

Filbert bounded farther up the hill and disappeared into the brush with the agility of a fellow half his age.

The pack animals jostled and jumped in place. The General shied right up to the cliff edge, and her hooves knocked bits of rock down into the ravine below.

Clark leaped at Vanderbilt and yanked the gun from his grip, knocking the man to the dirt in the process. "What were you thinking? You could have killed him."

Before he could react, Vanderbilt swept Clark's ankle out from under him with a quick foot. Clark landed hard on his back, the air rushing from his lungs. He cradled the weapon against his chest before rolling to his hands and knees and fighting for a breath.

"What do you think I was trying to do?" Vanderbilt clambered to his feet. "That hobo's a lunatic. He's dangerous."

Clark shoved the pistol into his belt as he regained his own footing, ready for the man's next lunge.

Vanderbilt's momentum carried him past Clark and into the rocky slope. Clark grabbed his arm and bent it behind his back, pinning the coward against the craggy ground. Placing a shoulder against the larger man's back, Clark prayed he'd stay put. "You told Olivia you'd unloaded and stowed that gun until the end of the trip. Now it's mine. Care to argue?" He gave an extra shove for good measure.

The fight seemed to have left the man, and Vanderbilt shook his head.

Clark stepped back, allowing the deflated bully to get back on his feet.

Vanderbilt wiped some grit from his cheek, glaring. "You shouldn't have done that."

Clark unloaded the gun, dropping the shells into his vest pocket. "I should've done it earlier."

The women huddled together, wide-eyed. Olivia spoke first. "Marcus, the old man was defenseless. Anyone can see that his wits are muddled. He was no danger to us."

The businessman's eyes narrowed. "He's a menace." He lifted a pointing finger and jabbed it in Clark's direction. "And you're making excuses for him. What sort of guide are you—letting us get attacked by miscreants? And I'll be speaking to the rangers about letting tramps and vagabonds live in the park. They need to ferret out that man and lock him up, not let him wander around here accosting good people."

"Good people?" Clark huffed. "I hope you're not including yourself in that group."

Vanderbilt scowled and stalked over to the lead horse. Snatching the

General's reins, he swung up on the mare's back. "Come along, Sophie. We're done following this man."

His wife stood motionless for a long moment before her face firmed into a stony frown. She folded both arms across her petite frame. "I'm staying."

Vanderbilt's eyes went cold. He jabbed his heels into the horse's sides and took off up the trail, dust rising from the General's hooves.

Clark turned away and added the empty pistol to the supply box on Chieftain's back.

Olivia hurried up behind him. "He took your horse. Your best horse."

"The General won't go more than a half mile or so without me. It'll give Vanderbilt time to cool down." He glanced back to where she stood. The tears in her eyes tugged at him. "And in the meantime, it will give us a little breather as well."

He was going to need the time to figure out what to do about Filbert. He'd never mentioned the man's presence to John or any of the other rangers, knowing it would put them in an awkward position. The government didn't allow squatters on park land—and with good reason. But Filbert was as much a part of this place as the monoliths themselves. And Vanderbilt seemed determined to cause trouble for him.

What would Filbert do if he were turned out of the park? Disappear into the High Sierra? Wander the streets of Sacramento begging for a scrap of bread? Clark couldn't let that happen. *Inasmuch as ye have done it unto one of the least of these my brethren, ye have done it unto me.* The old man certainly counted among the least.

Unfortunately, Clark wouldn't be at Yosemite much longer unless he agreed to take the ranger position. And if he saddled himself with a park-service badge, he'd be required to enforce regulations. Either way, Filbert might be on his own.

Nine

O livia clung to the saddle horn, locking her attention on Goldie's expressive ears rather than the view. If she glanced down the cliff side one more time, she was going to lose her lunch. Her stomach still roiled from watching Marcus ride off without them. Honestly, she'd been glad to see the back of him. Sophie had collapsed in a teary mess as soon as he left, leaving her and Clark to pick up the pieces of the woman's tender heart.

A heaviness spread through her chest. Frank had been counting on her to obtain Marcus as a benefactor while on this trip. She'd mostly hoped for the Vanderbilts' friendship—or Sophie's at least. How long had it been since she'd had a true friend?

She studied Sophie's rounded shoulders ahead of her. If it weren't for Louise and Frances, Olivia would never have agreed to any of this. When had Frank begun making all her decisions? He wouldn't care a lick that a marriage was crumbling before her eyes—in fact, he might even view it as an opportunity.

She dreamed of being so talented that she didn't need anyone's affirmation or social connections. But few artists achieved that level of success within their lifetimes. Frank never tired of telling the stories of Gauguin and van Gogh, both of whom died penniless but whose works' value soared shortly after their demise.

For the sake of two darling fourteen-year-old girls, Olivia needed success now, no matter what it took. If not Marcus, it had to be this Yosemite job. She needed these paintings to be beyond good. They must be breathtaking. They had to jump from the pages of the magazine and into people's hearts, transforming Olivia Rutherford into a household name. But how?

She looked up in time to see a riderless horse trotting down the hill toward them.

Clark, walking in front of the group and leading Queen Elizabeth by hand, glanced back toward Olivia. "Didn't I tell you she'd return on her own?"

Sophie frowned, pulling her mule to a stop on the narrow trail. "But where's Marcus? Did the horse throw him?"

The guide moved to catch the loose mare. "I doubt it. The General probably put on the brakes and refused to go any farther. I thought we'd run into them both waiting for us. Evidently your husband decided to continue on foot."

Olivia shifted in the saddle, trying to ease the pressure on her backside. Today's ride had been a bumpy one. "So we'll catch up to him, right? If he's on foot?"

"We're not far from Glacier Point. He might beat us there, depending on how far the General took him." The guide gathered the horse's reins in his hand and patted her neck. "That's a good girl." He placed his foot in the stirrup and swung up into her saddle.

They continued climbing the long switchbacks but never encountered Marcus Vanderbilt. By the time they drew up to the hotel, Olivia's muscles were aching as if she'd been the one carrying the pack load. She couldn't imagine how tired and grumpy the animals must be. She dismounted and rubbed Goldie's soft ears. "You've earned a good feed, my friend. Thank you."

As Clark took the reins from her hand, he gestured toward the lookout. "Go take a gander. I think you'll enjoy the view."

As Sophie hurried toward the hotel to look for her husband, Olivia sauntered down to the overlook. The Yosemite Valley spread below like a rumpled blanket tucked between the granite cliffs. Patches of lighter green meadow broke up the forest below. *Emerald green, viridian, cobalt green...* She needed to check her supply of colors and possibly even blend some new ones to match what she was seeing. She lifted her eyes to the cliffs opposite, tracing the rounded apex of Half Dome, its odd shape putting her in mind of a generous slice of pound cake left behind on a platter. The variety of tones and textures in the rock stole her breath. The steep face even had streaks of black mixed in with the gray and brown tones.

A surge of excitement burned through her system. She couldn't wait to get started. The enormity of this landscape would play well with the broad-stroke technique she preferred. Hopefully *Scenic* wasn't looking for detailed or realistic paintings. She pushed away the distracting thought. They hired her, certainly they were aware of her signature style. Besides, it left room for the imagination. If the goal was to draw people to the park, it would be best to provide a taste of what lay here rather than replicate it perfectly.

Ten minutes later, Sophie reappeared and joined Olivia at the overlook. "He's not in the hotel lobby." She turned and sat down on the short rock wall, the curve of her shoulders matching the dome in the distance.

Olivia crouched in front of her, laying a hand on the woman's knee. "I'm sure we'll find him. Did you check the veranda? He's probably there right now, having a nice iced tea."

Sophie lifted her head, her lower lip trembling. "Do you think so?"

"I'm certain."

"This trip has been a washout." Her brow furrowed, and she placed a hand behind her neck as if rubbing away the tension. "Marcus spent more time looking at you than at me."

A hot flush prickled across Olivia's skin. "That's not the case. Please, Sophie, let's go find him. You two need to mend fences." She helped her friend to her feet.

Entering the lobby of the Glacier Point Hotel felt like stepping into a dark cave, even with the glare from the windows opposite. A blazing fire crackled in the oversized fireplace. Olivia sighed, making a mental note to curl up on one of the overstuffed chairs this evening.

"We only spent a few nights camping, but I feel like we've been gone for a month." Sophie rolled her eyes. "I need a hot bath."

"And a good meal." Olivia added. Clark did a decent job of cooking over the campfire, but she'd really enjoy a fine supper in the hotel restaurant.

Sophie led the way to the front desk and inquired about rooms for the night. The clerk frowned at the ledger book. "I only have one room available, I'm afraid."

Sophie glanced at the upside-down book. "Has a Mr. Vanderbilt checked in, by chance?"

He drew the book closer as if shielding it from view. "No, I'm afraid not."

She drew back and turned to Olivia. "What if that horse threw him and he went over that dreadful cliff? Or that crazy man—maybe he did something to my Marcus."

Both ideas sent a chill through Olivia. "We'll speak with Clark. He'll know how to find him." She squeezed Sophie's wrist. "Why don't you check the porch?"

After Sophie left, the clerk leaned forward. "Miss, were you referring to Clark Johnson? Is he here?"

Olivia nodded. "Yes, he's been our guide this week."

A big grin swept over his face. "Oh, good! I found a message waiting here at the desk. It's for someone in his group." He rifled through a long drawer. "Let me see." He paused. "Oh, yes, here it is. Do you have an Olivia Rudd traveling with you?" He lifted an envelope.

Olivia's heart jumped to her throat. She snatched it from his hand. "I'll get it to her."

Sophie reappeared at her shoulder. "He's not there, either."

Olivia tucked the envelope behind her back. "You go ahead and take the room, Sophie. When Marcus shows up, he'll be able to find you."

Sophie lowered her head, blinking. "Olivia, I'm sorry for what I said. I know it's not your fault." She stepped close so the man at the desk wouldn't overhear. "Marcus appreciates beauty of all sorts, so he'd be foolish not to notice you." With a sigh, she turned back to the clerk. "Miss Rutherford and I will share the room." She shot a glance toward Olivia. "If Mr. Vanderbilt does show up, he can go sleep with the mules."

Olivia squeezed the paper in her trembling hand. "All right. I'll meet you up there, though. I need to retrieve my paint box."

"You don't trust Mr. Johnson not to drop it again?" Sophie collected the key.

"Right." Olivia forced a smile. "You know me; I don't really trust anyone with my supplies."

Olivia hurried back through the front door, pausing on the steps to examine the envelope. She slid a trembling fingertip along the Ahwahnee logo before breaking the seal and pulling out the folded note.

A little songbird told me Livy Rudd was back in Yosemite, and I could scarce believe it. I need to see you. I've held onto these secrets for far too long.
~Gus

Gus Kendall. She'd been so careful to avoid him—how could he have found out?

A little songbird?

The image of Clark with his camp guitar shot through her memory. He must be the person Kendall was referring to. Hadn't Clark admitted to being on the run himself? It made sense he'd be friends with a man like Kendall. Her stomach turned. How long before her news was all over the park and then the city beyond?

⌐

Clark tipped a little extra feed into the General's nose bag. She'd earned every bite. He would have paid admission to see Vanderbilt's face when she parked herself on the trail. Hopefully he didn't treat her too badly when she refused to obey. He'd seen Vanderbilt's type of arrogance before, and men like that usually didn't take well to being humiliated.

He'd placed Olivia Rutherford in the same category, based on their first encounter, but she'd surprised him. On each step of their journey together, it was as if something chipped away at her granite exterior, revealing a tender spirit within. Or perhaps it had always been evident, and God had simply removed the scales from Clark's eyes.

She might look—and occasionally act—like a Hollywood starlet, but inside she had the sweet disposition of country girl. Had his own prejudice blinded him? His heart picked up its pace, as if he'd hiked up the trail to Glacier Point rather than letting the animals do the hard work. Perhaps with the Vanderbilts busy at the hotel, he could invite Olivia out on a walk. Nothing overly romantic, mind you. Just to help her choose some good spots to set up her easel.

The image of her standing in front of the massive landscape, a brush balanced in her fingers, the mountain breeze ruffling her smart black hair… the very idea sent chills down his spine. He needed to stop thinking such things.

He lifted Olivia's paint box from the pannier then paused. Would he forever avoid women because of one bad experience?

The recollection of what had happened at his church still tore at him, the memory circling through his mind on a regular basis like a horse on a lunge line. He'd been so focused on helping the woman, he'd been oblivious to her growing attraction for him. Or so he told himself. To be honest, it had been flattering, and that realization now turned his stomach.

When the woman's wounded ego erupted with false accusations, it had torn away any shred of trust his congregation held for him. He'd essentially stood before them naked as the day he was born. *"For false witnesses are risen up against me, and such as breathe out cruelty."* He'd never understood the psalmist's cry better than in those dark days.

Clark lowered the box to the ground, and then wiped a hand across his forehead. He needed to leave the disgrace in the past where it belonged. He closed his eyes, thankful it was now Olivia's face that jumped to his mind. He might barely know the woman, but at least she wasn't attached to painful memories. Maybe God placed her in his life—if only as a friend—to help him put the horrible incident behind him.

Crunching footsteps jerked him to alertness. The object of his thoughts was striding toward him at an alarming speed.

He shook away the feelings, in case they somehow registered on his face. "Olivia?"

Her stiff-legged gait came to an abrupt halt at the corral gate. "Does the Park Service know what you are?" Her sharp voice launched at him as she balled her fists. "Is this blackmail of some sort? Or do you have some sort of devilish scheme I haven't discovered yet?"

Several heads popped up from the nearby veranda, and Clark stumbled back two steps. "I-I don't know what you're talking about."

She lifted a piece of yellow stationery, clutching it in her fingers until her knuckles whitened. "You told Kendall I was here. What is it you *think* you know about me?"

The rage in her eyes cut like a hunting knife even as she shoved the paper against his chest. "Kendall who?" He encircled her wrist with his fingers, lifting her hand so he could inspect the paper more closely.

"You're friends, aren't you?"

Clark struggled to grasp the threads of this conversation. *Kendall. The maintenance man at the Ahwahnee? Quiet fellow.* "Gus? I know him, but I wouldn't call him a friend. I'm not sure he has any."

"And you told him I was here."

Clark swallowed hard, his ears buzzing with the intensity of her voice. "I haven't had cause to speak to Gus in a month or more. Certainly not about you. Why should I? What's going on, Olivia?"

She yanked away from him. "It's none of your business."

He choked down a laugh. "Well, I think it is, if you're claiming I'm guilty of something—by association, it would seem. So what is it?"

Her blue eyes filled, the ferocity melting away like grease in a hot frying pan. "It's a note. Addressed to me. Well, not exactly to me. But no one could have known about it unless they'd gone through my things."

"Your things?"

She looked pointedly at the box next to his feet.

"Your paint box." His chest tightened like a girth being cinched. "You think since you saw me in your box the other day—"

"You realized my connection to Kendall and told him I was here. You're the only one who could have known."

"You've got this all wrong." He had to clear this up. If he lost another job, he'd end up like old Filbert, living on scraps from the land or handouts from men.

"Why should I believe you?" Her face crumpled. "How did you know my name?"

"You told me your name." He pressed a hand to his forehead. Did she realize how crazy this sounded?

Her tortured expression broke down any thought for himself. He managed a step forward, fighting the urge to take her in his arms. She'd likely pummel him to death if he tried. "Olivia, I'm not lying. Please. You have to believe me."

"Why? Why should I?"

His throat closed. *Because no one else had.* "Olivia, I barely know Gus Kendall. And if I'd discovered something in your things, why would I tell anyone? And when? I've been on the trail with you. What would I do—strap the news to a homing pigeon?"

Her mouth opened and closed like a brook trout gasping for air. "He said a songbird told him."

"This park is full of songbirds. You must be aware of that. Besides the obvious ones with feathers, there are countless entertainers at the hotels and camps." He spread his arms. "As best as I can see it, I'm the least likely. What does this letter contain that has you so concerned?"

She turned away, pressing the paper against her chest. "It's personal."

Her voice had softened. Had he finally convinced her? "And Kendall—is he threatening you?"

Olivia unfolded the message and stared down at the scrawled words. "Not exactly, but he knows something that—that could cause problems for me."

Clark leaned close, reading over her shoulder. "'Livy Rudd.' Is that you?"

"It's who I used to be, anyway." The words came out as a strained whisper.

"That's what you meant about your name?"

"Yes."

He glanced back at the letter. "He doesn't actually say anything menacing here. Is there a chance he honestly wants to see you?"

She crushed the paper in her fist. "He was an associate of my late father's. I wouldn't want to hear anything the man had to say."

Now that sounded like a story. One she was unlikely to tell him. He stepped back and rubbed the stubble sprouting on his chin after several days on the trail. "I could make some inquiries, if you like."

She looked up, eyes wide. "I most certainly would *not* like that. I want to keep this quiet. Please."

This woman was a puzzle, that much was certain. "Well, I'll help however I can." He glanced up at the hotel. "Did you find Vanderbilt, by chance?"

"No." Olivia pressed her hands up into her hair, the tension of the past few moments seeming to leak out of her. "And Sophie's a mess."

He resisted touching her arm in comfort. *She doesn't want your help, remember?* "I'll look around. Maybe I can locate him. Did you take a room?"

"Sophie and I are sharing one."

"Why don't you go get some rest, and we can check the viewing porch during dinner. If Vanderbilt is around someplace, he's got no food with him. I think he'd show up for a meal."

Olivia frowned down at her flannel shirt and riding breeches. "I haven't got anything suitable for fine dining."

"This isn't the Ahwahnee. The porch at Glacier Point has the best view of the valley. Folks won't be looking at you."

She ran a hand across her shirtfront. "If you're sure."

He fought to tear his eyes away from where the flannel hugged the curve of her hip. *Not if I can help it.*

C lark strode into the Glacier Point Hotel. A burning sensation sim-
mered in his gut, like his best campfire stew straight from the pot.
He'd never had reason to doubt Kendall before, but then he'd never had
reason to think anything of him. The man did his work and stayed out of
the way. Is it possible he was trouble?

Olivia had asked him not to stir up questions, but would a single call to
John hurt? He didn't have to inform him why he was asking. Then again, if
the man had bad intentions, maybe it was best to keep Olivia clear and be
done with it.

Clark hurried to the desk, surprised to find a friend working the front
counter. "Charlie, I thought you were moving down the hill to Camp Curry
this month."

The young man grinned. "Not 'til next summer, I guess. I made the
mistake of flirting with one of the soda girls down there, and Ma Curry had
a fit. At least I get to keep doing the Firefall from this end, though. I told my
girl every time she sees it to imagine I'm doing it just for her."

"You're never going to learn, are you?"

"Hey, you put a pretty girl in front of me, am I not supposed to look?"

He lowered his voice. "Speaking of which, those two dames came in a little bit ago said they were part of your tour. How did you get so lucky?"

"Is that what you'd call it?" He glanced over his shoulder. "I heard you received a message for one of my clients. Can you tell me who delivered it?"

Charlie shook his head. "I only found it about ten minutes before those two birds walked in. Sitting right here on the register like it was waiting for them."

"Any ideas who might have left it?"

"I figured it was the courier, but it could have been anyone, really. Folks are in and out of here all the time."

Figures. "No chance it was Gus Kendall?" Olivia might not want him asking around, but since she seemed convinced the man was up to no good, Clark wanted to know if he was there.

"From the Ahwahnee? Why would he venture clear up this way?"

Clark blew out a deep breath. "He wouldn't. I was merely curious. Don't tell anyone I asked, would you?" He turned to leave, then stopped. "Have you seen a tall, lanky fellow? About six foot two?"

Charlie squinted. "What's going on, Clark? What's with the third degree?"

"One of my tour group went off on his own—bit of a hothead. He was heading to Glacier Point, but no one has seen him. I'd hoped we could clear the air."

"No, can't say as I have, but like I said, folks are in and out all day. Have you checked the veranda? Most visitors end up out there eventually. And if he came from one of your trail rides, he's probably looking for a decent meal."

"I'll check. Thanks, Charlie." Clark tapped the desk.

"Hey Clark, that dark-haired gal from your group—she spoken for?"

Was she? Clark leaned forward, keeping his voice low. "Let's say, she's not in the market."

The clerk shrugged. "Too bad. There's a dance tonight. I'd love to have a doll like that on my arm."

"What about your girl from Curry?"

"Yeah, well that's three thousand feet down the hill, isn't it?"

Olivia hugged the fluffy towel around her body as she dug through her bag. She'd only brought one dress? She simply couldn't be seen downstairs in trousers. She had a reputation to maintain. If she'd known she'd be dining at another hotel, she'd have packed her black dress. It never failed to capture men's eyes.

But now that's exactly what she needed to avoid. Would Kendall come here? Why had he sent a note rather than confronting her himself? A tremor ran through her gut. Typically Frank instructed her to be "seen" wherever she went in order to keep her name on people's lips. But he probably didn't anticipate that same name being smeared through the mud. Perhaps someday she'd be able to be herself without constantly minding her public image.

Was it possible Clark was right? That Gus Kendall only wanted to talk? She closed her eyes for a moment, trying to picture the man she remembered. He and her father had been drinking buddies. She had a hard time even picturing Kendall sober.

Olivia shook out the simple day dress she sometimes used for painting. It was clean and unstained and—best of all—not wool. *A few wrinkles won't hurt anything, right?*

Sophie's quiet breathing suggested the poor girl had finally drifted off to sleep. She'd cried for an hour, moaning about all of Marcus's shortcomings. The girl deserved to rest. Olivia shimmied into the dress without making a peep, even while wrestling with the buttons on her back.

Sitting at the vanity table, Olivia stared at her reflection in the mirror.

Her carefully sculpted image was crumbling around the edges after this crazy week. As Clark had pointed out, Kendall hadn't actually threatened her, but just the hint of it was causing her to fall to pieces.

She pulled a boar-bristle hairbrush through her damp hair and noticed that the light brown roots were unmistakable along her part line. *I'm sure Clara Bow and Lillian Gish never have this problem.* It'd be a shame to waste her expensive lash darkener, but she could stand only so much imperfection. One magazine had recommended mixing coal soot with petroleum jelly, but this might not be the best time to experiment with new concoctions. She dabbed on the color, as if she were touching up a painting.

At least with her smooth Dutch-boy cut, she didn't have to worry about finger curls or Marcel waves. Even after putting her hair in a net, Sophie would be a mess when she woke. Chances were, she'd sleep through dinner anyway. Her friend barely ate enough to keep a cricket alive. The slim, boyish figure was popular, but as Marcus had stated—in such a boorish manner—he'd appreciate a few more curves on his young wife. What woman could eat when she was constantly worried about her husband's roving eyes?

Olivia fastened a jeweled clip in her hair, one of the few frivolous items she'd brought along on the trip. She wouldn't normally wear it with this dress, but one couldn't be picky at such times.

Letting herself out of the room, she locked the door behind her and made her way downstairs to the dining room. As she stepped out onto the long viewing porch, the vista once again stole every other thought from her head. Round tables were pulled up adjacent to the railing, and a large awning provided shade to the guests. She walked to the rail and stood, leaning against one of the posts and gazing down into the loveliest valley in the world. What had Clark said about it? *"God saved up the best bits of creation and spent them here."* Viewing it from this angle, she could almost imagine a divine artist smiling as He carved the valley away from the giant monoliths.

"It's quite a sight, isn't it?" Clark's voice sounded soft over her shoulder.

She didn't turn to look at him, unable to draw her eyes from the vision before her. "Don't you think it's a bit unfair to the rest of the world? To have all this beauty hidden here?"

"It's not hidden anymore. Especially not with folks like you putting its face on magazines."

She heard the sound of a chair being drawn away from the nearby table and turned to see Clark holding the seat for her. "Thank you."

"Nothing makes a view finer than a nice meal."

Olivia smiled. "How can you even think of food when you're looking at something so beautiful?"

He didn't move his attention from her face. "It's a peculiar talent of mine."

She took the seat, her cheeks warming even as the man sat opposite her. They ordered and enjoyed the view as they waited for their food to arrive.

"I'm fighting the urge to run and get my easel right now. This would be a delightful place to paint."

"You'll do better on a full stomach. We'll eat first, and then you can set up here for the rest of the afternoon, if you like. I'll see if I can figure out what happened to Vanderbilt. If no one has actually seen him, I'll ride back down the trail apiece and make sure he didn't pull off somewhere."

"Will we stay at Glacier Point long?" The idea sent a shiver through Olivia. If Kendall wanted to expose her, she'd prefer to be ten miles down the trail in the opposite direction.

"I need to find out what happened to Vanderbilt. He's my responsibility." Clark leaned back in his chair. "You should be safe enough here."

She swallowed any protests. After all, what good had running done her so far? "I'll try to focus on what I've been sent here to do."

He smiled. "That's all any of us can do."

The waitress placed soup and sandwiches in front of them before heading back to the kitchen.

Olivia picked up her spoon. "What will you say to Marcus when you find him?"

"I'm not certain. I haven't had much luck talking to him so far, but I have to try. There's a brokenhearted woman in there who deserves better than what he's handing her."

An ache grew in Olivia's chest. He was right. Her own needs were nothing compared with what Sophie was now enduring. "You're still a pastor at heart, aren't you?"

"It's not only a minister's job to care for others; it's everyone's. We can't leave it all to the paid staff."

"Of course, but it hardly seems like the job of a wilderness guide." She wiped her mouth with a napkin. "Maybe you should go back into the ministry."

A shadow crossed his face. "That doesn't seem to be the trail God's laying out for me. I've been offered a job with the Park Service."

"Here at Yosemite?" Olivia scooted closer to the table. "That's wonderful."

"I knew my packing days were coming to an end." He took a sip from his water glass. "God's been working on my heart, lashing it back together after what happened at my church. I'd hoped eventually He'd guide me back to His work."

"And being a ranger isn't doing His work?"

"It isn't what I had in mind."

"My mother used to say, after my father…left—" The words slipped from her tongue before she could grab hold of them. Shaking her head, she plowed forward. "She said, 'God sometimes drops surprises in your path.'"

"Your mother sounds like a smart lady." He tilted his head as if studying her face. "You haven't said much about your family before."

"I've been on my own a long time now. She died six years ago. Tuberculosis."

He frowned. "I'm sorry to hear that."

Olivia folded her napkin and dropped it beside her empty plate. She couldn't let him wheedle his way into her affections. Her life. She had enough to worry about. "Thank you for the meal. I'll go retrieve my paints and wait to see what you come up with. Good luck with Marcus." She pushed back her chair and stood.

"I'm afraid I'm going to need it." He sighed. "Because I'm determined to find out what he's up to."

It took only a moment for the mask to drop back over her face. Clark shook his head as she walked away. Every time he got an inch closer, she took two steps back. At this rate, it'd take a lifetime to learn what made her tick.

Livy. He liked the sound of the nickname. It suggested she'd once had a real life, surrounded by family and friends who loved her. People who saw her as more than a paint slinger. Though truth be told, her talent brought him to his knees. When the magazine editor laid eyes on these paintings, he'd be thrilled. There was no question that the images would sell magazines. When the readers flooded into the park to see the wonders she depicted, John would be forced to hire a whole crew of extra rangers.

The idea curled in his gut like a lariat. Why didn't the ranger job appeal to him? Because he'd have to part with the mules? That would happen, regardless. Because of Filbert? John and the others would find him eventually and run the old man off the land.

Or was it because it meant his dream of pastoring a church was truly dead?

The thought of leaving Yosemite burned like day-old coffee reheated over the fire. John and Melba had become his family. These trees were his home. The wind of Yosemite was the breath in his lungs.

So take the job.

Clark dug his hand into his vest pocket and clasped the silver compass his father had left him. He didn't need to read the inscription to bring it to mind. *"Ye have compassed this mountain long enough: turn you northward."* *Deuteronomy 2:3.* He flipped open the lid, glancing down at the needle. It pointed directly at the valley. So, did that mean stay or leave? Whatever God had in store for him, he was ready to follow. But it'd be nice if the Almighty would make it clear—and soon.

⌒

Fifteen minutes later, he was checking the grounds near the hotel when he finally spotted Marcus Vanderbilt, leaning against the corral, a cigarette in hand.

Clark pushed down his irritation at seeing him so close to the General and the mules. Now wasn't the time to cause a scene. "Glad to see you made it in one piece."

The man snorted, resting his foot on the lowest rail. "Surprised you care."

"To be perfectly honest, I don't. But there's a little gal back at the hotel who does. Two of them, in fact."

"Well, if we're being honest, I'm in no hurry to put either of them at ease."

The General wandered over and thrust her nose up under Clark's arm.

Vanderbilt snorted, flicking some ashes on the dirt. "Loyal animal, isn't it?"

Clark cupped a hand under the horse's whiskery chin. "Loyalty follows kindness and trust—at least with critters."

The man drew off his hat and turned around to face the hotel. "With people, loyalty follows money. That's the only reason either of those women are with me. I'd like to believe it's my charming personality and wit, but I know it's because of my stock portfolio."

Clark leaned against the rail fence. He'd like to think Olivia was beyond such practices, but hadn't she told him as much?

Vanderbilt knocked his hat against his knee. "When Sophie turned her back on me, I knew I deserved it. But then your blasted horse?" He spit on the ground. "I couldn't even get a stupid animal to obey me."

"Maybe it's not about being obeyed. It's about respect."

"What do you mean?"

Clark patted the General a second time, then shoved his hands into his pockets. "I've rarely had more than a couple of coins to rub together at a time, but as I see it, money only takes you so far. People will follow you to Timbuktu if you earn their respect."

"I'm better at earning dollars than respect." Vanderbilt eyed him. "The ladies seem to respect you. They chose to follow you."

"I put their needs first. I don't know if you read the Scriptures, but Christ said, 'If any man desire to be first, the same shall be last of all, and servant of all.'" He drew a peppermint from his pocket for the General, hoping he could slip it to her without the mules catching wind of it. "Who would you rather follow? A leader who seeks to meet your needs, or one who's more than capable of doing so, but can't be bothered?"

Vanderbilt dropped the cigarette to the ground and crushed it under his boot.

"It seems to me your wife is quite devoted," Clark continued. "She's been in tears ever since you left."

"Truly?" The man's face softened.

Sad to think a woman's suffering would brighten his day, but maybe Vanderbilt simply needed his pride mollified. "Now Olivia—she's tougher to decipher. She's got her head in the clouds half the time."

"You can say that again." The fellow smirked.

"How long have you known her?"

"A month or so. Sophie introduced us at an art showing in Sacramento. My wife was smitten with her immediately." Vanderbilt shrugged. "I'd seen better, but I was pleased to see Sophie take an interest in the art business. If she wanted a little artist pet, who was I to quibble at her choice?"

Clark's stomach dropped. Just when he was starting to soften to the man. "Really? You all seem so close. I thought maybe you'd known each other for years."

Vanderbilt thrust his hat back on and tipped it against the late afternoon glare. "She's pretty new to the art world, or so I gathered. I'm not sure she'll be around long. This bold, modern style... It's a passing fashion. Too simple. Anyone could do that sort of thing. The true masters are the ones who focus on the subtle details, not brash colors." He straightened his jacket. "At least she's easy on the eyes."

Clark kept his hands firmly in his pockets. He'd already had one fist-fight today, he'd hate to be guilty of instigating a second. "She's a rare beauty."

The man cleared his throat and glanced back up at the building. "I suppose I should go and apologize to Sophie."

"That would ease things considerably, I imagine."

As Vanderbilt strode off toward the hotel, Clark turned back to give one last pat to the General. "There's one crisis averted. At least until the next time he opens his mouth."

Eleven

Olivia squinted at her watercolor paper in the deepening twilight. The light was fading too fast. She'd only caught the rough edges of the shapes scattered in front of her—Half Dome, Liberty Cap, Nevada Fall, Vernal Fall, and so much more. There was far too much to grasp in one painting. But the evening light falling across the domes was entrancing. She'd barely noticed as the staff had cleaned up and put things away. She and Clark had eaten midafternoon, so it hadn't dawned on her to order anything else. A server had come by a few times and tried to offer her something, but she'd waved him off.

She glanced around, her stomach grumbling its complaint. That was always the problem when she got busy painting, life slowed to a gentle crawl—at least for her. The rest of the world went on without her.

Clark stood at the far end of the porch, gazing out over the view. He'd likely been waiting a while, not wishing to bother her. Over the past week, she'd probably tried the man's patience multiple times as she disappeared into her world of paints and colors, leaving everyone else behind. He'd not complained once.

She tapped the water droplets from her brush, then left it to sit in the narrow tray under the easel and glanced back at the guide. He gripped the railing, his arms spread as he studied the valley below. The sky behind him shifted from orange to purples, casting the man in shadows as he blocked a portion of the fading light.

Olivia lifted her easel, balancing the cup with one hand, and sidled her way to the rear of the porch, hugging the building until she was directly behind Clark. When he stood perfectly silhouetted before Half Dome, she lowered the three-legged stand to the floor and scampered back to retrieve her brushes and paints.

Opening her box, she checked the clip holding all her finished paintings in place. She ran a finger across the large stack, a surge of energy flooding her chest. Yosemite had been a good muse so far. At this rate, she'd finish early.

She selected two mop-head brushes and closed the lid. Tiptoeing to her previous spot, she swirled her brush through the paint, layering dark colors along the bottom third of the picture. The vertical slats in the porch railing were topped with a cross-shaped cutout, glowing in the dusky illumination.

"I know you're back there." Clark's voice carried like a gentle touch through the evening air.

"Don't you dare move." She outlined his broad shoulders and the rakish angle of his hat, filling in the shadowy image with Payne's gray and indigo. The sun's radiance still played off the summit in the distance, the details in the granite exposed by the long reddish rays blending light and shadow.

"Please tell me I won't be here all night."

"Shh." Olivia's breathing slowed, releasing her fingers to capture the image before the moment was completely gone. The framing of the porch provided the scene with much-needed boundaries, and Clark—well, Clark gave it life.

Warmth rushed through her at the thought. She'd known the man only a week, but he was already framing her thoughts in much the same way. She'd not known what was missing in her life. It was too much like that great view—terrifying freedom and no focus. Her brush stilled for a heartbeat as she watched the man leaning against the railing. She traced the lines of his back and shoulders as if her hands slid over the gentle arc between his neck and shoulder.

"Are you finished? You've gone quiet." Clark asked, unmoving.

The brush slid in her trembling grip. She couldn't give in to these longings. Too much was at stake. A dalliance with a mountain man would do nothing for her upscale reputation. Unfortunately, her heart no longer cared. She'd been away from the city too long. She needed Frank's solid presence reminding her to focus on the prize.

He turned, glancing over his shoulder. "Olivia?"

She blinked, her eyes stinging. Words refused to come, her tongue refusing to cooperate, as if in defiance.

Clark's brows drew low over his eyes. He moved toward her. "Is everything all right?"

His motion knocked her loose from the trance she'd become entrapped in. "I—yes, I'm fine." She shook herself, ducking her head in case the emotion was still splayed across her face like paint spilling across the page. "Yes, I'm finished."

Clark glanced down at the paper. "It's lovely. Except for that big, ugly fellow in the way."

"Nonsense. He's the best part." She nearly choked as her throat tightened. "The best."

He caught her eye, a smile playing about his lips. "If you say so. I suppose it will make magazine readers feel they're looking through my eyes."

"Or over your shoulder at the very least. It's intimate." Warmth rushed to her cheeks.

"It takes an artist to turn something that vast into something so personal. You've got a gift, Olivia."

Her fingers trembled from the hours of exertion. "It was seeing you standing there that inspired it." She glanced up at him. "Did you find out anything?"

His expression grew somber. "I found Vanderbilt. He was licking his wounds, but I talked to him. I still don't care for the man, but he was on his way to apologize to his wife when I last saw him. Hopefully she'll accept his olive branch, and we can get back to our journey."

Music wafted from the open porch doors. Olivia turned, and the sight of couples milling in the lounge area caught her attention. "Oh! What are we missing?"

"Charlie from the front desk said there's a dance tonight, after the Firefall."

A dance? Her heart skipped. "Here in the hotel?"

"They were hanging Japanese lanterns as I came in." Clark cocked his head. "Are you interested?"

"Are you inviting me?" The coy words spilled out before she could catch herself.

He tipped his hat. "I'm ever at your service, miss. You know that."

Her heart dropped. Suddenly having him in her employ hung heavy. Clark wasn't showing interest; he was just being kind. Someone like Olivia Rutherford wouldn't turn his head. He needed a sweet little church girl, not a woman who blackened her hair and her eyelids to play a part another had set out for her. "Then I grant you the evening off, Mr. Johnson." Olivia ran a hand through her hair, hoping the short locks had dried smooth in the afternoon sunshine. She glanced around the gathering crowd and sighed. "I'm sure I can find someone who knows how to spin a girl around the dance floor."

Clark's lips pressed together for a moment, and he offered a quick nod. "Very well, if that's what you prefer."

It isn't. She tried to brush away the hollow feeling growing inside. "Do you think the staff would mind if I left my painting on the easel here to dry?"

Clark glanced at the small easel. "There's a supply closet beside the porch. I'll put it back there—your art box, too, if you'd like."

She glanced down at the box. "You're sure it'll be safe?"

"I'll ask Charlie to keep an eye on it."

"Then I'll go freshen up. Thank you for posing for me."

He folded his arms across his chest. "All part of the job, right?"

The words turned to dust in her mouth. "Right."

Clark returned to the corral, his pride soothed by the General's soft whicker of welcome. "At least you're glad of my company."

He hadn't expected Olivia to want him to escort her to the dance, but her brash dismissal cut to the bone. Of course he wasn't in her class. Now that they were back in civilization, their differences shone brighter than a sunrise over El Capitan.

He'd been a fool to fall under Yosemite's romantic spell and believe that a woman like Olivia would give him a second glance when there were so many better options available. She was cut out for a gentleman, not a mule packer who probably smelled little better than the stock. Clark grabbed his shirt collar and drew it up toward his face, inhaling deeply.

Olivia had smelled like the azaleas that grew along the stream banks— or something similar. She was probably fresh from a bath at the hotel.

What had he been thinking? He wouldn't even want to dance with himself.

He reached for his bag he'd slung over one of the railings and dug through the clothes, drawing out a clean shirt, jacket, and tie. She may have declined his offer, but he was determined to stay close by. The note she'd shown him earlier—and the fear in her face—had sent his thoughts in a sickening downward spiral. A woman like her would be a target for any gold-grubbing opportunist. As long as she was under his charge, he was determined no one would frighten her again. But he couldn't do it looking like a vagabond.

Forty minutes later, he slipped into the crowd mingling in the great room, hoping he smelled more of Ivory soap and brilliantine than of mule.

The jazz combo was in fine form, and he recognized several of Melba's musician friends from Camp Curry Village. Evidently the staff at the Glacier Point Hotel had wooed them away for the evening. Even Charlie was busy fox-trotting with a charming young woman on his arm. Hopefully the musicians wouldn't carry that observation back to his camp sweetheart.

Clark took a glass of punch from a server making the rounds with a tray. He scanned the gathering and the festive decor. He'd rarely seen the hotel dressed in its finery. The furniture had been pushed back, the large rugs rolled up, and the doors and windows to the wide porch stood open.

A few romantic couples chose the relative privacy of the outdoor tables, moonlight mixing with the glow from the rice-paper lanterns. The sight jabbed at his pride. Dances were for lovers, not for men like him. Besides, the jaunty music floating over the porch and out into the starry sky wasn't his idea of a peaceful night in the park. He'd rather listen to the wind rustling the tree branches and the owls calling out their mournful songs.

Vanderbilt and his wife made a fine picture as they danced near the center of the floor. Apparently he'd succeeded in earning Sophie's forgiveness. God had redeemed far worse men than her husband. Clark reminded himself to continue praying for the couple.

He paced to the far end of the room and scanned the crowd but failed to spot Olivia. He frowned. Last week at the Ahwahnee, eligible young bachelors vying for her attention had surrounded her. Maybe he just needed to search out a circle of preening Casanovas.

As he maneuvered around the dancers, his friend Charlie caught his arm and grinned. "There you are. This party is quite a blow, ain't it?

Hey, I wanted to introduce you to Maizy. She's the one I was telling you about."

Clark managed a smile for the young woman. "From Camp Curry?"

She nodded, her feathered headband bouncing with the motion. "Mother Curry hired me and several of my chums from Stanford. I'm having the best summer. There are so many young people working here, and the music—I met cowboy crooner Glenn Hood last week. I can scarce believe it." She pulled a tiny autograph book from her pocket and flipped it open. "Look! He wrote, 'Wishing you fair weather and an easy trail through life's journey.'" She grinned. "He even kissed my hand."

"Hey." Charlie scowled. "I don't want fellas kissing my best gal."

Maizy patted his arm. "He didn't kiss me, just my hand, silly."

Clark glanced past the young couple, still trying to locate Olivia. "I'm pleased to meet you, miss. Charlie must be quite a catch for you to climb up the trail to Glacier Point."

"Oh, no. We're not allowed to go up the Ledge Trail. It's too dangerous. I rode up with the musicians." She giggled behind one hand. "I'm not sure that would be condoned, either, but I didn't ask."

"Never take the Ledge Trail." Clark folded his arms across his chest. "It's not even safe for goats. Take the Four Mile Trail. It's better."

Charlie hooked his arm around the lady's waist. "I've risked the Ledge Trail a few times to see Maizy."

"You stumble off that ledge, and she'll be a lonely girl." Clark knew many of the staff took the path regularly, even racing to see who could make the journey the quickest. One of these days someone was going to fall to his death. Scrambling across some of the rockier parts, you had to hug the cliff face to keep from catapulting off the edge. It wasn't worth it for a simple shortcut. He glanced around again. "Charlie, have you seen Miss Rutherford? The dark-haired woman from my group?"

"Yes sir. She's right out there." He pointed to the window overlooking the far corner of the porch.

Clark turned, spotting Olivia sitting on the porch railing, her back against one of the tall support posts, gazing out over the dark night.

He excused himself from the group and headed to join her. "I thought Olivia Rutherford was always the life of the party."

She lifted her head. "Maybe your wilderness experience has ruined me for civilization."

He tried not to laugh. "I don't think we ever made it to the wilderness. We never got more than a few miles from the village."

Olivia shrugged. "That's farther than I've made it in a decade."

Her melancholy tone tugged at him. "Didn't find that man to sweep you around the dance floor?"

She turned her eyes on him as if seeing him for the first time. "Not one I wanted to."

"Then will you do me the honor? I'm no wealthy art connoisseur, but I know my way around a fox-trot." Clark extended a hand. She might refuse him, but what harm would it do?

She stared at it for a long moment before placing her hand in his and lowering her feet to the floor. "I'm not as shallow as all that, you know."

The words pricked at his conscience. He squeezed her fingers as he led her inside to the dance floor. "I didn't mean it as an insult. You have standards. I understand."

She glanced sideways at him as she stepped into his arms. If only he could read her thoughts. Unfortunately, she seemed to have disappeared into some inner vault he couldn't reach.

He settled his arm around her stiffened back, stepping out to the rhythm of the song. Within a few minutes, her rock-hard posture seemed to be uncoiling, and she eased into the flow of his lead. "You're good."

"Don't sound so surprised. You assumed I'd be a complete heeler?"

"No, well...it's just...I didn't picture a mountain guide knowing all the current steps."

"I haven't always been a guide."

She smiled, the first of the evening. "Ministers dance?"

"Some do. Remember, I'm a musician, too." He turned her in a quick circle before drawing her back, a sneaky way to reposition her closer in his arms.

"A man of many talents."

"Sure, I suppose. But I'd trade a few for some direction."

She tossed her head, a little of the spark back in her eyes. "I'm your boss, remember? I can provide direction."

His throat tightened. Perhaps not the sort of guidance he needed. The last time he'd followed a woman's lead, it took him right over a cliff. "I think I need divine wisdom for this particular problem."

"Whether or not to take the ranger job?"

"Among other things."

"So you're waiting for God to give you all the answers?" Her lips drew down into a frown. "Do you think that's what He really wants from you? Blind devotion?"

"I wouldn't call it that, exactly. But trust, yes."

"It seems to me, if you wait too long, you'll have no job at all. Am I right?"

He took a deep breath, the night air a tonic. "That is true, yes."

"Maybe the Park Service is right where He wants you."

"Perhaps." Tonight he wanted to focus on other things. He pulled her an inch closer, skirting around the edge of the dance floor until they were near the open windows. The fresh air might help clear his thoughts "You look lovely, by the way."

She laughed. "Only you would say such a thing. I'm not suitably dressed for such an event."

"I enjoy seeing you like this. And dressed for the trail. What about tomorrow? What tickles your fancy? South to the Mariposa Grove or north toward Tioga Pass? We could even scramble up one of the domes, if you like."

She tensed in his arms. "I spoke to Sophie. She told me Marcus was planning to return to Sacramento. He's offered to take her to Europe for the rest of the summer. That won her over completely, I'm afraid."

Good riddance to him. An instant later he understood the problem. She wouldn't dare to venture out on the trail with him, unaccompanied. His heart sank. "Oh, I see."

"I'll miss Sophie. She's become a good friend." Olivia wrinkled her nose. "She's excited about going to Paris. I imagine she'll find other artist friends— she and Marcus."

"I think she will miss you, too." Clark squeezed Olivia's hand as they danced. The freedom to touch her overwhelmed his good sense. Clark lowered his eyes, gazing at the nape of her neck, imagining the softness of her skin under his fingers. Yes, alone on the trail would not be wise.

The song ended and he drew back, releasing her like the overheated handle of a frying pan.

She pulled the blue sweater tight around her sides. "It's chilly over here by the doors. Perhaps we should move closer to the fire."

Chilly? He hadn't noticed. Clark glanced out across the valley to where the moonlight shimmered off the top of Half Dome. Moving away from the romantic view would definitely be a good idea. The night air was playing with his judgment. Next he'd be trying to steal a kiss. If she didn't trust him before, such a move would drive a nail into that particular horseshoe.

Twelve

O livia led the way farther into the great hall, the massive granite fireplace spilling heat into the large room. Still she shivered, though as much from Clark's touch as from cold. This little adventure had gotten far out of hand. Her thoughts and her heart had taken flight like one of those silly camp-robbing jays Clark had pointed out their first day on the trail. One moment she was all common sense, the next she was consumed with the idea of—well, of ideas best left unspoken.

Had Clark even noticed the song the band had been playing? No matter what he was saying, all she could hear was his gentle voice back at the campfire and the sound of his simple guitar strings. *"I'll be loving you, always…"*

Would a man ever whisper such things to her? Her throat grew thick with emotion. But no one could promise "always." Always was nothing but sentiment. And she didn't have time for empty vows.

Olivia strode to the fireplace and held out her shaking palms to the flames. A few couples lingered nearby.

Clark followed, drawing up next to her. "I hardly noticed the cold. I'm sorry." He shrugged out of his jacket. "Here." He wrapped it about her shoulders, the silk lining sliding along her bulky cardigan.

"Won't you need it?" She spoke the words even as she wrapped her fingers in the lapels, drawing the jacket close around her neck, the warmth of his body lingering in the fabric and enveloping her. Did it smell of pine needles?

"No, I'm plenty warm."

"This is a lovely party. Real people dancing to real music."

"Instead of waltzing to Strauss and Beethoven, like back at the Ahwahnee? Do you prefer jazz to dead composers?"

The reminder of the Ahwahnee sent another shiver through her, and she snuggled deeper into the jacket. "I appreciate all types of music, but jazz has a sort of infectious energy. And an 'everyman' appeal." She spotted Marcus and Sophie standing outside the door, their voices raised. "Oh, no. Are they at it again?"

"I thought he'd come to his senses earlier."

Sophie dashed inside and darted up the long stairway, leaving Marcus frowning by the doorway.

Olivia slid Clark's jacket off her shoulders, instantly missing the soft embrace, and handed it back to him. "It's my turn to speak some sense to him, I suppose. Will you excuse me?"

Clark folded the jacket over his arm. "I'll be here if you need me."

Olivia hurried over, following Marcus into the cool night air. "Marcus—where are you going?"

He turned, one brow hitching upward. "Olivia. Such a pleasure to see you." He tipped his head in the direction his wife had disappeared. "I'm glad some ladies still deign to speak with me."

She grasped his sleeve and tugged him toward the far end of the porch where the shadows could give them a moment's privacy. "What's gone wrong this time? I thought she'd forgiven you."

He reached for Olivia's wrist, running his finger up her arm. "She's a sensitive soul. A feisty lioness. Not unlike yourself."

She drew her arm away, moving back against the rail. Had he been drinking? "Perhaps if you kept your attentions focused on her, she'd be more content. Sophie's no fool."

Marcus tipped back his head in a laugh. "Then you don't know her as well as you believe. She is indeed a fool. A pretty little fool. How do you think I convinced her to marry me?"

Olivia's stomach turned. What was the use of talking to this man? She moved to slip around him and return to the party.

He snagged her hand. "Dance with me, Miss Rutherford. Let's show this dreary little party how it's done."

"No, I don't think so. Besides, we can hardly hear the music out here." She freed her fingers from his grip and swallowed the bitter taste in her mouth. This was the man Frank wanted her to win over? Did her dealer realize what type of two-timing lizard he'd foisted on her?

"We don't need it." He leaned in close, placing a hand on the small of her back "I adore your energy and spirit, Olivia. It's a shame the art world hasn't discovered you yet."

She turned her head, sickened by the sour smell of rye whiskey on his breath. Where had he laid hands on it?

"I can help with that, you know. Sophie and I are heading back in the morning. If I could take a few of your paintings with me, I could show them around to some key art critics."

Olivia's breath caught. "The paintings I've done at Yosemite? They're for *Scenic*. I can't sell them."

"No, perhaps not. But just to give them a sense of what you've accomplished in your short time here." He brushed his face up against her hair to speak softly in her ear. "And if they *were* to make an offer on one—you could always produce more. There's enough scenery in this park to choke a horse." He chuckled and drew back. "In fact, with what I think one of my friends would offer, you could set yourself up here for an entire year."

Olivia's heart raced. Or she could pay for the girls' schooling. "Just one?"

"Let me take a few to choose from. I'll only sell one, if that's what you want." He slid his other arm around her waist, his fingers toying with one of the buttons on her back.

She twisted, but his forearm cut into her lower back, locking her in place. "Marcus. Give me a little space, please."

"Shh." He ducked his head into the nape of her neck, nuzzling her ear. "Don't be like that, Livy. It's a beautiful night; how can I resist a beautiful girl?"

The world seemed to tilt under her feet. She landed both palms on his chest. "Don't call me that."

He lifted his head, his ice-blue eyes catching the light of the moon. "A beautiful girl?" Before she could speak, he gripped her chin and kissed her lips, driving her back against one of the porch supports.

Olivia gasped, the sudden shift catching her off balance. Her hip collided with the porch railing. She wrenched her face away from his searching mouth. "Stop."

His other hand gripped her side, pinning her in place. "Olivia, you're a natural. I'll have your name on every art dealer's lips. Just say you'll give me what I want."

"Are we still talking paintings?"

His laugh was a slow, deep rumble. "Mmm, yes. Paintings. Sure." Marcus slipped his hand between her sweater and dress and pressed his fingers against her ribs. "But I'd be open to other suggestions as well."

Suggestions? A chill swept through her. What if Sophie saw the two of them? She grabbed his wrist, trying to push him away from her. "Marcus, the paintings aren't mine to sell, not to mention I already have an art dealer. *Scenic* paid for my trip, they have first rights to anything—"

"Don't be ridiculous. An artist can't be bought like some common street harlot."

The vulgar words spun her thoughts into a tangled mess. "You should speak to Frank. If he says—"

"Olivia, Frank Robinson is the only reason I'm here. Well, that and Sophie's fascination with you."

"Wha-what do you mean?" She shoved him back another few inches, trying to give herself room to think.

"Frank Robinson asked me to keep an eye on you, sugar. He wants his investment protected." He lowered his head close to hers again, his breath hot on her forehead. "Of course, the man's one tiddlywink away from bankruptcy anyway."

Bankruptcy? A chilling wind swept up from the valley below, teasing the backs of her legs. Frank had never hinted at such a thing. And he'd certainly never referred to her as an investment. He treated her like a daughter. He cared about her future—and the girls' future too.

"Plus he mentioned your little crush on me. Now how can a man resist such an offer?" Marcus managed to snag the edge of her skirt this time, dragging the hem with it.

"My what?" Olivia took an instinctual step back, forgetting she was already against the railing. Her heartbeat roared in her ears. She gripped his roving hand, digging her nails into his wrist. "Let me go. I'm not interested in—in your attentions *or* your deal." She swung at his face with the heel of her hand.

Marcus turned his head, catching her glancing blow about the ear rather than the cheek where she'd aimed it. He stepped back, his eyes glowering.

"Make sure you know what you're giving up here, Olivia. I have my fingers in every art deal from here to Los Angeles."

Clark's voice sounded from over his shoulder. "I don't doubt you do."

Olivia stepped out from under Marcus's arm, her breath catching.

Marcus pointed at the guide. "This is none of your concern."

"Do I look concerned?" Clark folded his arms. "I thought I'd ask the lady for a dance. By the way, your wife is looking for you."

Marcus jerked his head around, glancing down the porch toward the door. After ascertaining Sophie was nowhere in sight, he glared at Clark. "We're talking business here."

Olivia ran a hand down her skirt, assuring everything was in place. "Not any longer. I've no interest in your offer. You can go tell your backers the same. My deal is with Frank and with *Scenic*."

Vanderbilt sneered as he yanked on his cuff as if to cover the marks on his wrist. "Frank Robinson is a sinking ship. You can see the rats deserting in droves. And we'll see how long the magazine deal lasts once I have a word with them."

Olivia's stomach dropped as he stormed off.

Clark grunted. "He's bluffing."

"I don't think so." She stepped closer to him, suddenly longing for the comfort of his arms to wipe away the sensation of Marcus's touch.

Clark sucked in a deep breath, the anger clawing at his chest like a trapped animal. When he'd spotted Vanderbilt with his grubby paws all over Olivia, it had taken every bit of control not to grab the man and hoist him over the railing. Seeing her belt the weasel had given him the moment he needed to gather control of his senses. He'd been a fool to leave her alone with him. "Should we go inside where it's warm?"

"No." Olivia shook her head, her voice low. "I need a minute."

He stepped back to give her space to breathe, but she grasped his elbow. "Stay, please."

Clark didn't need another word. He moved closer and slid his arm around her back. "I'm not going anywhere."

The woman's sigh nearly undid him. She lowered her head to his chest. Clark pulled her into his arms. "I'm sorry. I should have stayed closer."

"I've ruined everything." Her voice was little more than a whisper.

"What? No." He straightened. "You can't let a skunk like Vanderbilt undermine what you've achieved. Whatever it is he thinks he knows, it doesn't overshadow your talent. The paintings you've done since you arrived —they show the life and breath of Yosemite. Everyone will see that."

"I wish it were that simple."

"It is." He grasped her shoulders so she stood square to him. "God's given you a gift, Olivia Rutherford. One man's words can't steal that away."

She took a long, shuddering breath, wiping the back of her hand across her cheeks as she glanced up at the hotel. "I can't stay here."

"No." Clark turned around. The music had changed, signaling that festivities were winding down. Vanderbilt had stalked off down the porch, but now his white dinner jacket was nowhere to be seen. This might be the best time to act. "Are you up for a moonlight ride?"

She looked at him with widened eyes and nodded.

"It'll be a rough go of it, but we can make it down the hill before dawn. Just you and me." He squeezed her shoulders.

Olivia stepped back. "I'll need to get my things. I only brought in the small bag. Are my paint box and easel still in the supply closet?"

He grasped her hand and led the way, angling past several couples taking advantage of the area's relative privacy. The knob was icy to the touch as he opened the closet door and pulled the chain dangling from the single bulb.

Olivia's gasp froze his heart.

Her supplies were strewn about the small space, the paint pots smashed underfoot. Clark stepped inside the room and surveyed the damage. Everywhere he looked, scraps of Olivia's beautiful paintings lay shredded and tattered. A fragment of Yosemite Falls lay atop a chunk of El Capitan. A heavy weight descended into his gut.

She pushed past him, falling to her knees in the mess, her trembling hands gathering up pieces of her work. "It's ruined—all of it."

Clark bent down and picked up her wooden box, the hinges falling free and the last few brushes slipping to the floor. He jostled the bottom, remembering Olivia's hiding place. Lifting out the wooden panel, he stared into the box's lower compartment. Empty.

Thirteen

Olivia gave the mule her head to follow the General down the moonlit trail. She leaned forward and let her tears fall onto Goldie's neck. *My pictures. My paints. My life.* Nothing was left. She gulped, a sob burning its way through her ribs.

Clark had gathered every scrap and broken paint pot, jamming them into the box as she stood dumbstruck, unable to process what her eyes were telling her. Every bit of work she'd done over the last week was ruined or missing completely. The views of Yosemite Falls, Nevada Fall, Bridalveil Fall, El Capitan, even today's painting of Clark in front of Half Dome. How could this have happened?

Marcus hadn't wasted any time exacting his revenge. Had she and Clark lingered outside for that long?

Next, with whatever information he had, he'd ruin her. *The newspaper article.* Why had she brought that along? She could have left it in Sacramento or tossed it in the fire years ago, like she'd always wanted.

The image of Frances's and Louise's faces danced through her mind. Did he know he was destroying their future in the process? Would he even care?

Clark glanced back over his shoulder, as if aware of her thoughts, his face barely visible in the dim moonlight. He tipped his head at something in the distance, lifting one hand to gesture.

She studied the underbrush to the right, finally spotting the coyote standing at the trees' edge, its bushy tail silver in the dusky light. Two little ones tumbled nearby in play.

The wildness—yet intimacy—of the moment quieted her soul and loosened the knot in her stomach. After she lost sight of the animals, she turned her eyes back to Clark riding ahead of her, his steady presence a life-line in the night. The evening breeze touched her damp cheeks.

She closed her eyes, the steady clopping of hooves and the creak of the saddles among the few sounds lingering in the still air.

Where was the brash Olivia Rutherford now?

She felt more like plain old Liv than she had in years. And when Marcus was done, likely that's all she'd ever be.

⟶

Clark had never been so glad to see the light post at the entrance of Camp Curry, its glow spilling out in a welcoming circle. His neck ached from the countless times he'd glanced back at Olivia. A lot of people would have opted for the shorter Ledge Trail, but there was no way he was going to risk it to-night, not with the troubled woman riding behind him. With the end of the road in view, the exhaustion of the day hung heavy over them both.

Spotting the two familiar figures waiting for them, their horses tethered on the rail nearby, lifted the burden somewhat. Melba hurried up to his side. "You made it."

Clark blew a long breath between his lips as he slid to the ground. "You two are a welcome sight."

John pulled his ranger Stetson from his head. "Welcome to Camp

Curry, Miss Rutherford. When I received Charlie's telephone call from Glacier, Melba and I came especially to make sure a tent cabin was ready for you." He held Goldie still as Olivia dismounted.

Melba stood near the General's head. "I didn't like the idea of you two riding down that trail at night. It makes me nervous."

"Better than the other option." He leaned close, lowering his voice. "Take care of her, will you? She's had quite a shock. She needs a friend."

"You know I will, Clark." She touched his sleeve. "And it looks like she's found one in you." She took Olivia's arm and walked her to the tent cabins.

John adjusted his hat. "She looks a different woman than the one who left here a week ago. I'd have hardly recognized her. Rough trip?"

"Not so much, until today." Clark turned to unload the saddlebags. "But today was rough enough to count for a week's worth of bad."

"Charlie told me a little about what happened. Should we have someone speak to this Vanderbilt fellow?"

"I think he and his wife are planning to leave at first light, so I doubt we'll have any more trouble. Other than destroying Miss Rutherford's paintings, I don't think any laws were broken—and we can't prove that was him." Clark rubbed his stiff lower back. "Oh, and there's this." He reached into the saddlebag and drew out the small pistol. "I took this off him on the trail. I'd rather you took possession, if you don't mind."

"Happy to." John took the gun and turned it over in his hand. "If he wants to retrieve it, it will give me the opportunity to give him a piece of my mind. I don't take kindly to men behaving badly around our female visitors. I asked Mary Tresidder to hold the neighboring tent cabin for you. I thought it might be best if you stay close until Miss Rutherford decides what she wants to do next."

"I appreciate that, John."

"Superintendent Thomson is adamant that this partnership with *Scenic* go well. I'm afraid we might be on tough footing now. Do you think she'll quit and go home?"

Clark lifted the panniers from Chieftain's back. He'd left the other animals and most of his supplies in the care of a friend at Glacier Point. "I can't say. She'd done some beautiful work, and now it's all gone. That's quite a blow."

John tipped his head. "You weren't real keen on this artist gal when you left the Ahwahnee last week. Have you changed your tune?"

"A man's got the right to alter his opinions here and there."

A grin spread across his friend's face. "I'd like to hear more."

Clark turned back to his animals. "I've got to bed down the stock. They've had a long day, too."

"I'll walk over there with you. I think after riding out here in the middle of the night, I deserve some good news."

Fourteen

A clanging bell jarred Olivia awake. She glanced around the canvas-tent frame, her mind taking a moment to clue her in as to where she was. The memory of last night settled over her like a wet blanket, and she fell back against the pillow. Everything—every single painting—ruined. How could Marcus be so evil? He knew she was counting on that *Scenic* cover.

She should have seen through the man the first time she met him. And his so-called love and adoration for Sophie? To him, she was nothing more than another art treasure. How many of those had he disposed of after the initial excitement wore off? Olivia's stomach turned. The realization that he'd zeroed in on her for his next acquisition made her queasy. Her heart ached for her friend.

Olivia's only focus had been that fancy school for her sisters. That and the idea of being famous and successful. A prickle eased its way across her skin. Was she much better than him? It probably appeared as if she'd used Sophie's offer of friendship to gain his wealth and influence. No wonder Marcus thought she'd risk everything to secure his patronage.

No more. She'd telephone Frank and tell him the job was off. Between Marcus's threats and the ruined paintings, she could forget ever seeing her work on a magazine cover. The article about her father's crime was not among the scraps of ruined paintings, which meant it was likely in Marcus Vanderbilt's pocket. She might as well have handed him her past—and her future—on a silver platter. And there was still Gus Kendall lurking about. She'd nearly forgotten him in the milieu. Her stomach turned.

Olivia crawled off of the cot as the bell rang a second time.

"Breakfast! Breakfast! Last call!" The fragrance of bacon and coffee floated through the morning air.

She reached for her riding breeches, coated in trail dust, and pulled them on. Maybe a good cup of coffee would shine some light on this day.

"Miss Rutherford?" Clark's hesitant voice sounded outside the tent flap. "Olivia? Are you awake?"

She finished buttoning her shirt and ran quick fingers through her hair. She probably looked little better than day-old toast. "Yes." She hurried over to the tent flap and poked her head out.

The sight of Clark dressed in a smart blue suit sent her heart into her throat.

He grinned. "There you are. I was worried you might miss breakfast. Camp Curry serves the best hotcakes this side of the Sierra. You don't want to miss them."

She ran a hand across her limp, stained shirt. "I'm not sure I'm ready to face a crowd. I just woke up."

"You look fine. Wonderful." He held out a hand. "Come on, all these folks have been camping. You'll fit in fine."

She dropped her fingers in his without a thought and then stared at them dumbly. When had that motion become natural? Olivia pulled her hand back, a flush burning up her cheeks. "I—wait—I need to put on shoes and stockings. I don't think they'd appreciate me showing up barefoot."

He chuckled. "Mother Curry might frown on that. I'll wait for you."

She ducked back inside the tent cabin and glanced down at her rumpled attire. Rummaging through her bag, she pulled out the dress she'd worn last night and quickly changed. After drawing on her bulky sweater, stockings, and shoes, she found her compact and checked her reflection in the tiny mirror. How had she not ruined the man's appetite?

She patted a little powder across her nose, skipping the rouge. Nothing was going to make this face look presentable. Nothing but a day in the beauty salon.

As Olivia stepped out of the tent, Clark's smile sent a jolt of energy through her. She tamped down the ridiculous sensation. She'd be leaving soon, and this infatuation couldn't follow her back to Sacramento.

"You look beautiful."

And that doesn't help. She smoothed the front of her skirt. "I wouldn't say that, but at least I'm dressed."

Clark hadn't lied about the hotcakes, but the coffee was even better. Olivia sat at the long table with both hands wrapped around the stoneware mug, breathing in the fragrance. One more cup and she might be able to figure out whom to ask about using a telephone.

Clark could barely eat two bites in a row before another waitress or busboy came by to chat with him. She blinked through her weariness and tried to follow their conversations. Much of it seemed to be advice about hiking and fishing spots, though one attractive young woman named Maizy asked if he was singing tonight.

After she left, Olivia leaned over. "Singing where?"

He ducked his head. "I sometimes help out in the camp shows. Mostly I play guitar for Melba when she sings, but I've been known to belt out a ballad or two when they're low on paid entertainers."

"And are they now?" If he was going to sing, maybe she should stay another night.

"Possibly. Apparently there's a summer cold going around. Lots of laryngitis among the staff."

Olivia managed another sip of coffee, her head starting to clear a bit.

Clark pushed back his plate. "I know you're concerned about your supplies. There's an art and photography studio down in the village. We could probably find most of what you need—paints, paper, and such. Obviously the paintings are irreplaceable." A shadow darkened his face. "But we could revisit the locations. You could make more, right? More...paintings?"

Olivia's throat tightened. "I-I don't think so, Clark. I need to telephone Frank and speak with him about it."

He searched her face, his brown eyes unwavering. "You're leaving."

"I think it might be best." She pushed her plate back and stood, her mind finally settled to the decision. "Can you take me to a telephone?"

He sat for a long moment without speaking. "Yes, but we have to make one stop first."

⁓

Olivia stared up at the small chapel, her heart jumping to her throat. "Church? We're going to church? Here?"

Clark chuckled. "Well, we sometimes meet outside, but it rained a little last night, so it's damp."

She turned on him. "That's not what I meant."

"I know. But it's Sunday morning, and I like to stop in whenever I'm in the valley."

She buttoned the sweater up to her neck. "If you'd warned me, I would have made myself presentable."

"If you were any more presentable, you...you'd..." He shook his head slowly. "What I mean to say is, you look fine."

The sound of a reed organ filtered out the open door, beckoning them inside.

She narrowed her eyes at him, trying in vain to finish the sentence he'd begun. But he'd already started up the steps. What choice did she have but to follow?

They took seats in the back of the rough building, which was almost colder than the outside air. A haze of smoke filled the room.

Clark leaned over. "And that's one of the reasons we often meet outside at 'Church Bowl.' The stove is piped through the window, but it never draws quite right. This whole building is a mess. Someone needs to take it in hand."

"I can't believe there's a chapel in the valley."

"It's just about the oldest building in the park. The congregation wants to replace it with a larger structure, but I'm not sure it's going to happen anytime soon." He shrugged. "There are more people living here than you think. Not just the rangers, but the staff at the hotels, the camps—and the visitors, of course. Someone has to see to their spiritual needs."

Olivia sat back and studied the odd collection of people. Some were sporting their best glad rags, while others—like herself—looked as if they'd been living off the land for weeks. Melba and her ranger husband sat near the front. She almost didn't recognize him dressed in a gray suit. She'd never bothered to look beyond the forest-green uniform.

The plaintive notes of the organ tugged at her heart like a child asking her to come and play. Olivia closed her eyes and let herself drift with the sweet sound. A few minutes later, she was jostled as the worshippers rose to their feet, including Clark. She scrambled up, embarrassed she'd somehow missed the subtle cue.

Melba stepped to the front and started a hymn, the rest of the crowd joining with her lovely soprano voice.

Clark opened a small hymnal and held it out. His arm bumped against hers, the strength of his presence calming her heart. Olivia hadn't stepped in a church in years, but the gentle peace she remembered from such places in her childhood remained. She'd nearly forgotten the sensation. Even the tune tickled at the edges of her memory.

Melba led two more songs before closing the hymnal and gesturing for the congregation to sit. She pressed the book to the bodice of her lace dress. "I'm afraid I have sad news this morning. Reverend White is feeling under the weather, like so many of our staff. So we're going to sing a few more songs, and then I'm hoping one or two of you will share something that's on your heart that might be a blessing to others here. You can be praying about it while we sing number one-twenty-five."

Olivia sat back and let the words of the hymn wash over her. "What a friend we have in Jesus, all our sins and griefs to bear. What a privilege to carry everything to God in prayer."

She'd been drawn to Clark's assertion that divine hands had sculpted this majestic landscape, but it was a huge step to actually consider this Creator God a friend. Would He truly listen to her? She glanced at the man sitting beside her. Sure, to someone like Clark, perhaps. But she'd worked and schemed for every bit of goodness she could obtain. And prayer? She couldn't think of the last time she'd gone that route.

Clark leaned forward, head down, bracing his forearms against his knees as if a mighty weight hung on his shoulders. His eyes were closed.

Is he praying? Right now?

She swallowed hard, glancing about her. Everyone was singing or praying, and yet she just sat. What did God want from her here? Was she supposed to be doing something? Olivia squeezed her eyes closed, replicating Clark's posture to the best of her ability. If she could pretend to be the flamboyant artist, she could certainly play the part of a sweet church girl. Right?

She moved her lips as if reciting a prayer. What had been that prayer her mother had always said before kissing them goodnight? *"Four corners to my bed, four angels round my head."* Somehow it didn't seem to apply right now. And would Jesus really want to hear her recite a children's rhyme?

The song ended and the room grew silent. Olivia opened her eyes. Keeping her head lowered, she glanced at Melba standing in the front. Was she staring back? A jolt of panic traveled through her. Melba couldn't be expecting *her* to say something, could she?

Clark shifted in his seat, his fingers gripping and regripping the edge of the bench.

Olivia shrank back against the seat as all eyes turned their direction.

Melba smiled. "Clark, I'd hoped you might speak to us."

Standing, he cleared his throat. "Yes, well, I didn't intend to. Didn't really want to. But"—he ran a hand across the back of his neck—"it seems God had something else in mind. As a friend recently told me, He likes to surprise us sometimes."

"Come up, please." Melba beckoned him forward.

As Clark stepped out of the row and walked down the central aisle, Olivia tried not to fidget. He'd said he was a minister, but she hadn't expected to hear him preach. It was hard to imagine the rough mule packer doing such an unusual thing.

He stopped at the front, his back to the group, and paused for a long moment, as if studying the cross at the front of the small chapel. After a long breath, he turned and faced the room. "For three years I've been leading pack mules through these mountains, but I think that short walk felt longer than any trip I've done yet."

A soft laugh rippled through the gathering.

His attention wandered the room, settling for a long moment on Olivia. "Sometimes one step is all He wants us to take. For some the path is easy. For others, it's like scaling Half Dome. But if we trust in Him to lead us, He guides our feet. There's a place in Psalms where David wrote that God set him up on the mountains and gave him feet like a deer's." Clark glanced down at his boots. "Mine are a little more like a mule's." He smiled. "Some people here would say I'm a bit muleheaded, too."

Gentle laughter carried through the room a second time as people smiled at him and each other.

"But we all know that a mule is the best choice for treacherous trails. The good Lord brought me to these high places for a reason." His attention wandered through the crowd. "And He brought each of you here too. He's doing a work in us, right here in this place. We might not even know what it is." He shrugged. "I still don't know why *I'm* here. But I want to feel Him moving in my life, so I say, 'Here I am, Lord. Use me.'

"Maybe He's asking you to do the same. Some of you are here for only a season, or even one day. But I hope you take this time to seek Him out. God is here, in this valley. You sense that, right?"

Murmurs of agreement sounded from around the room.

Olivia's heart seemed to be inching upward in her chest as Clark spoke. She'd come to Yosemite for one reason—to paint. God couldn't have anything here for her.

Clark cleared his throat. "Today is the Lord's day. Whatever you end up doing today, give it to Him. Give Him *this* day." He lifted a hand and gestured to the windows. "You can have tomorrow for yourself. The rest of the week. The rest of your life. But give Him today. See what He does with it. Can you do that?" His question hung in the air as the room fell silent. Clark didn't move, his focus lighting on her.

Olivia held her breath as a shiver raced across her skin. Was he asking *her* to stay for another day? Without giving it another thought, she offered him a slight nod.

One day.

∽

Clark released a little fishing line, playing the lure out over the Merced as the chilly water rushed around his legs. "See? Gentle wrist action."

"Like a brush stroke." Olivia struggled with her pole. "Only heavier. And longer." She cast a second time, almost hooking the tree branches behind her. "I'm going to need far more than one day to get the hang of this."

Clark hadn't known what he was going to say when he stumbled up the church aisle, but his legs had propelled him forward without asking permission. The last time he'd faced a congregation, he'd walked out in disgrace. Was this God's way of finishing the job?

One day? He'd said the first words that poured from his heart. Was it wishful thinking or a divine message? Was God promising him an answer to his question by the end of the day?

Olivia's large eyes and subtle nod had taken him equally by surprise. Maybe the message wasn't even for him. Perhaps God was working in her heart and only using Clark as the messenger.

He glanced back at her standing in the rushing water, her trousers rolled over her knees. When had his heart started beating faster at the mere sight of this woman? "You'll get it. It takes patience. Yosemite trout are smarter than the average fish. The streams are so rich, they don't really need our flies. So you've got to wait them out."

"Or they have to wait *us* out." She stared down at her legs. "Look at me—I'm knee deep in your 'river of mercy.'"

One step at a time. Clark flicked the line forward, sending the lure skimming over the surface of the water. A splash followed as a trout leaped in time.

"Oh!" she sputtered. "Did you get one?"

"Not yet. But it shows you they're out there."

Her expression steeled. "I'm going to get one."

He couldn't resist smiling at her determination. When she'd postponed leaving until tomorrow, he knew the last day in Yosemite had to be special. What could chase away the memories of what Vanderbilt had taken from her? He'd considered taking her to Nevada Fall or even hiking part way up Half Dome, but a quiet word had swept away all his plans. *Give the day to God. See what He does.*

If he couldn't follow his own advice, what good was it? It didn't matter where he took Olivia. This was between her and the good Lord.

And Jesus spent time fishing with His friends, didn't He?

Clark balanced his way across the shifting rocks until he stood behind Olivia. Taking her wrist in his hand, he guided her arm back and forth, forcing himself to focus on the line and not the feel of her skin under his fingers. He'd been praying she would meet God in this place; unfortunately his thoughts weren't as holy. The last thing she needed was him confusing the issue.

Besides, it was only one day.

She moved her feet, leaning into his arm. "I didn't see you helping Marcus like this."

He chuckled. "I don't think he would have accepted my advice. The man seems to think he always knows best."

"That's a prerogative of having money, I think."

"Money makes you wise?"

She laughed, glancing up at him. "No. But it makes you important."

"That depends on what you do with the money." He released her arm, the touch of her skin driving him to distraction. "But let's not talk about him, shall we?"

"Agreed." She returned her focus to fishing.

Standing beside her, he watched her measured movements, already like steps of a dance. "You're a natural, Olivia."

"I'm good with my hands."

His throat tightened. There was no safe response to that. He moved away and prepared his own cast.

"Clark, do you really believe what you said this morning?"

He thought back over the morning. "Which part are you referring to?"

"That God brought each of us here for a reason?"

"Yes, I believe He orders our steps."

She sighed, lowering the rod. "I came to do a job, but it's all a mess now. So, if God brought me here to paint…" She blew out a long breath. "I don't understand why He'd bring me—when I don't even follow Him—and then take it all away."

Clark shifted his weight. "I don't pretend to know His mind. But maybe painting isn't the only reason He asked you to come."

The tiny lines that formed on her brow as she considered his words sent tremors through him. *Jesus, how do I lead her? Give me words because I don't have the wisdom. But I'm here.*

"Painting is all I know."

"It's not, Olivia." The certainty swept over him like a gentle rain. "There's much more to you than art. It's just all you show anyone, like a mask. There's a depth to Olivia Rutherford—deeper waters where fish swim unseen below the surface."

She backed up, lowering the rod until the tip dragged in the stream. "I don't know what you mean."

He remained motionless. Was there a way to reel it back and try again? "You don't have to share that with me. But if you want to meet God—truly meet Him—you need to take off the mask you wear. He knows the real you anyway. He knit us together in our mothers' wombs. He knows you better than you know yourself."

A shadow dropped over her face, and she blinked hard several times, as if fighting tears. The sight tore at him, but he remained silent. If God was at work here, Clark didn't want to step in the way.

A long moment passed before she lifted her head. "I've spent the past few years creating someone people would care about. The real me isn't worth knowing."

"I don't believe that." His heartbeat quickened. "I admire this Olivia far more than the one I met back at the Ahwahnee. It's like I can see little bits of you shining through the cracks in your facade."

Olivia's lips pursed, an uncertain look darkening her eyes. She took a deep breath and whipped the line out over the water, tickling the surface. In an instant, a trout leaped, snagged the lure, and disappeared under the ripples. She shrieked, nearly dropping the pole.

"Now set the hook like I showed you." Clark held his breath as she lifted the rod. After a few minutes, she was reeling in one of the most beautiful rainbow trout he'd ever seen come out of this river.

Fifteen

Olivia brushed off the legs of her trousers as she and Clark took a seat in the Camp Curry amphitheater. They'd arrived early, so most of the benches were still deserted. "I can't believe we managed to catch so many of those little guys."

"Little guys? You caught a four pounder." He laughed.

"I think I caught him twice. Apparently he isn't the brightest of fish. I thought you said Yosemite fish were clever."

"Perhaps it had a taste for McGinty flies. It's just fortunate we were releasing the fish today. If we'd been out on the trail, we'd have had a tasty addition to our frying pan."

Olivia ran fingers through her hair. "I've had enough of your panfried trout for a long time. I was glad to see the roast and potatoes on the menu here at camp. That was a treat."

"Starting tomorrow you'll be eating city food again, I suppose."

"Yes, tomorrow." Back to scraping by on what little she could make from small gallery showings after sending most of her cash off to Aunt Phyllis for the girls. Would she have to pay the editor back for her expenses from the past few weeks? They couldn't be expected to cover her hotel and food when she returned empty handed. "How much is *Scenic* paying you for guiding me?" She blurted the question before thinking how it might sound.

He raised a brow. "They're not. They're paying the Yosemite Transportation Office. My contract's with them."

So she'd owe them money too. A bit of this afternoon's shine wore off. She couldn't let herself think about it until tomorrow. She'd agreed to give Clark today. Or had she agreed with God? The moment was hazy.

Clark's eyes fixed on something over her shoulder, and he laid a hand on her arm. "Olivia."

The concern in his face made her stomach tighten. She jumped to her feet.

Clark's ranger friend walked down the aisle toward them with Gus Kendall at his side.

An icy chill spread through her system, from the depths of her chest out to her limbs. She grabbed Clark's arm for balance. "I told you not to say anything—"

"I needed to know you were safe, Olivia. I didn't think John would bring him here." Clark took her hand. "But let's hear him out. He'd be foolish to try anything with the chief ranger right next to him."

It wasn't physical harm she feared. Kendall could ruin her with a word. She pulled her hand free from Clark's grip, fighting the urge to run for the trees.

"Miss Rutherford." Ranger Edwards spoke to her, then nodded to his friend. "I'm sorry to interrupt."

Does he know? Olivia sank down on the bench, no longer trusting her legs.

Kendall rubbed the back of his neck. "Fellas, I think Miss Rutherford and I should speak privately."

"Not a chance." Clark folded his arms.

Olivia's heart beat so hard she could feel it in her throat. "Clark, please. He's right." Was he going to demand some type of payment to stay silent?

Ranger Edwards pointed to the edge of the stage. "We'll be right there if you need anything."

Clark's eyes darkened as his focus bounced from Kendall back to Olivia. "Are you sure?"

She nodded, biting her lip. The last thing she wanted was to be alone with the man, but even more frightening was the thought of Clark hearing her secrets.

His brow remained furrowed as he backed several steps before turning to follow his friend.

Olivia stared at the ground, studying the pine needle–strewn dirt rather than face the last man to see her father alive.

Kendall cleared his throat, as if struggling to find his voice. "Do you mind if I sit, Miss Rudd—I mean, Miss Rutherford?"

As he lowered himself to the bench, she finally allowed herself to look at him, studying his stooped shoulders and lowered head. This wasn't how she remembered the hot-tempered individual who'd often been at her father's side. "What do you want?"

He lifted his chin, meeting her eyes. "I could ask you the same thing. Why are you here?" Kendall's voice trembled.

Words failed her. She stared at him in silence.

"When Melba told me about the artist she'd met, I knew it had to be you. I've followed your career."

The songbird. Melba. "I'm—I'm here on assignment. I didn't know you'd be here."

"I'm a different man, Olivia." He scrubbed a palm over his face. "I've stayed sober and out of trouble ever since that day. It changed me."

"It changed *you?*" A flush crept up her neck. "I grew up without a father." She lowered her voice. "And knowing my father was a killer."

"I know. I'm sorry. You can't believe how sorry I am." He ducked his chin. Silvery stubble dotted his neck. "But you showing up here—it could ruin me. Not that I don't deserve it. But I don't want the world to know my secret."

She pushed up to her feet. "Your secret? *Your* secret?"

"If the truth comes out, I stand to lose everything here. The police will think I was involved in the murder. They'll send me up the river."

A lump formed in her throat. She hadn't considered that he had as much to risk as she did—or more. "But you *were* involved. The newspaper said Givens left with two men. If my father was one, you must have been the other."

His shoulders slumped. "I was there, yes, but I didn't kill him. I saw it happen. That's enough."

"Why should I believe you?"

"You've got no reason to." His voice cracked. "When your father ran off into the woods, he left me holding the bag." He took a long, shaking breath. "Me—I couldn't do it. Couldn't leave. My memories got me chained here. I did not lay a finger on that man—but I may as well have."

"Aren't you afraid of someone finding out?"

He faced her, eyes hollow. "Every living moment."

After Kendall left, Olivia slumped on the bench in exhaustion. She dropped her face into her hands. Whether or not she believed his story, it didn't sound as if he was ready to announce her identity to the world. She could remain Olivia Rutherford for another day.

Clark charged down the aisle. "So?"

She blew out a long breath. "A misunderstanding. You were right."

He looked taken aback. "Really? Well, that's good, right?"

Good, yes. But if Kendall spoke the truth, it meant her father acted alone. And bore the guilt alone. The grief over her father's choices flooded her anew. She glanced up at the man standing in front of her. Thankfully it also meant Clark would never have to know the truth. Not him or anyone else—at least not from her or Kendall. Marcus Vanderbilt might be another story.

Campers were starting to stream into the amphitheater, families with children and older couples holding hands. So wonderfully normal. She leaned back on the bench. Normal. Was that even within her grasp?

Clark sat down beside her. "Do you still want to stay for the show? It should be a good one. Melba is singing."

His presence soothed her frazzled nerves. "Of course. I've been looking forward to it. She told me she met Ranger Edwards when she visited Camp Curry as part of a vaudeville act. I'm still trying to figure out how a vaudevillian and a park ranger would have anything in common."

"John followed her from theater to theater, he was so smitten—driving hours from Yosemite each time to see her."

The idea curled around Olivia's heart like a ribbon. To find someone so devoted would be a dream. She glanced sideways at Clark. The man was handsome and sweet, but he would never fall for someone like her. Especially if he knew the truth. She'd been on her own since she was young. There was no reason to expect anything different.

He brushed her arm, his fingers warm even through her sleeve. "Have you considered letting me replace your paints? I thought maybe after today, you might want to paint the stream. Maybe your little fish friend."

Those brown eyes—a girl could get lost there. "No. I don't think so." The idea raised goose bumps on her arms. Move forward with the project after she'd lost so much? Move forward without the influence of someone like Marcus at her side?

She never should have taken this job in the first place. Olivia Rutherford was nothing but a tottering house of cards. Facing Gus Kendall had proven that. One stray word and everything she and Frank had built could come crashing down.

And now she had Marcus to worry about.

The crowd hushed as the music started. A cowboy clambered to the stage to croon ballads and tell silly stories. Her mind wandered as she studied Clark leaning forward, his elbows balanced on his knees.

One painting she'd be sure to re-create—him silhouetted against the Glacier Point view. She could do that from memory. She could still feel her brush mapping the curve of his arm.

After a magic act and a comedy routine, Melba finally took the stage. Her lilting voice captured the crowd as she belted out "Don't Bring Lulu" and "Red Lips Kiss My Blues Away." Quite different from the sweet hymns she'd led this morning, but equally delightful.

With a grin, she wandered over to the piano and stole the man's straw boater. Sauntering across the stage, she launched into a saucy version of "Button Up Your Overcoat." As she sang about the merits of flannel underwear and eating healthy, the crowd roared with laughter. People young and old clapped and sang along with the comical love song.

Clark sneaked an arm around Olivia's shoulder, leaning close to whisper in Olivia's ear. "Didn't I tell you?"

"She's a delight. She should be in the pictures—talkies."

"Probably could. But then she'd have to leave all this behind. And John, too. His life is here." He shrugged. "Though he would give it up for her. He's so in love, I can't imagine who he'd be without Melba. They're like two trees that have grown together until you can no longer see where one starts and the other finishes." He shook his head. "But she'd never ask him to do that. Yosemite is in his blood. Now it's in hers, too."

Olivia sat back against the wooden bench, relishing the warmth of his arm against her back. In the seat in front of them, a tiny girl was nodding off on her daddy's shoulder. This place was magical. It could get under one's skin. "What about yours? Is it in your blood?"

"Yes." His smile faded. "But my life doesn't belong to me. I dedicated myself to God's work when I was young. Where He leads, I will follow." Clark withdrew his arm so he could applaud with the rest of the crowd.

Olivia clapped too, but a hollow space had opened in her chest. As attractive as she found Clark, she knew they could never have a future together. A man of God and a woman of lies? The idea was so farfetched, it was funnier than Melba's whimsical tune. Olivia could never have anything like what Melba had found with her ranger husband. And she wouldn't settle for less.

Melba lifted the microphone. "And now I want to invite a friend of mine up here to help me out on this next number. Clark, come join me."

He chuckled. "I thought she might do this."

Olivia touched his hand. "Oh, go—please. I want to hear you two sing together." She refused to let a melancholy moment destroy her last night in the park.

Clark turned and stared at her for a long moment. "You do?"

She nodded.

"Anything for you." He rose, much to the delight of the surrounding folks who began cheering. Making his way forward, he lifted a hand, waving to the group.

Anything. If only he meant that.

He borrowed a guitar from the lovesick cowboy and joined Melba on the stage. "What are we singing?"

"I think you know." Melba scanned the audience. "This goes out to my special ranger."

The crowd hooted and clapped.

Olivia turned in her seat to catch a glimpse of Ranger Edwards, grinning by the amphitheater's entrance. He tipped his hat in his wife's direction.

As Clark picked out the notes on the plunky guitar, Melba settled the microphone back on the tall stand, running her hand along it like a jazz singer in a sultry speakeasy. With a soft voice, she eased her way into the song "Always," her focus never straying from her husband's face.

It felt like months had passed since the night Clark had sung the same tune by the campfire. Her heart warmed to the memory.

Clark stepped close to his friend, adding a line of harmony to Melba's lilting soprano. Their voices were a lovely blend, like a mixture of cobalt blue and vermillion red that created an entirely new shade wherever the two touched. Olivia couldn't resist sighing and leaning forward, like many of the young woman in the audience. Were they all wondering if the handsome guitar player was taken?

A shiver raced through Olivia as she blinked against the tears stinging at her eyes. One day, that's all she'd given him. Not always.

He lifted his eyes as if searching for her in the crowd.

She jumped up and hurried out the back, unable to bear the pain welling up in her chest. *Always* was something she'd never have.

⟿

Clark watched Olivia dart out the back, wishing he could follow her. Did she realize how attached he'd grown in just a few short days? She couldn't. If she did, she wouldn't be waltzing out of here tomorrow with half of his heart.

Melba glanced over at him, her brows lifted, a smile playing about her lips even as she sang.

That woman never missed a thing, did she?

He couldn't let Olivia leave Yosemite without telling her what she meant to him. That must be what God was impressing on him this morning. The message hadn't been about the ministry or the ranger position. He was prodding Clark to follow Olivia. To make her his own.

After strumming the final chord, Clark handed the guitar back to the other musician. "I'm sorry Melba; I've got to go."

She touched his elbow. "I know. Go get her." Her whispered words weren't caught by the microphone, but they rattled around in his heart anyway.

He launched himself off the edge of the stage and raced down the aisle. Their day was almost over, but there was still time. He'd make sure of it.

Olivia had walked all the way to the corral in the short moment before he caught up to her. She leaned against the rail, her hands cupping Goldie's face. Was she talking to the mule?

He slowed his pace. "Olivia."

She glanced toward him, tears on her cheeks.

The sight tore him up inside. Had he caused this? Or was she still thinking about Vanderbilt? "What's wrong?" The words felt flat. That was the best he could do? Maybe this moment didn't deserve words.

She turned back to Goldie and lowered her forehead against the mule's nose.

Clark joined her at the rail, adding a hand on Goldie's neck. "You've been good to this old girl."

"I'll miss her." Olivia's voice crackled in her throat.

He could no longer resist the pull of her presence. He placed a hand against the small of her back, stepping close enough that her shoulder brushed against his chest.

She turned toward him, lowering her head against his shirtfront, her breath coming in short bursts. "Clark, I don't know what to do."

Stay here with me. He swallowed the words. This morning had started with God's words, could he really end it with his own selfish desires? Hadn't he learned anything from his last experience with a woman? "Olivia." He loved the feeling of her name in his mouth. "Olivia, you need to seek God's will for your life. I won't—I can't speak for Him." But, oh, how he wanted to.

"I don't know how to do that."

He closed his eyes, burying his hand in the hair on the nape of her neck. He needed to step back.

She slid her fingers down his arm, raising goose bumps with every touch. "He hasn't answered *you* yet, has He?"

"Not yet." His throat thickened.

She lifted her eyes. "Then I'm not sure I want to know, either."

In the distance, the stentor's call ran out, echoing through the valley. "Let the fire fall!"

A distant reply sounded, like a voice from the heavens: "The fire falls…"

Clark pulled his attention away from her blue-eyed gaze, his pulse quickening with every breath. The first embers of the Firefall cascaded over the cliff face, plummeting down through the darkness like so many falling stars. "Look."

Olivia leaned into his side, as she watched the spectacle in the distance. Her body melded against his.

He slid his hand across her back, the wool sweater doing little to distract his fingers from the enticing curve of her hip. Clark lowered his face until his lips brushed her hair, the scent of her soap still making her smell like a mountain meadow. *Lord, I need her.*

As the final flickers of flame died away in the night, she lifted her head, brushing her forehead against his and lifting one palm to stroke his jaw.

He groaned, the touch driving a final spike into his heart. He couldn't resist this woman. Bending forward, he pressed his lips to hers, his heart leaping as she returned the kiss. For a long moment, he lost himself in the touch of her mouth, pulling her close as if he could convince her to stay simply by the warmth of his body.

Olivia's hands trembled even as she slid them against Clark's forearms. She could feel herself falling into the kiss much like the sparks that had tumbled from the cliff face and dove free into the waiting air below. Or was this as much of a passing illusion as the Firefall? She'd never known anything could be this good—this safe.

He kissed her again, the gentle brush deepening until a shiver coursed through her. If only she could stay right here forever. If he'd stay...always.

Clark drew back a hair, the warm sensation of his breath on her skin sending a shiver through her.

Even that short moment of separation made room for a sliver of doubt to creep in. This would end. It always ended. One more heartbeat and he'd be gone, and she'd be left standing here cold and alone, staring off into the woods. She latched on to his arms. "Don't go."

He nuzzled her cheek. "I'm not going anywhere."

Olivia lifted one hand to touch his jaw in wonder, sliding her fingers down to the edge of his chin. He wasn't going. She was. Tomorrow. Her throat tightened. "Clark, I don't know what we're doing. How is this going to work?"

"I've no idea." He kissed her lips again, the soft touch weakening her knees. "But I know I've wanted to do that for a while now."

He did? "You don't know anything about me. Not really."

"Then tell me." He settled his arms around her waist. "I want to know everything."

Her breath caught. "You don't. You want someone sweet and loyal, like Melba. But I'm nothing like that. I've playacted my way through life." She stepped back. "I'm not worth it."

"You have no idea of your own worth." He clasped her fingers. "I can see your heart, Olivia. You've hidden your past from me, but I don't care. You're a child of God."

"I'm not anybody's child."

He closed his eyes for a moment, a pained expression crossing his face as if she'd physically struck him.

An ache grew in her chest. She fought the urge to kiss him again, if only to chase that look from his face. But this was too important. He had to hear the truth, while she could still disentangle herself. If he was going to walk out, best he do so today. Because with the memory of his kiss lingering on her lips, it might already be too late for her. "I need to know I can trust you— count on you not to walk off into the woods if I tell you something difficult."

He moved closer. "I understand."

She intercepted him with a hand to the chest before he could lean in again. "I'm serious. Sleep on it."

He placed his palm over her hand, the warmth of his skin soaking through her fingers. "I will. But you need to think about what I said as well. You deserve good things, Olivia. Great things. Things beyond even what I can provide."

His words sank into her spirit. *Good things.* This time when he moved forward to claim her lips again, she didn't resist.

Sixteen

Olivia rose early the next morning and crept out of her tent before first light spread through the tree branches. Sleep had been hard to come by, her mind and heart too busy puzzling out the revelations of the day. Coming to Yosemite had been difficult enough. Leaving was going to take every last shred of her strength.

Had she really kissed Clark, or had she only dreamed it? One more complication in her life was definitely not on her schedule. She needed to go back to Sacramento and figure out her next steps, away from the entrancing nature of this place—and this man.

She walked through the quiet campground with no real direction in mind. Across the road, three deer grazed in the meadow. One lifted its head, swiveling tall ears in Olivia's direction. She stopped to watch them, the morning birdsong providing the musical score. Without even thinking about it, she lifted a hand, splaying her finger and thumb to frame the edges of the scene.

You deserve good things, Olivia. Clark's words rattled around in her soul, bouncing off the walls she'd spent years building. The only good things she'd ever achieved were those she'd clawed out with her own two hands—

her friendship with Frank, the safe home for her little sisters, this opportunity with *Scenic*. The latter was already crumbling around her. How long before the others did as well?

How would Clark fit into her life? Could she—like Melba—give up her own dreams to stay here in the park? She shook herself. It was far too soon to think such things. Couldn't she just enjoy it while it lasted? Allow herself this one good thing?

A chill raced across her skin, and she rubbed her forearms trying to get her blood moving. Last night's kisses had teased open a chink in her heart she'd not even realized existed. She wanted more. *Please, God.*

Clark would probably frown on her praying for such things. His spiritual nature intrigued her. She lifted her eyes to study the outline of the granite cliffs framing the valley's edge. God's presence was in Yosemite; she couldn't deny it. Every blade of grass, every breath of wind, even the light passing over the polished granite and dancing through the waterfalls' spray seemed touched by His spirit. It was easy to believe in the Almighty here. But what would happen when she returned home? Back to the galleries, the showings, and the parties. Was He there, too?

Clark's life seemed so in tune with the divine, as if the Lord ordered every beat of his heart. She couldn't imagine a time when she'd understand Christ in the same way.

The sound of an approaching automobile caused the deer to lift their heads and peer down the road.

Olivia backed from the roadway, pulling her sweater close around her shoulders and watching as the car slowed at the Camp Curry entrance. The familiar lines of the vehicle pulled at her. As it rolled to a stop, her heart jumped. "Frank?"

Her art dealer pushed back his battered straw boater, its green and gold petersham ribbon matching his wide tie. Frank jumped out, spreading his arms. "Liv, this is early for you. Has life in the wilderness changed you so much?"

She stepped into his embrace. "You wouldn't believe me if I told you."

"I might. I hear you've had some adventures." His grin faded. "I think we need to talk."

"I planned on telephoning you." She glanced back at the Curry entrance, the large wooden archway casting a long shadow across the road. "How did you know where to find me?"

He leaned against the automobile's door. "I drove through the night, then stopped at the Ahwahnee. They told me you were here." He glanced out over the sleepy tent village. "Not the sort of digs where I'd expect to find Olivia Rutherford."

"A lot has happened, I'm afraid. You drove all night? Why?"

Lines formed around his eyes. "I had a visit from Marcus Vanderbilt."

A sickening sensation descended into her stomach. "Frank, the man's a snake. I don't know what he told you—"

"He told me enough to know that you failed to gain his favor. Quite the opposite, in fact." Frank shook his head. "I thought I taught you better than that. These people's opinions matter."

"The man was all hands. He wasn't interested in my talent. He wanted..." She swallowed. Frank was the closest thing she had to a father, which made this topic uncomfortable. "He's a married man. And his wife is a friend." She straightened her shoulders. "I couldn't stomach his advances."

"Sophie Vanderbilt isn't your concern. She's incidental. Vanderbilt is a collector. He purchases large amounts of artwork from all over California." He pulled off his hat and smacked it against his knee. "Liv, without him you are nothing. Nobody."

Her throat tightened. "I know, but what was I to do—give in to his demands?"

"You're smarter than that." Frank thrust his hand into his pocket. "But you could have strung him along, left him room to hope."

"I can't believe you would suggest such a thing." She swallowed against the sour taste rising in her mouth. "And he wanted to sell the paintings I'd done for the magazine—"

"Then let him." He spread his arms. "Honestly, Liv, you're a working artist, not Rembrandt. You want to eat? Then you've got to sell."

"They belonged to *Scenic.* I signed a contract."

"So paint more. That's a good problem to have."

A hot flush surged up her neck, her eyes blurring with tears. "Are you taking his side?" Had she really been so naive?

"Don't develop morals on me now, girl. With this business you've got to strike while the iron's hot—sell as much as we can while your look is fashionable. Tomorrow you go back into the dust heap where I found you."

Olivia's knees trembled, threatening to buckle underneath the weight of her friend's words. "I-I…" Her throat closed.

His expression softened, and he reached out a hand to cup her cheek. "Look, Liv, I don't mean to be harsh, sweetheart. But you've got to be sensible. Think of the girls."

Sensible. She'd been that once upon a time. When had that changed? She blinked away the tears. "So what do I do?"

"Finish the job you came here to do. I might be able to salvage the *Scenic* contract. I convinced Vanderbilt I'd talk some sense into you."

Her stomach twisted. "He's not coming back here, is he?"

"No, no. He and his wife are headed for Europe. But you might want to consider sending him a painting or two as a gift."

A wash of red flooded her thoughts, and she spun around to face Frank. "A gift? You're joking." Anger washed through her.

"A peace offering."

"Frank, he destroyed every painting I'd made. I've nothing left to send him."

"He what?" Frank's mouth dropped open. "He didn't say anything—"

"Of course he didn't. Because it shows his true colors, doesn't it? I stood up to him, and that's what I got in return. And you want me to go groveling back and seek his renewed favor? I won't do it."

Frank ran the back of his wrist across his forehead. "It doesn't make any sense. He wanted me to get a few of your pieces to bring back to him. If he'd destroyed them, why would he ask?"

"To embarrass me further?" She curled her fingers into a fist. "He'd been drinking. Maybe he was too spifflicated to remember, though I find that difficult to believe. He seemed quite in control of his actions, if you ask me."

"They're *all* gone?"

"They're in tatters, Frank. That's why I was going to call you. I think it's time to go home."

"No!" His bushy brows cast dark shadows around his eyes. "You do that and you will never work again."

A jay swooped over them, shrieking out into the meadow beyond.

"I can't just start over. Even if I do, Marcus is still out there." She lifted her hands. "He's waiting to ruin me, Frank."

Frank's nose wrinkled. "Well, he can't do that from Europe, now can he?"

Her thoughts jumbled. "Not easily, I suppose."

"Then we've got some time. You're going to have to do your best to re-create those paintings—and make more. Do enough so you can buy off Vanderbilt and still have ones for the magazine. We can pull this off, Liv." His Adam's apple bobbed as he glanced heavenward. "You have to."

"What do you mean?"

He gripped her shoulder, steering her back toward the automobile. "I'm in trouble, Liv. I need this contract even more than you do."

The warmth of his palm seeped through her sweater.

This man had been everything to her. She couldn't fail him any more than she could walk out on the girls. "Why? What's happened?"

"I owe some people money, love. And it won't go well for me if they don't see it soon."

"Oh, Frank." A weight descended into her chest. Frank's artists had drifted away, one by one, each complaining of mistreatment or of not getting paid—sometimes both. *Sour grapes. Not every artist made it.* Besides, with each departure, she'd garnered more of his attention.

"You've always been loyal to this old man." He tipped his head, gray wisps of hair peeking out from beneath his boater. When was the last time he'd gotten a trim? "I'll be all right, Liv. But we need to close this deal." His eyes narrowed as he enunciated the final three words.

"All right. I'll try." Olivia took a deep breath, glancing back over her shoulder toward the camp.

"Good girl. Oh—one more thing." He dug in his coat pocket and pulled out a long, battered envelope. "This came for you." He glanced down at his hand. "It arrived the day after you left, so I opened it, to make sure it wasn't urgent. I—I'm sorry. In retrospect, I shouldn't have."

A shiver coursed through Olivia. Not more cryptic messages. She couldn't take any more.

He thrust the envelope toward her. "It's from your father."

⟳

The rich fragrance of broiled ham, eggs, and coffee followed Clark as he hurried through the dining hall, searching the crowd for Olivia. His heart had jumped into his throat when he'd found her tent empty. Had she left during the night? After a harrowing minute, he realized her belongings were still there. She might still be leaving, but at least she wasn't doing so without saying goodbye.

A deep ache settled in his middle. When she'd first walked into his life, he'd never dreamed he'd fall for the raven-haired flapper. Now he was already having trouble imagining Yosemite without her.

The park had worked its magic, as John suggested it might. Olivia had given herself over to the beauty of this place. He'd never expected to fall for her—or for her to return his affection. That kiss...the very thought of it sent a shiver down his spine. Now she was walking out of his life. Would he ever see her again?

Every seat in the hall was taken, the room echoing with conversations and laughter, but Olivia was nowhere to be seen.

Clark turned to leave and bumped into a man on the front steps. "Excuse me."

The fellow pushed back a straw boater and held out his hand. "Are you Mr. Johnson—the guide? I'm Frank Robinson, Olivia Rutherford's art dealer."

Clark shook the man's hand, his muscles suddenly wooden. He'd come to collect Olivia already? "It's a pleasure to meet you, sir."

"It's going to be a scorcher today, isn't it?" Mr. Robinson swept off his hat and wiped his brow. "Look, I wanted to speak to you about what happened to Olivia's artwork. Can you shine any light on that?"

Clark followed the man off the porch, the warm breeze swaying the canvas awning. "It was quite a shock. I know Miss Rutherford was distraught—as well she should be. She'd done some fine work."

Mr. Robinson shot him a glance as if studying his face. "Olivia told me that she believes Marcus Vanderbilt to be responsible."

"It sure appeared that way. I saw him accost her. The man's a bully."

"True. But when you're worth three million dollars, you can afford to ruffle a few feathers."

"Th-three million?" Clark thrust his hands in his pockets. No wonder the man was so full of himself.

"The stock market has been good to him, I'm afraid. And if he wants to squander it on women and art, who am I to argue?"

Clark chose his words carefully. "Artwork sure, but women typically aren't for sale, at least not the ones I know."

"You'd be surprised. Anyway, I'm curious—is there any chance Vanderbilt was not responsible for the damage to the paintings?"

"Well, it wasn't mice, if that's what you're suggesting."

"Did you see Vanderbilt near them?"

Clark thought back over the evening. "No. But I didn't see anyone else, either. And he was pretty steamed. Maybe he figured if he couldn't have them, no one would."

"I suppose so." The man rubbed a hand over his chin.

Clark ran a hand down his vest front. "I'm sorry Miss Rutherford will be leaving us so soon."

"Leaving?" The man jammed the hat back on his head. "She's not going anywhere. Not until she finishes the job."

"Oh, I didn't realize…." Clark's pulse quickened. "Well, that's good news." His mind raced. Where would he take her next? Perhaps up to Tuolumne Meadows or the Mariposa Grove. It could take a lifetime to show her all his favorite spots. And maybe discover a few new ones.

⌒

Olivia clutched the envelope in her hand, shaking as she hurried out to the meadow. The deer grazing there wouldn't care if she fell apart. They wouldn't point fingers and laugh. Or sneer with contempt.

Her father? How could he be alive?

Olivia's palm grew damp as the paper pressed against her skin. She stopped at a cluster of cottonwoods where the branches sheltered her from the glaring rays of morning sun spreading over the valley. She sank down to her knees in the dirt, holding the envelope to her chest. She closed her eyes, conjuring up the security of Clark's arms around her. Her first instinct had been to go and find him, but she still hadn't told him about this piece of her past.

She stroked a finger along her lower lip, remembering the touch of last night's kiss. A shiver raced through her. Who would think someone like him could ever be attracted to her? She'd worked so hard to create a glamorous disguise, but it was as if he saw straight into her heart. *"I can see little bits of you shining through the cracks in your facade."* She'd designed her look to attract the eye of men like Marcus Vanderbilt. She hadn't expected to draw a solemn, steady man of God.

Her throat tightened. *God.* That's where Clark would point her right now. Could his God see the scared little girl hiding behind her painted face and darkened hair? Maybe He, like Clark, could find the light within.

If there was any to find.

"God, help me. Please..." She opened her eyes as a brilliant green dragonfly darted close, hovering near her for a moment before swooping away, its iridescent colors glimmering in the morning sunlight.

Olivia focused on the letter, her name—her old name—scrawled across the front, followed by Frank's address. How had her father known where to look for her? It must be a hoax. Her father had died in the woods—the same forest that had witnessed his crime. A life for a life.

"Lord, Clark's right. I do need You." She whispered the words so only the grass and trees could hear. Not even El Capitan would be aware of her weakness. "No matter how I re-create myself, I can't hide who I am. And I want a father. I just don't want this one."

Sliding the paper out of the envelope, she unfolded the softened sheet. It felt like it had been folded and refolded, as if the writer had held on to it for a long time. She opened its creases and stared down at the handwritten lines, smudges marring the page.

She slid her finger across her name at the top. *"My Dearest Liv."* Olivia's gaze remained fixed on the greeting, the words touching down in a quiet place of her soul, like a bird alighting on a branch. She stayed there, savoring the sound of those words. Whatever followed was bound to scatter any good feelings.

Olivia sucked in a deep breath and forced her eyes down the page, skimming through quickly.

"I bet you never expected to hear from this old man, did you?

"I wish I could tell you that I've been searching for you and your sisters for years, but that would be a lie. I hope you can forgive me for that and keep reading."

Olivia staggered up to her feet, stumbling forward as if the steps could somehow free her from the pain cutting into her chest. He was *alive?* Worse yet, he was alive and hadn't *bothered* to look for her? A bitter taste rose on her tongue.

She flattened out the paper, driving through the words as if somehow they could help her understand.

"I read of your mother's passing, God rest her soul. I know it's no comfort to you, but the news broke my heart. I tried to write, but I found I couldn't put pen to paper.

"In a way, I've been dead myself. I thought you'd all be better off if I were, and I have to confess to trying to make it happen more than once. Although I did what I had to do, I'm still the coward who ran off that day in Yosemite.

"But, Liv, I don't want to die without seeing you girls again. I know the twins are with your mother's sister, so I'm going there first. I hope this letter reaches you so you can join me. It's time we had a real goodbye."

Olivia pressed trembling fingers to her forehead. A real goodbye? The last thing she desired was to have him walk back into her life for any reason. As far as she was concerned, she'd buried that man, that father, long ago.

Her stomach clenched as if the world had lurched into a dizzying spin. Louise and Frances didn't even know what their father had done. Whatever happened, she couldn't allow Albert Rudd anywhere near them.

Clark hurried back to the tents and spotted Olivia sitting on the front step of her tent cabin, a piece of paper in her hand. "I hear you're staying." The tearstains on her face stopped him in his tracks. "What is it?" He glanced down at the paper. "Not Kendall, again?"

"It's my father." She folded it twice and jammed it in her pocket. "I-I haven't heard from him since I was young."

He sank down on the step next to her. "I thought he was dead."

"That's what I was told." She stared off into the distance as if she couldn't bear to make eye contact with him.

A million questions raced through his mind. He pushed them away, settling for one. "How can I help?"

Olivia took a long, shaky breath. "I have to go."

"What? Your art dealer said—"

"Frank was wrong." Her tone grew sharp.

He'd never heard coldness in her voice, not even when she faced the tattered remains of her paintings. The sound sent his heart into a tailspin. "Olivia."

"No." She wiped away tears with the heel of her hand. Standing, she reached back into the tent for her broken art case and pulled it to her side. "I quit. I'm going home."

"To Sacramento?" Maybe once things calmed down, he could go see her. How long had John pursued Melba?

"My sisters live in Oakland. I'm going there. I need to see them."

Clark stood, a hollow forming in the center of his chest. The stiffness in Olivia's demeanor suggested the letter had already whisked her away in spirit or somehow returned her to being the stranger who'd walked into his life a week ago. What happened to the woman he'd held in his arms last night— the warmth of her kiss, her smile? "I didn't even know you had sisters." What did he know, really?

She rifled through the container, digging through the meager supplies that remained after the incident at Glacier Point. "Yes, I have two beautiful sisters living with an aunt who's evidently been lying to us for years." Her voice pitched upward. "They deserve better, and somehow I'm going to get it for them, no matter what it takes." She pulled out a cracked paint tube and stared at it. "I don't even know what I'm looking for. I'm never going to find any answers in this box." Olivia flung the tube back into the case. "It's time I faced the truth. I'm never going to be free of him. And art is never going to pay the bills." She shoved the box to the edge of the step where it teetered for a moment before crashing to the ground. Paint pots spilled across the dirt. Her chest rose and fell as if she struggled for breath.

Clark had to close this distance. He reached for her. "Olivia—"

She landed both hands against his chest, arms stiff. "Don't call me that." Her voice cracked. "Olivia Rutherford is nothing but a lie. She never existed."

He laid his palms over her hands. "Then tell me what to call you. I'll walk through this with you. But don't walk away."

She lowered her head, her dark hair falling forward to frame her face. "You don't even know me."

"Maybe not. But I want to." He held his breath until her elbows unlocked. He folded her into his arms. "I want to know everything."

Olivia laid her head against his chest, sniffling. "I have to go, Clark. Please try to understand."

"I don't." His throat squeezed off the words. He swallowed hard. "I don't understand. Because if last night meant anything to you...you'd trust me." He gripped her shoulders, lowering his cheek against her silky hair, his heart pounding. "Will you be back?"

"I don't know."

Seventeen

July 23, 1929

A week later Clark sat in John's office, his knee bouncing a steady rhythm as he tried to process his friend's words.

"Clark, I know your contract with Walker over at transportation has expired. It's time to make a choice." John rapped knuckles against the file folder sitting open before him.

God had led him to a crossroads but remained frustratingly silent. Clark closed his eyes, praying one last time for direction. "I don't mean to draw this out, but I never planned on being a ranger." He reached into his pocket and clasped the silver compass. "I came to Yosemite to escape from my life. I always figured I'd go back someday."

"And is that someday here? Are you leaving us?" John leaned across the small desk, his eyes intense. "Because I need a man in this post. We are already short staffed, and now I've got Ranger Gardiner out with a broken leg. Summer is well underway, and I can't wait on you any longer. I hate the idea of having to train someone new when we both know you could step in and do it without batting an eye."

"I don't want to leave."

"Good. Then it's settled." John yanked open a drawer and dug through it. He slid the badge across the tabletop. "I've got an extra uniform at home—at least until we can get one ordered. We're about the same size, I figure."

"John…"

"Clark." He folded his arms. "I need a man on horseback patrolling those trails. You need the job. Let's help each other. Stay until the end of the season, and then if you decide to go, I'll replace you."

Clark took the gold shield in his hand, the metal cold and unyielding. "Just until the end of the summer?" He and the General could spend long, lonely days patrolling the trails. No more groups of ungrateful tourists to haul around the park so they could gape at the scenery while complaining about the weather and his carefully prepared camp meals. Why was he even balking at this?

His mind traveled back to Olivia and the drawn look on her face when she left—an image he couldn't banish no matter how hard he tried. Riding through the wilderness would give him plenty of time to figure out what went wrong.

Her art dealer had assured him she would return, but the box of broken art supplies left behind suggested otherwise. She hadn't even left an address.

A summer dalliance. Is that all it was? All *he* was?

A dull throbbing ache lay in his chest, a constant companion since the morning Olivia boarded the green auto stage with so many other visitors and disappeared through Curry's "Farewell" arch. He stared down at the badge, rubbing his thumb across the engraved image of a pinecone. If he pinned on the Park Service emblem, he'd be here when she returned.

If she returned.

Olivia had suggested this could be God's new calling for him. But without her by his side, he was no longer certain he wanted it.

Three weeks later, Olivia settled back on Aunt Phyllis's buttery-yellow settee. It had taken several days for her to make her way to Oakland, only to find her aunt and sisters had boarded a train to Monterey to stay with one of her aunt's cousins. Maybe Aunt Phyllis was avoiding her father as well? By the time they returned, Olivia had worked herself into a state.

She tried not to scowl at the new draperies in her front window. Her mother's sister deserved nice things at this point in her life, but it made every request for additional money sting. "I can't believe you didn't tell me he was still alive."

Her aunt frowned. "Albert swore me to secrecy. He thought it would be better if you believed him to be dead. I should have known he'd change his mind."

"When did you last hear from him?"

"He contacted me in February." Aunt Phyllis picked up her cup of tea. "I told him I wouldn't allow a visit. You, Frances, and Louise have been through enough."

Olivia sat forward, all her nervous energy draining out her toes. "Thank you."

"I didn't realize he would write to you as well. You must know I have your and your sisters' best interests at heart. But I can't keep putting him off forever. Eventually he's going to show up on my doorstep. Then what will I do?"

"Call the police?"

Aunt Phyllis pursed her lips. "Do you really want to go through a trial and have your father's crime splashed back through the press? The girls don't even know what happened."

"Which is a very good reason to keep them away from him." Olivia folded her arms. "They're coming home with me."

"You're not even painting now. How will you provide?"

Olivia stood and paced across the room—anything to get away from the scent of stale cigarette smoke mixing with the fragrant potted gardenia sitting in the window. "I still have my room at the boarding house in Sacramento. I'll find work like my mother did."

"My sister worked herself into an early grave. It isn't what she'd want for you." The woman folded arms across her more-than-ample bosom. "I never wanted children, let me tell you, but these girls have been much better off with me than with a drifter like you. You're not in a position to take them now, either." She sat back in the overstuffed chair. "And they're not children anymore. They're young ladies, and they need proper schooling, not stuck here with an old lady."

"You're not old, Auntie."

"I'm old enough." She clamped her hands on her knees. "To tell the truth, they're full of beans, especially Louise. I've had no more luck stamping it out of her than I did you. Remember what you did at her age?"

I ran away and never looked back. Olivia's chest tightened. How could she forget?

"If we arrange for them to board at the Miss Ransom and Miss Bridges School for Girls, Albert will never need to know. I'll tell him you moved the girls to Connecticut or something."

"You'd lie to our father?"

"Honey, I've been lying to you for ten years. Why should I grow a conscience now?"

"But I don't have the money for the school. Maybe I *should* consider going somewhere he'd never find us."

She clucked her tongue. "They deserve better and you know it."

Olivia dug her fingers into her sleeves, pacing over to the window. The fear that her father could walk up the sidewalk and into their lives drove any sane thought from her mind. She wouldn't be able to plan anything until she knew they were all safe.

Olivia turned and headed for the kitchen. "Louise?"

The girl hid a book in her apron, grabbed a spoon, and began stirring a simmering pot of soup. "It's almost ready."

The sight tore at Olivia. Louise and Frances had lived a gentle life here with Aunt Phyllis. It seemed unfair to wrench them away. But what choice did she have? "What were you reading?" Olivia couldn't resist reaching out and tapping the square outline evident on Louise's apron front.

Louise hid a smile, drawing the well-worn copy of Wordsworth from under her apron. "I have a recitation for my thespian club next week. Miss Long says I'm doing very well. She thinks I could be an actress."

Another career with little return. Olivia studied her sister's rosy cheeks, flushed from leaning over the steamy stove. "I'm sure you'll be a star."

"Not like this, I won't." Louise touched her long braid. "Can you cut my hair like yours? All the girls at school wear bobs, but Auntie won't let me."

"All the girls?" Olivia ran her fingers through her own hair. The first thing she'd done after arriving in Oakland was touch up her dye job.

"And how." The girl glanced down at the soup pot. "Or at least, all the popular ones."

The wispy curls framing her sister's sweet face pulled at Olivia's heart. Is this what she'd taught them? "You don't need a special hairstyle to be loved, Louise. Your light shines from within." Clark's words sent a familiar pang through her chest. She missed him with every breath. Would that ease with time? It hadn't in the three weeks she'd been away from Yosemite.

The girl smiled, laying her head on Olivia's shoulder. "I'm glad you're here, Liv. I've missed you."

Tears sprang to Olivia's eyes. She wove her arm around her sister's waist and pulled her close. "I've missed you, too."

"How long are you staying?" Louise's face lit up. "Will you come see the Ransom Bridges School with Frances and me? Aunt Phyllis said you were going to get the money we needed."

Olivia lowered her head, hiding her face in her sister's shoulder. "I'll be staying for a while." Long enough to figure out what lay ahead. "And we'll have plenty of time to talk about school—I promise. That and more." Maybe it was time the girls knew the truth.

Olivia and the twins walked through Piedmont Park, the overhanging branches cooling the wooded path. Normally she would treat the girls to a night at the pictures, but this was better. The stream gurgled by, taking Olivia back to the Merced with Clark. She shook herself, trying to scatter the memories. Her thoughts returned to him again and again, no matter how much she fought against it. But every time she was reminded of him, a fresh wave of longing threatened to burst over her like water through a leaky dam.

She'd told the girls a few of the stories of Yosemite but had said little about Clark. They'd enjoyed hearing about the Firefall and the raccoons. And Filbert, too.

"You mean a man *lives* up there? In the woods?" Frances's eyes had widened, a dreamy look spreading across her freckled cheeks. "Wouldn't that be amazing?"

Louise frowned. "You're a loon. Why would you want to live in the woods?"

"It's not the woods. *It's Yosemite.* Do you know they've found over two hundred species of birds there? And there may be more that haven't been identified yet."

"Oh, you and your birds." Louise rolled her eyes. "The only thing I want to see with feathers is a new hat or maybe a gown. Did you see the boa that Bessie Love wore at the premiere of *The Broadway Melody*?"

Olivia shot her a glance. "You attended a movie premiere?"

"No, though I would in a heartbeat. I read about it in *Hearsay*."

Olivia stopped short. "Louise, you shouldn't be reading that smut. That's nothing but a gossip magazine."

Frances walked on ahead, her hands clasped behind her back. "I told you."

Louise flipped her braid between her fingers. "I read it for the Hollywood news. If I want to be an actress, I need to know which of the producers is stepping out with whom."

A pair of crows squawked in a nearby tree as if echoing the twin's bickering. The noise set Olivia's head pounding. How could three sisters be so different? She massaged her temples. "Here I thought you were busy studying poetry and literature, but instead you're reading trashy magazines."

The girl's lower lip protruded like a scolded five-year-old's. "You're only vexed because you haven't been named in there like some other painters. But when you're famous, they'll do stories about you, too. First you need a secret lover, because that's what they like best—oh, and crimes of passion. But that doesn't seem like you."

Frances turned, eyes wide. "Lou, you shouldn't talk like that."

Olivia lowered her face into her hand. The girls were growing up too quickly. If only Mother had lived. "No secret loves, I'm afraid. And no reason they'd ever want to write about me. Listen girls..." She found a seat in the grass, the long blades tickling at her legs. "I want to talk to you about school. I was thinking"—she paused, searching for words while her sisters sat down—"I'm thinking about moving. Maybe Chicago or Boston. You would come, too, of course. We could be a real family. I'm sure we could find a good school there for you to attend."

Frances's mouth fell open, her hands flying to her lips.

Louise's posture went rigid. "Miss Long says I need this school. I told her I was going to run away to Hollywood, but she insisted I study classical acting first. The Ransom Bridges School does a Shakespearian play every spring. Miss Long says actresses who are fluent in the classics will get better roles in the talkies. If you pull me out now...I'll...I'll—" She jumped to her feet and darted away to plop down by the water's edge and cover her face with her hands.

Frances sighed. "You see why Miss Long thinks she'll be a good actress."

A sudden chill sank into Olivia's stomach. "Does Louise mean what she says? Running away to Hollywood?"

Her sister glanced down at the ground. "Lou talked of nothing else for months. But she told Miss Long she'd wait and do one more year of school."

"She's fourteen. She can't run away."

Frances frowned. "We'll be fifteen next month. Nearly as old as you were when you struck out on your own."

A bubble of panic welled up inside. When had time started passing so quickly? "What about you? You're not running away, are you?"

The girl shook her head. "No. School is too important to me. I'm going to be an ornithologist."

"A what?" How could she not know these things? Had she been so fixated on her own problems that she hadn't bothered to ask these questions?

"I'm going to study birds. When you wrote about Yosemite, I thought maybe you'd invite us to come with you. I'd simply die to see the place. My favorite bird is the great gray owl, and that's one of the best places to see one."

Olivia put her arm around Frances and drew her close. At least she didn't have to worry about this one—yet. Maybe tomorrow the girl would be packing her bags to run away to Yosemite.

The image of the giant cliffs loomed large in Olivia's memory. How many times had she painted the outlines of those rocks, the waterfalls, and the trees? Had she even noticed the birds, except for adding a little life to the scene? Here her sister longed to see one, just for its own special self. She stared toward the creek where Louise sat, her shoulders shaking with sobs.

How had Olivia strayed so far from her family?

No matter how similar they appeared, both of these girls were unique, as if God had taken the same vibrant colors and then used them to create two entirely different paintings. Louise and Frances each knew exactly who they were and what they wanted from life.

What of her? The only things she truly wanted, she'd left behind. Was she prepared to leave California too? She'd never see Clark again.

"Frances..." Olivia bit her lip as she thought, her fingers closing around an imaginary brush. "I want to paint your portrait. You and Louise."

The girl perked up. "Here? Now?"

"No." She took a deep breath. "Not here." She still needed to tell them the truth about their father. And there was only one place she wanted to do that. "In Yosemite."

The last place her father would ever look.

$\backsim$

Clark leaned over the General's neck and adjusted her bridle. He'd been in the saddle six hours riding over rough terrain and had another fifteen miles to go today. The country was beautiful, but the lack of good tree coverage at this elevation meant the sun had been beating down on his back far longer than he preferred. He pulled out the canteen and guzzled a few swallows of water, then spilled a little on his hand and wiped it across his face and neck.

So far he'd seen two pack strings and one lone hiker over near Polly Dome. Patrolling the high country was lonely work. He lifted a pair of binoculars to his eyes and scanned the valley below, where stands of evergreens gave way to the rocky outcroppings. What was there to see other than beautiful views? Signs of smoke? Trouble? Other than a lone coyote trailing through a clearing, he saw little that would even be worth reporting.

Clucking to the horse, he continued down the trail, the General's hooves clattering against the stony surface. "Well God, if you wanted to keep me away from temptation, I guess this was a good way to do it."

The General's ears swiveled back at the sound of his voice.

He patted her neck again. "Don't worry, girl; it's only our second week. I'm not going loco yet. Just talking to the Father. You should be used to that. Between you and Him, that's pretty much all I've got to converse with." Truth be told, he'd spent about as much time talking to Olivia. Only she wasn't there to answer him.

As he straightened, a tiny plume of smoke in the distance caught his eye, down along the Murphy Creek drainage. He lifted the binoculars again. A campfire, most likely, though it was an odd area for someone to be staying. Maybe a hiking party had gotten lost? He lowered the eyepieces and stretched his back. Going to investigate would add miles onto his day, but wasn't this why he was out here in the first place? He pulled off his new ranger Stetson and ran quick fingers through his sweat-dampened hair.

Clark turned the General in the direction of the smoke and headed down into the valley, humming to himself. The climb back up to the ridge would be a killer, especially since the mare was already tired. Maybe he'd skirt around the valley's edge and work his way up tomorrow. If the fire was no concern—and he couldn't imagine it would be—he could easily get back on track in the morning. Besides, it wasn't as if he needed to return to see anyone. Melba and John were busy with the overflowing campgrounds; extras camped in all the meadows. He should thank God he was out here and not trapped in the village. A peaceful night under the lodgepole pines was exactly what his spirit needed. Except every minute he spent alone was one more he spent thinking about Olivia.

He pushed against the stirrups, lifting himself out of the saddle for a moment as the General picked her way through the loose rubble on the steep trail. As he readjusted, he bumped his elbow against the revolver on his hip and grimaced. He'd nearly hidden the thing away in his saddlebag, but John had insisted he wear it. Part of the uniform. Clark tugged at the shirt collar. He was a bit broader through the chest than his friend, so John's shirt left little room for movement.

The horse sidled down the dry riverbed, the smell of campfire growing stronger as they approached.

Clark had expected to see people before this point. They couldn't miss the sound of the General shoving through the underbrush. Could it be these folks were clear out this way because they didn't want company? He laid a hand on his gun, as a reminder to himself. He was official now, no need to go pussyfooting around. "Hello? Anyone there?"

There was no sound but the wind stirring through the pine boughs and the cry of a hawk in the distance. He urged his mount forward until he reached the campsite, the fire still smoldering and the scent of cooked fish lingering in the air.

Clark dismounted, keeping the General's reins in his hand as he scouted the area. "I don't want trouble, just wanted to check that you're all right."

"I's fine." The familiar voice sounded behind him.

Clark spun about and spotted Filbert coming out of the brush. He laughed. "I should have known. What are you doing clear out here?"

The man pushed his long, matted hair away from his face and shrugged. "Didn't want no more run-ins with that one fellow." He sniffled, running the back of his hand underneath his nose. "Not going back."

Clark looped the reins over a branch, not that the General would take off without him. "Vanderbilt? He's long gone and no one's asking you to go anywhere. Got any more of that trout?"

The old man grinned. "Two more." He hustled over to where he'd hung the basket in a tree. "I can cook 'em up real good." He opened the wicker lid so Clark could admire the contents, and then he pointed to the uniform. "New duds. You gone official."

The reality of the situation dawned on him. Filbert was squatting *and* fishing without a license. His appetite faded. "I guess you could say that." What was he supposed to do—run the old man off? Arrest him? "Look, Filbert—I shouldn't stay. And…" He swallowed against the sudden ache in his throat. He'd spent years earning the man's trust. "Have you ever thought about moving outside the park boundaries?"

Filbert threaded the fish onto a green stick and laid it across a couple of large stones so the trout hung suspended above the coals. "Sure. But this land belongs to all of us. The other land belongs to certain folks. Here nobody bothers me. 'Cept fellows like that one you was running around with."

"He was no friend of mine, I can tell you that much."

Filbert smiled his familiar gap-toothed grin. He jutted a finger Clark's direction. "Because of that crow head, right?"

Was he so obvious? He crouched by the fire, watching dinner cook. He was the only ranger for miles—who would know or care? "Didn't help, I suppose. But I'm not fond of his kind."

"So what happened to the little lady?"

The smell of the food was reawakening his stomach. It growled in response. "Went home."

"Shame. She was a good one."

"I agree." Clark took off his hat and set it on the ground next to him. "How do you know?"

The corners of Filbert's eyes crinkled as he squinted at Clark. "She brought me breakfast."

"Olivia did?" The man got confused sometimes, but Clark appreciated the thought.

The man bobbed his head. "No one but you ever done that. She'll be back."

He wished that were true. Sometimes Filbert seemed crazier than a fox with his tail caught in a trap; other times he was like a wise old owl. Trouble was, you were never sure which was which. "What makes you think so?"

"Saw the way she looked when you was singing. Smitten."

Clark had forgotten that Filbert had waited around that night. "Maybe so. But it doesn't mean she still feels the same. I pushed my luck, I'm afraid."

Filbert ran a hand over his whiskery chin. "She'll be back."

Clark pulled the stick from the coals before the fish burned. His heart settled on the old man's words. He might not know what he was talking about, but at least the hopeful thought granted a measure of peace. "I pray you're right, old friend."

"I'll pray on it, too." Filbert took a swig of water from his canteen. "Not good for a man to be alone. Makes you a bit loose in the head."

Eighteen

August 10, 1929

Rays of light filtered through the treetops onto the wooden archway gate at Camp Curry as Olivia stepped from the auto stage, her muscles stiff from being crammed in the long automobile with ten other tourists. She took a deep breath, picking out a hint of pine needles beyond the overwhelming smell of car exhaust. She reached back to give Frances a hand. Hopefully Frank could smooth things over with *Scenic* so she could afford to pay Aunt Phyllis back for the tickets.

The younger girl was already swiveling her head like an owl, taking in every sight she could lay her eyes on. "I can't believe I'm here. I've read so much about this place."

Louise nudged her. "Get a wiggle on, Frances. We're not officially here until you get out. Olivia, are you certain we must camp? I thought you stayed in a hotel?"

Olivia smiled. "I did at first, but you'll like Camp Curry better. There are more people your age, and they have singing and dancing every night."

Her sister beamed. "Well, that part I like. You said one of your friends is a singer?"

"She's a very new friend, but if we bump into her, I'll make sure to introduce you. I think Melba would love to meet both of you." Melba seemed to love everyone, and Olivia hoped that would include the girls. The ranger's wife might be a better influence than she'd ever succeeded in being.

Louise bounced out, her skirt swishing about her knees. "Do you think she'd let me be in the show with her?"

"I don't know about that."

The girls helped the porter load their bags into a wooden cart, Louise chatting up the young man the whole way to their tent cabin.

"Well, look who's returned. Yosemite always brings them back." Ranger Edwards hurried to meet them. "Frank Robinson telephoned to say you were on your way. He sounded quite pleased."

Melba walked at his side, leading her husband's horse. "We were pleased, too. Welcome back, Olivia."

Olivia shook the ranger's hand, suddenly feeling as light as thistledown. It was odd how quickly these people felt like family. Maybe that's because she was so lacking in that area. She glanced around, hoping for one more familiar face. She hadn't been able to focus on anything—or anyone—else since they stepped into the automobile. Her heart had threatened to climb up her throat as soon as they entered the park. What would she say to him? "Is Clark here, too?"

John pushed his hat back an inch. "I'm afraid he's on patrol up in the northeastern section of the park. I haven't been able to reach him."

Her heart thudded back into place. "He's out with another tour group?"

The ranger shook his head. "I finally talked him into taking the seasonal ranger position."

At least he was still here. And that might give her a day or so to decide how she should apologize to him. Would he even still want to see her? "I do need to re-create some of the paintings we did together. Do you think…" She bit her lip for a moment. "Would he be able to take me back to some of the spots we visited before? And maybe a few more?"

John frowned. "I can arrange another guide for you."

Another guide? Her spirits sank. "I'd really prefer Clark."

Melba turned to her husband, taking his arm. "John, you can't send her out with a stranger. It must be Clark."

Her knowing smile flooded Olivia's cheeks with heat. What had Clark said to her?

"Well, maybe we can work something out. Let me look at the schedules, and I'll speak with him."

Melba handed the reins over to her husband and joined Olivia next to the tent. "Perfect. Now I want to hear everything you've been up to while you were gone."

John tipped his hat before swinging up on his horse's back. "I'll stop by the Rangers' Club and see if Clark has returned yet."

After introducing Melba to her sisters, it was a definite case of love at first sight. Within minutes, they'd convinced the ranger's wife to give them a tour of Camp Curry, Louise practically begging to see the stage area.

Olivia gathered her new paints. She hoped Clark had saved her old ones, because she could barely scrape together the money for a few basic colors. She clamped the pad of paper under her arm and headed for the entrance. She needed a picture of the Camp Curry archway with the Glacier Point cliff rising in the background. It might not be the most jaw-dropping view in the park, but it would always hold a special place in her heart.

⌒

Clark guided the General up to the chapel, the weight of the past few days pulling at his shoulders. Obviously God wanted him to remain here at Yosemite, but why? He still dreamed of leading a congregation in worship, but

with each day that passed, it seemed less likely. No church would hire a park
ranger to be the pastor, particularly when he'd left his first church in
disgrace.

And then there was Olivia.

As he patrolled the park, his thoughts bounced between her and his future. Would she care to be a part of it? She hadn't even bothered to write.

His uniform was one more barrier between him and the people he
wanted to reach. How could he minister to someone like Filbert when his
primary duty was enforcing park regulations? His heart lay with people—
guiding them along the steps to salvation, not down forested trails. He could
no more be a ranger than John could be a banker. God had designed him for
a different calling, and he could feel it in the depth of his being. But if that
was true, why was he still stuck here? Why did his soul still reach for the
mountains?

Clark had promised John the summer, but he couldn't stay beyond that.
He didn't know where God would lead him, but there must be something
else out there. He pulled his father's compass from his pocket, rubbing his
thumb across the inscription. *"Ye have compassed this mountain long enough:
turn you northward."* The verse from Deuteronomy mocked his indecision.
But what was "northward" in God's lexicon?

Clark dismounted and fastened the horse's lead to the hitching post
outside the chapel. He'd spent the past week in prayer in God's granite cathedral, but—for at least a moment—he needed to talk to the Almighty in
a house made by men's hands. He brushed the trail dust off his trousers and
clomped up the stairs. Entering the house of worship, he pulled off the
Stetson and tossed it onto the coatrack, glad to be rid of it for a moment. The
late afternoon light poured in through the windows, dusty sunbeams spreading across the wooden pews. The floor creaked as Clark made his way down
the aisle and sank onto the front bench.

"God, I don't even know what I'm doing here." He spoke the words to the silent room, thankful that God's presence was as obvious inside the building as it was outside.

"Maybe I can help shed some light on that."

The voice brought Clark vaulting back to his feet.

Reverend White walked down the aisle toward him.

A wave of heat traveled up his neck. "Reverend, I didn't see you."

"I'm sorry. I was over in the corner working on my sermon. I hope you don't mind."

Mind? It was his church, wasn't it? "No, of course not. I apologize for interrupting your work."

The older man smiled. The lines on his face spoke of years spent bearing others' problems. "This is as much my work as anything else. You know that better than anyone, Clark."

Clark's muscles uncoiled a notch. "Yes, I suppose I do."

"Sit, sit. I can leave you to pray alone, or I can stay if you'd like to talk." The minister came alongside him and gestured to the bench.

"I've been praying steadily for a week. Longer, really—ever since I came to Yosemite. But I'm not getting answers." Clark sank back into the hard wooden pew. "Sometimes I think He's not listening."

"You know that's not true." Reverend White sat down next to him.

Clark shared a little of his story, though the pastor knew much of it already. He'd been one of the few privy to Clark's situation before coming to Yosemite. Clark fell silent when the tale got to Olivia.

Reverend White leaned forward in the seat, studying Clark's face. "So you've hit a fork in the trail."

"I guess that's one way to put it. But it'd be nice if God saw fit to give me a signpost or two."

"Is that what this is really about?"

Clark glanced out the window, the shape of El Capitan looming in the distance. "I don't want to leave here, but this…" He ran a hand across his shirtfront, pausing at the badge. "This isn't me. Enforcing regulations, giving directions, issuing permits?"

"No, it's not. And that's where your problem lies."

The man was speaking in riddles. Clark ran a hand through his hair. "What should I do about it?"

The minister sighed, sitting back. "Clark, I'll ask you the same question I ask many who drag themselves in here. Who are you?"

Clark stopped. "I'm a guide. A former pastor. A—"

"No." The minister held up a hand, palm forward. "Stop right there." He turned to face Clark square on. "I didn't ask what you *do*. I asked who you *are*."

"I don't understand."

"No, because you haven't stopped to think about it. You're frustrated because God won't give you direction, but maybe that's because you don't understand how He made you. What He made you." Reverend White cleared his throat. "Let's put this simply. In Christ's eyes, who are you?"

The bold question sent a quiver through Clark's chest. "Well, I'm…I'm a child of God."

"Right." The reverend paused, as if waiting for more.

Clark plowed ahead. "I'm loved. Forgiven. Redeemed."

"So you know the words. Then why aren't you acting like it?"

"Pardon?"

Reverend White leaned back and braced his arm against the back of the pew. "When you talk, Clark, all I hear is how you think others view you. You were wronged by your church, true. They believed lies about you. But when did these lies become your truth?"

"They're not."

"The moment you left that church, you decided you weren't worthy to serve God. You weren't worthy to help your fellow man." The minister's eyes narrowed. "Now who are you, Clark? A guide? A ranger?"

"I'll always be His servant, but I left in disgrace. How can I ever go back?" The familiar ache burrowed into Clark's chest.

Reverend White rapped the bench next to him. "*Dis*-grace is a human term, Clark. God invented grace. No one can take it from you." He leaned closer, his voice growing in intensity. "You want to know why God isn't showing you which direction to go? Maybe it's because you're not ready to listen yet."

Clark pushed to his feet, turning to face the cross in frustration. "That's all I've been doing. I've walked these trails for almost three years, listening."

"Really?" The reverend sat back. "Because, I've been watching you. I think you've been wallowing in that disgrace."

Clark turned back to face the man. "I hate to disagree with you, Reverend."

"Why? Afraid I'll kick you out, too?"

The statement sank into the pit of his stomach. Clark took a step back from the pew. "I need to get back to work."

The pastor stood. "Seek your identity in Him, Clark. Everything else will come clear. He hasn't stopped speaking to you; you just think you're not worthy to hear it."

⁓

Olivia dipped her brush into the hunter green and let the water diffuse the color around the edge of her painting, touching the distant trees with breath. Months ago the idea of a forest would have sent her into a panic. Now the myriad greens spelled out life. Is this how God felt when He created Yosemite? Like He was playing?

The archway framed the lower half of the painting, the letters of "Camp Curry, Welcome" spelled out in lengths of cut limbs. The cliff face of Glacier Point provided a glorious backdrop behind the trees. Her heartbeat settled into a steady rhythm as she gave herself to the process. A mosquito landed on her arm. It paced up and down, looking for the perfect spot to dig in, before she bothered to flick it off.

Melba and the girls sat nearby, their conversation blending with the birdsong. If only she could capture that as well. She had added a few vehicles and figures around the edges, but resisted the urge to include a handsome ranger and his horse walking up the road even though she'd glanced over her shoulder countless times hoping it might be true. Clark, a ranger? It wasn't so different from what he'd been doing, but something about the idea felt strange. Maybe when she saw him in uniform.

If she saw him.

When she'd left Camp Curry three weeks ago, she'd flung her supplies at his feet and cast his affections aside just as easily. He'd offered her tenderness, and she'd walked out. The realization sank low in her chest, like a weight pulling her under the water. Olivia Rutherford, avant-garde artist, carefree genius of the art world—had her charade become such a part of her that she no longer knew her own mind? Or her heart?

The picture blurred as she blinked away tears. Perhaps he'd already moved on, disappearing into the backcountry without a backward glance. How could she expect anything more? She dropped her brush into the water cup, green droplets splashing against her blouse. Olivia pressed one hand against her eyes, the deep stirring in her stomach sending a wave of regret through her.

Melba's soft voice caught her attention, and Olivia glanced up. Her friend pointed down the road.

The sight of a ranger on horseback sent her heart into her throat.

"Clark?" Even after hours of waiting, she still had no idea how he'd react to seeing her again. Would he be angry? Distant? She held her breath even as she hurried over to meet him.

As Clark pulled the horse to a stop and then slid from the saddle, all her well-intentioned apologies flew from her mind, and she could only gulp down breaths to try to steady herself.

He shoved back his hat. Dust had settled into the tiny grooves around his warm, brown eyes.

"Clark, I—"

Clark stepped forward and scooped her into a hug so big it lifted her off her feet. "I can't believe you're back."

A tiny cry caught in her throat like a mixture of a sob and a hiccup. She pressed one hand to her lips, gripping the back of his neck with the other. "I-I can't believe I left." Her arms trembled as she let his warmth flood her skin. The man smelled of campfire, horse, and sweat. He smelled like heaven.

He pulled back for a moment, gazing down into her face. "When someone mentioned you were here, I didn't even stop to ask for details. I just took off."

"I'm glad." She laced her hands behind his back in fear he might let go. "I had to return, Clark. I couldn't stop thinking about you—and about this place. Its story needs to be told. Even if I never make a cent off it."

A grin spread across his face, softened by what looked to be exhaustion. "Are you staying here at Camp Curry?" He glanced behind her. "Tell me you didn't bring the Vanderbilts back with you."

"I received a delightful letter from Sophie Vanderbilt, written as she was on her way to Paris." A laugh bubbled up in her chest. "I brought someone better. My little sisters."

"More Rutherford women? We'll have to keep an eye on the camp boys."

"Louise has already been surveying the offerings. Frances only cares about birds, thank goodness."

He pulled off his hat, displaying a clean line where it had protected him from the elements. "Olivia, I'm sorry I pushed you so hard. You can tell me as little or as much as you like."

"No, you were right. I want to know everything about you. It's only fair that you have the same right."

He smiled, pulling her close. "I'd love to get started right now, but I need to report back."

Her shoulders grew heavy. *So soon?* "Your friend John thought he might be able to arrange for you to guide me again."

Clark's brows rose. "Would that be completely appropriate... considering?"

His sweet nature brought a smile to her face. She couldn't resist lowering her head to his shoulder, the shirt rough under her cheek. "I'm not sure I care at this moment. But we should be able to work something out. Perhaps Melba and the girls could join us. Would that be enough chaperones to put you at ease?"

He slid his hand up her back. "A month ago I'd rarely had a woman out on the trail. Now I'm going to have four? Lord, help me." He glanced heavenward. "Olivia, I haven't even drawn a paycheck as a ranger yet. I don't think I can get the time off."

She pulled back and looked up into his face. "So for a week, I had you all to myself and I didn't fully appreciate it. Now that I long for such an arrangement, I have to share you with the National Park Service?" It didn't seem fair.

"I'll see what John has in mind." He tightened his grip on her waist. "If only I could toss you up on the General's back and take you on patrol with me. It'd sure make the trip more interesting."

The thought sent a quiver through her. "And you're worried about 'appropriate.'"

He grinned. "Yes, well, I didn't say it was a *good* idea, just an intriguing one."

Olivia couldn't resist his draw a moment longer. She lifted up on her toes and pressed her lips to his cheek.

He turned and met her mouth with his, the soft brush deepening into a long moment that stole the breath from her chest. When they finally parted, he chuckled. "I've been thinking about that for weeks."

She ran her hand down his shirtfront, touching the gold badge. "So have I, only I wasn't certain it would happen again."

"I wouldn't mind it happening another time or two, if you're open to the idea." He ducked his head toward hers.

Girlish laughter behind them stopped all forward momentum. Olivia stepped out of Clark's embrace, a flush warming her cheeks.

Melba smiled, the twins flanking her. "Sorry, I held them back as long as I could."

Louise bounced to Olivia's side, grasping her hand. "You do have a secret love. I knew it!"

Olivia sighed, her lips still warm from Clark's kiss. Why, exactly, had she brought her sisters along on this trip? "Louise, Frances, this is Clark Johnson."

"*Ranger* Clark Johnson," Melba piped up, her smile golden.

"Pleased to meet you both." Clark nodded.

The girls took turns shaking his hand before Frances turned to Olivia. "Melba's husband is a ranger. Are you going to marry one too? Then I could come to Yosemite any time I wanted." Her eyes widened, her face taking on a peculiar glow. "You'd *live* at Yosemite then, wouldn't you?"

Clark shuffled his feet, reaching down to adjust the leather puttees covering his lower legs. "I'm only a temporary ranger. I don't think I'll be here long enough to…to…"

Olivia had forgotten how easy it was to embarrass the man, not to mention how sweet he was with red-tipped ears. "Frances, you'll need to hold off on the wedding plans. Mr. Johnson—Ranger Johnson—and I are just…" She glanced his direction, barely able to meet his eyes. What were they, exactly? "We're good friends."

Louise giggled. "Mm-hmm."

Melba took them each by the arm. "Girls, why don't we head over to the amphitheater? I think the band might be setting up for tonight's show." The enticement worked, and she managed to draw the girls away, leaving Clark and Olivia in peace. Or as much peace as could be found in a busy campground.

As soon as the girls disappeared around the bend, Olivia reached for his arm again. "So now you've met all of the Rutherford sisters."

"What a first impression I made." He glanced down at her hand on his forearm, a smile touching his lips. "Look, I should go. I have to talk to John and get cleaned up." He glanced around. "If you'd like, I'll come back this evening for the Firefall—out of uniform. I don't want the Currys complaining about rangers kissing guests."

"All right. I should finish this painting anyway." She drew her hand back to her side, her stomach fluttering. "I look forward to this evening."

He grinned. "So do I."

Nineteen

C lark hurried to headquarters, urging the General to a faster clip than the tired horse deserved, the memory of Olivia's touch burning through his system. He'd despaired of her returning to Yosemite, and here she was—and happy to see him. His heart raced. What in the world was God doing?

Hopefully John had some idea of how they could work this out. He'd committed to the Park Service for the rest of the summer, and the new guide outfit had already taken over. He'd been sad to see Goldie, Bess, and the others trot off behind the new man, but in reality they belonged to the park—not him. At least he owned the General straight out.

Clark tied her at the hitching post and gave her a quick pat. "I'll be right back to give you a good rubdown at the stable, girl. You've earned it." He took the three stone steps in one leap, pulled the door open, and headed for John's office.

"Welcome back." His friend sat back in his chair, lacing his fingers behind his head. "From the look on your face, you stopped at Camp Curry on your way in. It went well, I take it?"

"You could say that." Clark dropped down in the seat on the far side of the desk. "I can't believe she's back."

"Melba was pretty certain you two were an item. I guess she was right."
He smirked. "Now where does this leave us? My romantic bride wouldn't
forgive me if I went and separated lovebirds."

Lovebirds? He should be annoyed with his friend's teasing, but he
couldn't help the goofy smile that had probably claimed his features. He
pulled off his hat and scrubbed a palm down his face to get hold of his emotions. "It might be a bit early to make such claims, but—"

"But you don't want to head out on patrol again just yet."

"Is it that obvious?"

John leaned one elbow on the desk, dropping his chin into his hand. "I've
been there, remember? And not all that long ago." After a moment, he drew
back and pulled a file from his desk. "I've been looking over the assignments
for the summer. I can't release you from duties, but I can make some swaps.
Joseph Morris has been working traffic in the valley here, but he's young and
eager. I think he'll jump at the chance to get out in the field." John shot Clark
a dark look, pointing a long finger his direction. "But I hired you because of
your knowledge of the backcountry. Morris is new to the area. If he goes and
gets himself lost, I'm sending you after him—unpaid. Got it?"

"Yes sir." Clark leaned forward in his seat. "So I'd be working here?"

"Yes. Directing cars, dealing with campground bears, finding lost kids,
making sure folks aren't falling in the creek, that sort of thing. Not the most
glamorous job, but it has to be done. And you'll have at least some of your
evenings free."

A couple of weeks ago, he'd never have accepted a post directing traffic,
but if it kept him closer to Olivia, who was he to quibble? "So no guiding
then?"

"What you do on your own time is your business." John sat back. "But
don't take any money for it, or you might come to blows with the new guys."

"I wouldn't dream of it."

"And you'll keep Melba and me informed of any interesting develop-ments. I think I've earned that much, and I don't want her pestering me for information all the time."

"Speaking of which, I'll probably invite Melba along while Olivia paints. I don't think it would be a good idea for us to be alone in the woods, if you know what I mean."

John's brows lifted. "A little time alone might not be the worst thing, but I'm sure she'd be willing to keep an eye on you two."

The telephone on John's desk broke the silence, the metallic ring vibrat-ing the tabletop. Clark stood, but John motioned for him to stay.

After listening to the caller for a few moments, John's face darkened. "Hold on for a moment. I have a man here who can deliver the message for you." He held the receiver to Clark. "Frank Robinson, Olivia's art dealer."

Clark frowned, accepting the telephone from his friend. "Clark Johnson here." He hadn't gotten used to using the title *ranger*, yet.

"Mr. Johnson. Perfect. You're the guide, right? I assume Olivia arrived safely back in the park, is that correct?"

"Yes sir. She's staying over in Camp Curry."

"I'm hopeful you can pass a message on to her for me. It's great news, actually, albeit a bit surprising. I need you to tell her that one of her Yosemite paintings has surfaced."

Clark's breath caught in his chest. "How is that possible?"

"I'm not sure, but it's definitely one of hers. It went up for sale at a local gallery, and before I could get down there, it had already sold for four thousand."

Clark nearly dropped the phone. "Dollars?"

"I could hardly believe it myself. The painting shows a view of the mountains with a silhouette of a man in front, leaning on a rail. It's stupen-dous. Her best work yet, by far."

He shut his eyes, a weight settling in his gut. The man was him. "How can they sell it without her permission?"

"It's already done. I'll work on figuring out who's behind it, but you were probably right about Vanderbilt. The good news is, folks are clamoring for more. She's going to be an overnight sensation. Tell her to get busy. By this time next week, I'll have buyers lined up around the corner. But she's got to fulfill the *Scenic* contract first. That woman's going to have more money than she knows what to do with."

His throat tightened. The money she needed for the girls.

And the money that would take her away.

~

Clark stood in an empty row at the Curry amphitheater, the mouth-watering smell of meatloaf and gravy filtering down from the pavilion. He'd managed a quick shave and a bath before throwing on clothes and hurrying back to the camp to deliver Robinson's news. At this rate he'd wear down the path between headquarters and Camp Curry.

"I don't understand." Olivia plunked down on one of the long benches.

Clark ran a hand over his throat, wishing he could push the words back. Olivia's distraught face had caught him off guard. "I don't understand it myself. I thought all the paintings were ruined."

"I assumed they were. I didn't look too closely. It would have hurt too much to play jigsaw puzzle with them."

That whole evening was a blur. The storeroom had been a mess of shredded paper. Had Vanderbilt truly gotten out of there with a painting? A thought struck him. "Maybe he took more than one. How many did you have finished?"

She balled her fists in her lap. "None of them were *finished*. I wanted to add touches to them. And some were little more than sketches." Her face pinched. "There were over a dozen, but the one of you at the Glacier Point Hotel was my favorite. I wasn't even going to sell that one."

The crack in her voice pulled at him. He sank down on one knee, drawing her close. "I'm sorry. If I'd realized any were missing—"

"If I'd known he'd taken them, I'd have gone after the lout myself." She jumped to her feet. "How dare he steal my paintings and then sell them without my permission. I could have him arrested. He thinks because he's wealthy and privileged, he can get away with anything."

Clark ran a hand across his jaw. "Your dealer seemed to think it was a good thing."

She turned away, her shoulders curving forward. "Of course he would. He's looking at future sales. For pieces I haven't even completed yet."

"You will. You have a gift, Olivia. And those sales will help you with the girls and their schooling. It's what you wanted, right?"

"I suppose. Only I didn't expect it to happen like this." Her hands squeezed closed. She turned back to face him. "Someone really paid that much?"

"That's what Mr. Robinson said." He slid a finger down the side of her arm, unable to resist touching her. "And worth every penny, I'm sure."

Like dawn breaking over the mountains, a tiny smile appeared. "I suppose that means you'll have to sit for me again."

"The painting didn't sell because of me."

"You were the model." She cocked her head. "And the muse."

"And maybe it would have gone for more without me stuck in the middle of the view."

That earned him a laugh. The beautiful sound sent a thrill through him. He'd like to hear more of that. "So, what should we do next? It's a little late for painting tonight, but I could meet you here at daybreak, and we could spend a few hours at Yosemite Falls before my shift starts."

"Sounds perfect. What about this evening? Any plans?"

He held out a hand. "How about supper? It might not be the Ahwahnee, but Camp Curry does make an excellent meatloaf. And then the Firefall, of course."

She placed her palm in his and stood. "Dinner and a show? It's practically a real date."

A date. After two weeks on the trail, exhaustion weighted every muscle in his body, but how could he resist? "There's nothing I'd like better."

Nothing besides sneaking a kiss during the Firefall while everyone else was enjoying the view.

———

Clark led the way up the path, Melba and Olivia and the twins trailing behind him. He placed a hand on the center of his chest, the emotions swelling inside his heart causing a physical ache. Three years in Yosemite, and he'd never been this eager to lead a group, and he wasn't even getting paid for it. Hitting the trail in the predawn hours after the world's most perfect evening—who could ask for more?

"I remember this spot." Olivia panted behind him. "Only, I don't remember it being so steep." She hefted the canvas bag higher on her shoulder.

"You were riding Goldie last time."

"I miss her. And that's not just my feet talking." She sighed. "What happened to her and the others?"

"They weren't mine. They belonged to the transportation office. Though after working with them for several years, it didn't feel that way."

"I can imagine. I hope the new fellows are taking as good of care of them as you did."

"I'm sure they will. My fear was they'd end up as rentals. Then any Tom, Dick, or Harry could rent them for the day. The rental mules get pretty testy."

Olivia frowned. "Can't you buy them from the park?"

He chuckled. "Maybe you can, Miss Successful Artist."

She jutted her chin. "Perhaps I will."

"And what would you do with a pack string in Sacramento?"

She laced one hand through his arm. "They could carry my paintings to the gallery. Except for Queen Elizabeth. She'd sit home with her hooves up."

They climbed the last little stretch to the falls, the sight bringing a surge of excitement as it often did. No matter how many times he visited the various falls, they always put on a fresh face.

Olivia shrugged off her pack. "It looks different."

"The weather's been dry. You should see it in the early spring. It roars so loud, you can feel the tremors in your chest."

"I'd like to. I'll have to come back." She pushed a strand of hair out of her face, meeting his eyes.

Where would they be next spring? Clark fought against the urge to take her in his arms in that very moment. He wanted to swear his devotion to her right then and there.

Instead, he pulled off his own backpack and helped her set up the easel. There was no use promising what wasn't his to give. *"A man's heart deviseth his way: but the LORD directeth his steps."* The proverb had been a comfort to him during the past couple of years, but suddenly it hung about his neck like a millstone. Right now their feet trod the same path, but how long would it last? His parents had found love to last a lifetime, and John and Melba had made sacrifices to be together. But he couldn't see his future three months away, much less for a lifetime. *Lord, I need her. Please. Couldn't our steps be together?*

The artist and the...the what? The ranger? Guide? Reverend White's words came back to him. *"Clark Johnson, who are you?"*

Melba and the girls caught up to them. Frances ran up to Olivia. "Mrs. Edwards says she'll take us to the top of the falls while you're painting, if that's all right with you."

Olivia smiled. "And here I was worried you'd get bored sitting here watching me work."

"I could never be bored here." Frances glanced around.

Louise tucked her long braid up into her straw hat. "I could. But the falls are pretty."

"Please be careful—and stay far away from the edge." Olivia's brow furrowed, making her look more like a nervous mother than an older sister. "And make sure you come back this way. I want to add you two into the painting, right there along the stream bank." Olivia gestured down to the edge of the water. "I had my friend Sophie perched there last time, but I think it will be even prettier with the two of you."

The girls beamed.

"We'll be back. It won't take too long." Melba glanced pointedly at Clark. "But you don't need us hanging around distracting you from your work."

He hid his smile by snatching Olivia's rinse cup and meandering down to the stream. He had plenty in his canteen, but there was something about touching the water that always grounded him. He dunked the cup under the surface, letting the icy creek wash across his skin. No matter what his identity, this place had woven itself into his bones and the water was part of his blood. He closed his eyes for a brief moment, the desire to stay rooting itself deep in his chest. How could he even consider leaving this place? He might as well leave his own soul behind.

He stood, shaking the droplets from his hand. There had to be another answer. And with any hope, Olivia would be part of it. He turned, gazing toward where she'd perched herself and the easel. She stared up at the falls, the early morning light touching her face with a glow that went beyond simple sunrise. By now he knew her well enough to realize she was tracing the lines of the river with her eyes, disappearing into the scene like the tiny water ouzel birds that darted through the waterfalls' spray.

Olivia wouldn't speak for hours as she worked, as if her very spirit had left her body and dipped right into the painting itself. But that was okay. He would be content to stand here and watch.

She glanced his direction, using her hand to shade her eyes. "Are you bringing that back?"

Clark jerked back to alertness. The water. "Oh, yes, of course. I got caught up in the view."

Olivia placed a hand on her hip. "You've got your back to it."

"That's what you think." He climbed back up the bank and fixed the cup into the hole in her easel. "I can only stay a couple of hours. If you need to be here longer, Melba can walk you back."

She laid out a line of brushes. "It's not far. I could get back on my own." She darted a sweet glance at him. "Not that I don't love the company."

What had happened to her fear of being alone? Perhaps this place had captured her as deeply as it had him. "I don't want you alone on the trail." He stepped close, pulling her into his arms for a brief moment. "I'd stay forever if I could."

Olivia nuzzled her forehead into the curve of his neck, sending his blood racing. "I know you have to work. I'm thankful John was able to give us this time at least."

He touched her hair, relishing the smooth strands under his fingers. "Melba would never have forgiven him. She's been trying to pair us off since you stepped foot in the Ahwahnee."

She laughed. "I find that hard to believe. Do you remember our first meeting? I couldn't have foreseen this happening. How could she?"

"She's a cupid, that one. Won't be happy until the whole world finds love." And he was never going to argue with her about that again. Clark stepped back. "I should let you paint. That's why you're here. This isn't helping you any."

"Oh, I wouldn't say that." She lifted her chin, a smile brightening her face. "I find this very inspiring. But I will get started—after you kiss me."

"Now there's the bold Olivia Rutherford I remember." He chuckled. Leaning in, he placed a kiss on her lips, careful not to linger. If he permitted himself, he'd never be able to leave.

She tossed her head, the short dark bob reminding him of her flapper ways. "She's still a part of me. That's true."

"Hey," he tugged her back for a moment. "When you left before, you told me Olivia Rutherford wasn't real. Should I still call you that? Or would you rather I call you something else?"

Olivia tipped her head. "Like what?"

"I'm not sure. Sweetheart? Darling?" The endearments felt foreign on his tongue. He stared down into her face, admiring the cute little upturned nose. He slid a fingertip across her cheek. "Are those freckles? How did I not know you have freckles?"

She turned into his hand until her jaw nestled in his palm. "I usually powder them away."

"I like them. You shouldn't cover up anything, Olivia. You're perfect, just as God made you."

A shadow passed over her face. She lifted a hand to touch her hair. "Then you should probably know that my hair isn't really black."

He chuckled. "What is it, then?"

"Plain old mousey-brown."

"Hey, mice can be pretty cute, at least when they're not jumping out of your supply bag." Clark laid his cheek atop her head, which was quickly becoming his favorite place in the world, and breathed in the scent of her hair. "I hope I get to see it sometime. It sounds lovely. I'm quite partial to brown, Olivia."

"Liv." She ran her fingers along his chin, drawing back to gaze into his eyes. "You can call me Liv."

Twenty

O livia stood back and surveyed the painting, the familiar ache between her shoulder blades telling her it was time to stop for the day. The sun beat down on her hat and shoulders, so different from the predawn hours when she'd met Clark and Melba and headed out on the trail.

After Clark returned to work, she, Melba, and the girls hiked back to Camp Curry. Frances and Louise had already befriended some girls at the next campsite, so Olivia packed up her easel and spent a few more hours painting in the meadow. Now as she glanced around, she realized the solitude wasn't grating on her as she'd feared it would. The sounds of the river trickling in the distance and the wind rustling the grass were like a gentle whisper to her heart.

A couple of deer grazed at the far end of the field, so Olivia stretched and walked toward them for a better view.

When she turned back, two men were standing on the trail looking at her easel. Their automobile waited nearby on the road. Her chest tightened as she hurried back.

"Is this yours? It's remarkable." The older man smiled.

"Yes. I just finished." She wiped away a bead of sweat on her forehead.

People had often stopped to admire her work in the past. What did she think was going to happen? They'd grab her paper and run?

"You must be Miss Rutherford, the artist, then." The younger man stepped forward, pushing his hand toward her in greeting.

She drew back. "I-I am, yes. How did you know?"

He dropped his arm, awkwardly. "We met Frank Robinson at the gallery. He told us you were working up here. I'd hoped to speak to you."

"Frank sent you?" Why would he do such a thing? Suddenly she wished she had someone nearby.

"I'm Amos Baker. I own a gallery in San Francisco. We'd like to feature your Yosemite paintings in a showing next month." He drew a calling card from his vest pocket. "In fact, I'll take this one now, if you agree. As a deposit."

"It's not even fully dry." A throbbing ache grew beneath her temples. Was Frank selling her work before she'd gotten started? What about *Scenic*? "No, I need to speak to my dealer first. I'm sorry."

Mr. Baker stepped to one side, as if keeping the easel in view. "Look, Miss Rutherford—gallery space is limited in the city. You know that. We need to get you positioned for the best exposure, sales-wise. I'm certain this type of work would make a big splash, but we need to jump on it right away."

The older man folded his arms. "If she's not interested, Amos—"

"I didn't say I'm not interested." Olivia's breaths came quickly. "But I can't send this with you now. It's cockled, and I still need to stretch it. And I should speak to Frank. I'm under contract already, and I believe—"

"We can take care of all the details back at the gallery. We'll put our best people on making sure the painting is ready to display. You should go on with your work and let us focus on the frivolous details." Mr. Baker cleared his throat, digging in his trouser pocket, then pulled out a bulging billfold.

"I can offer you three thousand, right off the top. I'm sure the painting will go for more, but this is a start."

"Three thousand?" Her voice cracked. She'd never even seen that sort of money, much less held it in her hand. *One painting would cover the girls' schooling. For years.*

"It's a deposit." The man smiled. "But I'd have to take it with me. I need something to show my partner at the gallery. He wasn't able to attend the last sale, so right now he's just going on my say-so. That only takes me so far. In order to secure the event, I need to have something in hand."

"But..." *Scenic* was waiting. Hadn't Frank said to fulfill that contract first and then paint others? Had he changed his mind?

Mr. Baker pulled the bills back as if sensing her hesitation. "I can't hold this offer, I'm afraid. We have other artists waiting in the wings. But I can throw in an extra $500 if it makes you feel better."

"It's not that." She stared at the roll of bills squeezed in his palm. "I need to speak—"

"I tell you what. You have your dealer call me." He shoved the money back in the billfold, shadows forming around his eyes. "He was quite eager when I spoke to him yesterday."

Frank had mentioned money troubles. Of course he was eager. They hadn't seen the money from the last sale, and now here she was dragging her feet. "Very well. But just this one. After that, I need to fulfill what I promised for the magazine."

A look passed between the two men. The older fellow stepped over to the easel and unclipped the fasteners holding the damp paper in place.

Mr. Baker retrieved the wallet once more and yanked the money out. "It's nice doing business with you, Miss Rutherford. Mr. Robinson told me you were a shrewd businesswoman, but I hadn't expected you to make me sweat like that."

The money felt warm in Olivia's hand, like Baker had been clutching it tightly. "Please, be careful with it." She gestured at the figures at the bottom of the picture. "Those are my sisters there. So it means a lot to me."

The gallery owner smiled. "Of course. We'll take every precaution, trust me."

His associate nodded. "Nice meeting you, Miss. I hope you have a lovely day."

"Thank you," Olivia murmured. Watching her painting walk away with the two gallery executives turned her stomach. For years, she'd dreamed of selling paintings so easily. Now people were buying them before she'd even gotten them home? She closed her eyes, trying to slow her fluttering heart.

After a deep breath, she gathered her paints and tumbled them back into the box. The trees and cliffs were closing in. She needed to get back to camp.

⁓

The stuffy air of the chief ranger's office made it hard to draw a decent breath. Olivia sank lower in the chair and pressed the telephone to her ear.

"Liv, are you still there?" Frank's voice crackled on the line.

She clutched the edge of the desk, turning away from John and Clark's sympathetic eyes. *How could I have been so foolish?*

Frank's voice echoed a second time on the long-distance. "I don't know what you're talking about, Liv. I didn't send anyone out there."

Bile burned at her throat, but Olivia swallowed against it. "They said— they spoke of a gallery in San Francisco. They said you were excited about it and told them to come. If they didn't speak to you, how did they know where to find me?"

"What's the name of the gallery?"

She pulled the calling card from her pocket, together with the roll of bills. The crooked type on the smudged card glared back at her. "Market Street Gallery for Fine Arts."

There was a long pause on the line. She laid the pile of money on the desk, the feel of it turning her stomach.

Clark gestured at the stack of bills with a questioning glance. "May I?" he mouthed.

She nodded, still waiting for Frank's pronouncement.

"Liv, I've never heard of them. I swear, I knew nothing about this. Did you give them anything?"

Tears stung at her eyes. She pressed shaking fingers against her lids. "I did. I knew something didn't seem right, but they knew your name and—"

And I'm an idiot.

"I'm coming up there. I think you shouldn't be alone right now. This is getting out of hand."

"I'm not alone." She glanced up at Clark and John. "You don't need to come, Frank. I'll be more careful." She curled her fingers and pressed them against her leg as she finished the call and lowered the phone to its cradle.

Clark scowled as he flipped through the hundred-dollar bills. "You won't be alone, again. One of us will be with you at all times."

Olivia stood, locking her knees to stop their trembling. She'd embarrassed herself enough for one day, she didn't need to crumple in a miserable heap. What a stupid, childish mistake.

He held up one of the bills to the light. "And I hate to tell you this,"—he sighed, his eyes meeting hers—"but these aren't real."

She dropped back into the wooden chair, a wave of nausea rising in her stomach. She should have realized from the moment the man waved it under her nose. The money was as fake as Olivia Rutherford.

Twenty-One

C lark leaned close to the dusty black Ford. "I'm sorry. The campground is full."

The man frowned beneath his overgrown mustache. "How can it be full? It's a huge park."

The vehicle's rattling motor nearly drowned out any conversation. Clark lifted his voice to be heard over the din. "The official campgrounds are already filled. If you'd like, you can park your vehicle in the meadow and pitch a tent there. No facilities are available, though." The exhaust fumes made Clark's eyes water.

The man's wife leaned over, lines around her mouth and eyes spoke of hours of frowning at the children filling the car's rear seat. "We always stay at Camp Curry. Jenny Curry is a personal friend."

Clark ran a hand across the back of his neck, his skin raw after nine hours of standing in the glaring sunshine. The temperature only now was dropping under eighty degrees as the sun dropped low in the sky. "Is she expecting you?"

"Well, no, not exactly." Her brown eyes flickered toward her husband. "I told you we should have written ahead."

"It's a big park," the man repeated. "Plenty of open space."

"Yes, but I wanted to stay in one of those nice tent cabins, not on the ground."

Clark pointed them to the overflow camping area, trying not to choke on the cloud of exhaust spewing from their tailpipe. It had been a long day. A long week. For the past seven days, he'd risen before dawn to hike with Olivia, spent all day on his feet in the valley, then returned to Camp Curry for the evening show or to watch Olivia paint the sunset.

Since being swindled out of her painting last week, she'd buckled down and painted five more—each more astounding than the last. Another woman might have fallen apart under the pressure, but instead it seemed to have honed her determination. Clark had stayed by her side every minute he could spare, and Melba or John accompanied her any time he could not.

Those men might have wanted nothing more than to steal the painting, but Clark wasn't taking any chances. What if she'd refused them? Would they have taken it by force? They'd obviously put a lot of thought into how to steal her work. Not only had they faked the card and the counterfeit bills, they'd found an opportunity when she'd be alone and unable to contact Mr. Robinson for advice. Clark broke out in a cold sweat just thinking about it.

And if they'd harmed her... The thought nearly drove him to his knees. *Lord, protect her.*

He should have realized the stir her art would make in the world. He knew he liked it, but he was certainly no expert. Several pictures by famous artists hung in the valley's hotels, but Olivia's style was unique—it triggered deep emotions when you studied it. In his eyes, the beauty of her paintings was unparalleled by anything except the original view. And perhaps the beauty Clark saw as he watched her create. The fact that she'd give him more than a second glance still staggered him.

Ten more cars waited in line. Clark took a deep breath and paced down the road to the next one. Everyone from the city must have had the same idea this weekend. The trails would be crawling with people.

No wonder young Morris was eager to trade positions with him. Who would choose traffic duty in the valley over solitude in the high country?

Only a man crazy in love.

Olivia wiped her face with a damp handkerchief, longing for a breath of air in the sweltering campground. She clenched the short scissors between her finger and thumb as she eyed Louise's golden-brown mane. "Are you sure?"

The girl bounced slightly on the wooden stool. "I've never been more sure of anything."

Melba smiled. "Come on, Olivia. She'll be adorable."

Frances sniffed, pulling her own braid over her shoulder. "I like mine as it is. Short hair seems like a bother. All those Marcel waves." She grabbed her hat and tossed it on her head. "Who's got time for such nonsense?"

Louise wrinkled her nose at her sister. "You don't even know what a Marcel wave is, Frances."

"And I don't care." Frances turned to Olivia. "Can I go visit the bird-man? He said he'd show me his most recent drawings."

Her sister had wasted no time befriending the bird-loving nature artist camped down near the kitchens. He had tamed several of the camp's Steller's jays, teaching them to eat peanuts from his hand. Olivia had already purchased two of his cute little pinecone bird figures to take home to Aunt Phyllis. They'd bring a spark of whimsy to her stuffy home. "I suppose. But don't make a pest of yourself."

Melba laughed. "Don't worry about that. Frances will make Mr. Sonn's day. He enjoys talking birds to anyone who will listen. Everyone loves the birdman."

Frances gathered her bird books. "I want to be just like him. He told me that University of California at Davis is the best place to study ornithology. He collects specimens for one of the professors there. I can't wait until I'm old enough to go to college." She hurried off without a backward glance.

University, too? Olivia pushed down the traitorous thought. If Frank was right, they'd be seeing real money soon enough. She just hoped it would come in time to pay for the girl's tuition this fall. She'd worry about college when the time came.

"Now let's get on with it." Louise tipped her head back. "I'm tired of being the only girl at school with long hair."

The only girl. Had she been so prone to exaggeration when she was fourteen? "All right." She ran her fingers through Louise's long, thick hair. It seemed a crime, but the determined set of her jaw wasn't going to be denied. If Olivia fought this, Louise might run off and cut it herself. And then who knows what she'd turn up with.

The scissors trembled in her hand.

Melba sighed. "Give me those. I think you're too nervous."

Olivia handed the tool off, the tension in her arms unclenching. "Thank you. This isn't my type of art."

"I've done it plenty of times. I cut all the rangers' wives' hair. Most of us can't afford the stylist at the Ahwahnee."

Melba had become a true friend. It was a shame Sophie wasn't here too. The three of them would have had fun together. "I don't know what I would have done without you this week."

Melba rewarded her with a quick embrace. "I've enjoyed spending time with you and the girls, Olivia. I adore John, of course, but sometimes I miss my carefree single days. I come down here and hobnob with the actors as much as possible, but they didn't hire as many women acts this year.

For John's sake, I don't spend much time with the male performers." She winked.

That sounded wise. Olivia watched as Melba began clipping at Louise's hair, locks dropping to the dirt like fall leaves. If possible, her sister grew even more beautiful as the hair cupped around her sweet face. She certainly looked older. What would their mother have thought?

Olivia smoothed the front of her riding pants. Clark was borrowing John's auto to drive her up to Glacier Point this evening to see if she could capture some of the sunset before the night claimed all the light. Perhaps she could talk Melba into staying with the girls until they returned. They were old enough to be on their own at fourteen, but why ask for trouble?

⟡

Three hours later, she clutched her paint box on one knee as the car rumbled up the steep, winding road. "This is sure different than riding up that frightening trail on Goldie's back."

Clark chuckled. "It's a beautiful drive, but I'd rather be out in the open air." He placed one hand over hers. "Though this is rather cozy, sitting next to you, Olivia—Liv."

Hearing Clark say the name still sent a charge down her spine. Clark's voice softened every time he said it, and it made her smile.

"That's for certain." She slid closer along the seat, weaving her hand through the crook of his arm. The warmth radiating through his shirt sent her feelings spiraling out of control. No matter what had happened since she'd first stepped into Yosemite National Park, being able to wrap her arms around this man was by far the best. *Thank You, God. Thank You for sharing him with me.*

"Are you going to try to re-create the painting from the Glacier Point Hotel porch?"

She closed her eyes, burying her nose in his shoulder and breathing in his scent. "I don't think so. It's still out there, somewhere. I'll try to get it back eventually. But I don't want copies floating around."

"It's a shame. That handsome model might have sold a lot of magazines."

A laugh bubbled up from her chest. "True. But I've featured him in a few of the other paintings."

"I remember walking onto the porch and seeing you sitting on the porch railing. Now that was a beautiful sight." His voice rumbled against her ear.

The thought stirred deep within. How precious of this man to think of her in those terms. Even though she'd stopped applying the lip rouge and face powder, he seemed to appreciate her more. If only she could get rid of the ridiculous black hair color. For the first time in her life, she yearned to stand in front of someone as…as herself. As Liv.

Maybe someday he could love her as she was. *Love.* He hadn't actually used that word. Would he? A tremble rushed through her. Did she love him?

As they came around a bend in the road, a sprawling view of the valley spread beyond them. She leaned forward, bracing herself against the dashboard and studying the granite monoliths. "Everything about Yosemite seems oversized. Like some giant toddlers were playing in a sandbox and left their building blocks behind."

Clark smiled. "It puts our troubles in perspective." He rubbed a thumb along her wrist before returning both hands to the wheel.

Like what the future held—or didn't. "I don't ever want to leave."

His brows pulled low. "Then don't." He pulled the roadster into a small turnout at the side of the road, overlooking the picturesque vista. "I know your life is back in the city. Your galleries and galas, grand parties in crystal ballrooms, and such."

She laughed, moving her hand to his shoulder and squeezing. "You have far too glamorous a notion about the artist's life."

He shrugged. "Perhaps. But I know you're needed there. I"—his focus darted away, down toward the valley, before returning to her—"I hope it's not just Yosemite that drew you back."

Her throat tightened. Is that what he thought? "No, of course not. But Clark, you're a part of this landscape, at least in my mind—like how the colors meld together when I add water. I couldn't separate you out if I tried. It wouldn't be Yosemite without you."

He sat quiet for a long moment. "And what if I go elsewhere?"

Her thoughts tumbled free, like a loose stone down the bank. "Is that what you've decided?"

"I'll go wherever God calls me."

Of course he would. She could hear the question in his voice. *What then?* She let her hand slide down his arm. Would she follow him? Is that what he expected of her? Was it him she loved—or this place?

He didn't wait for an answer. Turning forward in the seat, he guided the vehicle back onto the road.

The wind tousled her hair as they moved along. Olivia lowered her free hand to her knee, her other arm gripping the paint box tight against her side. They'd almost reached the top of Glacier Point. How would she concentrate on painting when this man had essentially laid his heart in her lap—and she hadn't known what to do with it?

━━━

Clark leaned against the railing at the Glacier Point Hotel watching her paint. Usually her focus was unwavering, but today Olivia fidgeted, her attention bouncing from the paper to him, even though she wasn't including him in this latest masterpiece.

Obviously he was a distraction. As much as he hated to leave her unaccompanied, considering everything that had happened, he wandered down to the far end of the porch to give her some peace.

He never should have laid his feelings out there like he had. He'd put her on the spot. They'd known each other less than two months. What did he expect from her? That she'd throw away her life and follow him into ministry—even as her own career was taking flight? His stomach twisted. He'd always pictured himself married someday, but he'd never considered what it would be like to have a wife who was in the public eye. Would she still be the great Olivia Rutherford—even if she someday became Liv Johnson?

Liv Johnson. It had a lovely sound to it. He glanced up to see her bending over her easel in the distance, her dark hair falling forward and hiding her face. The simple moniker didn't fit this incredible woman. He was dreaming to think it might.

He shouldn't assume this was a courtship. He'd read about these creative types. Didn't they move from one relationship to another with abandon? Clark turned away, leaning against one of the support posts and gazing out into the canyon below. So the mighty artist had lowered herself to a summer flirtation with park staff. How many summer romances had he seen spring up between young tourists and the college kids working at Camp Curry, only to wilt when vacations ended? He was arrogant to believe this was anything more.

Yet, she hadn't spoken of other men. In fact, Olivia seemed quite innocent. Was that another act?

The evening light colored the granite with its long rays. She should be frantically trying to capture every glimmer of light, but even from this distance the tension in her shoulders was obvious. He swallowed and turned back to face Half Dome. She'd come to the park to complete a job, and he was here to keep her safe. Even if that's all it ever turned out to be, he'd take it. The Lord would help him with his heart in the aftermath.

As if summoned by his thoughts, she appeared at his side. "Let's go. This isn't working tonight."

"I can't help feeling like it's my fault. I shouldn't have said what I did in the car. It was selfish."

A half smile smoothed the shadows on her face. She touched his wrist. "Clark, I don't think you could be selfish if you tried."

He captured her hand, pulling her a step closer. "Watch me."

She came to him, moving into his arms like she'd always belonged there. "There are several things standing in our way, I'm afraid." She drew in a deep breath. "If we're going to have any hope of moving forward, you need to know the truth."

A cool breeze swept up from the valley, the hint of autumn already in the mountain air. "Whatever you need to tell me, I'm ready to hear it. I don't think it will change how I feel."

She looked up at him, her blue eyes filling with tears. "I wish I could believe that."

⁓

Clark opened the roadster's door, holding a hand out for Liv. Hopefully the engine hadn't woken everyone in the camp. He didn't want to explain to anyone why they were driving in at two in the morning. Still, the cooler air was a welcome change from the heat of the past week.

They'd taken their time, talking the whole way and stopping at every turnout. Liv had disclosed the facts of her father's crime, and the grisly story echoed through his memory. He'd already heard the fearsome tale, told and retold by staff since he first stepped into Yosemite three years ago. Olivia— the daughter of Albert Rudd? The thought cut into Clark like a knife. No wonder she was hesitant to speak of her past—especially in this place.

How would he break the news to John? John was the one who had recovered the body of Chester Givens from the base of the falls. The incident had left an indelible mark on his friend, not to mention never seeing the killer brought to justice. How would he feel knowing that Rudd's daughter had stood right in front of him and never said a word? Clark swallowed back the nausea building in his gut. The woman he loved...

The sight of Olivia's head drooping in exhaustion pulled at his heart. He wrapped an arm around her shoulders as they walked toward the tent. She needn't bear the stain of her father's mistakes, no matter how heinous the sin. But would the world agree? The fact that she'd changed her name and her sisters' would offer some protection at least.

Camp Curry was oddly quiet considering every cabin and tent overflowed with campers. But that's what they got for returning at such an hour. A sliver of lantern light showed in the entrance to the Rutherfords' tent. Clark frowned. Were Melba and the girls waiting up for them?

He should have returned her at a decent time, but every minute felt precious. He hated the idea of wasting any in sleep. "I hope I haven't ruined your reputation keeping you out so late."

She squeezed his waist. "Who's going to know?"

The door flew open, and Louise's head popped out. "There you are." Her high-pitched voice shattered the stillness.

Clark sighed. He'd hoped to kiss Liv goodnight before heading back to his quarters, if for no other reason than to reassure her of his affection after their heart-rending conversation. No chance of that now.

"You've got to see this." The girl surged out the door and waved a magazine before jumping down the steps and landing with both feet hard in the dirt. "You're in *Hearsay Magazine*."

Melba followed, her face drawn, a second magazine clutched in her fist. Frances followed, yawning and pulling a dressing gown tight around her middle.

Olivia stepped clear of Clark's embrace. "You girls should be in bed. Louise, you're not even undressed yet."

"How could I sleep after reading this?" She grasped Olivia's arms, jumping up and down like a little girl. "You're famous!"

The color drained from Olivia's face. "What? That's not possible." She pulled the fluttering magazine from her sister's hand.

Melba frowned. "Olivia, I'm not sure you want to read it."

Louise jabbed at the pages with her finger. "Look. See the headline? 'Olivia Rutherford makes a splash in the art world.' It's not as good as being a film star, but it's still so thrilling. My sister's famous. All the girls at school will be green with envy."

Clark placed a hand under Liv's elbow, the sudden loss of color in her face alarming him. "Is that some type of art magazine?" He glanced toward Melba, her dark expression speaking volumes.

"No, silly." Louise giggled. "It's news about the stars. They sometimes write about artists. They had pictures of Georgia O'Keeffe last month. But this is so much better."

Olivia lifted the article close to her face, squinting in the darkness. "I can't read it."

Clark fetched the lantern from the cabin. The girl's excitement was contagious, though Frances was quick to lean against his arm and close her eyes, swaying on her feet.

He hated the idea of the younger girls out here by themselves, even if Melba was nearby. He pushed down the protective nature that welled up in response to Olivia's story. They deserved someone to look after them—all three of them.

Olivia sank onto the bench, her mouth falling open. "Oh no. Oh no, no, no."

"What's wrong?" He hurried to her side.

"It reads, 'Sacramento's darling artist Olivia Rutherford is busy painting up a storm at Yosemite National Park, adding a dash of much needed style to the out-of-doors. She spends her days painting vistas and nights dancing and dining with the social elite at the luxurious Ahwahnee Hotel. There have even been rumors of a heated summer liaison with…with…'" She dropped the magazine into her lap.

Clark's stomach hardened. How dare they turn this into something coarse? What he had with Olivia was precious. He snatched it up, skimming through the sordid lines. "With…married art connoisseur, Marcus Vanderbilt."

Olivia leaned forward, burying her face in her hands. "I'm going to be ill."

The feeling was mutual. Of course the magazine wasn't talking about him. *Vanderbilt.* "It's a lie."

Louise shrugged. "That's what sells magazines." She plopped down next to her sister, squeezing her arm. "Olivia, don't worry. This is great. Everyone will be talking about you. It's an honor."

"An honor?" Olivia straightened. "Lies and scandal are not an honor. I'm not trying to be a star. I want to be respected."

Melba crouched in front of her. "No one believes that trash."

Louise frowned. "But won't you sell more paintings if people know who you are? Everyone's going to want an Olivia Rutherford original now. Keep reading. It says Buster Keaton bought your last painting. Buster Keaton, Liv!"

Clark lifted the pages, focusing on the lines that followed. "It does say that."

Melba stood and brought the second magazine out from under her arm. "And I hate to be the bearer of bad news, but evidently that's an older copy.

There's a follow-up is this week's issue." She held onto it for a moment before handing it to Clark.

Why hadn't she given it to Olivia? He read the story in silence, every word sending his heart sinking further toward his stomach.

This rags-to-riches story has caught the attention of the state and the nation. Could a little backwoods girl really grow up to be a famous artist? **Hearsay** *writers have dug into her history and were shocked to learn that she is the daughter of famed murderer Albert Rudd. Rudd shot and killed a young Yosemite employee, Chester Givens, after a quarrel. Givens's body was found at the base of the famed Yosemite Falls.*

He lowered the page and focused on Louise. "Did you read this one?"

"No, not yet. Melba took it away from me. She said it wasn't suitable. Why, what does it say?" She reached toward his arm.

"No matter." He stood, pulling it out of her reach. "More lies." Only they weren't.

Melba met his eyes, the haunted expression cutting into his soul. Olivia's secret was out. How would his friends react to the truth about her?

After a long moment, she sat down beside Olivia and took her hands. "Those reporters don't know their ears from their elbows, Olivia. No one will believe it. Especially not when they see your gorgeous portrayals of Yosemite in a real magazine."

Clark tore the article out and ripped it into multiple pieces, fully intending to feed it in the next campfire he saw.

Louise jumped to her feet. "Why did you do that?"

He set his jaw. "No one needs to read that."

Twenty-Two

O livia tossed and turned on the camp bed, sleep eluding her no matter how hard she tried to shut out the world.

She'd heard Melba and Clark whispering outside long after she'd retired with the girls. The sad tones in their voices tore at her heart, yet she couldn't bring herself to join them. Facing Melba—or anyone—seemed like too much to bear on this horrible evening. What must she be thinking? The only details of the conversation Olivia could make out through the heavy canvas were that Clark convinced his friend to drive the auto home and that Clark was going to bed down out front with blankets borrowed from the camp.

Knowing he was still there brought an odd mixture of relief and dismay. He couldn't maintain this pace forever. He was already working dawn to dusk—and now sleeping on the hard ground?

The look on his face when he'd torn up the article had sent a chill through her. She knew in that instant that whatever they'd written was far worse than the lies about her and Marcus Vanderbilt. They must have uncovered the truth—her real name and her father's sordid connection to Yosemite. Marcus had promised to ruin her. Perhaps he'd delivered the stolen newspaper clipping to the magazine's editors. Apparently destroying her work wasn't enough. He needed to devastate her as well.

The only comfort she had was that *Hearsay* was known for printing lies and half truths. No one expected them to actually get it right.

She wrapped both arms around her pillow, the memory of the long ride back to the camp bringing a small measure of peace. At least she'd managed to tell Clark the story first. He'd taken it in stride. Perhaps nothing would shock the man.

The thought took some of the sting from the day.

She rolled over once more, the cot squeaking as she did so. Could Clark hear every sound from where he lay? Probably so, since she could hear the woman next door snoring. Olivia sat up and reached for her bulky sweater, drawing it on over her nightdress. She ran her hand over the thick blue fibers. Melba had loaned her the garment before she left on the first hike with Clark. Olivia had tried to return it, but Melba insisted she keep it. The sweater had become like a trusted friend.

She tiptoed to the door and slipped outside without making a sound. The girls needed their rest. They'd been up far too late.

Moonlight painted the campsite in silvery-gray tones. Clark lay curled on his side in front of the tent, his head resting on one arm.

Olivia sank down on the step, staring out over the somber scene, for once not longing for a paintbrush. This picture was far too precious, and she didn't want to share it with anyone. Especially not if someone could take it from her as easily as they had taken her others. She pulled the sweater close, burying her chin in its softness. What would the morning hold? More painting? Her stomach churned. Maybe spending one day without touching a brush would help. She'd been working too hard, the "job" now sucking any joy from the act of creating.

Frank had carefully crafted the image she presented to the art world, but the misshapen costume no longer fit. How would people view Olivia Rutherford now? The artist who apparently carried on with married men? The daughter of a murderer? Her life had gone into a tailspin, and she didn't know how to stop the madness. If only the rest of the world could see her as Clark did.

He stirred, lifted his head, and then sat upright. "Liv? What's wrong?"

"Shh." She stood and walked toward him. "I couldn't sleep. I didn't mean to wake you."

"Here." He sat cross-legged and patted the blanket beside him. "Sit down. You didn't wake me. When I opened my eyes and saw you over there, I thought maybe I was dreaming."

She sat close, laying her head on his warm arm. He smelled of pine needles. "Let's say you are."

He stifled a yawn. "Good. Then I'll be rested come morning."

"I think it is morning. Hear the birds?" All around them, the tiny forest birds of Yosemite were waking, trilling their excitement to the world. "Frances could tell us their names, if she were awake."

"Mmm. Good morning, then." He wrapped one arm behind her back, pulling her into the safety of his side and planting a kiss on her forehead. "A fresh, new day. 'But though our outward man perish, yet the inward man is renewed day by day.'"

"What's that from?"

"Paul's second letter to the Corinthians."

"The outward man. That's what haunts me now—my outward woman."

He ran his fingers along her arm. "You're not worried about that trashy magazine, are you?"

"How could I not be? They made me sound like a harlot. And then telling the world about my father?" Her throat squeezed. "I suppose that part's true, but I've barely come to terms with it myself—and now the whole world knows."

"So what? Let them know. It doesn't diminish who you are. You're still the woman God made you to be."

"At least on the inside." The touch of his hand sent cracks through her reserve, emotion seeping out. "Recite the verse again, will you?"

"'But though our outward man perish, yet the inward man is renewed day by day.' Later Paul wrote, 'While we look not at the things which are seen, but at the things which are not seen: for the things which are seen are temporal; but the things which are not seen are eternal.'"

"What does that mean?"

"That all this"—he gestured around them—"it's all temporary. Here today, gone tomorrow. Much like the story in that insipid magazine."

"Which is now in a hundred pieces, thanks to you. Louise may never forgive you."

He glanced down, sheepishly. "I didn't think that one through. But I didn't want her to read the rest." He brought his attention back to her face. "Like the verse says, everything that's seen crumbles eventually. Even our outer bodies. But the inside, the unseen…" He brushed a finger against the base of her throat. "Is eternal."

"Eternal. Me?" She laughed. "I'm not so sure."

His brows knit together. "He grants eternal life to those who believe."

"I do believe, but I doubt He's pleased with how I've turned out."

"He sees your heart. As do I." He took her hand, running his thumb along her knuckles. "And I think it's beautiful."

Olivia glanced up to where the sky was warming with color. "Renewed day by day?"

"Yes ma'am."

"No matter what magazines say. Or what people whisper about me." She took a deep breath, the ache in her chest lessening with each passing moment. Maybe she could still do this. She turned to face Clark, the hairs on his unshaven jaw revealing a hint of red among the brown—burnt sienna and raw umber. This man was a constant surprise. "You're quoting Scripture a lot this morning."

"I guess that's what happens when you spend the night in prayer—when I wasn't sleeping, anyway."

"Prayer? For me?" The thought tugged at her.

He laid his palm over her hand. "Always, love. Always."

The words wove themselves through Olivia's heart. *Not Liv. Love.*

Rain coursed down the outside of the office window, the fourth day in a row. Summer seemed determined to end early, no matter Clark's wishes. He stared out at the gloom as he pressed the telephone against his ear. "Another article? When are these wolves going to let up?"

Frank Robinson's voice crackled at the far end. "Not while there's still interest. Now they're claiming she's on the verge of a nervous breakdown. Heartbroken over Vanderbilt's sudden departure."

"That's total malarkey. She was never interested in him in the first place." The very idea made his skin crawl.

"But listen, it might work in her favor. Instead of a nameless woman up there painting sweet nature scenes, she's a heartsick artist seeking solace in nature—that or a woman scorned. And you know what they say about those."

"How does any of that help?" He gripped the coffee cup John had set in front of him.

"Trust me. I know how to sell art, and it's as much about selling the artist as it is the paint on the page. I'm going to work on getting a few more articles printed. Maybe in some other magazines. Liv needs to make use of this publicity, get folks interested in her story. Then they'll be interested in her art."

Selling the artist. Clark grimaced as he hung up the phone. Olivia may view Robinson as a father figure, but every conversation with the man left Clark feeling like he'd just walked through a spider's web. He scrubbed a palm across his face.

John leaned against the doorframe, a mug cradled in his grip. "That fellow doesn't seem concerned about long-distance charges. This art business must be pretty lucrative."

Clark sat on the corner of the desk. "I'd be happy if he showed a little concern about his artist."

"I'm still stunned to hear she's connected with the Givens murder." His friend's face darkened. "I thought that story was long over."

"She's not connected. Her father was." Clark let a long breath escape his lips. "We cannot hold her responsible for a tragedy that happened when she was a child. She's lived under a terrible burden ever since."

"I suppose that's true." John crossed his arms. "How's she handling the pressure?"

"She's focusing on the job she came to do."

"Seems to me she's focusing on you." He raised one brow.

Clark smoothed a hand across the front of his uniform jacket. "I won't complain about that."

"I must say, I never pictured you with a flapper."

The offhand comment further soured Clark's mood. "She's not, and I'd appreciate you not referring to her as such."

John raised his hands. "No offense intended. Hey, I married a vaudeville star. I endured more than my share of ribbing, let me tell you. Still do."

Clark pushed down his anger. If anyone could understand the situation, it was John. "But we know who they really are, on the inside." He took a sip of coffee.

"Indeed. And that's why we jump to their defense so quickly." The ranger cleared his throat. "Speaking of moving quickly, Melba thinks you should propose to the girl."

Clark choked. After a quick swallow, he wiped the back of his hand across his mouth. "Isn't it a little early for that?"

"Not if you know what you want. Are you in love with her? Because it sure looks that way. You spend every waking moment with her."

"I"—Clark shook his head—"I'm not ready to have this conversation."

"With me, or with her?" John cocked his head.

"You've always been too nosy for your own good, you know that?"

"A woman like that isn't going to stay around here long. Melba and I have done everything we can to clear the path for you, but you can't wait on this forever. Sometimes you don't seem to recognize a good thing when it's in front of your face. That's where we come in." He lifted his cup. "You do love her, don't you?"

"Of course I do." The words sounded hollow at best. "But I have nothing to offer her. As of September, I've got no job, no home, no future."

"And soon—no girl."

He shot a look at the chief ranger. "How can I ask her to follow me when I don't know where I'm going? What if God calls me back into the ministry?"

"Maybe he wants you to follow her. Have you thought of that?" John chuckled, shaking his head. "And for a preacher man, your faith is pretty weak. If God calls you back into ministry, He'll decide those details. Not you, not her. Him."

"That's a little too easy."

"That's faith, Clark. And trust. But I shouldn't have to tell you that."

"I'll think about it." As if he'd been thinking of anything else the past few days. Every time he looked into her blue eyes, all he could think about was keeping her close forever. But didn't she have enough on her mind right now?

John grunted. "So how much longer before she's finished?"

The question tugged at his heart. "Soon. The rain slowed her down a little, but she still wants to do a few more paintings. We're going up to Mirror Lake tomorrow."

"About that..." John leaned back in his chair. "Traffic's eased since the weather's turned. I think we can spare you for the day."

A whole day with Olivia? He couldn't imagine anything better. "Are you sure?"

"If you don't mind missing out on a day's wages. I have a couple of guys looking for extra hours. It'll make everybody happy."

"It certainly will. Thanks, John." With a whole day at their disposal, they could go farther afield. Olivia had met some rock climbers at camp and was fascinated by their stories of scaling Half Dome. If the weather cooperated, they could get a closer look and give her the opportunity to capture the view for the magazine. He glanced out the window. Not that it looked promising. Right now it was raining hammer handles.

The chief ranger's brow furrowed. "And Clark, if she is getting...disturbed by any of this gossip, keep a close eye on her. We don't want any accidents on the trail. I've heard those artist types can be pretty sensitive. Givens wasn't my first time recovering a body. My second month here, I saw a girl throw herself over one of the waterfalls because of a lost love. I still wake up in a cold sweat sometimes thinking about it."

"She's not like that, John. And there's no lost love—remember?"

"Sure. Just be aware."

"I am. But she's got the girls to think of. Don't let that magazine trash fool you."

"Of course." John nodded. "I just never want to see something like that happen here again. Not on my watch."

Clark slipped out of the ranger's office, eager to solidify plans for tomorrow. They could hit the trail early and be back before the Firefall. The evening entertainment had become a ritual for them, and last night's dance had given him the opportunity to hold her in public without any raised eyebrows. Melba had even worked Louise into the program, as an assistant to a local magician. Olivia's starry-eyed sister was having the time of her life and really was quite the light on stage.

Thankfully, the rain had cleared enough each evening to allow the show to happen. It had been a solace to the campers driven inside by the poor weather. The storms had also sent him back to sleeping in his quarters in the Rangers' Club at night. He'd camped in rain plenty of times, but Olivia insisted she wouldn't be able to rest knowing he was out there in the damp.

He decided to leave the General munching on her hay and walk over to Camp Curry to meet the Rutherford girls. The walk would give him time to consider how to break Robinson's news to Olivia. It seemed strange how easily this magazine had gathered dirt on the story. And why was anyone else interested?

Clark picked up his walking pace, Frank Robinson's words still bouncing around in his head. *"It's as much about selling the artist as it is the paint on the page."*

The dealer had sent Liv here to illustrate a story for a magazine. When had Olivia Rutherford *become* the story?

⸻

Rain dripped from the trees limbs, pattering on the canvas roof of her tent. It had taken Olivia more than an hour to explain the truth about their father to the two girls. Afterward, Louise disappeared to spend time with her new friends next door. Olivia hoped she wouldn't share any details from their conversation. Frances, looking exhausted, surrounded herself with her notebooks and bird manuals and refused to look up.

Olivia sat on the edge of her cot, adding a few more details to the Glacier Point painting. She glanced at Clark, leaning against the foot of Louise's bed and watching her work. "Why do they bother writing about me?"

Clark shook his head. "I don't know. I must say, this new obsession with learning about strangers' lives—it's pretty distasteful. People should focus on their own problems."

Olivia studied the painting, adding a little extra cobalt blue to the sky. Something about the rain made her want to make the sunny picture even brighter. Rather than including Clark's silhouette the way she had for the stolen painting, this time she'd done a self-portrait based on his description of her sitting on the railing the night of the party. With the cloche hat and the shadowy dress, it could have been anyone.

He came and stood next to her. "I wish I could afford to buy that one."

"If *Scenic* doesn't claim it, I'll save it for you. You've earned it a hundred times over. And Melba told me you stopped accepting the magazine's money when you took the job with the Park Service."

"I'm no longer your guide."

"You've been at my side nearly every time I've left the campground."

"And all day tomorrow, I'm pleased to say."

Her heart lifted. "All day? That's wonderful." She turned back to stare at the painting with a critical eye. "I think I have almost enough to satisfy the editor." *And then what?* She let the question fade. Better to enjoy this evening and tomorrow. Let the future worry about itself. "So where will we go? Mirror Lake or Half Dome?"

"I suppose it depends on the weather." He propped open the tent-cabin's door, the sweet scent of rain-freshened air rushing in. "We don't want to go near Half Dome if there's a chance of lightning."

"I trust your judgment. Oh"—she straightened and turned to face him—"the girls won't be coming along. They agreed to help Melba with a special act the camp is putting together for this weekend. Both girls will be in it, right Frances?"

Frances finally lifted her head. "Yes. I'm doing birdcalls for one of the musical numbers. Mr. Sonn has been teaching me. We'll practice tomorrow."

"Isn't that wonderful?" The idea of an entire day alone with Clark brought a warm flush to Olivia's cheeks. "Melba has been so good to us."

"That she has." Clark walked to Olivia's side, reaching down to grasp her hand. "A day alone? Remind me to thank her later."

Olivia ducked her head. "How much more could I besmirch my reputation? It's already in tatters."

"I'll be a gentleman, I promise."

She'd expect nothing less. "I'll order some box lunches from the dining hall. Wherever you decide to go, I'll be ready."

He sat down beside her, the cot creaking under his weight.

Wish we could go right now. She set the brush down, wrapped her arm around his waist, and leaned against his shoulder. Could she get away with kissing him since Frances had her nose in a book? She glanced over at her sister. Best not risk it. She contented herself by running her fingers along his wrist instead. "Tomorrow will be here before you know it."

Clark grasped Liv's hand, helping her navigate past a rocky point in the trail barely visible in the early morning shadows. Her skin was cool to the touch, so he tucked her hand inside his arm and placed his other hand on top of it. "Are you cold?"

"Not too bad. The hiking will warm me up. At least it's not raining."

"We're not going very far. Mirror Lake is a short distance up Tenaya Canyon. But it's a lovely spot."

"I'm looking forward to seeing it. With a name like that, it sounds picture perfect."

Clark glanced upward, surveying the sky. "I wish the weather promised to stay nice. We'll be lucky if we make it through the day without another thunderstorm. We may have to head back early. That's one of the reasons I decided to stay in the valley."

She shivered. "I've had splendid weather for most of my stay, so I can't really complain now."

He'd managed to squeeze all her supplies into one large canvas backpack, but the edge of the box dug into his side. "So how many paintings have you finished?"

Olivia squeezed his hand. "Well over a dozen, thanks to you. I hope the editors will be pleased."

"They're fortunate to have hired such a talented artist."

Her brow furrowed. "I'm sure they wish they'd found someone less scandal ridden. I had no idea this gossip would get so out of hand."

He turned to study her face. "Have you ever met the *Scenic* editor?"

"No, but Frank has."

He dropped her hand in order to adjust the backpack again. "They've been very quiet through all this. Is it possible they don't mind the rumors?"

She stopped in the middle of the trail. "Why would you think that?"

"For the publicity. Frank said your paintings are becoming more valuable as people talk about you. That in turn would sell more magazines, wouldn't it?"

"Frank also seemed concerned they would drop the contract. I made the mistake of humiliating Marcus back at Glacier Point. So when he found the newspaper article about my father, he probably couldn't wait to deliver it to *Hearsay*." She started walking again.

Just hearing her say Vanderbilt's name sent a jab through his chest. He hoped never to run into that man again. "You were right to refuse him, Olivia. The man is a bully."

"Marcus even claimed that Frank told him I was interested in a liaison. So he's more than a bully; he's deluded."

Frank told him. It seemed like he'd done little to help her out of this situation—especially considering he'd put her up to the charade in the first place. Granted, Robinson was a businessman, but it seemed like a shady way to sell paintings.

As they approached the lake, she gasped. "Oh, Clark. It's beautiful."

It was. Even with the cloud cover, the lake brilliantly reflected the mountains behind it. "I was afraid with as hot as it's been this summer, it might have dried up. But then, it's been raining all week."

"It's perfect. So serene. Oh, imagine what it must look like in winter."

"It's beautiful. Tenaya Canyon is one of my favorite places." He glanced around the small valley, granite peaks rising on all sides. Even better, they had the area to themselves. Most park visitors favored the waterfalls for their stunning vistas. This quiet spot went largely undiscovered. "John says the lake's gotten a little smaller every year. Eventually it'll fill in and become a meadow.

Olivia frowned. "All the more reason to capture it now. Oh, I wish the girls were here. I'd love to paint them down there by the water."

Clark slung off the pack and pulled out her wooden easel, then assembled it with practiced ease. "If you finish early, we could walk up the Snow Creek Trail for a few miles. It's a steep climb, but there are some pretty views of Half Dome along the way.

"We have all day, right?"

"If the weather holds." He pulled her into his arms, planting a kiss on the top of her head. In a few minutes he'd lose her to her work, so he wanted to snatch the moment while he could.

"Then I suppose there's no hurry." She gazed up at him, her eyes shining in the morning light. Wrapping her arms around his waist, she pulled him close.

"I'm a lucky man." He ran his hands down her lower back, appreciating the way she fit in his arms.

"You could say that again." She smiled. "Or you could just kiss me."

Rather than give in to her demand right away, he leaned down and buried his face in her neck, breathing in the scent of her. "You smell sweet—nutty."

"It's probably the soap I borrowed from Frances. Honey and almond. Do you like it?"

"Be glad I'm not a bear." He slid his nose up along her ear and nuzzled her temple. "But if I kiss you now, I might not let you ignore me for the next few hours."

Her eyes remained closed, but her lips curved upward in a faint smile. "I couldn't ignore you if I tried. I can always feel you nearby, like the warmth of a campfire."

He slid his fingers through her hair, focusing on the soft tickle of her breath against his skin. "After you finish capturing that lake with your brush, I'll kiss you. But not before. I don't trust myself."

"But by then, there might be others up here, picnicking by the lake."

"Then we'll add a few lines to your scandal sheets. 'Artist caught in embrace with a nobody park ranger.'"

"No." She drew back and lifted her eyes to meet his. "It'd be, 'Artist falls madly in love with rugged man of the mountains.'"

Despite the teasing lilt of her voice, the words wrapped around his heart. It took every bit of strength he had to follow through on his promise, when every fiber in his being wanted to kiss her soundly right now.

He rubbed his thumb down the side of her cheek, tracing the curve of her jaw. "These past few weeks have been the best of my life, did you know that?"

She tucked her head against his chest, just under his chin. "I feel the same. I love being myself with you."

"That's because I love you just as you are, Liv." He pushed the words out, determined not to let this moment slip past, as he had so many others in his life.

She didn't move for a long moment. "You do?"

"I do." He squeezed his arms around her back.

"And I love you." She lifted her hand, brushing the tip of her finger across his lower lip. "So, it's really too bad you can't kiss me until later."

He sucked in a deep breath. "You do know how to torture a man."

Twenty-Three

Olivia paused to stretch her back as she waited for a layer of color to dry. The trees beyond the lake gave way to balding cliff faces above, misty clouds clinging to the rounded top of Half Dome. The mountain scene wrapped around this hidden glen and seemed to protect it from the pressures of the outside world.

Let the gossips say what they wanted about Olivia Rutherford, because here she was just Liv. *Clark's Liv.* The thought settled into her chest like a seed ready to sprout. If only she could remain here forever. Safe in his arms. In the arms of this place. Clark had called it a granite cathedral, so maybe she was safe in God's arms, too.

Her illustrations for *Scenic* were almost finished, but the idea of leaving Yosemite—of leaving Clark—seemed like an impossible task. Could she return to being Olivia Rutherford now that she remembered what it was like to be herself?

Clark crouched at the lake's edge, staring into the shallow water.

She let her eyes trace his lines, memorizing his physique and position so she could add his image to the final painting when she got to the detail work. Even now she could feel their time together ebbing away, and it fueled her desire to capture every moment before it was gone.

He loves me. She curled her fingers around the flat wooden handle of her squirrel-tail wash brush as she sealed Clark's form in her mind and heart. *That handsome, rugged, thoughtful man loves* me. The sentiment was too precious, too implausible to grasp. Securing the scene on paper was the only way she knew how to process the emotion threatening to overwhelm her senses. She cleared her throat. "What are you looking at so intensely?"

A grin spread across his face. "A salamander, working his way through the mud."

Less than romantic. She turned back to the drying painting. The sky overhead darkened with every passing minute. She needed to finish the picture before rain moved in to ruin her efforts. Olivia got to work, painting as rapidly as the watery medium would allow.

After a time, Clark stood, focusing on something behind her.

Approaching hoofbeats caught her attention as well. She turned to see John riding up, the General trailing behind, saddled and ready.

Clark hurried toward him. "What's wrong?"

John dismounted, his expression grim. "Remember when I said if Joseph Morris got himself in trouble in the backcountry, I expected you to go retrieve him? I'm calling in that promise."

Olivia shaded her eyes to study John's face. "What's happened?"

The ranger took off his hat and ran a quick hand through his hair, standing the short locks on end. "He's a day overdue, and I just received a report…" He took a deep breath, glancing down at his polished boots. "A visitor thinks he saw someone—a body—down a ravine. He couldn't get close enough to help, so he rode to Tuolumne for help. My man there telephoned headquarters."

"A body?" Clark's face went ashen.

"No need to jump to conclusions until we see for ourselves. He might be injured and unable to climb out."

"You think it's Morris? Has anyone seen his horse?"

"No. But I've got no other reports of people missing, and the location's about right."

Clark turned to Olivia. "Looks like our day has to be cut short. I'll help you pack up, and then we'll escort you back to camp."

She gestured at her easel. "You two go ahead. I'll be fine."

His brow knitted. "I'm not leaving you behind."

Her throat tightened. She didn't like the idea of being alone out here either, but it made no sense to delay them. "Just because some fast-talking con artists talked me out of one painting doesn't mean I'd fall for such antics again." She glanced back down the trail. "I'm less than a mile away from the road and close to Camp Curry as well. I can make my way there on my own. You two have a job to do."

Clark's gaze darkened. "Liv, with everything that's going on"—he looked at the steel-gray sky beyond the peak—"and another storm rolling in… Promise me you'll leave right away. I'm not comfortable with you here alone, close to camp or not."

"I'll pack up my supplies and head back. But I don't want you to wait for me."

Clark sighed. "I'll swing by Camp Curry and ask Melba to come meet you. You might need help to carry your easel and such."

"Melba and the girls are practicing for Saturday's show. I'll be fine." She reached out and squeezed his wrist. "But poor Ranger Morris might not be. You should go."

John had stepped away to give them privacy, so she didn't hesitate as Clark pulled her close and murmured into her ear. "I'll bring you back tomorrow so you can finish. Otherwise I'll never get that kiss."

She laid her head on his chest, listening to his heartbeat through the warmth of his shirt. "Please, be careful. Both of you." The image of a broken body at the bottom of a ravine sent her thoughts spiraling in unwelcome directions. She'd never truly considered the danger of Clark's job.

"We will." He backed up, giving her one last lingering glance before swinging up onto the General's back and following John down the trail.

Olivia took a deep breath, fighting the urge to run after them. The valley that had seemed so comforting minutes ago now crowded in on all sides. She shook her arms, releasing the tension building in her muscles.

She glanced at the sky and her nearly completed work. In the short distraction, the clouds atop Half Dome had thickened, the light changing as it swept over the granite outcroppings. Olivia tried to imagine Clark still crouched at the water's edge, but his absence sent a jab through her heart. Other than his worry for her, he hadn't hesitated to jump to this man's rescue. He was probably praying for Ranger Morris with every step. Clark's concern for others was what drew her in the first place. Had anyone in her life shown her the level of compassion that this man had?

Frank's face floated through her mind, but in recent weeks, she'd even begun questioning his sincerity. All his careful attention, his grooming of her career—was that really for her sake?

Olivia emptied the water cup on the nearby grass and piled the paint pots back into her box at a rapid clip. She could organize them later in the tent as Louise plied her with anecdotes of her newfound fame on the Curry stage.

The fresh scent of rain picked up on the breeze as a few droplets splattered down on her paint box. "No, not already." She slammed the lid closed and fastened the latch before springing up and looking around. She should have planned better. Scooping up her easel, she dashed for a nearby grove of trees, clutching the painting in place. After setting it down, she hurried back, snatched up her wooden box and tucked it under her arm. She could wait out the worst of the cloudburst in the shelter of the limbs.

Olivia shivered in the damp shade of the trees, waiting as the rain shower worked its way through. As it began to ease, a man appeared on the trail, coming from the direction of the road, decked out in rain gear and a sturdy canvas pack. Olivia's heart jumped, but she forced herself to relax. Just another hiker out for the day and caught in the cloudburst.

She bent down to fold her easel.

"Olivia?"

She spun toward the male voice. Clark couldn't be back so soon—and without the General. Squinting, she watched as the man drew back his oil-skin hood.

"Frank?" Her heart jumped. She rushed at her friend, pulling him into a quick embrace. "What are you doing here? How did you know where to find me?"

"I heard you were finishing up, so I wanted to see what you'd accomplished in such a short time." His lined face was dotted with raindrops. "A young woman at the campground told me where you were hiding today."

"Look at you—you're dripping." She laughed. "Why didn't you wait until I returned?"

"I know you, Olivia. If you were in the midst of a masterpiece, a little rain wasn't going to stop you." He grinned and spread his arms. "See, I was correct."

She wrapped her arms around herself and shivered, bouncing up and down to stave off the chill. "Actually, I was just leaving. Let me stash this piece in my box, and we can head back to camp together."

Rain still pattered down around the valley, bouncing in heavy splats on the rocky trail, but the branches protected them from the worst of it.

He folded his arms, his coat rustling. "Do I get to see the latest painting?"

Frank hadn't seen any of her work since she arrived. She picked up the paper, curling around the edges from the damp and shielded it from any stray drops. "It's still rough. I have more to do." The scene brought a smile to her face even now. The brilliance of Half Dome mirrored in the lake, stretching down to touch Clark's image in the lower corner, his hand brushing the mountain's reflection. "Clark once said, 'Faith can move mountains, but time spent in the mountains sometimes moves us toward faith.' That's what I was thinking of when I painted this."

The mountains had moved her a few steps toward faith—but this gentle man had done far more. Olivia hoped he was safe now, wherever he was. *Lord, watch over him.*

Frank studied it in silence, the lines deepening around his eyes. "Liv, you've changed. This place has changed you."

She turned back to the painting, her stomach tightening. *Changed?* She tried to see it through Frank's eyes, comparing it to her earlier works. Her style had shifted somewhat in the past month, matured. Her broad strokes of color had given way to a gentler rendering. Yosemite had changed her, from the inside out. "I suppose that's true. But hopefully for the better."

He stepped closer, taking the edge of the paper in his fingers. "It's breathtaking."

"But will the editors like it?"

"No question about it. You've exceeded everyone's expectations." He turned his attention to her. "In more ways than one."

"I don't understand."

"All of this hoopla about you—"

A jolt burst through her chest. "They're firing me, aren't they?" She lowered the painting. "Everything we've worked for, Frank. All the careful sculpting of my image…"

He chuckled, shaking his head. "Liv, Liv. You've got it all wrong."

"What do you mean?"

Frank walked to the edge of the trees and studied the clearing sky. "Why did we create Olivia Rutherford in the first place?" He turned back to her. "The name, the clothes, the makeup?"

"So I could mingle with the wealthy art collectors without making a stir."

"Wrong." He pointed a finger toward her. "Making a stir was exactly what we wanted. Olivia Rutherford, the avant-garde flapper artist. The dramatic hair and makeup, the carefree attitude—she was poised for crazy success."

"And look at her now."

A huge grin crossed his face, and he spread his arms as wide as Santa Claus welcoming the children to a Christmas party. "Yes, look at her now. On the mind of every art buyer in the country."

"But for what? Not my talent."

"Who cares about your talent?" Frank snapped, his voice taking a hard edge. "This is about business."

She shivered, her sleeves damp from the rain. "So it doesn't matter that they're firing me? Is that what you're saying?"

"They're not firing you, sweetheart." One corner of his mouth quirked upward. "But I've got bigger plans for those paintings. And for you. *Scenic* is a waste of your time. I've got an idea that will skyrocket Olivia Rutherford into everlasting fame."

⌒

Clark hunched his shoulders against the smattering rain, trusting the General to pick her steps with care along the slick trail. His heart hammered in his chest as if it were *his* legs doing the work rather than the horse's.

He pushed away any thought of what they might find at the end of this journey. He couldn't let himself think that far. The reports were sketchy at best. Just because the man was inexperienced and far overdue didn't mean he'd met his demise. Clark swallowed against the knot tightening in his throat. And because someone spotted something they thought *might* be a body. The story was far too murky.

But his imagination had already latched onto the grim picture as if it were truth. Clark had taken the plum post in Yosemite Valley, casting an inexperienced ranger out into the field alone. Clark knew every rock, stream, and trail in the park. He should be the one at the bottom of the ravine. Not Morris.

John called to him to slow. "We need to pace ourselves, Clark. It's going to be a long day in the saddle." The wind whipped away his words.

Clark turned to give his response the best chance of reaching his friend's ears. "If he's injured, we need to hurry."

"We won't be any help to him if we don't arrive in one piece."

Clark pulled up on the reins, giving John a chance to come up beside him. "It's my fault he's out there."

The ranger's horse bobbed his head, likely shaking water from his ears. John's expression was grim. "I gave the orders. Not you."

"If I weren't so enamored with the idea of Olivia's attention, I wouldn't have taken the trade."

"You're a man in love, Clark. That's a good place to be." John shook his head. "Morris wanted this posting. He'd been pestering me about it for months. He imagines himself as some great explorer. I should have realized —that level of enthusiasm makes a man careless."

"We don't know what happened."

"I'll tell you what happened. He was trying something foolish." John scowled. "I knew better than to send him out there unaccompanied. Young and stupid. It'll get you killed every time."

Clark used a bandanna to mop the moisture from his face. "You know what that makes us? Old and cautious."

"I wouldn't say old. You're not even pushing thirty. But a little caution goes a long way out here."

"And that's why you're the chief." Clark urged his mount forward as the trail narrowed. John might be his boss, but it was Clark's heart at stake if this man was dead. Losing a church because of a weak moment was one thing. Losing a man's life? That would be more than he could bear.

A movement in the distance caught his attention. Rising in the saddle, he squinted against the afternoon light. A man was riding along the far edge of the valley where mist clung to the tops of the trees. His green coat nearly blended with the forest backdrop, but the black and white pinto stood out against the landscape. Clark reigned his mount to a stop and held up a hand to John.

Pointing at the rider, he swiveled in his saddle. "Any chance that's him?"

John came alongside and pressed a set of his binoculars to his eyes. "By golly."

Clark sank down in the seat, his arms falling loose at his sides. "Thank You, Lord."

"It's Morris, all right." John lowered the field glasses, water dripping off the eyepieces. "But he's not safe yet. After the day I've had, I might just shoot him myself."

Olivia gripped her upper arms with tight fingers. "I'm here on contract,

Frank. I signed it myself." Her stomach recoiled. "These paintings belong to *Scenic.*"

Frank splayed his fingers. "I need you to take a deep breath, Liv. I did this for you, and everything's settling into place like clockwork."

When had Frank turned into a stranger? A greedy stranger.

"I've been pushing you since you were a child, Liv. Not just the painting, but everything about you. Now is the time to strike. You're poised on the edge, waiting to dive in."

Dive into what?

"When we are done, there will be hundreds of buyers lined up, clamoring for an Olivia Rutherford original." Frank took the picture from her hand and fastened it into her art box. "I've got our next step all figured out, Liv."

She'd never minded Frank using her childhood nickname, but now it jabbed like a needle. "You've lost the right to call me that."

Frank snapped the lid closed. "I'll call you whatever you want, but mostly I call you a sound investment. I told you I was up to my neck in debt. You're my last client. My only client. I asked you for help, and what did you do? You ran off to Oakland without producing anything. I could have been ruined."

"I came back."

"Yes, you did." A smile spread across his face, the white bristles of his mustache twitching with the sudden motion. "And that's when it dawned on me." He stepped close. "You came out here to illustrate a story, but the bigger story is you. That's why I spilled some juicy tidbits to *Hearsay.*"

Her breath caught in her chest. "That was you?" Her knees weakened. "Why would you do that?"

He shrugged. "Publicity, Liv. Everything that happened pushed you further into the limelight—and made you work harder. The perfect combination. The job, the Vanderbilts, the travel, even the theft—it all made you interesting to buyers. But when I read the letter from your father? It explained so much. I knew you had a silly fear of Yosemite, but I didn't realize the extent of the…uh…situation." He tipped his head, wisps of hair floating about his face. "It was too good to pass up. With a little work, we could push this story beyond California. You could become a national phenomenon."

Would she never be free of her father? "Those weren't your secrets to tell. I can't believe you'd do that to me." The realization cut through her. "To my family." She snatched the box out of his hands. "I've played enough of your games."

"I think you've forgotten something, sweetheart." Frank's eyes narrowed. "You signed an exclusive contract with me years ago. I have the rights to sell your work as I deem fit. That was our deal." He pulled off his raincoat. "Which is why I stopped by and collected all the paintings from your campsite before I came to meet you."

Her stomach dropped. "You—you what?"

"Don't worry, they're safe. I've got a vehicle stashed down the road."

"Those are supposed to pay for my sisters' schooling. It's my whole reason for taking this job. You can't take that away from me."

"I'm not taking anything away, Liv. We're still in this together."

Her thoughts scrambled. Frank wasn't making sense. She clutched the box to her chest. "No, we're not. You're threatening to sell my work out from under me. We're not 'together' on any of this."

"Listen." He dug in his coat pocket. "The press isn't done writing about you yet. When they are, that's when I'll release these paintings for sale—at the height of public fascination about the mysterious Olivia Rutherford. Not a moment before."

"What else could they have to say? They've already raked me through the mud. I've got no secrets left to hide."

He pulled a newspaper from the inside pocket of his coat, unfolded it, and held it for her to see. "*The San Francisco Chronicle*. We've grown beyond *Hearsay* now."

"*America's darling artist—lost in the wilds of Yosemite.*"

Olivia's skin crawled. "That's ridiculous. Why would they think I was lost?"

His expression grew solemn. "Because that's what I told them."

Twenty-Four

C lark dismounted, stretching his back after a long day in the saddle. He walked to the far side of the horses in an attempt to hide his amusement as the young ranger endured the brunt of John's relief-turned-to-anger.

Morris threw up his hands. "I'm only one day behind. How could you expect me to see everything on this trail in seven days? It's not unusual for men to come in late."

John scowled. "You're two days late now, and you failed to check in at Tuolumne Meadows when you passed that way."

"That's because I took the long way around. There's more to see on the far side of the mountain."

Clark ran his hand down the General's neck, shaking his head. "Wrong answer."

The veins on the side of John's temples stood out. "Do you realize we've been riding all day in a rainstorm because someone thought you were dead?"

Ranger Morris shuffled his feet, creating grooves in the mud with the park-issued boots. "Well, I'm not. That's good news, right?"

Clark joined them in order to keep his friend from doing his colleague any permanent damage. "That's great news, Joseph. We're very glad you're alive." He eyed John, hoping the chief ranger had the good sense to agree. "But as I see it, we still have one problem."

Morris glanced up. "What's that?"

John sighed, pushing his hat back. "Who's at the bottom of the ravine?"

⟶

"But I'm not lost." Olivia pushed her hands into the arms of her sweater, glad for its warmth, damp though it was. "I imagine they'll figure out the truth when I show up for the Firefall tonight."

"The public doesn't care about the truth. You know that." Frank reached down and collected her canvas bag. "Besides...you're not back yet. Liv, listen to me." Frank stepped closer, the scent of his cologne mingling with the fragrance of the wet leaves. "This is our golden opportunity. Stay out here a while longer. Let 'em sweat a little."

"Let who sweat? My sisters? My friends? Clark?"

Frank cocked his head. "That's the second time you've mentioned the guide. Is there something I should know?"

Olivia pulled the empty bag over her shoulder. She'd tuck the box inside once she was away from Frank. "Let's see—is there something I should know about your dealings with Marcus Vanderbilt?"

"I already told you about that. The man's a chump for a pretty face. Look at the Little Bo Peep he married."

"He told me you asked him to keep an eye on me. Did you also tell him to steal one of my paintings and destroy the rest? Is that part of your publicity scheme?"

"Of course not." Frank folded the long coat over his arm and pushed back his straw boater. "But you were shortsighted enough to spurn a man of his status and wealth. Vanderbilt feeds off his pride. Why do you think he buys and donates so much art? It's not from the goodness of his heart. Sometimes he bores of his prize, but usually it's because he's building his name—something akin to a gigantic bronze statue of himself. And you had the gall to spit on it. You, Livy Rudd of backwoods California." He huffed. "You think men like him take kindly to being told no?"

"I suppose not."

"Of course, excitement over the sale of that rogue painting helped speed things along, so it actually worked to our advantage. Now about this guide—"

"That's none of your business." Olivia shot him a look. At one point, she'd have been happy to tell him her news, but likely as not he'd find some way to twist it against her as well.

He shrugged off her response. "I'd hoped it wouldn't come down to this, but the *Scenic* deal won't bring in enough money to pay my debts. While you've been up here enjoying the finer life, I've had sharks breathing down my neck. I can't wait any longer. You'll help me, Liv, won't you?"

Olivia ducked out from under the tree. She'd heard enough. Now she knew why so many artists had walked out on him. Turning, she strode back toward the trail.

He hurried to catch up. "Not that way, sweetheart. We're going this way." He grabbed her elbow.

She snatched her arm back. "I'm not going anywhere with you."

"That's too bad. Because you'll never see a red cent, if that's what you decide. Olivia Rutherford has a contract to fulfill. And two baby sisters to support. Head back now, you'll have nothing but a ruined image. I own you, Liv; you know that."

Her throat squeezed. The summer was coming to a close, and the girls would be starting school. Even if she could finish another painting in time, could she sell it by herself?

"Now." He patted his bag. "I've got enough supplies for a couple of days. So what's say we head this way?" He jerked his head to the trail winding up the cliff face.

"I'm not going with you, Frank."

"Just listen to my idea first."

"Fine. What did you have in mind?" She crossed her arms. Maybe if she let him talk, he'd ramble his way back to his senses.

"We stumble back into civilization in a few days, and I'm a hero for rescuing you from the wilderness. The paintings sell for thousands—each."

"And if I don't go?"

His brow furrowed. "I didn't want it to come to this, Liv, but I've got too much riding on this deal." He reached into the pocket of his coat and drew out a revolver.

He set his jaw. "If you don't cooperate with my plan, there will be one final news story. 'Lovelorn artist casts herself off waterfall.'"

Twenty-Five

Clark eased back and edged over the lip of the cliff. He and John had rigged a doubled rope in a *Z* shape, circling it under Clark's thigh and up over his shoulder for stability. Even with the extra help, his arms trembled as he struggled to maintain his grasp. "John, you got a good grip? I don't like the looks of this first stretch." His boot slid against the wet granite as he searched for a toehold.

"I've got you." His friend braced the line from above.

"There's a good crevice off to your left." Morris lay on his belly on the rock, guiding from the higher vantage point. "Take it slow."

Clark sucked in a deep breath, leaning back against the makeshift harness and controlling his descent with the line in his right hand. "Slow is good." He lowered his voice, muttering under his breath. "If I'm going to die down here, I'd like a minute to pray." The fibers scraped against his neck, the friction searing his skin as he dug his toe into the crack.

Once he cleared the challenging first section, the descent went fairly quickly. Reaching the lower ledge, Clark cast a glance at the battered body lying to the side by a clump of brush. The angle of the limbs suggested that whoever had last made the trip down the cliff hadn't been as fortunate. *Lord, have mercy.* He released the rope and called up to Morris, who was peering over the edge. "Tell John to relax. I'm going to take a look."

Pushing down the sickening sensation in his stomach, Clark ran damp palms over his sleeves. A single thought had haunted him since finding Morris alive and well: *no one would report Filbert missing.* The last thing he wanted to do right now was look into the face of a dead man, particularly if it was a friend. Unfortunately, someone had to do it. He picked his way across the talus slope, littered with chunks of weathered rock.

Clark held his breath as he approached the mangled form. The clothing —a green jacket and pants—seemed strangely clean. A dark knit cap covered the head; gloves and boots intact.

He stopped, several feet away. *No blood. No scavengers.* Clark wiped a hand across his mouth. Something was off. He squinted, searching for a sign of life. Flies, anything.

Air rushed into his lungs as realization dawned. He stepped forward, dropped to his knees, and rolled the jumbled garments over. The sight of the crumpled clothing stuffed with rags like a scarecrow sent a weird combination of emotions through his gut. "What kind of sick joke?"

He pushed up to his feet, his stomach lurching almost as if it hadn't yet realized the truth. Turning back to the rangers above, he raised his arms. "There's no body. It's a hoax."

John appeared at the edge, leaning over for a better look. "You're kidding me. First Morris, and now this?"

The younger ranger shot him a hurt look.

Clark lifted the dummy, giving it a good shake before casting it back onto the ground. "Someone went to a lot of trouble to get us all the way out here."

His world stilled as the thought swept over him.

Olivia.

The trail grew rockier as they ascended. The winding switchbacks slowed their pace, and Olivia dragged her feet whenever possible, digging at the ground with her heels. Clark would come searching—eventually. Any traces she could leave behind would make his job simpler.

The missing ranger still weighed on her mind. Clark and John would be focused on him—as they should be. Frank might be carrying a gun, but as long as she cooperated, there'd be no need for him to use it. In time, she'd find a way to escape and make her way back. At least she wasn't lying at the base of a ravine somewhere. Yet.

She lifted her eyes from the trail and gazed at the view. Even in this bizarre situation, it was impossible not to glory in the incredible beauty of this place. Half Dome rose in granite splendor, misty clouds clinging to its upper reaches.

She studied Frank as he walked beside her. Rather than looking like an avid outdoorsman, Frank leaned heavily on a walking stick he'd found, puffing as he climbed the steep incline. She suddenly realized she didn't know as much about this man as she thought she did—other than his proclivity for art. It was five years since he'd discovered her painting caricatures of strangers outside the gates of the state fair, trying to make enough money to buy food. He'd sat for his portrait before informing her of his career. Probably a good thing, too, or she'd have been too nervous to paint. After that he'd taken her under his wing—offering more and more for each picture. He sold her pieces at small galleries where her work shared wall space with some of his more successful clients. And he kept that tiny caricature in a gold frame on his desk.

She hoisted the heavy pack higher on her shoulder. She didn't need to rush. After a day in Yosemite's wilderness, he'd start making mistakes. As

he'd already taught her, sometimes you had to wait for the perfect opportunity. "Where are we going, exactly?"

He paused, chest heaving. "If I told you, you wouldn't be lost, would
you?"

"So, in other words, you *intend* to get lost. That sounds like a foolproof
plan."

"I know where we are." His face was red, dots of sweat lining his forehead below his boater. "We need to lay low for a few days. Stay out of sight.
According to this map, there's some pretty secluded areas on the other side of
this ridge."

Olivia turned her attention forward again. If only she'd brought a map
herself. She'd expected to spend the day with Clark, and he knew every trail
like the back of his hand. What had he said about this area? Snow ridge?
Snow trail? Something like that. Hopefully that description didn't hold true
this time of year. Next time they stopped, she'd need to get a look at Frank's
map for herself. When she got free of him, it wouldn't help to get lost for real.

"So this Johnson fellow—you two an item?"

Hearing Clark's name sent a pang through her. "Why? Do you need
more material for your gossip campaign?"

Frank turned toward her, tugging at his ear. "I know you're angry, Liv,
but I do care about you."

A sour taste rushed her mouth. "Care about *me*? You're marching me
along at gunpoint, and you say you *care* about me?"

His bushy brows pulled together, making him look like a disgruntled
squirrel. "I've nurtured your career for years. There would be no Olivia
Rutherford without me. I *made* you."

Olivia's jaw ached from holding it closed against the barrage of words
welling up in her chest.

"Look, Liv. You're talented, sure. But you'd still be trying to rub two nickels together if it weren't for me. Now you're staying in luxury lodges, dressing in expensive gowns, dining with millionaires. Who did that, Liv? Who?"

"You did." The truth leaked out with her breath.

"I did. You wanted big money. You wanted fame. Who made that happen?"

She turned away, plodding on up the trail rather than answering.

"I did that, Liv. Me." He crunched up behind her, grabbing onto her pack and swinging her around.

She stumbled on the steep slope, her foot turning under her. A sharp pain ripped through her ankle, but she managed to stay upright.

He glared at her. "Now you want to go it alone, do you? You don't know the first thing about selling your art. Because it's not about selling pretty pictures, Liv. It's about selling you. And until you get that, you're going to need me—every step of the way."

Hot tears burned at her eyelids as she rubbed her ankle.

"You want to support those little girls? Want them to be more than you are yourself? How's that going to happen if you throw it all away now?"

"I-I don't know." She gripped the straps of her pack and hoisted it higher on her back. "But I don't like the lies. I'm tired of pretending to be somebody I'm not."

A cold wind swept up the side of the hill, catching her damp clothes and sending a chill across her skin.

John yanked off his hat. "You're getting paranoid about that woman, Clark. What would make you think this has anything to do with her?"

Clark's knees trembled after the harrowing scramble back up the cliff face. In his hurry, his damp palms had trouble finding good holds. If it hadn't been for the rope, he might not have made it in one piece, and he'd bloodied one palm in the process. "I just know. This was staged, John. You must see that."

"How would they know I'd come after you? And that Olivia would be alone?" The ranger tugged at his collar. "There are too many variables here."

"That dummy could have been set out at any time. They were waiting to make the call until Olivia and I were alone on the trail. And of course you'd call me. Who knows this region of the park better than me?"

"We tried to take her back to Curry."

"And maybe they were waiting for her there." Clark reached for the General's reins. "I'm wasting time talking to you about this."

John grabbed the bridle. "Your horse is exhausted, Clark. If Olivia doesn't show at camp tonight, Melba will sound the alarm. But if you ride back to the valley at a breakneck pace, you put both you and your mount at risk. We'll leave at first light. I think you'll find she's tucked up in her tent, tired from a night of dancing with Melba and the rest of the campers. You'll be lucky if she hasn't set her cap on one of those jazz musicians they've hired this year."

The common sense in his friend's words didn't settle well. "Remember what I said before about old and cautious?"

John stepped closer, his jaw set. "Remember what I said about young and stupid?"

Morris lifted his head. "I don't think I like this turn of the conversation. Were you talking about me?"

Clark maintained his grip on the horse's reins. "I can't stay, John. Not if there's a chance she's in danger."

"It'll be long past dark when we reach the valley—if we reach it." John sighed as he released his grip on Clark's horse.

"We?"

"I might be old and cautious, but I'm not letting you do this alone. And if nothing's wrong, we'll both be dancing with pretty girls at Camp Curry tonight."

Clark swung into the saddle. "I pray you're right."

Twenty-Six

They'd left the trail two hours ago, crunching through the underbrush and stumbling over rocks as they descended into a steep river canyon. Olivia's ankle throbbed, but it bore her weight.

The storm clouds hanging low over the granite domes obscured her view of the landmarks. It had rained off and on all afternoon and now as the sun was dropping low in the sky, Olivia's clothes were soaked through. The exertion had built a little heat, but her teeth still chattered. She pulled the sweater up around her chin. The scent of wet wool and Frances's nutty soap filled her mind with thoughts of the girls. "What sort of supplies do you have in that pack? Is it too much to hope for a tent and warm blankets?"

He darted her a look. "I'd hoped for better weather."

She shivered. "Dry clothes? Food?"

"Food, yeah. We'll build a fire, maybe."

Olivia wrapped her numb fingers around her arms. A fire, with plenty of smoke—that would bring Clark in a heartbeat, assuming he was even looking for her yet. She splashed through a small stream, the water soaking her boots further. "How far are we going tonight?"

"I want to get plenty of distance between us and that boyfriend of yours. Of course, it helps that I sent him off on a wild-goose chase."

Olivia stopped, a lump rising in her throat. "That was you?"

Frank smirked. "I'm not stupid, Olivia. If this was to work, we couldn't have the rangers swooping in to the rescue before you were even lost."

She managed a deep breath, one strand of the tension clamped about her chest easing. Ranger Morris was alive. She turned, staring back in the direction they'd come. But no one would be able to find them in this mess. And worse—no one was even looking.

⌒

The campsite was dark and cold. Clark slid out of the saddle, his hand gripping the wet horn. The trip had taken longer than expected. The camp show would be long over. "Olivia?" He hurried to the tent, calling the girls' names before flinging the door open. "Where is everyone?"

John was a few minutes behind him at most, but Clark had urged his horse to a gallop as soon as they struck the valley floor.

Now as he turned back to study the dripping circle of trees, a heaviness rode in his chest. The General stood to one side, sides heaving. Clark gathered the reins in his fist, below her chin. "I'm sorry, girl. You worked hard today, and you deserve a good rubdown and feed."

Somehow he'd manage that—as soon as he figured out where everyone was. The gloom that had fallen over his heart the moment he'd discovered the sham had only deepened on the long, dark ride. He'd not expected to find the tent empty, especially at this time of night.

The sound of hooves drew his attention as Melba rode up on her stout little mare, John at her side.

Clark rushed forward. "Tell me you know where they are."

She pulled her horse to a halt, her eyes wide. "The twins are at our house. I didn't want to leave them here alone."

Alone. He gripped the General's saddle, his knees weak.

"Clark, I'm afraid you were right." John's face was grim. "Olivia never returned."

—

Olivia scooted closer to Frank, desperate for his body heat even though the idea sat in her gut like curdled milk. The fire had largely been a smoldering waste of time, barely putting out enough heat to warm the can of beans he'd packed, much less stave off the chill that had sunk into her bones. At least he'd given her a dry shirt and wool socks, plus his oilskin coat. The rest of her wet things hung draped over the pitiful fire.

The art dealer snored, as if he bedded down in a wet forest every night.

She sat up, clutching the coat around her. *I could sneak away right now, and he'd never know.* She just needed the map. And maybe the gun.

And her clothes might be nice, too. She pulled her bare legs up under the coat's hem.

Olivia squinted in the darkness, almost able to make out the pile of supplies on his far side. Was the revolver in the pack? If she got away and hid until morning, she could probably figure out her location based on the mountains. She wasn't far from North Dome, and Yosemite Valley had to be on the far side of it. Probably. She thought back through their journey.

Definitely.

She slid her feet into her damp boots, wincing as she tightened the laces around her swollen ankle. It would be light soon. Best to gather her things and leave now, while she still had darkness for cover.

A twig cracked in the distance and she froze. Something was moving in the dark beyond the campsite. Could it be Clark?

She drew her feet back under her and strained to see through the darkness. The sounds grew more pronounced. There was definitely something coming through the night, and it wasn't bothering to mask its movements.

Olivia stood and scampered to the supplies, rifling through the bag. Now would be a really good time to find that gun.

The supplies rattled as she dug through cans and cooking implements. It seemed all Frank thought about bringing was foodstuffs. At least they wouldn't starve—assuming they survived whatever was blundering their direction.

"Frank!" She picked up the bag and hurried back to the man's side, nudging him with her boot as she continued scouring through the pockets. "Frank, there's something out there. Do you still have that gun?"

He grunted and sat up, wiping his eyes with curled fists. "What? Yeah."

As he spoke, her fingers curled around something smooth in the pack. A pocket knife? Palming it, she turned to him. "There's someone—some-*thing*—out there. Hurry."

Frank stood up, still scrubbing at his eyes. He drew the revolver from the back of his belt. "What do you suppose it is? A bear?"

The thought sliced through her. What else could make that sort of racket? She remembered the raccoons from the first night on the trail with Clark. This was no raccoon. The crashing sounds flooded her ears, her heart hammering in her chest. "The pack is full of food. It must be hungry."

"Come on." Frank grabbed her elbow. "Let's back away and see what it does."

Olivia stumbled after him, pulling the coat tight around her middle. "Shouldn't we climb a tree or something?" Why hadn't she just slept in the wet trousers? At least she had her boots on.

Frank scooped up a lantern. "Don't they climb trees?" He stumbled through the woods, holding the lamp he hadn't bothered to light.

Olivia followed on his heels, the idea of a bear attack more pressing than escape.

The sound seemed to stop for a moment around the vicinity of their campsite.

Olivia ducked behind a large tree, digging her fingers into its thick bark as she tried to peer around it. She could smell Frank's breath, arriving in nervous puffs just over her shoulder.

"Can you see anything?"

She studied the glow of the campfire. A large dark shape crossed in front of it, as if pacing back and forth. "It is a bear. You were right."

He grunted. "There goes our breakfast."

"Let him have it. At least that means we're not on the menu." She crouched, tucking her bare knees up inside the coat. "I hope you brought enough to satisfy him."

"Bacon. I hope it leaves some for me."

"I hope he leaves my clothes."

"Now that's a picture." Frank's chuckle transported her back to better days, but the moment was short lived. He pushed up to his feet. "Oh, my lands. What about the painting?"

She yanked him back down. "What's he going to do—eat the paper?" And even if he did destroy it, at least that would be one less for Frank to sell. She'd already lost a picture of Clark; the idea of this one being auctioned to the highest bidder sent a chill through her heart.

The bear lumbered around the camp, occasionally crossing into view when he passed in front of the fire. After about ten minutes, Frank sighed and sat down with his back to the tree. "It's going to be light soon." His low voice barely stirred the air.

"So we can clean up camp and head back to the valley. One night 'lost in the wilderness' should be enough to satisfy your gossipmongers, shouldn't it?"

He pulled a handkerchief from his pocket and swiped it across his nose. "No, it's got to be a few days. We've got to worry some folks. As is, they've probably hardly noticed you're missing."

"A few days?" Olivia's voice pitched upward.

"Shh." Frank glanced around the tree. The camp had grown quiet. He waited another ten minutes, then stood up and took a few steps toward the fire. "I think it's gone."

"We can't stay out here for days." She waited while Frank walked back to the camp. If someone was going to get mauled, she preferred it be him.

He strode around the campfire, his steps growing more confident. He picked up the mangled backpack and poured out its remaining contents.

Olivia stood, clutching the tree for strength. Her legs trembled. She glanced over her shoulder. *I could run. I'd just have to make it far enough to hide.*

If only there wasn't a bear loose in the woods.

She dug her hand into the coat pocket, closing her fingers around the small knife. It wouldn't do much against a wild animal, but it gave her a rush of strength all the same. She would run, eventually. But when she did, she wanted her pants.

Picking her way through the darkness, she walked back to the campfire. "Frank, I cooperated. Now take me back. We can return to Sacramento and sell the paintings. You'll make back your investment and then some, and I'll have enough to send the girls to school. Then we can decide what comes next."

"Next?" Frank huffed, piling the busted food cans and wrappers together. "There's no next."

She retrieved her shirt and trousers. They'd been strewn through the dirt, but seemed unharmed. "What do you mean?"

He straightened. "Look, sweetheart. This is the end of the road for us.

You've got to see that." He wiped his nose. "I'm making my million, and then I'm out of the business for good."

"My paintings won't be worth a million."

"They will be by the time we're done."

Olivia squeezed the blade handle between her fingers, her heartbeat slowing in time with her breathing. For the past year Frank had been fixated on the stories of Paul Gauguin and Vincent van Gogh, artists whose work had become priceless after their deaths.

Frank glanced back over his shoulder. "Come on, Liv. It's high time we got moving."

She pulled on her clothes as the knot in her stomach tightened. She was Frank's last painter. His last hope.

And there was only one way she'd be worth the kind of money he had in mind.

Twenty-Seven

C lark and John hiked down the Mirror Lake trail as dawn's light peeked around the side of Half Dome.

Clark ran one hand down the front of his Park Service jacket. He hadn't worn it during yesterday's search, because he was technically off duty. Today he'd grabbed the forest-green coat, desperate for the air of authority it provided. Hopefully the gold badge on his pocket would be enough, because he could barely conceive of using the revolver strapped to his hip. John might be a war veteran, but Clark had never aimed a gun at a man before.

But for Olivia—anything.

"I can't figure out what happened." He repeated the words for about the third time this morning. John must be tiring of his speculations, but Clark couldn't smother his thoughts. "She wasn't far enough down the trail to have gotten in trouble on her own. Of course, there is always the chance of a rogue mountain lion or bear."

"Maybe she turned an ankle and decided to stay put rather than hike out?"

John's statement fell flat, and they both knew it. Unless the prank had been a bizarre coincidence, they'd been lured away. That only left one frightening possibility.

Clark's stomach turned at the thought. "So who could be behind this?"

"How about that Vanderbilt fellow?" John led the way toward the lake.

"The man's a rat, but he didn't seem devious enough to pull this together. And to what end? Olivia already rebuffed his advances."

"Revenge, perhaps? But I don't understand why he'd wait until now."

Clark ducked under a low limb. "Perhaps Olivia's father tracked her down." The thought sent a shudder through his stomach. "But why go after her? And why not the twins?"

"Maybe to extort money from his newly successful daughter."

Clark brushed his hand over the revolver at his side. He'd rather face a grizzly than a murderer any day. At least a bear behaved as nature intended. A man—you never knew.

The lake spread before them, reflecting the blues and purples of the morning sky. A jay screeched out a warning to the world as they approached. Mirror Lake had never looked more deserted, as if even the wildlife had fled. *Lord, I know You're here at least. Help me find her.*

He strode to the lake's edge. His footprints from yesterday remained in the mud. Had it been less than twenty-four hours since he'd stood here and proclaimed his love? He turned in a short circle, studying the trees and grasses. Somewhere there must be a sign. But running around like a rabid chipmunk wouldn't help.

John was walking slowly around the perimeter. His friend's steady presence settled Clark's lurching heartbeat. At least one of them was thinking straight.

Clark looked up, searching the surrounding landscape. Wedged between Half Dome and North Dome, the tight canyon limited the choices as to where she'd have gone—or been taken. Of course, they could have returned down the trail toward camp and made it out to the road. If she'd been forced into a waiting vehicle, she could be anywhere.

Clark curled his fingers at his side. Better to focus on the possibilities he had some control over. His eyes traced the Snow Creek Trail as it skirted the edge of Basket Dome and up into the backcountry.

He hurried over to where he'd left her the day before. He could see the imprints of the easel in the ground, the divots filled with water from yesterday's rains. Clark bent down and touched the muddy surface, as if it could show him something about where Olivia had gone. With all his years of guiding, he'd never been asked to track a human. Usually he focused on not letting them get lost in the first place. He lifted his head, thinking back over the previous day. He and John had been soaked through, riding in search of Morris. What if Olivia had still been out here at the lake when the storm broke? He walked toward the nearest grove of trees, scanning the ground with each step.

It took twenty minutes, but he and John finally found smaller boot prints around the base of one of the larger trees. There was no way to know if they were Olivia's, but an odd rectangular indention could have been her paint box set on end.

"Look over here." John crouched down, pointing to some larger prints. "She did meet someone."

"Or he met her." Clark examined the soft dirt. "And three more round indentations—her easel."

"But where did she go from here?"

Clark shouldered his pack. "Let's head up the Snow Creek Trail a ways. Maybe we can see something from the higher vantage point.

John nodded. "You think they're still around here somewhere?"

"That's what I'm praying for."

Olivia unfastened the latch on her paint box, then slipped several brushes and paint pots into her pocket alongside the knife. Maybe she could drop a few along the path like breadcrumbs. If only she could splash a big arrow on the side of one of the granite boulders. The idea brought a halfhearted bubble of laughter to her chest. *"Just a moment, Frank. I want to paint this rock."* Watercolors weren't exactly designed for leaving signal markers.

Hopefully leaving a brush or two along the way would catch someone's attention—if anyone was looking.

"Let's go." Frank's voice rang out. "I want to get some distance from the valley before too much daylight passes."

She fastened the box. "I was checking on the painting. With all the moisture yesterday, I wasn't sure how it fared."

"And?"

She glanced over her shoulder at the grizzled man. "It's fine."

"Good. That one ought to bring in a pretty penny."

She should dump it in the creek while she still had a chance. Olivia slid the box into her pack. "Have you seen my sweater? It was with the other things by the fire, but I can't find it."

Frank stomped around the campsite and kicked against the charred logs. "Maybe it fell in when our visitor was busy. That or there's a bear sporting blue wool this season. My hat's gone, too. At least he's well dressed."

She stood and brushed the dirt off the knees of her trousers. Her throat tightened. The sweater had been a gift from Melba, and the thought of leaving it behind stung.

Frank slapped his arms, as if trying to get the blood flowing. "It's brisk this morning, but it looks like the rain is finished. Blue skies today. Heaven's favoring us."

"Somehow I doubt that." Olivia adjusted her load and glanced about the messy campsite. If Frank was thinking straight, he'd clean up the area. If anyone bothered to check on the "lost in the wilderness" story, they could clearly see that more than one person had spent the night here.

She bent over the spent fire, checking to see if any fibers from her sweater remained among the ash. There was no sign of it. Perhaps the bear had dragged it off somewhere. That's what she got for washing it with that ridiculous honey and almond soap. If she made it out of this, that soap was going in the trash. She'd buy Frances a new bar—any one she wanted as long as it didn't smell of nuts.

Frank led the way through the undergrowth, loosely following the creek's path through the canyon. He was a better hiker than she'd suspected yesterday. At this pace, they'd make several miles before lunch.

"Do we have any food left after last night's escapade?"

He glanced over his shoulder. "Hungry already?"

"I'm curious if I should be watching for berries or something."

"I brought some fishing line."

That should slow them down. Fishing was a patient business in Yosemite. Clark had taught her as much. She dug in her pocket, pulling out a cobalt blue paint pot. With Frank focused on blazing a trail, she set it on a nearby rock. It wasn't much, but perhaps the bright color would attract someone's eye. Why didn't she think of this yesterday? She could have dropped one every couple of yards. Would the rangers even know where they'd left the trail? *You foolish girl. Lost in the wilderness is right.*

Olivia slowed her pace, letting Frank draw ahead. There was no need to be quite so cooperative in her own demise. She rolled the knife in her palm. Would she have the courage to use it?

She pulled off her hat, running quick fingers through her hair. It had been under Frank's tutelage that she'd dyed her hair, covered her freckles, and painted her face. She'd allowed him to transform her into a mere caricature of herself. Olivia pushed past some low branches, ducking her head as she walked. *But God knit me together in my mother's womb.* Isn't that what Clark had said?

"Stop dragging your feet. What's your problem?"

Olivia forced a limp. "You saw me turn my ankle yesterday."

"Well, you're walking on it, so it's not broken. Come on." He waited until she reached his side, and then prodded her ahead of him. "Don't play games with me, Liv. I invented most of them, you know." He laid a hand on the revolver. "If I think you're toying with me, I'll end our little march here. No one will ever find you."

She blew out a long breath and pushed ahead through the brush. Perhaps he wouldn't notice if she altered their direction slightly. If they could just get closer to the main path, she would have a better chance of finding help.

Far off to her left, a tree limb bounced as if a particularly fat squirrel had alighted on it. She studied the branch until a second motion sent a rush of certainty through her chest. A hand gripped the bough. *Clark?*

Olivia glanced back at her dealer, the gun in his belt glinting in the morning sunshine. She needed to warn Clark, somehow. "Frank, I need to stop and rest. My ankle." She crouched and rubbed her leg, working her fingers against the leather of her tall boots.

"No way." He scowled. "Get up. Now. I don't know what you're playing at." He latched onto her elbow and hoisted her back to her feet, jarring her forward.

"Since when do you carry a gun, Frank?" She lifted her voice, hoping it would carry far enough to be heard. "It doesn't seem like your style."

"When you've got thousands of dollars on the line, you take precautions." He gripped her pack. "Let me carry that for a while. That ought to get you moving."

Olivia paused and shrugged out of the shoulder straps. She'd rather keep the last painting in her possession, but it did seem wise to lighten her load in case she needed to run.

Frank stopped, staring in the direction she'd been trying hard not to look. "What's that? Another bear?"

She dropped the pack at his feet. "Maybe the same one. He's probably tracking us."

The dealer turned back, eyes narrowed. "You take me for a sap, don't you?"

"Why wouldn't he? You're still carrying the food bag, aren't you? And it reeks of spoiled meat now."

He pulled the straps off his shoulder, handing it to her. "I'll carry the paint box. You take this one."

"So you don't mind if I get eaten." She took the lighter bag, careful to school her expression.

Frank jostled her forward. "Let's not stay here and find out. Move."

Limping with every step, Olivia glanced over her shoulder. Clark was back there. She was sure of it.

As their pursuer drew closer, Frank quickened their pace and pulled the gun from his belt. "I don't like it. That thing—whatever it is—is getting too close. I think I can smell it."

"You're paranoid." The sight of the weapon in his hand sent her pulse racing. "I was joking about the bear, Frank. There's nothing there. You're getting jumpy."

He stepped behind her and shoved the barrel into her back. "Yes, I'm jumpy. I don't feel like getting eaten."

"You're imagining things."

His brows drew together. "I saw it. I'll show you." He turned, holding the revolver outstretched.

Olivia grabbed at his arm. "No, don't."

He squeezed off a shot before she could stop him, the sound bouncing off the valley walls.

Her heart jumped into her throat. This had been a wild shot through the trees. Would his next one be aimed straight at Clark? A chill swept over her. If she led him to his death, how would she live with herself?

"There. Maybe that'll convince it to leave us alone. The bear"—he turned and faced Olivia—"or the person. Now, let's get moving."

The sound of a gunshot tore through air, echoing along the cliff faces. Clark jerked back to look, thinking little of his precarious footing. *Liv.* His pulse raced. "God, tell me that wasn't aimed at her."

John called to him from the trail above. "It was over the ridge, far side."

Clark slid several more feet down the embankment and snatched the blue garment he'd spotted from overhead. It was wedged between a scrubby tree and a boulder, the yarn unraveling in his fingers as he tugged it free. He'd hardly seen Liv without the sweater since the day they'd first headed out from the Ahwahnee. *No bloodstains.*

He yanked off his pack and jammed the sweater inside. She wouldn't want it back in its condition, but he certainly wasn't going to leave it behind. "How far?" he called up to John.

"Couldn't tell. I'll scout that way. Stay put."

Stay put? Not likely. As John disappeared from view, Clark used both hands for balance as he struggled up the hill, clambering at a reckless pace. Loose stones kicked free by his boots tumbled downslope, the sound causing a racket in the quiet afternoon.

Halfway up the slope, he noticed a straw boater sitting upside down, wedged against a stubby tree. He scrambled toward it. The hat was in shambles, its gold and green ribbon hanging by a thread. Clark frowned as he scooped up its remains. He'd seen it once before—the day he'd met Frank Robinson.

Clark crushed it in his fist. He should have realized who was behind this. The art dealer had always looked after his own self-interests, but Liv's grateful heart had blinded her to the fact. What was the man up to now? *Lord, I need to find her.*

He tossed the hat away, scrambling the rest of the way up the steep bank to the trail and then setting out in pursuit of John. If that shot had been meant for Olivia, Clark wanted to be the one to get his hands on Robinson.

Twenty-Eight

O livia and Frank had been walking for hours, hiking through another canyon, fording a small stream, and climbing the opposite ridge. The afternoon had clouded up, and once again, raindrops began to fall, dampening the trail and making the rocks slick under her feet. The distant rumble of yet another creek—or perhaps a waterfall—sent Olivia's heart pounding.

Frank's steps behind her grew more hurried and erratic with every passing minute. He knew it wasn't a bear following them, that much was obvious. The harried look on his face and the way his hand repeatedly tightened on the gun's grip caused her stomach to lurch.

Assuming Clark was back there, he seemed to be biding his time. Olivia hoped he wouldn't put himself in the line of fire. "Where are we going?"

Frank didn't answer. He seemed consumed by putting one foot in front of the other, the sound of the falls growing louder with each step.

She halted. "I'm not going any farther." She squeezed the knife handle, the blade exposed inside her pocket. It might only be an inch long, but she had the element of surprise. With a well-placed jab, she could get the gun out of his hand. At the least, she could draw blood. She wasn't sure how that would help, but it seemed better than plodding along to her death.

He shoved her forward. "You'll move when I tell you to."

She swung around and lashed out with the knife, catching him across the wrist.

Frank's eyes widened as he cried out in pain. He gripped the arm with his other hand, the revolver still firm in his fingers. He lifted the weapon, his hand shaking. "You—you—"

She'd given away her one advantage. Olivia ducked to the side. Scrambling forward, she threw herself through the brush not caring what might lie ahead.

The shot never came, but from the sound of branches cracking, she knew Frank wasn't far behind her.

Her breath came in ragged pants. She clutched the pocketknife in her damp palm as she ran. Ducking through brush, she tripped once, but scrambled up in less than a step. There had to be a place to hide.

God—Lord—anything. Please.

Where was Clark? She'd been sure he was behind them and must have heard their altercation. But now all she could hear was Frank's footsteps pounding in her ears. At least he hadn't shot at her. Was there a chance he actually wanted to keep her alive?

The ground sloped downward toward the river. What would she do when she reached it? There'd be nowhere to go. She could tell from the sound that it was too large to ford, probably swollen from last night's rain.

She stumbled out into the open, the creek cutting through the scrubby forest and plunging down a series of swirling cataracts. Her breath caught and she backed. *Artist throws herself off waterfall.*

Frank appeared out of the trees, his face red and splotchy. "I gave you a chance, Liv. I didn't want it to come to this." He still had his hand locked on his wrist, blood oozing between his fingers. He gestured with the gun. "Sit down."

Not sure what else to do, she complied, lowering herself onto a boulder near the swollen creek.

"Drop the knife and take off the coat."

She laid the knife down and shrugged out of the raincoat, the cold raindrops soaking through her shirt in short order.

He gestured with the gun. "Downstream."

Olivia turned to study the water flowing past her as Frank picked up the coat. They'd traversed for miles southwest along the high country on the north side of the valley, largely staying off the trail, meaning they should be just about…

She thought through the various trips she'd taken with Clark during the previous five weeks.

Yosemite Falls.

Clark picked up the red-handled brush, the color standing out against the rocky path.

John jabbed at the map. "I thought they'd turn north and head overland to Tioga Road. It doesn't make sense to stay this close to the valley. We can track them too easily. What is he thinking?"

Clark ran his fingers across the soft squirrel bristles. "If he'd wanted a road, why not just go out the valley road?"

It had been several hours since they'd heard the gunshot, and other than the single paintbrush, they'd seen no sign of Olivia and Frank. What's more, the rain had started again and they were quickly losing light.

"We're going to be caught out here overnight if we don't get a break soon. We've no way to know how far ahead of us they are." He slid the brush in his breast pocket. She'd obviously left it for him to find—trusting him to be coming after her. His chest tightened. It was hard to know what the art dealer was planning, but if it involved forced marches and gunshots, it couldn't be good.

He took the map from John's hand and flipped open his compass. If only the device could simply point the way to Olivia. In this situation, it was useless. They needed a sign.

John straightened, gesturing down the trail. "Someone's coming."

Clark pushed back his hat, surprised to see a hiker out in this weather. His heart jumped when he recognized the shoddy-looking old vagrant loping toward them. A wash of emotion spilled through him. "Filbert! I have never been so glad to see you."

The man stopped, breathless, and swung his beat-up derby at them in an obvious gesture. Then he scurried back the way he'd come.

Follow. Clark had answered that call years before when he'd first stepped foot in a church as a boy. The call was just as clear now. He set out after the man at a dead run, John falling in behind.

Olivia's stomach lurched as they approached the top of the falls. In one sweeping glance, she took in the distant domes and cliffs all the way to the valley floor, the last rays of sunset adding a reddish tinge to the normal grays and greens of the panorama. What a painting it would make, wisps of spent clouds softening the harsh angles of the scene. At her feet, the churning creek disappeared over the distant edge to plummet thousands of feet to the rocks beneath.

The Ahwahnee sat somewhere below them, likely little more than a mere dot in the distance. For a moment she was back there, casually viewing the falls from the patio on her first night in the park, determined not to set foot on the Yosemite trails.

Heart numb, she turned to Frank. "You've been like a father to me. Is this really what you want?"

He grunted. "I've slaved for three decades matching artists with art lovers, everyone looking to make their fortune. It's my turn."

She set her jaw. Every minute she stalled was another minute to live. "I'll do whatever you want. You want me to woo Vanderbilt? Fine. You want me to give you rights to every painting? You can have them."

"I've already got them, Liv. And I don't think Vanderbilt would give you a second look now that he knows about your old man."

The wind lifted the spray, pushing it back toward them. The fine mist coated Olivia's face. Frank had chosen his location well. She stood right where her father had murdered a man in cold blood, then tossed him over the falls to try to hide his crime. Her death would play well in the papers, like a real-life Shakespearian tragedy. Readers would believe she ended her life rather than live with the shame. She pulled off her hat, clutching it to her middle.

"I met him, you know," Frank said.

She twisted to face him. "You met my father?"

He offered her a half smile. "A couple of weeks ago. He came looking for you. Right after you returned to the park."

"What did you tell him?"

"I thought about bringing him for a visit to see how you'd react, but I realized you'd probably go off the rails again. I needed you focused." He shrugged, gesturing loosely with the weapon. "I told him you weren't interested in the ravings of a murderer."

"And yet here I am—listening to you." She tried to imagine her father as she had last seen him, but the picture was too foggy. A vague memory of jumping into his arms when she was very little—before Louise and Frances came along. Too bad he hadn't always been there to catch her. How did the man she knew become a killer?

She pushed her back against the rocky outcropping, trying to take stability from the cool granite. Clark had spoken of how the cliffs were formed by God's hands and then shaped by glaciers. Was God watching now? *Lord, if I go over this cliff, tell me You'll be waiting.* The thought of a loving Father —so unlike her own—standing with arms wide to catch her quieted her pounding heart.

But it would mean leaving the girls. And Clark. Their faces flooded her mind. *Lord, watch over them.*

"Enough reminiscing. I'm not your dad, even if you tried to use me to replace him. And you're not my girl, no matter how much I tried to plan your future. There were times"—Frank paused, clearing his throat—"I kind of wished you were my daughter, Liv."

She turned to look at him, the low light deepening the grooves on his face, droplets of mist settling on his whiskers. "Don't do this, Frank. Don't."

Frank took a moment to gaze out across the darkening valley, the breeze fluttering the edges of his white hair. "I wish I didn't have to, Liv." He blinked hard before turning back to her. "But we're here, and there's no going back."

⌒

Clark pushed forward, leaving John and Filbert behind him. The sun was slipping past the horizon, long shadows obscuring the landscape, but the rumble of Yosemite Creek sounded in the distance. It was often dry this late in the season, but the past few days of rain had sent it surging back to life. His heart thundered in his chest, matching the sound of the roaring falls.

If they'd arrived too late, he'd...he'd... He had no idea what he'd do. He couldn't entertain the thought.

But as Clark approached the lookout, he spotted them. Liv and Robinson stood close together on one of the lower ledges near the falls, rock at their back, spray at their feet. For a brief moment he hesitated. They looked more like old friends than captor and victim. Olivia's expression was soft, as if she was comforting the man rather than pleading for her life.

Clark skidded to a stop on the slippery trail, his thoughts scattering. Had he somehow misinterpreted the situation? "Liv—" His voice cracked as his tight throat protested the sudden use. She'd never hear him over the roar of the water. "Olivia!" He shouted her name.

As Frank lifted a hand toward her, Clark spotted the revolver in his grip. Reaching for his own, Clark dropped to one knee to aim. He couldn't risk hitting Olivia. His shaky hand and their precarious footing could be a deadly combination.

He jumped back to his feet and edged closer. He could almost make out their voices.

A few more steps, and Olivia met his gaze over Frank's shoulder. Her eyes widened as she stared at him for a long moment, her black hair dripping and plastered to the sides of her face.

He wanted nothing more than to lurch forward to grab Frank Robinson and yank him back away from her, but Liv's expression froze him midstep. Sadness lay heavy in the blue-gray depths of her eyes, a deep penetrating sorrow that cut into his heart.

Clark fought to take a breath. "Robinson." His voice finally lifted enough to carry through the sound of the falling water.

Frank turned. His eyes landed on Clark. He crouched slightly against the rock, one hand flying back to grasp at the stone. His brow furrowed, a flash of awareness on his face, as if he recognized the impossibility of his situation. Unfortunately, it didn't stop him from raising the weapon he gripped in his left hand.

Clark flattened himself against the rock face, clutching his own gun in his damp palm.

Olivia watched Frank turn, his arm shaking as he pointed the revolver toward Clark. John stood frozen several yards beyond, and both rangers had their guns drawn. Her heart had gone cold, as if it was happening on a silver screen rather than in front of her eyes. The spray and the slightest rumble in the rocks beneath her feet dashed any hope that she was imagining the situation. *I'm to blame for all this. They shouldn't be here.*

She threw herself into Frank's side, slamming him against the cliff face. In the sudden motion, they both slipped. The gun flew from his hand and clattered across the stones down into the churning water. Frank landed hard on his side, his head cracking against the granite.

Olivia fell against his legs, clutching at his knees even as her foot slid over the edge. Scrabbling her fingers against the fabric of his loose-fitting trousers, she pedaled her legs trying to reach a foothold.

Frank's eyes glazed as he looked down at her, blood oozing from a gash in his forehead.

She gripped the edge of his high boot, lacing her fingers between the leather and his leg. "Frank, help me."

Even as she said the words, Frank's eyes rolled back. His limp body skidded a few inches along the slick surface, his mouth gaping open.

A few more seconds and they were both going over. The sudden awareness coursed through her, but her fingers were locked. She could no more release him than she could willingly let herself drop.

Clark lunged forward and grabbed her fingers, wrapping his other hand around her wrist. "Liv, hang on! Don't let go of me."

She clasped his wet fingers, the sudden shock of his skin against hers sending a wall of emotions cascading through her like the water plunging over the drop. "I won't."

As he hoisted her a few inches, Olivia's toe made contact with the rock face. She dug in and managed to hook a leg over the ledge and scramble up to her hands and knees. Clark's arm wrapped around her midsection.

Frank lay prone on the wet granite, eyes at half-mast.

John appeared over Clark's shoulder. "I'll take the man. You get Olivia back to safety."

Olivia's eyes blurred with tears—or spray—as Clark pulled her up into his arms. She pressed her face into his neck, a long buried sob throbbing in her chest. "I knew you were back there, somewhere. When he shot at you, I thought…I thought…" Her legs shook as she pressed against him, her knees threatening to buckle.

He drew back, looking down into her eyes. "That wasn't me, love. It was Filbert. He was tracking you."

The name bounced through her mind, finally settling on the image of the scraggly old man from the wilderness. "The hermit?"

"John and I weren't far behind. Finding your sweater and brush helped. But Filbert took us the rest of the distance."

She laid her cheek against his chest, the beating of his heart evident through the park jacket. "I knew I wasn't alone. I could feel it."

"You're never alone." He pulled her back along the cliff edge to a wider spot as John helped Frank sit up. The older man looked shaky, blood trickling down from his forehead.

She laced her fingers through Clark's, staring down at the frothing foam of Yosemite Creek, barely visible in the fading light. Her tremors deepened as if her body was somehow just now realizing how close she'd come to joining the creek on its descent.

He shrugged out of his jacket and laid it around her shoulders. "We need to get you back to the valley and thawed out."

She leaned against his side, pulling the jacket close and breathing in the warm scent of him. "It's not the cold. Not really." She glanced up at his face, locking onto the intensity of his brown eyes. "It was the idea of leaving you and the girls—and everything I've grown to love."

He gripped the edges of the jacket and pulled it closed across her front, like a hug. "When you were hanging off that—" His voice cracked and he paused, shaking his head. "I thought I'd lost you." Clark brushed cold knuckles against her cheek. "And I'm still learning who you really are."

She blinked back tears for a second time. "Now we've got plenty of time to figure that out."

He wrapped his arms around her back and pulled her to his chest. "A lifetime, if you'll let me."

She stared out over the darkening valley, an orange glow on top of one of the cliffs opposite. "Is that..."

Clark pulled her close, his breath warming her cheek. "Glacier Point. The Firefall."

She held her breath as the embers drifted off the edge, cascading through the night like thousands of falling stars.

Twenty-Nine

After Sunday's church service, Clark walked out the door of the Yosemite Chapel, Liv's hand firmly clasped in his. Out of sheer necessity, he'd let her go last night so they could both get some much-needed sleep, but he had every intention of holding on to her this entire day. Or at least until his hands stopped shaking.

He'd woken three times in a cold sweat, and he couldn't imagine she'd done much better. Hopefully a morning spent in worship and then a quiet afternoon walk might start them on the road to healing. They'd yet to speak of the future, but before this day was out, he intended to. He still had little security to offer, but after watching her nearly pitch off the ledge into Yosemite Falls, security seemed like an artificial construct. It didn't exist, so why wait for it?

Other worshippers hurried past, but he was content to wait on the steps a moment, listening as the final strains from the organ spilled out the open doors. Louise and Frances had already disappeared with John and Melba; the couple had offered to treat them to lunch and ice cream at the Ahwahnee Hotel.

Olivia smiled and squeezed his arm, as if understanding his desire to linger until everyone made their way from the small building. "It was a lovely service."

"It was a joy to have you next to me."

"There's no place I'd rather be." She leaned against his arm.

They sat down on the sun-warmed steps, enjoying the fresh morning air. Clark's eyes were drawn to Yosemite Falls on the cliff face opposite. The stream's flow had decreased overnight until it was little more than a wispy line, the breeze blowing the slight curtain of water up against the granite wall. He pulled his gaze away, the sight a little more than he could manage right now. Pulling her hand into his lap, he studied her long fingers as they wrapped around his own. "It wouldn't surprise me if you wanted to leave Yosemite forever, after what's happened."

Olivia scooted closer, adjusting her hat against the glare. "It wasn't Yosemite; it was Frank. If anything, it makes me fearful to leave."

"You shouldn't be afraid. After the doc patched him up, John put him in the jail for the night. He'll be transferred to another location soon. Kendall turned himself in, as well. He told John it was the only way to gain his freedom. Though how he gets freedom in jail, I don't understand."

"I do. Lies hold us captive, but there's freedom in the truth. I probably understand better than anyone." She fell silent for a moment, and then frowned. "Yosemite has a jail?"

"It does." He chuckled. "I've only seen it from the inside once."

"Now that sounds like a story I should hear."

"The chief ranger doesn't take pranks very well—even when his wife is one of the instigators. He locked all of us in for the night."

She laughed, tipping her head back to look him in the eye. "He arrested Melba?"

"Well, he let her out after a few hours. The rest of us weren't so lucky."

Footsteps behind them drew Clark's attention. Reverend White stood, arms folded across his chest. "Clark Johnson, exactly the man I'd hoped to see."

Clark stood, helping Olivia to her feet. "Reverend, we were just saying how much we enjoyed your sermon."

"Hmm. Yes, I heard." The minister's brow lifted. "Something about jail time. Makes me think twice about my offer."

"Your offer?"

The minister shuffled down the steps to Olivia, ignoring Clark's question. "Welcome, Miss Rutherford. I don't think we've formally met."

She shook his hand, her face lighting. "Pastor, thank you for your teaching this morning. It was a joy to hear."

"Thank *you*, my dear. Clark here has told me much about you. I'm pleased to finally meet the woman herself."

A shiver raced across Clark's skin as he tried to remember exactly what he had said about her.

Reverend White turned back to face Clark, the grooves around his mouth deepening as he smiled. "Clark, I'd hoped to speak to you before I address the congregation next week. I've thought a lot about our last conversation. In fact, it's been weighing on my heart ever since."

Clark's chest tightened. "I'm sorry. I didn't mean to upset you."

The pastor chuckled. "No, no, nothing like that." He looked out over the valley, his attention seeming to roam across the road, the meadow, and the mighty waterfall beyond. "But you said you were waiting on God's call. That you wanted to return to ministry, yet you didn't want to leave here."

"Yes sir. He still hasn't answered me on that, though you were right about one thing."

Reverend White glanced at Clark, one brow lifting.

"I was living in disgrace—wallowing, as you put it. It kept me from hearing God's voice." He met Olivia's eyes briefly, the affection he saw there warming him to the core. "I couldn't see that I was still serving him, even as

I worked here. A wilderness guide isn't so different from being a pastor. You're helping people find their way. And if I'm called to be a ranger, I'd be protecting both God's people and His creation." Clark squeezed Olivia's fingers and released them, dropping his arms to his sides. "So if He wants me to stay on, I'll find a way to serve His people in everything I do."

Olivia smiled, the sight causing his heart to jump in his chest. He couldn't wait to be done here. As soon as he could break free from this conversation, he'd walk her across Sentinel Meadow and get down on one knee right—

Reverend White clamped a hand down on Clark's shoulder. "I'm happy to hear you say that. Because God's been speaking to my heart as well."

Clark turned away from Liv, trying to focus on the man in front of him. "He has?"

"I've compassed this mountain long enough." A misty look settled in Reverend White's eyes.

The familiar words echoed in Clark's spirit, like the whisper of his father's voice. He reached into his pocket and closed his fingers around the silver compass. *Turn you northward.*

"My tenure here is coming to an end, Clark. I'm planning to retire. I'd like to put your name forward to the board as my replacement."

Clark grabbed the stair rail, his thoughts spinning off in all directions like a flock of swallows. "My name?"

Olivia touched his arm, her lips parting in a quick breath.

Clark's attention darted up the face of the small building. "For the Yosemite Chapel?"

"I know it's not much." Reverend White sighed. "The building needs work—a lot of work. It's falling to pieces. But the people here, they're what matters. The rangers, the staff, the visitors. It's an odd flock at best, and it takes a certain sort of man to lead them." He shook his head slowly. "Your whole journey has been leading to this. It is *your* church, Clark. Your people. I've just been holding on to them for you."

"But you know what happened—"

The reverend lifted a hand to halt Clark's words. "Grace, remember?" He chuckled. "And I also telephoned your former parish and spoke with one of the elders—a Mr. Lambert?"

A wave of cold washed over Clark's skin. The man who'd led the charge against him.

"He informed me that some other"—he wrinkled his nose—"facts had come to light after you left. Facts that proved your innocence. But they had no way to reach you. And evidently, you never spoke out against your accuser."

Clark's throat tightened. "She had her reasons for doing what she did."

"We usually do. Anyway, I don't see any cause for your history to stand in the way of you accepting this post."

Like water through a crack in an earthen dam, the news seeped into him. Clark managed a nod, words escaping him.

The minister grinned. "You'll consider it, then? We'll talk more, but I'm already packing my things. I have a little granddaughter in Mariposa who's growing up too fast. I don't want to miss it."

"I'm honored." Clark finally pushed out the words, hoarse though he was. "I'm deeply honored."

"It's always a joy to see the Father at work." Reverend White glanced at Olivia. "And never have I been so aware of His activities than during my time at Yosemite. He does mighty things among the people here, and I sense He's doing something truly special here with the two of you."

He walked down the steps. "Close the door when you leave, will you?" Without another word, he sauntered off toward Yosemite Village.

Clark sat down hard, his knees no longer willing to hold him. *Pastor— of Yosemite?*

Olivia sat beside him, easing her hand up under his arm and squeezing it. "Your God—He's pretty amazing."

He closed his eyes, pulling her close. "He's your God, too, love."

"Yes." She sighed, as if the air had gotten too big to hold inside her lungs. "He is."

~~~

March 1, 1930

Frances and Louise huddled near the stove in the chapel, trying to get the smoke to draw up the little chimney pipe. Olivia smiled at the picture, her fingers already unconsciously outlining the image as if in preparation to paint—or perhaps a charcoal sketch would be more appropriate. But today would be far too busy. The snow falling outside was a welcome surprise, but it did complicate things for their guests.

Melba laced her arm through Olivia's. "We should have done this at the Ahwahnee. They have such lovely weddings in the Great Hall and the Solarium."

"I know, but I like it here." Olivia turned, studying the simple chapel. "It's Clark's chapel. It feels right to have the wedding here. It was God who brought us together after all."

Melba shivered. "Yes, but you first met at the Ahwahnee, and it's much more glamorous. With as many paintings as you've sold, you deserve the best."

Olivia thought back to her first meeting with Clark. "I was a different person then. I like this Liv better. Glamour isn't my first thought anymore."

"Clark's a different person, too. I'm still surprised every time I see him in the clerical collar. But it suits him, doesn't it?"

"It does." Emotion welled up in her chest. Clark's heart was always evident in all he did. Now the rest of the world could see it as well.

Louise gave the stove a kick. "It's hopeless. It won't draw."

"I'll have John come take a look at it. He's pretty good with ours when it's being difficult." Melba sighed.

Frances rose, hurrying over to Olivia's side. "I'm so glad you spoke to the headmistress, so we could come. I missed Yosemite. And you, too, of course." Her face reddened.

"You had to be here. We'd have waited until summer vacation if necessary." Secretly, Olivia was glad the headmistress had agreed. She liked the idea of sharing her first spring in Yosemite with Clark, already wed.

"And we will spend the summers and holidays with you, won't we? All of them?"

"I wouldn't have it any other way."

Melba clapped her hands. "We'll have to polish up our act, girls."

That got a grin out of Louise, a sight that warmed Olivia's heart.

The sound of Clark and John coming through the front doors sent Melba and the twins squealing. They grabbed Olivia and shoved her behind them.

Melba scowled at the men as they stomped snow from their boots. "You can't see the bride. What were you thinking?"

John pressed a kiss on his wife's cheek. "The same as you, it seems. That we needed to get that stove working before the guests arrive."

Clark glanced around at the room, a smile spreading across his face. "You girls have done a beautiful job. I've never seen the chapel so beautiful." The room was festooned with armloads of evergreen garland wrapped with yellow ribbons. Cream-colored crepe paper gathered in flowered buntings hung above every window.

Olivia couldn't help but smile at her groom's enthusiasm, even as she ducked behind the organ, playing along with the tradition. "I'm so glad you're pleased. The girls helped me with it last night."

He'd taken such an interest in cleaning and painting the quaint little chapel, and now it shone brightly.

Louise jumped in front of the menfolk. "We'll blindfold him." She giggled, holding up a line of crepe paper.

Clark held out his hands in front of him. "How about I close my eyes?"

Melba retrieved a scarf from her handbag. "This will do nicely. Now sit down."

Her husband chuckled. "I think we're outnumbered here, Clark. You'd better do as she says."

Clark sighed as the twins grabbed his arms and steered him to a pew, allowing Louise to tie the blue silk scarf around his head. "I won't be of much help like this."

"You should have thought about that before you came in here." Olivia stepped back into the open.

John got to work on the stove. "I am trying to keep the man busy so he won't get cold feet."

"If I've got cold feet, it's only from walking over here in the snow."

"You poor man." Melba sighed. "Meanwhile, Olivia and I are here in our pretty shoes, because who wants to get married in their boots?"

"I do?" Clark lifted a hand.

Olivia laughed. "Save your *I do's* for later." She sat down beside him and placed a kiss on his cheek.

"Oh." He grinned. "Well, then. I'll wear whatever shoes you like, ma'am."

Olivia snuggled her cheek down on Clark's shoulder as everyone else got back to work getting the chapel ready for the festivities. "Don't tell the girls, but I'm glad you came by," she whispered.

He tipped his head down to meet hers. "So am I. Even if I have to wear this silly getup."

"It'll be worth it when you see me coming down the aisle, right?"

His chest rose and fell in a deep breath. "True. I'll be right there waiting for you."

"Did you ever imagine this moment, back when we first met?"

He smiled, barely visible below the scarf. "I couldn't imagine anything past your red lips."

Olivia smacked him in the chest. "That's not true."

Clark lifted one shoulder and dropped it. "That's what you think. But now..." He reached for the scarf.

"No, don't." She stilled his hand. "I have one more surprise for you. I don't want you to spoil it."

He lowered his arms to his sides. "Why does that worry me a little?"

"You'll like this one. I think." She touched her turban head wrap. *I hope.*

"Then I'll wait. I've waited months now. I can last a few more hours."

"You didn't think I was going to marry you the moment you asked?"

He hooked an arm behind her back, drawing her closer. "I'd hoped."

The aroma of candles and freshly cut evergreen boughs brought a smile to Olivia's face. "It was tempting, but this is better. We needed to put all the unpleasantness behind us. I didn't want us to wed with the pall of a court case hanging over us." She shivered. "I still can't believe John didn't toss me out on my ear when he learned the truth about my father."

He fumbled for her hand and squeezed it. "It was a shock to the folks here, but no one can blame you for your father's sins."

She sighed. "Now that he and Frank are both behind bars, maybe everyone can rest easier."

"It's unfortunate we had to lose Gus, as well. At least he got a lighter sentence for cooperating."

"And now we can put all that nonsense behind us."

"And the paintings."

"Are you calling my paintings nonsense?"

"Heavens, no." His lips drew down. "I meant—"

"I'm teasing, Clark." She laughed. Without his eyesight, he seemed quite unable to read her. This could be fun. "I know what you meant. I'm glad we got most of them sold before the economy fell apart. I don't know what Sophie and Marcus will do now."

"He was pretty heavily invested in the stock market, I take it."

"Yes. And in art, of course. But who's buying art now?" She smoothed the front of her skirt. "Unless things pick back up, I won't be selling anything for quite a while. At least, not at the prices Frank had been hoping for."

"It'll turn around. The president didn't sound concerned."

She nestled against him, taking advantage of the blindfold to study the curve of his arm and the line of buttons going down his chest. She needed to commit this to memory as best she could so she could re-create it for a wedding portrait. Clark's friend, Ansel Adams, said he'd come by and take some photographs. Maybe she could work from them.

Clark squeezed her waist. "I'm glad we saved a few of your paintings, anyway. I don't like the idea of selling your artwork to strangers. Each one is like a piece of your heart."

How well he understood her. "Each one is like a child. But eventually even children go out into the world and make their own way." The image sank into her heart. How beautiful would it be to raise their children here in Yosemite. God's valley as their play yard.

John came down the aisle to stand beside them, wiping his soot-coated fingers on a dirty handkerchief. "All done, no thanks to you." He hooked a hand under Clark's arm and helped him to his feet. "Now if you'll excuse us, Olivia, I'll make sure this fellow is decked out in time for the nuptials."

"I'm wearing my suit, John, not the Park Service formal uniform."

"Lucky for you, I accepted your resignation." He clapped Clark on the shoulder. "Otherwise, it'd be park green for you."

Clark leaned close to Olivia who had risen to stand beside him. "I escaped just in time." He managed to land a kiss on her lips, even with the blindfold. "I'll see you soon."

She blinked back bleary tears. "Yes, you will."

⟵⟶

Cold winter sunlight sparkled off the snow as Clark checked the bells on Goldie's harness. She flicked her long ears, a puff of foggy breath rising from her huge nostrils. It was good of Mr. Walker to let him buy the mule from the transportation department. A wedding mule probably wasn't the most romantic gift for a bride, but Clark felt confident Liv would be delighted, regardless.

They'd gone to visit the mules two weeks ago and the bond between the two ladies—rather, *mule* and lady—was still evident after all the months that had passed. Mr. Walker had retired Queen Elizabeth to a pasture down in Groveland, and the other stock seemed content with the new guides.

He couldn't wait to see Liv's face when she came out of the chapel to see Goldie hitched up to the little sleigh.

He couldn't wait to see Olivia, period. The shenanigans earlier about the blindfold had been fun, but he was already missing his bride-to-be. In another hour she'd be his forever.

Forever. A shiver coursed down his back. Had God ever created a more beautiful word? It was right up there with *always*. The song never failed to make his Liv smile. He'd be sure to sing it for her tonight—and every night, if she wished.

It'd be much better than singing for a mule. Clark patted Goldie's neck and looked across the iced-over valley, the snow wrapping it in a perfectly silent blanket of white. Guests were arriving by horseback or snowshoes; a few came on skis. Where else could such magic happen?

Charlie had assured Clark the snow wouldn't stop him from trekking up to Glacier Point with some of the guys from the hotel. The staff was determined to celebrate his and Olivia's wedding with the most glorious wintertime Firefall the valley had ever seen.

He climbed the steps to the chapel, the ache in his chest growing every time he opened those doors. My chapel. My flock.

God had been good to him.

As he stepped inside, the wedding decorations sweetened the moment. *Too good, God. I'm not sure I can handle much more.*

"There you are." John hustled toward him, moving to brush the snow-flakes off the shoulders of Clark's suit. "I thought you said it would only be a minute."

"I got pulled in by the scenery. It happens."

"Just be glad the girls are running late too. Melba would have my head if you were out there when they arrived." John pinned a small yellow rose to Clark's lapel. "Now come on, *Reverend* Johnson, you're supposed to be up front."

Clark followed John up the aisle, reaching out to shake Reverend White's hand. "Thank you for doing this, my friend."

"My pleasure." The white-haired minister smiled. "Weddings are a treat. And for one of our own? Even better."

After a few minutes of talk, Clark couldn't help fidgeting. How long would it be until the ladies arrived? The guests were all seated, many of them with their eyes fixed on him in the front. For a disheartening moment, he was back in front of his old church, facing down the accusing eyes of his elder board and the congregation.

John bumped his elbow. "Doing all right there, Clark?"

"Yes." He swallowed, glancing back at Reverend White. What had the man told him? *"Dis-grace is a human term, Clark. God invented grace. No one can take it from you."*

The doors to the vestibule cracked open a hair, and Louise peeked down the aisle with a grin on her face.

As the organist started playing, Clark straightened his shoulders. He'd been imagining this moment for months. He'd never have thought, back when he first laid eyes on that exotic woman with her rouged lips and flapper dress and…

Olivia stepped into the aisle, her face glowing with a wide smile. Her white beaded dress caught the light flooding in the windows, her cap veil covering most—but not all—of her hair.

Her light brown hair.

Clark's breath caught in his chest. Of course, he'd fallen in love with the raven-headed woman who'd stepped into his life so many months ago, but since she told him that she'd dyed it, he'd been curious to see her as God had made her.

And she was every bit as lovely as he'd imagined.

Her hesitant smile moved his heart. He could see the question in her eyes as she moved down the aisle toward him.

He echoed her smile—the best he could as his eyes blurred with unexpected tears. As she joined him in the front, he took her hand and kissed her knuckles before reaching out to touch the locks of hair protruding from the filmy veil. "You're beautiful, Liv."

She smiled again, ducking her head for a moment before lifting her eyes to meet his gaze. She leaned forward to whisper in his ear. "I wanted to be sure you knew what you were getting."

Even though the entire crowd was watching, Clark couldn't resist pulling her close and brushing his lips across her forehead.

"You're an artist, Liv. Wrap yourself in any colors you choose. I'll love them all."

Author's Note

Dear Reader,

I hope you enjoyed this tour of Yosemite National Park as much as I delighted in writing it!

As our country was just getting started, the idea of preserving land for the purpose of a park probably seemed outlandish and even un-American. I sometimes wonder, when President Abraham Lincoln signed the Yosemite Grant Act back in 1864, did he realize that he was clearing the path for the many great national parks to come?

Even well before then, humans had interacted with Yosemite's landscape, marveling at the granite cliffs, high waterfalls, and giant sequoia groves; and few seem to walk away unchanged. It's almost as if, as we hike its paths and climb its domes, Yosemite somehow leaves footprints on *our* souls. The human/nature connection seems stronger in Yosemite than any other park I've visited, almost as if it's impossible to resist responding to the grandiose landscape through music and spectacle. As Olivia noted, people have become a page in Yosemite's story.

While I simplified the history of Yosemite National Park (particularly buildings) in order to fit the flow of the story, many aspects that I included are true. Here are a few.

- The **Glacier Point Hotel** was built in 1917, then burned to the ground in July 1969, along with the Mountain House (a neighboring hotel), and was never replaced. You can still visit the location and marvel at the spectacular views. Signs mark the location of the former hotels.

- The **Ahwahnee Hotel** opened in 1927 and was renamed the Majestic Yosemite Hotel in 2016 due to a trademark dispute with the former concessionaire.

- **Camp Curry** opened in 1899. David and Jennie Curry operated this campground as an inexpensive alternative to the park's hotels. David Curry passed away in 1917, but Jennie (a.k.a. "Mother Curry") and various family members continued to run the camp until daughter Mary Tresidder passed away in 1970. Also currently caught up in the legal dispute, Curry Village now bears the name "Half Dome Village." Many longtime visitors hope these name changes are temporary.

- Cowboy singer **Glenn Hood** was one of many entertainers who performed at Camp Curry. Singers, musicians, and Hollywood stars sometimes got their start entertaining hotel guests and campers at Yosemite. Other historical figures briefly mentioned include two NPS employees: **Charles G. Thomson** who served as Superintendent of Yosemite National Park from 1929 until his death in 1937, and **Enid Michael** who worked as a ranger-naturalist at Yosemite from 1920 to 1942. **Ansel Adams**, one of America's most beloved photographers, perfected his art while wandering the trails at Yosemite. Also featured is **Herbert Sonn**, the "birdman of Yosemite" who lived many years at Camp Curry, entertaining visitors (including Eleanor Roosevelt) with his birdcalls, stories, and whimsical pinecone sculptures.

- The **Yosemite Valley Chapel** still serves primarily as a house of worship for residents and guests, but the historic chapel is also a popular location for weddings. **Reverend James Asa White** was the presiding minister in 1929.

- The **Yosemite Firefall** started, legend has it, when the owner of the Glacier Point Mountain House, James McCauley, would build giant bonfires for his guests at the cliff's edge. At the end of the evening, he'd kick the burning coals over the side. Campers in the valley below enjoyed the odd sight and began to request it. Eventually McCauley and David Curry put together quite the elaborate tradition, complete with a loud call and response between Camp Curry and the cliffside fire tenders. The tradition lasted until 1968 when the National Park Service finally closed it down because the spectacle had grown so popular people would trample the fragile meadows in order to catch a view of the nightly event. Even though the Firefall is no more, you can see old photos and video of it online.

- There is also a **natural firefall** that occurs occasionally at Yosemite in mid to late February. When conditions are just right, the evening light will illuminate Horsetail Fall, creating a fire-like glow. This has become a much-sought-after event for photographers.

I hope that reading novels like *Where the Fire Falls* and *The Road to Paradise* encourages you to visit these incredible national treasures for yourself. There's no question in my mind that God put these landscapes together with special care and that spending time immersed in nature can provide us a special glimpse into our Creator's heart.

"Oh, these vast, calm, measureless mountain days....
Days in whose light everything seems equally divine,
opening a thousand windows to show us God."
John Muir, *My First Summer in the Sierra,* 1911

Blessings!
Karen

Readers Guide

1. *Where the Fire Falls* takes place in Yosemite National Park. Have you ever visited Yosemite? What are some of your favorite memories from the park? Which other national parks do you dream of visiting?

2. Clark says, "Scripture says faith can move mountains, but I've found time spent in the mountains sometimes moves us toward faith." Have you ever felt your faith grow after spending time in nature? Where did this happen?

3. Both Clark and Olivia struggle with identity in this story. Olivia hides hers, preferring to be seen as something she is not. Do you ever find yourself in situations where you pretend to be different than you really are? More accomplished? Happier? More affluent? Why do you think we do this? Is there anyone you feel completely comfortable being yourself with?

4. When the story opens, Clark is waiting on a "word" from God about his future—an answer he's already been waiting on for years. Even though both John and Olivia try to convince him that being a park ranger might be God's answer, Clark stubbornly resists moving ahead of God's plan for him. Are you patient in prayer, or do you tend to push through and look for your own answers? Do you know someone who embodies this persistence? Is there one prayer you've clung to for many years?

5. "*Dis*-grace is a human term, Clark. God invented grace. No one can take it from you" (Reverend White). Clark might have been cowering under the disgrace of false accusations, but all of us live with the knowledge of real sin in our lives. Does that dis-grace separate us from God's love and care? Has it ever prevented you from going to Him in your time of need?

6. John and Melba Edwards are favorite characters of mine, serving as an example of mutual love for Clark and Olivia to follow. What did they sacrifice in order to make their marriage work? Have any married couples in your life modeled a godly relationship for you? How does this differ from the fairy-tale type of marriage often demonstrated in novels and movies?

7. Early on, Melba tells Olivia, "Yosemite is a place of healing. It draws broken people—folks trying to understand why they're on this good, green earth." Is there a place you go when you feel like you need healing and rejuvenation? For some, it's in nature. For others, it's their home, church, gym, or even the library. What are some of your places of healing?

8. Olivia has a tendency to "disappear" into her paintings while she's working on them and occasionally feels like she's emerging from a trance when she's finished. Sophie called it coming "up for air." Do you have a creative side that sometimes consumes you? What do you like to do, and how do you feel when you are in the midst of it?

9. When Olivia and Clark are discussing God as artist, they decide that wilderness gives us a glimpse of the Creator's heart. *Outside of nature,* can you list some other places you see God's heart?

10. As soon as I set eyes on the Yosemite Chapel, I knew how and where this story had to end. (Hopefully you've read all the way through.) If you're married, where did your wedding take place? If you could imagine the most idyllic place for a wedding or vow renewal, what type of location would you choose?

   a. in my favorite national park, of course!

   b. in my home church, surrounded by my friends and family

   c. a rustic barn

   d. Italy or Greece

   e. on a beautiful tropical beach (no hurricanes allowed)

   f. a lighthouse

   g. the spot where we first met—no matter how quirky (Hello grocery store or post office?)

   h. none of the above. I'd choose…[fill in the blank].

Acknowledgments

Never has writing a novel seemed as much of a team effort to me than with *Where the Fire Falls*. From the early research all the way to the final edits, I've received aid and prayer from countless sources—many of which I'll probably forget to mention.

Here are a few of the "helping hands" from Yosemite:

- Tom Bopp, musician and historian at Yosemite's Wawona Hotel (Big Trees Lodge), provided me with a wonderful overview of the musical history of Yosemite National Park. If you ever get a chance to hear him perform at the Wawona, don't miss the opportunity. Make sure to ask him to play "Button Up Your Overcoat." It's a hoot!

- Virginia Sanchez, librarian at the Yosemite National Park Research Library, spent two long afternoons helping me cram in as much research as possible during my short visit.

- Zachary Naegele provided an informative historical tour of the Ahwahnee Hotel.

- Fellow author Grant Hayter-Menzies shared some wonderful stories and photos of his grandparents' adventures at Yosemite National Park—particularly at the Glacier Point Hotel and Camp Curry. I hope he'll see glimpses of their romance in this story.

- The Yosemite History Facebook group helped me locate research materials about the park and answered questions about the Yosemite Chapel.

Thank you to Rebecca Ondov and Cliff Turner for advice on horses, mules, and packing.

I could never forget my critique partners: Heidi Gaul, Marilyn Rhoads, and Christina Suzann Nelson. They helped shape Olivia and Clark into the wonderful characters they became.

To everyone who prayed me through this novel—you know who you are—I could never have finished this novel without your support.

I owe a debt of gratitude to all the folks at WaterBrook and Multnomah for catching the vision for these Vintage National Parks Novels and allowing me to run with it, especially the park-loving Shannon Marchese, Lissa Halls Johnson, Pamela Shoup, Jamie Lapeyrolerie, Chelsea Woodward, Mark D. Ford, and countless other behind-the-scenes folks that I never get to meet. I love being a part of this team.

To my brilliant agent, Rachel Kent—always my calm port in the storm—thank you!

And finally, to my family who endure research trips, countless nights of fast-food dinners, long hours when I'm off playing with imaginary friends, and the occasional emotional meltdown. Living with a creative soul can be a challenge, especially when she's facing doubts and deadlines. You're the best.